Death
of an
Unsung
Hero

ALSO BY TESSA ARLEN

A Death by Any Other Name

Death Sits Down to Dinner

Death of a Dishonorable Gentleman

TESSA ARLEN

Death
of an
Unsung
Hero

MINOTAUR BOOKS
A THOMAS DUNNE BOOK
NEW YORK

DEATH OF AN UNSUNG HERO. Copyright © 2018 by Tessa Arlen.
All rights reserved. Printed in the United States of America. For information,
address St. Martin's Press, 175 Fifth Avenue, New York, N.Y. 10010.

www.minotaurbooks.com

Library of Congress Cataloging-in-Publication Data

Names: Arlen, Tessa, author.
Title: Death of an unsung hero / Tessa Arlen.
Description: First edition. | New York : Minotaur Books, 2018.
Identifiers: LCCN 2017044450| ISBN 9781250101440 (hardcover) | ISBN
    9781250101457 (ebook)
Subjects: LCSH: Countesses—Fiction. | Upper class—England—London—
    Fiction. | Murder—Investigation—Fiction. | GSAFD: Mystery
    fiction. | Historical fiction.
Classification: LCC PS3601.R5445 D435 2018 | DDC 813/.6—dc23
LC record available at https://lccn.loc.gov/2017044450

Our books may be purchased in bulk for promotional, educational, or business
use. Please contact your local bookseller or the Macmillan Corporate and
Premium Sales Department at 1-800-221-7945, extension 5442, or by email
at MacmillanSpecialMarkets@macmillan.com.

First Edition: March 2018

10 9 8 7 6 5 4 3 2 1

To my father with thanks and love

Acknowledgments

At St. Martin's Press: thank you to my editor, Jen Donovan, whose meticulous attention to detail, insights, and suggestions contributed hugely to the finished story—much for the better! Thanks to my copyeditor, Fran Fisher, who has managed to achieve what my long-suffering English teacher at school gave up on—my rather eccentric relationship with punctuation. And thanks always to Kevan Lyon: ever patient and generous with her time.

Horses have always played a huge part in my life, but without John Meriwether's and Ermine Baguley's professional advice on foxhunting, steeplechasing, and plowing (or *ploughing* as we call it over there), and for their considerable knowledge on horse breeds from the English field hunter to the great Shire horses of England, Dolly would have been a rare animal indeed.

Thank you to Thomas E. F. Webb for his article in the *Journal of the Royal Society of Medicine*, " 'Dottyville'—Craiglockhart War Hospital and shell-shock treatment in the First World War", which helped me to understand the psychological impact of industrial warfare on those who fought, on all sides, in World War One and who suffered untold harassment and cruelty at the hands of the countries they so patriotically and selflessly served. And to one of my favorite writers of his time, Robert Graves, and his remarkable observations in *Goodbye to All That*—one of the most controversial chronicles of the war to end all wars—thank you for providing me with the inspiration, and the cheek, to write this story.

I don't know what I would do without Chris Arlen's generosity and wit, his willingness to listen when I manage to paint myself into a corner, and for his help in the design of this beautiful cover in such a luscious shade of red!

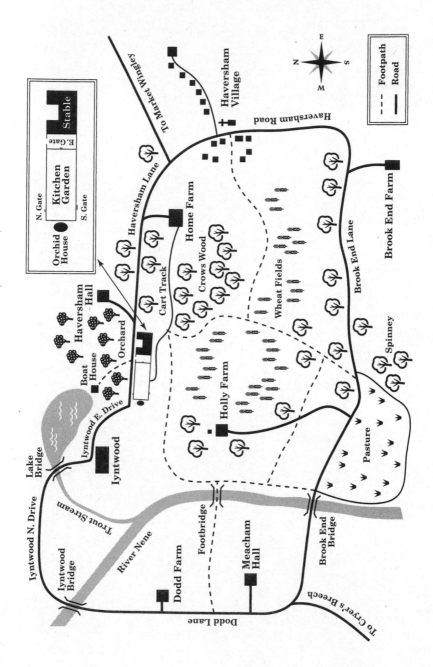

Cast of Characters

Haversham Hall Hospital

Major Andrews: Royal Army Medical Corps (RAMC), Commanding and Chief Medical Officer to Haversham Hall Hospital

Captain Pike: RAMC Medical Officer

Captain Sir Evelyn Bray: patient

Captain Martin: patient

Lieutenant Standish: patient

Lieutenant Forbes: patient

Lieutenant Fielding: patient

Second Lieutenant Carmichael: patient

Second Lieutenant Phipps: patient

Sister Carter: Queen Alexandra's Royal Army Nursing Corps (QARANSC)

Edith Jackson: Voluntary Aid Detachment (VAD) Quartermaster and amateur sleuth

Corporal Budge: RAMC Medical Orderly

Corporal West: RAMC Medical Orderly

Mary Fuller: VAD

Sarah Ellis: VAD

Iyntwood House

Ralph Cuthbert Talbot, Earl of Montfort: Clementine's long-suffering and loving husband

Clementine Elizabeth Talbot, Countess of Montfort: amateur sleuth and patroness of the Haversham Hall Hospital

Captain Lord Harry Haversham: the Talbots' son and heir

Lady Althea Talbot: the Talbots' middle daughter

Edgar Bray: guest of the Talbots' and brother of Captain Sir Evelyn Bray

George Hollyoak: the butler

Mr. Percy Thrower: the head gardener

The County

Sir Winchell Meacham: country gentleman at Meacham Hall

Colonel Valentine: the Chief Constable for Market Wingley

Inspector Savor: Market Wingley CID

Mr. and Mrs. Howard: the farmer and his wife at Holly Farm

Walter Howard: the Howards' eldest son

Mr. and Mrs. Allenby: the farmer and his wife at Home Farm

Davey Allenby: the Allenbys' youngest son

Mr. and Mrs. Anderson: the farmer and his wife at Brook End Farm

And assorted post mistresses, publicans, and sweetshop owners in Haversham village

Death
of an
Unsung
Hero

Chapter One

"How very nice, Mrs. Jackson." Iyntwood's elderly butler settled into his chair by the window. "Why, it's almost like old times again." George Hollyoak's glance took in the claustrophobic and over-furnished room: shabby velvet chairs jostled with a heavy mahogany desk, taking up far too much space in front of the windows, both of which were swathed in heavy curtains in a dusty but strident red plaid.

The dowager Countess of Montfort had died two years ago and her character, or that of the late Queen Victoria, whom she had revered, was still heavily imprinted on the dower house furnished as a faithful replica of the old queen's beloved Balmoral Castle. Bright and, to Mrs. Jackson's flinching eye, brash tartans dominated most of the reception rooms on the ground floor of Haversham Hall.

Mrs. Jackson was encouraged to see George Hollyoak sitting in her new office. It had taken weeks to coax him to visit her and now after all sorts of silly excuses here he was. Though even with her old friend and mentor sitting at his leisure with a cup of afternoon tea in his hand it wasn't really like old times, no matter how much they all wished it were. The war had changed everything.

Her face must have reflected her thoughts as she followed his gaze around the oppressively furnished room. "Perhaps not *quite* like old times." Her guest smiled as he observed a shaft of dust motes dancing thickly in the late summer sunlight. "I must say you are looking well, Mrs. Jackson, and so very smart in your uniform: Voluntary Aid Detachment or Red Cross?" This was the first time he had acknowledged that Iyntwood's dower house had been transformed into an auxiliary hospital.

"The hospital comes under the jurisdiction of the Red Cross, but I trained with the VAD. I am not an assisting nurse, so I am spared the traditional starched apron and the rather claustrophobic cap," she answered. Long aprons and linen caps, in her experience, were worn by cooks, and although Mrs. Jackson was not a snob, she was conscious of little things like rank and station.

In acknowledging Haversham Hall's new status the old man evidently felt he might ask his next question. He leaned forward, curiosity bright in his eyes. "And how are you finding life in your new abode?"

Mrs. Jackson hesitated before she answered. She had never liked Haversham Hall; it was as overbearing as the Victorian age it had been built in and an ugly building in comparison to the Elizabethan elegance of Iyntwood. But she had made the adjustment from being a senior servant to Ralph Cuthbert Talbot, the Earl of Montfort, at his principal country-seat, to the rank of quartermaster at Lady Montfort's new hospital far more easily than she had anticipated. The real challenge had come when their first patients had arrived, but this was something she was not prepared to share with Mr. Hollyoak—not just yet.

"It is not as different as I thought it would be. Haversham Hall is not Iyntwood, but it is a building I am familiar with, and my duties here are similar to those of my position as housekeeper at Iyntwood." *That's not strictly true,* she thought, *but it will do for now.*

Her new job was not at all like her old one, any more than this hospital was like many of the others that had sprung up all over the country in the many private houses of the rich and titled, speedily converted to cope with an unceasing flow of wounded men from France. At Haversham Hall Hospital there were no wards lined with rows of beds, no operating theaters with trays of steel surgical instruments, or hastily installed sluices and sterilizers. Certainly there was an occasionally used sick bay and a first aid room in what was known as the medical wing, but they were merely a token adjunct. And it was these differences that were the cause for Mr. Hollyoak's initial reluctance to visit her and for his searching question, *"How are you finding life in your new abode?"* because Haversham Hall Hospital was not a conventional Red Cross hospital, not by a long stretch of the imagination.

She raised her teacup to her lips and took a sip. If she was to help a man whose conventions were deeply mired in the nineteenth century to understand the value of the hospital's purpose, she must proceed with cautious tact. She decided to start with a prosaic description of the practicalities.

"I am responsible for the running of the hospital's housekeeping and for ordering all supplies, which means I spend most of my time sitting at my desk filling in requisition forms; the bureaucracy of wartime, her ladyship calls it. But we have plenty of nice young women from the Voluntary Aid Detachment to help with the housekeeping as well as some of our nursing duties. And I certainly need to be well placed here on the ground floor of the house to supervise them." She did not add "every step of the way" because that way of thinking made her resent how difficult it was to work with inexpert help. To go with her cheerful tone she exhibited her most optimistic smile. VAD girls from nice middle-class families were a nightmare to train in comparison to sensible, sturdy village women who were ready to roll up their sleeves and had no romantic illusions about their part in the war effort.

Having given her visitor the briefest outline of her duties, she decided that she would wait for him to display genuine interest—enthusiasm would be too much to hope for—in what they were accomplishing here before she continued. She offered Mr. Hollyoak a plate of sandwiches: delicate triangles of egg with cress. She had prepared them herself, mashing the hard-boiled egg finely with a narrow-tined fork and adding just the right amount of salt, pepper, and cress to spread on lightly buttered crustless bread. He took a sandwich and closed his eyes as he chewed and swallowed the first bite.

"Perfect," he said and smiled his appreciation, "quite perfect. I need not say how much you are missed at Iyntwood." He took another bite of sandwich and then slowly shook his head. "The house simply isn't the same without you."

She detected real regret in his voice that she was no longer his second-in-command in a servants' hall now staffed entirely with women. She knew how hard it had been for him to adapt to her temporary employment by the Red Cross, if it was indeed the Red Cross that paid her generous salary and not, as she suspected, the Earl of Montfort. *Perhaps this is why I am reluctant to talk about the hospital, because I find my new life so stimulating, and however inefficient they are, I enjoy working with young and lively women whose backgrounds are as varied as our duties.* However terrible this war was, it had certainly opened up a new perspective to those from other walks of life and in particular the staid and confined life of an upper servant to the aristocracy. All of this would be difficult to explain to a man whose retinue of perfectly trained footmen was serving in the trenches of northern France.

"I know it's wrong of me to say so, Mrs. Jackson, but Iyntwood seems so quiet, so empty now that we are not formally entertaining the way we used to. We all work, just as hard, perhaps even more so, to maintain standards but only because we have to make do with far less staff. I am sometimes hard put to remember our gracious lives before that terrible day in 1914." Mr. Hollyoak looked down into his empty teacup before he put it on the table between them and she poured him a second cup.

"I am quite sure that none of us will ever forget that day, Mr. Hollyoak." She nodded her head in commiseration of the old man's many losses. Others might remember the fourth of August, when Britain rallied to the flag, as one of the loveliest days of a perfect summer, the sort of day that Englishmen wrote poems about when they were far from home. But what fixed it in her memory was that it was a morning on which her ladyship had triumphed in a particularly tricky inquiry at neighboring Bishop's Hever and a murder of such audacious cunning that just remembering it still raised the hairs on the back of her neck. Tea poured, she offered her guest the sugar bowl and silently counted the three sugar lumps he extravagantly stirred into his tea. Mr. Hollyoak had always had a sweet tooth and sugar was in short supply these days.

"No word from Dick Wilson, I'm afraid, Mrs. Jackson. It's been nearly a month now, and Dick was always like clockwork with his letters before—we would have heard by now if there was bad news, wouldn't we?"

So it wasn't just curiosity that brought you here, then. More than likely the old man had come to see her out of loneliness, perhaps for solace. Iyntwood's hall boy at age eighteen had been one of the first to join the British Expeditionary Force to France in 1914.

She took a sip of tea. "Sometimes the post is a bit erratic, Mr. Hollyoak. Do you remember when we didn't hear from John for nearly two months? And then dozens of letters came, all in one go, each and every one of them asking us to send socks?"

He nodded, willing to hope that all was well with the youngest member of his servants' hall. "I certainly do." A faint smile as he remembered their fastidious second footman's complaints after a winter of rain-filled trenches. "That boy has enough socks for a battalion now."

She cut him a piece of Victoria sponge cake. "Ah, Mrs. Jackson, you spoil me." He sighed with contentment. "No time for a good sponge cake belowstairs at Iyntwood now that Mrs. Thwaite's kitchen maids have all left to become munitionettes at the Banbury factory." Her face betrayed no irritation but she inwardly bristled at the term "munition-*ette*," as the suffix made the dangerous job sound diminutive—dainty, even. *Is that what they are calling them now—what's wrong with "munition workers"? They are probably required to wear ridiculous little caps with frills, like waitresses at a Lyons Corner House, when they pack those shells with their bare hands.* She shrugged off her annoyance and presented a passive face as she listened to Mr. Hollyoak's gentle grumbling about lowered standards. "Lord and Lady Montfort are most careful not to overburden the staff these days, but Cook is so run off her feet without her kitchen maids that she is threatening to go and join them in Banbury. She says at least she would know what was expected of her." He shook his head that someone of Mrs. Thwaite's age and status would even consider factory work.

The image of the cook's angry red face flashed into Mrs. Jackson's mind. "She's the last person in the world to be in charge of explosives I would have thought," she said before she could stop herself.

Mr. Hollyoak chuckled. "Always a bit heavy-handed with the pots and pans is our Mrs. Thwaite, but the lightest touch when it comes to pastry and puddings. But, never mind all of that . . . how is life finding *you* these days . . . I mean, how do you . . ." he groped for the right phrase. "I mean *what* do you make of all this?" He waved the last bite of Victoria sponge around her office, clearly indicating that he was now ready to hear more about the hospital.

Mr. Hollyoak was well aware, as everyone was in the village and the county, that Haversham Hall Hospital had been one of Lady Montfort's bright ideas right from the start, which was probably why he was picking his words so carefully. Mrs. Jackson set down her cup and saucer. She had no difficulty in recalling how grim her ladyship's mood had been when she had returned from visiting an old family friend in Scotland. It had been a bitterly cold evening in early December last year. *She was certainly a woman on a mission, if there ever was one, when she came back from visiting that terrible place.*

"I have never seen such tragic young men," Lady Montfort had announced to her housekeeper as she stood in middle of her sitting room, still wearing her hat and gloves and with her fur huddled closely around her neck. "It was heartbreaking to see them, sitting so meekly in their corners, seemingly quite unaware of where they were."

"How is Mr. Barclay faring, m'lady?" Everyone belowstairs at Iyntwood was fond of Oscar Barclay, a particular friend of the Talbots' only son, Lord Haversham, who had alerted his mother to Mr. Barclay's plight: a casualty of the Battle of Loos, in France, and now a patient at Craiglockhart Hospital in Scotland.

"He is suffering from what the army refers to in their ignorance as shell-shock and what the doctors call neurasthenia, Jackson. I hardly know how to describe what has happened to that wholly decent and kind young man; you simply wouldn't recognize him. So pitifully thin . . . he shakes at any loud or sudden sound. When he tries to speak—he hardly uttered a word the whole time I was there—he stammers so, his mouth trembles, and he . . ." Lady Montfort's eyes filled with tears and she stared fiercely off into a corner of the room until she had regained her composure. "The hospital was generous enough to put me up in the staff wing while I was there. It is a dreadful old building: run-down, drafty, and cold. All night I could hear those poor young men crying out like souls in torment . . ." She had tailed off and Mrs. Jackson had almost reached out to take her hand, that was how distressed her ladyship had been. "They say nothing about their suffering, nothing at all." She had managed to continue in the flat monotone people of her class used when they were embarrassed about displaying emotion. "They politely lock down into stammering or silence. There is no release for them it seems—even when they manage to sleep they wake screaming from their nightmares as they relive over and over the horrors of battle." Lady Montfort had gazed down at the carpet for a moment to bring herself back under complete control. "One of the doctors at Craiglockhart, his name is Brock, believes that the act of functioning—of doing simple and useful tasks that engage the mind and body in healthy activities—is often successful in helping these men to mend, or at least recover something of their lives. All the way home on the train I kept thinking about them and what the doctor told me they were doing for them. It made me think that we might be of use."

However distressed she was, the Countess of Montfort was a resilient woman. High-strung? Certainly, and Mrs. Jackson was the first to acknowledge her ladyship's little ways, but her mistress was not without an inner strength and vitality that never left her, even during these terrible days of war. She had rallied from the horrors of her trip to Scotland, and after several long walks in the frosty woodlands on the estate with her husband had persuaded Lord Montfort not only to offer up Haversham Hall to the War Office as a hospital for those young men who were on the road to recovery from neurasthenia, but to make a substantial donation to its running and upkeep.

Mrs. Jackson had no intention of trying to explain the innovative new treatments used at the hospital to her doubting friend sitting across from her. It had taken her a while to overcome her natural skepticism in the first weeks of her employment, especially to this new "talking cure" that the doctors had come up with. It had barely made any sense to her at first and it was the last thing in the world she would repeat to the old butler.

She got up and opened the window to let a little air into the slight stuffiness building in the room. "I have made the adjustment quite nicely, Mr. Hollyoak, I am glad to say. It was difficult at first. I was completely unprepared for how deeply distressed our first patients were when they came here."

The old man cleared his throat. "If I may just say this, Mrs. Jackson, I am veteran of the Boer Wars and I am unfortunately familiar with the distress war wreaks on its soldiers. Conditions were indescribable at the Siege of Ladysmith when I was deployed there during the African wars. Our suffering was considerable, but none of us shrank from what we had to do. Why, most of us survived by eating rats and existing on a canteen cap of water a day. Typhoid carried off at least one-third of our number, maybe even more. But you see, Mrs. Jackson, real men do not hesitate to fight to the bitter end, no matter how hideous the conditions are. I am not saying there were no cowards in my day, of course there were and we gave them very short shrift." Mrs. Jackson concealed a smile and respectfully nodded along as he remembered his war. How often had Mr. Hollyoak regaled the servants' hall with graphic and bloody tales of the African wars? He had described getting over typhoid as if he had shaken off a chill caught on some sort of Boy Scouts camping trip. But what it boiled down to was that in Mr. Hollyoak's opinion, real men didn't complain, even under the worst of conditions, they merely got on with it; only a coward would hide out in a place like Haversham Hall Hospital and talk about the horrors of war with his doctor.

She summoned patience and tried again. "I understand, Mr. Hollyoak. Until I came to work here I thought of our patients as cowards too. Now I have to say I have had a complete change of mind. Every one of our officers say they want to return to the war as soon as they are able. Our job here, you see, is to help them function so they *can* lead their men in battle." She saw Mr. Hollyoak's look of disbelief and she stepped it up a notch. "They know they are thought of as cowards, they are painfully aware of it. What is the expression they use in the navy—swinging the lead?" Mr. Hollyoak acknowledged malingerers with a fervent nod. "We are low in numbers this week as thirteen of our twenty patients passed their Medical Board review and are now on their way back to the Western Front, to Mesopotamia, and Egypt. They went willingly and with brave hearts." She caught his eye and tried to hold his gaze but he turned, reaching for his cup. When he had it in his hand she sought his eyes again. "Strangely enough, most of them here were decorated for bravery—before they became seriously ill."

He raised his eyebrows and took a sip of tea. *Yes, I thought that might surprise you.* "There were six Distinguished Service Orders alone among our first fifteen officers, twelve of them mentioned in dispatches, and four Military Crosses in our second group. One of our officers was even recommended for the Victoria Cross. And it is quite remarkable that straightforward, useful work in the open air does so much to help restore our patients to normal life—we call it 'cure through function.'" He smiled politely and gestured with his teacup to the comfortable country house they were seated in, as if to say, *Who wouldn't want to hide out the war here?*

His eyes wandered to the little clock ticking away on the chimneypiece. She was losing him. She sought to change the subject. "Well, enough of my work. It must be wonderful to have Lord Haversham at home—is his arm healing well?" The old man brightened up at the mention of Lord and Lady Montfort's son, who was home on medical leave from the Royal Naval Air Service with a fractured arm.

"Just plain 'Captain Talbot' is the title Lord Haversham prefers these days," he said with paternalistic pride. "The highest scoring ace of his squadron and decorated three times, but of course he plays all that sort of thing down."

"He was always a modest young man." Mrs. Jackson did not want to precipitate another saga of heroic acts of derring-do from

Mr. Hollyoak. Any man who fought in this war had her admiration, and Mr. Hollyoak did rather go on. "I am glad to hear that all is well at Iyntwood, Mr. Hollyoak. It certainly looks like Lady Althea is doing a lot for the county with her Women's Land Army." The war had curtailed the Talbots' youngest daughter's love of travel, and now that she was safely marooned on the family estate she had involved herself in representing the government's volunteer force that provided local farmers with labor. "I can't believe the jobs those young women are taking on, can you, Mr. Hollyoak?" She took a bite of cake. "Up at dawn and out in all weather. You have to take your hat off to them, don't you? I simply don't know what our farmers would have done without them, especially with this bumper harvest."

The old butler sighed and pursed his lips. His handsome old head was imposingly leonine and when he slowly shook it from side to side, as he did now, it gave him all the appearance of an offended biblical elder—Moses when he returned from Mount Sinai to find the children of Israel had relapsed into drink and idolatry sprang to Mrs. Jackson's mind and she bit the inside of her cheeks to stop herself from laughing outright. "They wear riding breeches." Mr. Hollyoak put down his empty cup with some finality. "Most immodest and unattractive in the female form."

Chapter Two

Clementine Elizabeth Talbot, the Countess of Montfort, laid down her napkin and stood up from the dining room table. "Well, I must be off; I am going to look in on what Mrs. Jackson calls the cider detachment in the kitchen-garden courtyard this afternoon. Our Haversham Hall officers might be able to produce enough cider for the whole village for the harvest home supper this year."

"If you will wait a moment, I'm going that way too." Her husband rose to his feet.

"Harry?" Clementine turned to her son, who, half reclining in his chair, nodded to the butler to pour him another glass of hock.

"Not today, Mama, thanks all the same. I told Althea that I would drop in on Mr. Howard at Holly Farm with her. She is still trying to convince him to use her Land girls to bring in his wheat. He's running at least a week late and a heavy rainstorm would ruin the entire crop." Harry instantly had his father's attention.

"If he doesn't want help then Althea shouldn't push him. He will just dig in—such an obstinate fellow. However much I welcome your interest in the estate, Harry, I think I had better talk to our other farmers and see if they can lend a hand. Or," he turned to his wife, "perhaps some of your officers at Haversham Hall might pitch in. If Mr. Howard chooses to be finicky about using female labor then we must find some other way; every grain of wheat counts now that we can no longer depend on American ships to make it through the U-boat blockade."

Clementine was halfway across the dining room; she had no intention of being late. "I think we have two or three of our officers out at Brook End and Dodd farms already. I will ask Major Andrews if the others might be willing to help out."

"Do they know how to use a scythe?" It was unusual for Harry to be scornful of others, but he had made his dislike of the hospital known immediately on his arrival last week. Unlike his sister, Althea, he never joined in the many conversations about the hospital's occupants and had not once walked in the direction of his grandmother's old house. His judgmental tone stopped his mother in the open doorway. *Ever since he came home he has been withdrawn, almost sullen, and completely unlike himself.* Clementine wasn't sure how to be with this new Harry, just yet. *Give him time,* she thought, noticing the dark circles under her son's eyes. *As soon as his body mends and he has adjusted to not flying for a while he'll come round.*

Harry leaned back in his chair, stretched his legs out under the table, and lifted his wineglass. "If you don't support Althea's Land Army girls, Papa, then the farmers won't either." Two years ago, Clementine realized, he would probably have said much the same thing, but it would have been said with good humor and he would have accepted it, if his father chose to ignore any advice he might presume to offer about the running of his tenant farms. But the old carefree Harry was, these days, a far more burdened young man. *He is surely drinking far more than he did on his last home leave,* she thought as she watched him drain his glass. "Harry, I simply must dash, but I will see you at teatime," was all she said and was rewarded for her tact with his quick, sweet smile. For almost a moment she saw the old Harry.

"How do you find our son?" she asked her husband as they left the house and walked together down the east drive in the direction of the stables and the kitchen-garden courtyard.

He slowed his stride so that they might lengthen their time together and took her hand in his, as if they were still young and not a married couple of twenty-seven years. "It is more than he can stand to be at home," he said and she heard the sorrow in his voice. "I have never known him so impatient . . . almost irritable. He says his broken arm does not give him pain, but the other morning he drank brandy. Brandy at breakfast, Clemmy!"

She had been distressed to see streaks of gray in Harry's dark hair when he had come down to the dining room the night after he had arrived. And for the past two days he had either walked for miles alone with the dogs or sat motionless for hours in a chair. But she was curious to find out what her husband thought so she said nothing and waited.

"His moods change so quickly, when he was never moody before." He laughed and she realized that he was as baffled by this new Harry as she was. He glanced at her, perhaps trying to gauge how much he should burden her with what worried him most—she hoped he would. But he shrugged his shoulders and assumed the cover-up they all practiced even more thoroughly than they had before the war. *People like us must set an example for the rest of the country—even more so in these uncertain times. So instead of unburdening himself about our son he is going to make light of something we don't understand, something about Harry that worries us but he doesn't think we should refer to.*

"I have to ask him what he is talking about most of the time.

He calls bombs whiz bangs; he takes a dekko at something rather than look at it. He talks about kites, blimps, and someone called Archie. I am continually asking for a translation!"

"But surely that's not what worries you, all his flying friends use slang and talk as if nothing matters," she persisted. Lord Montfort whistled his dogs to heel as they walked past the orchard and the territorial flock of geese that grazed there in the afternoons.

"Strictly between us, darling, I am not angry about this war so much as saddened," he replied. "There seems to be no end in sight."

"And Harry?" she pushed, and her husband shook his head.

"Harry is a part of this war as much as we all are. He is doing his part." This was said with the stoic acceptance they all exhibited these days. *We must show fortitude and self-restraint; displays of emotion are bad form.* "I am far more concerned about Verity and our grandchildren. Why is she being so stubborn about leaving Paris for the safety of the Loire?" Their elder daughter, Verity, was married to a Frenchman. She and her two children had been visiting them when Britain had declared war on Germany. Both Clementine and her husband had begged her to stay on with them for the duration, but she had returned to her home in Paris, where, to Lord Montfort's consternation, she insisted on staying instead of retreating to her husband's estate in the Loire.

"She says she wants to be close-by, so that when Etienne has any leave she will be there for him. I think I would do the same thing if it were me." She nevertheless felt an undercurrent of anxiety for her daughter and their grandsons. "If the German army breaks through the line, she has plenty of time to run for the Loire." This is what Clementine told herself every night as she lay wakeful in her bed. But she did not want her husband to be sidetracked from their son's troubling withdrawal from ordinary life. She hesitated before she spoke thoughts that had not left her since Harry had come home. "Perhaps Harry might talk to Major Andrews while he is home on leave with us—it might help him to talk about . . .

16

you know, the war and everything. After all, Ralph, the major has done wonders for our officers at Haversham Hall," but she already knew the futility of her suggestion.

"Harry talk to Andrews? For God's sake, darling, Harry would no more talk to Andrews than . . . fly to the moon." He sounded affronted, as if she had found Harry wanting in some way.

She reluctantly turned away from the topic of their son to more-mundane matters. "About our guest, Mr. Bray—what time did he say he would arrive this afternoon?" She would have to keep her visit to the cider detachment brief and perhaps forgo a visit with Mrs. Jackson at the hospital if she was to be home and changed for the arrival of Mr. Bray, a man neither of them had ever met.

"He said he was motoring himself down and expected to be with us by five o'clock or so."

"Motoring *himself*? I thought you said he could only walk with the aid of a stick."

"Yes, that's right. Bad hunting accident apparently, left him without the proper use of a leg. That's why he is at home on the family estate and not off at the war."

"Well, he must have a driver or someone with him. Anyway, I have arranged with Hollyoak that he should stay in the Blue Salon so he doesn't have to negotiate the stairs, and there is plenty of room belowstairs if he brings his man with him."

The thought of entertaining a man who had come to visit his long-lost brother believed to have been missing in action in France but now a recovering patient in Haversham Hall Hospital had little appeal for Clementine and she guessed even less for her husband. *Especially since we will be joined by his monosyllabic brother,* Captain Sir Evelyn Bray, who had failed his Medical Board review again last week and spent his days silently double digging empty vegetable beds in the kitchen garden.

They had reached the open archway into the kitchen-garden courtyard. "With Harry's present mood of introspection, Althea's frustration with Mr. Howard at Holly Farm, and now this Mr. Bray, it will be rather a heavy going next few days," she said. He stopped and, turning her to face him, kissed her lightly on the mouth.

"Heavy going? Oh no, I don't think so! A man we have never met before is arriving to be reunited with his older brother who never says a bloomin' word and might never completely regain his memory after weeks in Dottyville; I can't imagine anything more enjoyable." He pulled her closer into his arms. "And in case you were not aware, Harry knows our Captain Sir Evelyn Bray— met him before the war. Says he was a complete wastrel—always in London, never went home to the estate, left everything to his brother while he was simply . . ."

"Unreliable with all the girls—yes, Harry did tell me. He also said that war heroes are made from very unlikely cloth and that whereas he didn't particularly like our Captain Bray he certainly admired him."

"Ah, jolly good—more dissension in the ranks!"

They laughed; theirs was not to be a peaceful end to the week it seemed.

The kitchen-garden courtyard is one of those quiet places that make me feel as if time has stood still, Clementine thought as she walked into the paved area between the back of the stable block and the tall walls of the kitchen garden. A long brick-and-glass potting shed had been built against the stable wall, with a smaller building attached to it, which in the old days had been where the gardeners gathered to brew tea, shelter from the worst of the weather, and enjoy a good gossip as they ate their noonday dinner. On its right-side wall was a heavy wooden door giving access into the kitchen garden. Encircled by walls that did not obstruct the sun, it was an intimately pleasant space to spend an afternoon.

She called out her hullos to three khaki-clad figures grouped around the apple press hard at work, in the methodical way of military men, making cider. A Royal Army Medical Corps hospital orderly, Corporal Budge, leaned up against a wooden keg, smoking a cigarette as he watched a younger man, wearing the single star of a second lieutenant on his uniform epaulette, shovel apples into the half barrel of the press. As the last apples rattled into the barrel, a tall man in uniform spun the handle attached to a heavy wooden screw, lowering the top board, darkened with many a cider pressing, slowly down into the barrel and the ripe apples. There was a satisfying crunching sound and the three men watched a cataract of golden juice pour into the wooden bucket below with evident satisfaction.

"It's the wosps yur gottur wotch," Corporal Budge said as he stood away from the keg and drew himself up to lift the two forefingers of his right hand to touch his cap to Clementine. "Afternoon, ladyship," he said in his thick West Country accent with its ripe round vowels and its generous burring Rs. "Thurr all drunk at this time o'year, tha's wha' makes 'um particularily aggressive." Budge was from Somerset, a county renowned for its cider, and Clementine suspected he knew about things like the hazards of wasp stings at cider time. She rather liked the corporal, a compactly built and prematurely balding man continually on the alert to the well-being of his officer-patients. She waved away hovering wasps and inhaled: countless late-summer days were carried back to her on the scent of crushed apples. "Delicious," she said appreciatively, remembering her first days at Iyntwood as a young bride when a much more sprightly Mr. Thrower had overseen the cider press. "You're right about the wasps though, Budge, much worse this year. It must be the heat.

"Captain Martin," she greeted the senior officer who was turning the handle to raise the board. The captain's appearance was deceptive: he was extraordinarily tall with broad shoulders and the physique of an athlete, but Clementine knew how frail

Captain Martin was underneath breadth of shoulder and well-toned muscle. He had failed his Medical Board review last week and had withdrawn even more into himself in the last few days, his old diffidence had returned, and his eyes had an evasive, almost defeated look. *It is almost impossible to believe he commanded a company of men through some of the worst battles in France, was mentioned in dispatches and awarded the DSO, when I see him standing here looking so uncertain and apologetic.* "Would you join us at the house for Sunday luncheon, after church?" she asked, turning to include the younger of the two officers, Lieutenant Fielding.

Both men looked up and Clementine was touched by their enthusiasm. "I say, how awfully nice of you!" Lieutenant Fielding clearly welcomed an invitation to be with a family again, sitting around a gracious dining table, in an elegant and comfortable house, with the fascinatingly beautiful Lady Althea dressed in a pretty summer frock.

The captain flushed with pleasure and said with only the slightest hesitance in his speech, "We should . . . bring . . . some of our cider." Captain Martin, DSO, gave the handle of the cider press a spin and down came the board.

"Yes, if you would prefer it to claret," she said, laughing.

Martin dug in his pocket and shook a packet of cigarettes up to his mouth, then stopped and looked for permission from Clementine.

"That's right, sir, light up a gasper," commanded Corporal Budge. "It'll keep the wasps away."

More apples were shoveled in and Captain Martin made a joke, beloved by an island race, about Lieutenant Phipps, who had gone with a wheelbarrow to fetch more apples being lost at sea. He made a brief attempt at command: "When you have shoveled that lot in, Fielding, you better go and find Phipps, probably sitting under a tree scribbling poetry."

Clementine momentarily closed her eyes to enjoy the sun on her face. She wondered what sort of poetry Phipps wrote; Major Andrews encouraged his patients to write prose, poetry—indeed anything that gave them the opportunity to express the inner world they were locked in.

As if summoned by the captain's words, the door in the wall to the kitchen garden was thrown open and Second Lieutenant Phipps came barreling through it from the kitchen garden.

"There you are, Phipps—finished skiving off . . . ?" Martin got no further than this.

Phipps staggered forward, his face as white as the plaster on the walls of the potting shed, his eyes wild. He stopped and cried out a few incoherent words and then froze in his tracks. He might be with them in corporeal form, but his eyes were fixed ahead and it was clear that he did not register where he was or even that he could see them. He was somewhere else completely. *And not,* Clementine thought as she saw his ashen, sweating face, and his blank eyes, *in a good place at all.* Corporal Budge stubbed out his cigarette and walked over to the stricken Phipps. He took him firmly by the shoulders and Phipps began to struggle and cry out.

"He's in shock," Budge said. He put a strong supporting arm around the lieutenant and gently lowered him to a bench, then crouching down next to him he spoke in slow, quiet tones.

"There now, sir, deep breaths. Remember the drill. Breathe easy, sir, nice and slo-ow." He was as gentle and soothing as a mother with a frightened child, Clementine thought. She turned to Captain Martin and Lieutenant Fielding standing by the cider press, all authority surrendered to Budge.

"Anything we can do, Corporal? Shall we get him back to Haversham Hall?" Clementine said as the young man began to sob, great shuddering, shouting sobs as he rocked back and forth in his anguish. "No, m'lady. He will be all right in a minute. Something happened to him in the orchard and it's sent him back. There, lad . . ." Budge spoke gently in his rough West Country burr, but he did not suggest that Phipps pull himself together. The young man, for Phipps was barely twenty, dropped his head and his sobs died to weeping.

"What happened back there then, sir?" asked Budge. Pulling a cigarette from his jacket pocket, he lit it and passed it to Phipps. There was silence. They all stood quite still, their eyes on the man on the ground, and waited for him to speak.

"Head smashed . . ." he managed, and then he started to stammer. He struggled for some moments, his mouth working to try to form words: "S-s-s-mashed, s-s-s-mashed . . . head all smashed in."

Budge nodded his head. "Yes," he said, "it were a terrible thing to happen." He looked up at Clementine even though it was Phipps he was talking to. "Pinned under three dead bodies when they found you in a water-filled shell crater, weren't you, sir? Been there for several days." Phipps lifted both his hands and pressed the heels of his palms into his eye sockets as if to force the memory away. Budge looked up at Clementine again. "His closest friend was lying immediately on top of him with his head . . . on his chest." He gestured with his hand to indicate half a head, and Clementine must have looked appalled because he hastily added, "Sorry to distress you, m'lady."

"No, no, not at all," she said. "Poor, poor man." Had this man, a boy really, lay in the mud under a pile of dead bodies with his friend's smashed head on his chest for three days? *No wonder he lost his reason.*

Phipps took a long pull on his cigarette and slowly exhaled. Then he spoke. "No, Budge," he said, his voice still wavering with the horror he had experienced three months ago and then again in his mind, just moments past. "You d-d-don't understand. Captain Bray . . ." he lifted his hand and jerked his thumb toward the open door into the kitchen garden, "lying . . . lying in the trench with his head . . . smashed in." He slumped forward with the effort of articulating what he believed he had seen.

"It was a hallucination, sir," Budge said firmly. "Just a hallucination, you know it was. Come on, sir, let's get you on your feet and we'll go and find Major Andrews. You can talk about it with him." He stood up and waited for the young man to rise to his feet.

"Don't be so d-d-damned daft, Budge," Phipps said, looking up at the orderly. He threw his cigarette down on the ground. "I haven't been 'seeing things' since I left Dottyville. Captain Bray is in the kitchen garden, lying facedown in the dirt with his head smashed in. S-s-someone"—he paused for breath and made the effort to keep his voice steady—"has bloody well done him in."

Chapter Three

Captain Martin started toward the door into the kitchen garden, followed by Lieutenant Fielding. Budge called after them, "If you please, Captain, might I go and look first? It would perhaps be best if you stayed here with Lieutenant Phipps." It was a request, politely worded, but nonetheless Corporal Budge was in charge here. Martin hesitated for a moment and then said in a voice that had probably not been as authoritative since the day he had given his first order to his men in Flanders, "Fielding, go and get the doc; Budge, you stay here with Phipps, and *that's* an order." He walked past Clementine and through the open gate. Clementine cast an apologetic look at Budge and followed him.

"Your ladyship," Budge called after her. "Perhaps best to wait here with me and Phipps?"

"I will be quite all right, Corporal." Clementine was already through the open gate.

The kitchen garden covered several acres within its old mellow brick walls, which supported the espaliers of pear, greengage, and apple trees. Clementine remembered that before the war the garden had been a thing of orderly beauty tended by a regiment of gardeners who, under the head gardener Mr. Thrower's direction, had produced a bountiful procession of vegetables and fruit in the abundant days of spring and summer. But she did not have time to notice that under the lesser competence of men who had never wielded a spade before in their lives, even at the Front, the kitchen garden had lost much of its aesthetic appeal over past years. But Clementine's mind was not on the loss of artistry in her garden, she was curious to see what had caused Lieutenant Phipps's hallucination. *Perhaps in his mind he ties the action of digging vegetable beds to the digging of trenches?* She suggested this to herself because underneath her outward composure she was beginning to feel distinctly uneasy. *And maybe Phipps did not hallucinate, and if that's the case then what on earth am I doing here?* When the captain paused in the center of the garden she stopped too, and they stood staring around them, both at a loss. "Where is he? I can't see him." Martin's earlier air of authority was deserting him, she thought; he looked around, doubting himself, perhaps hesitant of what he might find in this domestic scene so far removed from the acts of violence that had been part of his everyday existence just months ago. She noticed that the captain had lifted his arm as a polite barrier to prevent her from walking ahead of him.

"Bray told us at breakfast that he was going to dig over the potato rows," he said. And they set off down the gravel path together under a pergola heavy with fat green grapes for the table. At the end of the shady tunnel was an intersection of raked gravel pathways that radiated outward from a central irrigation fountain. They slowed only to negotiate an old wooden wheelbarrow overturned on its side, its load of apples strewn in their way. Abandoned no doubt by Lieutenant Phipps in his desperate need to run from a world where rotting bodies lay in rain-filled shell craters.

Clementine stopped at the end of the path and looked at the neatly turned root-vegetable beds to their right. At the end of each row lay the debris of potato stems and leaves, and piled in the center of the middle row was a carefully built hill of potatoes graded in size with the largest at the bottom.

Uncomfortably conscious that her heart was hammering as if she had run through the garden at top speed, Clementine looked around. *I can't see anyone,* she thought, *there is no one here at all. What can the poor boy have been on about? He must have imagined . . . Oh dear God, no!* Her gaze had passed over the dark, freshly turned soil of the potato bed, not seeing at first the well-camouflaged khaki designed to blend so well with the earth. It was Captain Bray's feet that she noticed first. He was lying across the last row of the potato bed with his booted feet on the grass lawn at the end of the garden's cultivated area. She narrowed her eyes and focused on the outline of a man's body facedown in the newly turned loam, with a potato spade planted in the ground next to him. She walked forward and stopped, and then took a few steps more as the outline came fully into focus.

There was a relaxed, almost nonchalant air to the body's position, as if the man had said, "That was a jolly good lunch. You go on ahead; I am awfully fagged by all that digging," and had flung himself, facedown to avoid the sun, on freshly mown grass for a postprandial nap. But this was not a daisy-speckled lawn, nor did the sprawled khaki-clad body appear to be asleep in the sun. She hesitated, feeling unsure and reluctant.

"Lady Montfort, I think it would be wise if you would perhaps . . ."

"Nonsense, Captain, he might be ill and in need of my help. I have done my Voluntary Aid Detachment nurses' training." Clementine started to go forward and to her relief was gently moved to one side as the captain walked past her onto the narrow dirt path to where the body lay.

Don't be silly, you have been trained for this sort of situation, she told herself, and coming up behind the captain she peered around his broad shoulders as he bent over the inert form on the ground.

It is true what Lieutenant Phipps said then, his head has indeed been smashed in, she found herself thinking as she took in the plight of the man at their feet in a snapshot of vivid detail.

Someone was awfully angry when they hit him on the head, was her next thought as she felt her stomach churn and clammy sweat break out on her palms and her nape, where her hair lay heavily coiled.

He has to be dead; he could not surely have survived an injury as serious as this. Her body felt as if it were made of wood, but she somehow managed to turn her head away and caught sight of the potato spade dug into the earth, standing upright like a sentry on guard.

Captain Martin, still bent over the body, started to turn the man over onto his back. "No, don't do that, don't move him. Feel for a pulse in his wrist." Her voice sounded to her own ears sharp in the quiet of the garden.

"No need, he is dead," Martin replied. Any man who had spent a scant twenty-four hours with the British Expeditionary Force in France recognized violent death when he saw it.

"It is Captain Bray then?"

"Yes," said Martin, standing up and brushing his hands on his trousers. "And someone has bashed the poor blighter's head in. Probably . . ."

As he reached for the spade handle, Clementine said, "No, Captain, whatever you do—do not touch the spade," with such authority that he turned and stared at her as if seeing her for the first time.

Clementine's stomach heaved and her mouth, moments before as dry as dust, filled with saliva. One moment she felt unbearably hot, the next she was chilled through and through, and there was a high-pitched ringing in her ears. "He has been murdered," she said and turned away from the sight of the stricken man to look out across the garden at the far wall, concentrating all her effort into bringing every brick into focus. *Listen to the birds, look up at the sky. There now, that's better.* Her hands still felt clammy as she walked away from the body, careful to stay on the path. She made herself look at the ground around the area; there were signs of disturbed earth everywhere. But there was order to the disturbance. The only footprints in the upturned soil were as orderly as the rows made by the man who had dug them. There was no sign of a skirmish, of a fight. The stamped-earth path between the root-vegetable rows was hard and at least three feet wide at this end of the bed. It looked as if the captain had been standing on the lawn at the bottom of the bed, had been hit on the head from behind, and had then fallen forward into the row he had just finished digging.

Now back on the main gravel path, she pulled a handkerchief from under the band of her wristwatch and carefully blotted her upper lip and the back of her neck. She walked down the path toward the lawn and into the protection of a nut tree growing by the garden's west wall. Its tall, wide branches gave shade to the bench underneath it, offering her a place to recover. She sat down and looked up into the green canopy until the crawling sensation in her scalp went away.

On the other side of the kitchen-garden wall was the orchid house. It would be full of flowers as bright as birds of paradise. She fixed on this image until the other one—the one of the man lying in the earth—began to recede. She heard the distant trickle of water from the fountain, and licked her dry lips, but she was too drained to walk to it for a drink.

After all these months of complete silence, enduring the torture of not knowing who he was and what had happened to him, why had this taciturn man on the edge of unlocking his identity been bludgeoned so ferociously to death in the carefully dug vegetable bed that had helped him to find himself again? She felt a flash of momentary anguish that after weeks of dedicated work this quiet man struggling to find his reason and his life had been denied both.

She exhaled slowly, unclenched her hands, and looked around her. *Who,* she asked herself, *could have come into this secluded place and killed the captain—apart from the obvious choice of Lieutenant Phipps?*

There were two heavy, arched oak doors in the ten-foot-high wall that surrounded the garden: the one she and Captain Martin had come through at its east end and the other, to her left, in its north side, which led to the drive she and Lord Montfort had walked up not half an hour ago. She noticed that it was closed. To her right, on the south side of the garden wall, was a pair of tall double gates to give entrance to carts. They stood half open at this time of year as the summer's now empty garden beds were spread with well-rotted manure for autumn planting.

The sound of voices, several of them, brought her head up to see a procession emerge at her end of the pergola. First came her husband, followed by Major Andrews—the hospital's commanding and chief medical officer—then Mrs. Jackson. They all stood in a group for a moment, hands lifted to shade their eyes, and then started across the garden toward her.

"Good God, Clemmy!" Her husband's face expressed both concern and exasperation. *Yet again I have discovered a dead body.* "Why on earth didn't you wait for us before coming in here?" He half turned back to the body in the potato bed. "Major Andrews said that given Lieutenant Phipps' recent progress it was highly unlikely that he was hallucinating."

"No, he wasn't." She looked over at the body in the potato bed. "Captain Sir Evelyn Bray," she said, as if making an introduction, "is quite dead." She looked around the garden, expecting to see someone else there with them standing under the shade of the walnut tree.

Her husband's concerned eyes sought hers, and he lifted a hand to her shoulder. "Clemmy, you are in shock, how sensible of you to come and sit over here." She noticed that he was standing directly in front of her to block the sight of the man on the ground. "As soon as you can, I want you to go back to the house. Mrs. Jackson will take you."

"Did you . . . ?"

"Telephone? Yes, at Haversham Hall before I left. Colonel Valentine will be here as soon as he can. I will have to wait here for him, of course."

As indeed I shall too. She thought Ralph had been very efficient in calling in Colonel Valentine, their chief constable for the county. *No doubt he's hoping to prevent* us *from involving ourselves.* She glanced at Mrs. Jackson, who was looking down her nose at the garden bed in which the body of Captain Bray was sprawled.

"I think I will sit quietly on the bench for a moment."

He was instantly solicitous. "Of course you should. Mrs. Jackson, will you see to her ladyship?" Then he turned away from them and went to consult with Major Andrews, who had carefully turned the body of Captain Bray onto its back. *He shouldn't have done that,* Clementine thought. *And why are they trampling the bed?*

She patted the bench next to her in invitation and Mrs. Jackson sat down. After a moment or two Clementine said, "Well, Jackson, what are you thinking?"

"I was thinking about the beginning of the war, m'lady, and our visit to Hyde Castle."

The murder of Rupert Bartholomew at Hyde Castle! Why, she hasn't spoken about that in two years. Clementine remembered how keenly Mrs. Jackson had participated in their investigation; Jackson had even persevered when she had been ready to throw in the towel, but she had learned that any reference to their involvement in unsavory matters after the fact were taboo. *Really understandable,* Clementine decided, *respectability would prevent her from ever admitting, probably even to herself, that she had been involved in anything as distasteful as prying. Does this mean she is prepared to be involved in this particular instance or is she reminding me in advance that she would prefer not?*

"Anything in particular that springs to mind, Jackson?"

"I was thinking that this was rather an angry sort of murder, m'lady, angry and violent."

"I would have thought all murders were violent, Jackson."

"Then I am not putting it very well, m'lady. Captain Bray's violent end makes me think that it was possibly a murder carried out on the spur of the moment. I am assuming that the potato spade was the weapon, which perhaps I shouldn't do. But my first impressions are that the captain's death was not planned and that the culprit evidently hit him more savagely than was needed to . . ."

"Kill him?"

"Yes, m'lady."

They sat in silence for a moment or two. "The obvious culprit is Lieutenant Phipps, Jackson. At least that is the most understandable connection and one that I expect the police will jump to."

She glanced at her housekeeper and noticed a very slight frown creasing her forehead. "I have been sitting here for a few minutes now and I am wondering why Lieutenant Phipps came into the kitchen garden at all. You see, he was coming from the orchard to the kitchen-garden courtyard with some apples for the press, so why didn't he wheel his barrow up the east drive on smooth going instead of taking a detour into the kitchen garden?" She waved in the direction of the closed north door into the garden. "He would have had to open that door, wheel the barrow in and turn and close it, then negotiate the paths with a cumbersome and heavy load. If he had wheeled the barrow up the drive he would have merely had to turn in through the archway—so much easier than this circuitous route."

"I am sure the police will pick up on that one too, m'lady, which means that Lieutenant Phipps might very well be arrested. And we have the War Office and Medical Board inspection next week. I am sure that a murder on the premises will not go down well with that lot."

"Oh dear heavens, Jackson, you are right, *that* will certainly be a problem. And how on earth are we going to break it to Mr. Bray that his brother, on the road to recovery, has been murdered while he was in our care?"

Chapter Four

"It only takes about twenty minutes to drive up here from Market Wingley—what is holding them up?" Lord Montfort asked for the fourth time as he and Major Andrews joined Clementine and Mrs. Jackson under the walnut tree after Captain Martin had left to return to the hospital. "What time is it now?" He took out his watch, then stuffed it back into his waistcoat pocket. "Nearly an hour since I put that blasted telephone call through. They must have had a puncture." And to his wife: "Clemmy, I really think you need not wait here, you still look awfully pale."

"I am quite all right." Clementine felt immensely tired, but she was determined to stay. "Look, here is Valentine now. Goodness me, he has brought half of the Market Wingley police force with him." She watched the chief constable for the county lead his men down the garden path toward them.

After a brief inspection of the body by both Colonel Valentine and his inspector, it was left in the competent hands of a police sergeant and one of the two police constables that had accompanied Colonel Valentine from Market Wingley.

"Lady Montfort . . ." The old colonel was holding his hat in his hands, and his lined face creased more deeply as he smiled down at her sitting on her bench. "What a terrible thing to have happened, it must been a most unpleasant thing to find." Colonel Valentine murmured all the conventional phrases to ladies who have had a horrid shock as he ushered them back up the gravel path toward the kitchen-garden courtyard. "Let us all go back to the Hall, perhaps a cup of tea?"

They filed through the garden door and into the courtyard. Clementine noticed that a swarm of wasps was enjoying the half-crushed apples left in the barrel. The smell of sweet juice drying in the sun was almost nauseating. *I don't think I will ever be able to drink a glass of cider again, without remembering Captain Bray lying in our kitchen garden.*

With her husband solicitously on her right and Mrs. Jackson on her left, they continued in silence on up the drive to the hospital. It was so breathtakingly hot that Clementine had never been so grateful to walk into the dim interior of the marble hall of the old dower house as she was that afternoon.

Mrs. Jackson, seeing Lord Montfort's hesitation, led the way into what once had been his mother's drawing room, and was now used as the officers' day mess. "Perhaps we might open the windows a little, Jackson?" With the windows open the heat in the room seemed if anything to intensify, but at least the smell of stale cigarettes began to lessen.

Tea was offered as Colonel Valentine made the introductions. "Just a glass of water please," Clementine murmured to a young woman in a VAD uniform, who looked startled and sped away, to return with a wet glass of tepid water in her hand.

Colonel Valentine's inspector was a tall, reedy man with a long, nervous face and eyes that slid about the room, taking in every detail. Clementine noticed that he had neglected to remove his hat when he had come into the house. "Lord Montfort, may I present Inspector Savor?" Colonel Valentine gestured to his inspector looking out of the window and whistling through his teeth as he shifted small change around in his trouser pockets.

"Saveur?" Lord Montfort asked in considerable surprise, taking care with his pronunciation. "Are you of Gallic extraction, Inspector?"

"Sav-*or*, your lordship." The inspector's correction was emphatic.

"Oh, I see, Sa*ber*, so not French then?"

"No, your lordship, I am not, and it is Sa*vor*."

"Right then."

What on earth is the matter with Ralph? Clementine knew that years of enthusiasm for the shoot had left her husband a little deaf. *Muffing the inspector's name so thoroughly makes him sound quite potty.*

"My apologies for our late arrival, Lady Montfort." She was grateful to Colonel Valentine for cutting in on the music-hall exchange between the two men. "We are alarmingly short-staffed at headquarters and have been taken up with a theft in the last day or so; a considerable amount of petrol seems to have been misappropriated." The chief constable bowed his head to her in apology for the hour they had waited in the kitchen garden. Clementine thought that he had aged in the past two years, his eyebrows were thicker and more wiry and his bearing a little less upright.

"Good God—stolen petrol—how much?" Her husband seemed far more shocked that valuable petrol had been stolen than he was by the death of Captain Bray.

"Well over eight hundred gallons."

"*That* much? Yes, that is serious."

Clementine guessed that this conversation would take up a considerable amount of her husband's time with his old pal Colonel Valentine, so she took over with the introductions. "Colonel Valentine this is Major Andrews. He is the Commanding and Chief Medical Officer of Haversham Hall Hospital. This is Captain

Martin, he is one of our officer-patients—the captain was with me when we discovered Captain Bray's body; and you have already met Mrs. Jackson, who was appointed as Haversham Hall Hospital's administrator just before we opened our hospital." Introductions made, the police constable was given a chair by the window so that he could take notes, and the inspector took off his hat, sat down, and made himself comfortable in a way that Clementine found both consciously disrespectful and rather defiant.

Colonel Valentine seated himself on a sagging green cretonne-covered sofa and everyone else pulled up straight-backed chairs and dutifully sat in a circle around him—everyone, that is, noticed Clementine, except her husband. Lord Montfort continued to stand, his hands clasped behind his back in the middle of the room. And it was he who was the first to speak.

"I would be grateful if you would talk to Lady Montfort first, Valentine. We must both be on our way; Captain Bray's brother is expected to join us at the house this afternoon." He glanced at the clock on the chimneypiece. "Good Lord, is that the time? We shall be late for him. What a lamentable state of affairs."

"Yes, I am so sorry to have kept you all waiting. Let's talk about what happened to . . ." Colonel Valentine looked down at a paper in his hand, "to Captain Sir Evelyn Bray. Perhaps, if it would not distress you too much to do so, would you tell me how you came to find the late captain, Lady Montfort?" Colonel Valentine's white-tufted brows rose to his hairline as he asked his first question.

Clementine straightened her back, folded her hands in her lap, and point by point gave him an account of what had happened from her arrival at the cider press to the moment when she had accompanied Captain Martin into the kitchen garden to find Captain Bray lying in his potato bed. "I think it would be helpful to you, Colonel, if Corporal Budge was to describe the state Lieutenant Phipps was in when he came into the yard through the east door of the kitchen garden." She respected Budge and believed that if anyone could, the hospital orderly would give the chief constable a better sense of the hospital, the work they were doing here, and the state of mind of their patients.

Corporal Budge was sent for and moments later he was with them, standing smartly to attention, his eyes fixed somewhere above his commanding officer's head.

"At ease, Corporal," Major Andrews said. "Just tell Colonel Valentine here what happened in the kitchen courtyard, please. Start from when Lieutenant Phipps came in from the kitchen garden."

"Lieutenant Phipps was in a state of considerable shock, sir, when he arrived in the yard at about half past two o'clock. It was a few moments before he was calm enough to tell us that he had found the dead body of Captain Bray in the garden—with his head, as Lieutenant Phipps put it, 'smashed.'"

"He had been able to identify him then?"

Budge paused. "Yes, he had, sir. He said, 'Captain Bray is in the kitchen garden, lying facedown in the dirt with his head smashed in.'"

"The captain was alone when Phipps found him?"

"Phipps did not mention anyone, sir, but I expect so, the captain always liked to work in the garden by himself."

"Do you mean to tell me that he worked alone in that extraordinarily large area, that he did not have any help?"

Corporal Budge cleared his throat and glanced over to Major Andrews for assistance, which he promptly gave. "Yes, the captain was rather reclusive. There were other officers in the kitchen-garden detachment, as we call it, since our officers are encouraged to garden and as you say it covers a large area—"

"Over two acres," interrupted Lord Montfort and looked at his watch.

"But when Captain Bray worked in the kitchen garden, he

preferred to work alone, and this was because . . . ?" Clementine could almost hear the derision in Inspector Savor's voice.

"He was still in the army, wasn't he?" A more polite inquiry from Colonel Valentine.

"To answer both your questions, he was still in the army; this is a military hospital, and active work for a positive purpose, like gardening or helping with the harvest, is a useful cure for our patients."

"A cure for what, Doctor?" Again that rather condescending tone from the inspector, and Clementine frowned.

"Actually my rank is major, and with respect, our patients' therapies are something I may not discuss with you, Inspector." Major Andrews did not look at Savor, and the inspector said, "We'll see about that."

Not only condescending but truculent too. Clementine glanced over at Colonel Valentine and the elderly man lifted his hand.

"If you would oblige us, Major Andrews, this is a murder inquiry." His quiet voice was a contrast to the lounging Inspector Savor's insolent tone. "Anything you can do to help us understand Captain Bray's circumstances, anything that would help us piece together the reason for his murder . . . is not only welcome, it is required."

"Certainly, Colonel, I will do whatever I can to help you."

"And I want to know where everyone in your hospital was, while Captain Bray was enjoying his solitude in the kitchen garden," Inspector Savor said, reclaiming his position as interrogator.

Oh dear, thought Clementine, *it seems the inspector doesn't like this hospital any more than our local people do.* Even their old friend Colonel Valentine seemed to have formed an antipathy toward the men they were treating here. *What is it about these old Boer War veterans that they simply cannot seem to grasp that modern warfare inflicts wounds on not just the body but the mind too?*

"If you wish to know where everyone was while Captain Bray

was gardening, Inspector, it will be simple enough." Major Andrews turned to Corporal Budge. "If you would be so good, Corporal."

"Only seven officers remain at present in the hospital as of this morning, sir. Thirteen officers passed their medical review and returned to duty last week." He said this with pride, but neither policeman seemed terribly impressed, Clementine noticed. Budge cleared his throat to continue. "Three of them are on farm detachment today: Lieutenant Forbes at the Home Farm, Lieutenant Standish at Dodd Farm, and Lieutenant Carmichael over at Brook End Farm; they all left after breakfast at eight o'clock this morning, sir, and will not return for another hour.

"The three officers who were with me in the kitchen-garden courtyard on cider detachment after lunch: Captain Martin and Lieutenants Fielding and Phipps spent the morning with either one of our medical officers: Captain Pike and Major Andrews."

"Thank you, Corporal." Colonel Valentine lifted a restraining hand to his inspector, who had started to chip in with a question. "Major Andrews, what about this morning and these three officers who were in the hospital, can you account for their time with you?"

"I was in consultation with Captain Martin at nine o'clock. He was with me until half past ten, and then I was with Lieutenant Phipps until . . . I think he was with me until noon. Captain Pike saw Fielding at about the same time, so you would have to check with him. Sister Carter gave all three officers their monthly physical when they were not in consultation. I can vouch that all three of the officers were with us in the medical wing until luncheon."

"Thank you, Major Andrews. Now let me see . . . you say three of your officers have been away from the hospital all day, so we will have to check at their farms. Hmm . . ." He ran his finger down one side of his mustache. "Luncheon was taken at what time? Was everyone present?"

Corporal Budge stood to attention as he answered. "Yes, sir, all the officers on cider detachment were present in the officers' mess for luncheon at one o'clock. The officers on farm detachment took their lunch at their farms. Captain Bray was given a sandwich in the kitchen garden—"

"Because he likes to be alone," interrupted the inspector.

Colonel Valentine ignored his inspector. "Did you say that Captain Bray is some sort of a recluse?"

"Captain Bray was an amnesiac, Colonel," said Major Andrews, and when the chief constable looked confused, he went on to explain: "He had lost all memory when he returned after the Battle of Beauville Wood in March; without his identity discs they would not have known who he was or what battalion he came from. At the beginning of this month his memory had started to improve, he remembered his name and who he was, but not much of anything else. By using certain therapies such as painting and gardening as well as medical consultation, we believed that he would gradually recall his memory not just in the last months but before the war, too. We were in fact very hopeful that this would be the case."

"Painting." Colonel Valentine's voice was not derisive, but he did not sound impressed. "Painting pictures, that sort of thing?"

"Yes, Colonel, painting helps to unlock images that aid in restoring memory. Occupational cures such as gardening, for example, or working on a farm; ordinary everyday activities like making one's bed, or the simple business of pressing apples for cider, help lessen the stress and tension of nervous disorders. In the case of amnesia, the patient learns new information to replace what was lost, or to use intact memories as a basis for taking in new information."

"Good Lord above, what a way to run a war." Colonel Valentine looked over at Clementine and her husband, saw that they were not with him in his thinking, and gestured to Inspector

Savor as if he had heard enough and that it was now his turn. *Oh no*, thought Clementine, *please don't tell me that this miserable clod is going to be handling this inquiry.* She looked across at Mrs. Jackson, who was sitting with her face composed as she gazed down at the green-and-yellow tartan pattern of the drawing room carpet.

Major Andrews evidently recognized dissenters when he heard them because he came to the defense of his patient. "Captain Bray was an exceptionally brave officer, Colonel. He was awarded both the Distinguished Service Order and the Military Cross in the first year of the war. He had been on continuous active service with very little leave for the first two years of the war, before the Battle of Beauville Wood. We have discovered in recent months that it is often our 'heroes,' the men who take the most risks, putting their men's welfare before their own, who continually perform acts of bravery, that are more likely to become victims of neurasthenia or shell-shock, as it is more commonly referred to, than other officers. Their men are devoted to these officers and trust them implicitly, and their senior officers value their courage and leadership. But under continued and increasing pressure and stress they suffer from depression, which deepens and often leads to manic acts of courage . . ." He paused for a moment. "And then if they are not killed in action, they simply break down."

"Really?" The colonel was being polite and Clementine's heart sank, as it was clear to her that Valentine was being tactful because of their friendship. *He doesn't like the sound of this at all*, she thought, watching his eyebrows waving up and down as he tugged the corner of his mustache. "Well now, where was the rest of the hospital staff when the officers took their luncheon?"

There was silence for a moment.

"VADs, orderlies, and nursing staff take their midday dinner in the servants' hall, sir. I am not sure . . ." Corporal Budge turned toward Mrs. Jackson, who had lifted her large, intelligent gray eyes from the carpet and had fixed them on Colonel Valentine as he turned and bowed his head to her. Sitting in a straight-backed chair by the window, her hair a halo of warm russet in the sunlight, Mrs. Jackson exhibited, to Clementine's mind, the dignity and bearing of a great lady. Even though her humble origins were reflected in her Lancashire accent, her well-modulated voice had everyone's attention, including, Clementine was amused to notice, a look of interest from Inspector Savor.

"I think I might be able to help with where the staff was today, sir."

"Ah, Mrs. Jackson, I am sure you know exactly where everyone was before, during, and after luncheon." Colonel Valentine smiled at the woman for whom he had the utmost respect.

Mrs. Jackson bowed her head in acknowledgment. "Since many of our patients have returned to duty, most of our staff are on home-leave this week and it will be easy to look at our hospital timetable to see where they all were today. Junior staff eat in the old servants' hall. The officer-patients and senior medical staff eat in the officers' mess dining room. Everyone in the hospital eats at the same time, at one o'clock."

"And what time did luncheon end?"

"Two o'clock, sir, same for everyone. Then we all went back to work."

"Are you telling me that you know where all the hospital staff was from one o'clock until half past two, when Captain Bray's body was found?"

"I know where everyone was supposed to be, sir."

"Well then, Mrs. Jackson, I would like you to remain behind so that you can give me a list of the staff and their duties, and I would like Corporal Budge to remain so we can go over his list of officers. Once we have an idea of where everyone was supposed to be, we will take it from there.

"Now, Lord and Lady Montfort need to return to Iyntwood for

the arrival of Captain Bray's brother," and turning to Lord Montfort: "When I have finished here, I will come over to Iyntwood to meet with Mr. Bray, and perhaps have a word with Lady Montfort if that would be convenient. Unless, Lady Montfort, you would prefer I return to talk to you tomorrow morning?"

But Lord Montfort, ignoring Colonel Valentine's desire to consult further with Clementine, said, "In that case, why don't you join us for dinner this evening, Valentine?" His invitation was not extended to the inspector sitting in the most comfortable chair in the room.

"No point in rushing things." Lord Montfort tucked Clementine's arm in his as they walked down the steps of Haversham Hall and out into the late afternoon. "We are already woefully late to greet our guest."

As they set off for home, three men came into sight walking up the drive toward them. They were in uniform, and it was clear from their sunburned faces that here were the officers who had spent the day on farm detachment. As they approached, the second lieutenant in front stopped, drew himself up, and saluted.

Lord Montfort nodded a greeting. "Looks like you have put in a good few hours today, all of you," and to the young man who had saluted: "And where were you working today?"

"Brook End Farm, my lord."

"Aha, so your harvest is nearly in; and you are?"

"Ian Carmichael, I am with the Glosters, Lord Montfort." His already rosy complexion deepened in hue as he hastily corrected himself: "I *was* with the Glosters at the Battle of Beauville Wood." Lieutenant Carmichael had none of the diffidence of his brother officers; his earnest expression together with his bronzed cheeks and clear blue eyes made him a perfect candidate for one of Lord Kitchener's recruiting posters.

"And these gentleman," Clementine extended a hand to the other two bringing up the rear, "are Lieutenant Forbes, who has been working at our Home Farm"—a very young officer, perhaps barely nineteen, saluted—"and Lieutenant Standish, who was working . . . where today, Lieutenant?"

"At . . . Dodd Farm, Lady Montfort. Harvest will be in by . . . tomorrow." There was still a hesitation in Standish's speech, as if forming his consonants came with effort.

"Nice enough sort of chaps," her husband remarked, after they said goodbye and continued on down the drive.

"They all are," Clementine said loyally, "every single one of them; it is what makes me so grateful you agreed to our hospital." And as they walked on together: "I hope that Harry and Althea were around to take care of Mr. Bray. I don't know about you, but I feel pretty shaken up by the idea of telling him that his brother is dead."

Her husband stopped and turned to her, his face expressing more than concern. "Clemmy," he said as he studied her face, "if you are not up to it then please don't feel you have to join us for dinner. I will tell Valentine that you will talk to him tomorrow." He watched her brows come up as she opened her mouth to protest, and he laughed. "What was I thinking? Of course you will talk to Valentine." They walked on in companionable silence for a few moments and then he said, "You don't think that one of the inmates at the hospital went stark staring mad and killed him, do you? Thought he was a Hun digging a trench and whacked him with the spade?"

She laughed. "'Inmates'? You make them sound like the criminally insane. You heard Mrs. Jackson; it was easy to account for all of our officers since we only have six of them, not including Captain Bray, at the hospital this week. And none of them could have murdered the captain." She didn't like to think about the stammering Lieutenant Phipps being hanged for this murder.

"Six? Aren't we getting any more?"

"You sound rather competitive. There will be a War Office and Medical Board inspection next week and if they are satisfied with the work the hospital is doing, they will send us some more. Major Andrews told me that the numbers of men suffering from chronic neurasthenia has risen considerably since the Somme offensive."

He stopped again and turned to her in the golden light of early evening. " 'If they are satisfied'? You didn't tell me about the War Office's need to be satisfied—there must have been dozens who have come and gone from the hospital in the past ten months, most of them sound enough to return to the war." He looked so affronted that she almost laughed. She could only imagine how much her hospital had cost him, both in patience and money.

"Major Andrews told me that the War Office's greatest concern is how long it takes him to help our officers return to a useful life. After all, an officer must have at least some semblance of confidence to lead his men into battle. There is a chap in London called Dr. Yelland who specializes in mutism and he claims he can 'cure' men suffering from shell-shock in less than a week, but he only works with soldiers. We take sometimes as long as three months and the War Office think that perhaps Major Andrew's talking cure and our cure through function are what they call 'too soft,' that if there are malingerers among our patients they can swing the lead for months."

'What does Yelland do that he is so effective?"

"It is pretty barbaric stuff, it basically comes down to torture— electric shock treatment he calls it: a quick remedy maybe, but certainly not a cure." They resumed their walk along the drive.

"So none of these seven patients we have now could have killed Captain Bray then, I mean because they were seeing things or whatever Andrews calls it?"

"Hallucinating? I really hope not. And we have six patients, Captain Bray was the seventh. As to who could have killed him, I think it all depends if Captain Bray was killed before lunch, during it, or half an hour afterwards. It would have been difficult for any of the officers helping at nearby farms to have found their way to the kitchen garden without their absence being noticed. And of the three officers making cider, only Phipps had the opportunity to murder Captain Bray." In her mind she saw Lieutenant Phipps staggering into the courtyard and felt a moment of fierce protection toward the young man. "Anyway, it doesn't matter what I think, it matters what Mrs. Jackson thinks. She pretty well runs the hospital. But there might be others at Haversham Hall who had a reason for murdering that poor man."

"Aha," he said as they walked on again. "Then I expect Mrs. Jackson will be over to the house, bright and early tomorrow morning, to report in." Clementine glanced at her husband out of the corner of her eye. He was laughing at her, encouraging her to admit that she was already summoning her resources for a new inquiry. Her only response was to give him her brightest smile.

"Of course you should investigate what happened, Clemmy. I am the last to say a word against it."

Her smile broadened but then lost some of its warmth when he said, "Just as, you know, you don't go mad."

"Go mad?" *What on earth does he mean?*

"Yes, precisely that. Exercise restraint. When you are nearing the truth, hand it over to Valentine to finish it off; let his be the back that bears the burden, especially if you unearth truths we would all rather not know about."

They had drawn level with the kitchen-garden courtyard and Clementine noticed that the strong aroma of apple juice still hung in the air; its concentrated sweetness permeated her thoughts as she enumerated possibilities, ticked off names, and asked questions. The hospital was an institution with a rigid timetable; it would be easy to establish alibis for their patients, and then they would be left with who on the hospital staff or in the surrounding area would have a reason to kill a man who had no memory of his life six months ago and who had appeared not to have made a friend or an enemy since he had come to them.

Her husband interrupted her mental note-taking. "I expect that dreadful jumped-up Inspector Saber will arrest Phipps by the end of the day, after all he is the obvious choice, and it struck me that Saber is possessed of a commonplace mind."

"It's Savor, darling, not Saber."

"Yes, isn't that what I said? Come on, we must go and dress for dinner and then find Mr. Bray and tell him our wretched news."

Chapter Five

Mrs. Jackson said good night to Colonel Valentine at the front door of the hospital, and then glancing at her watch made her way downstairs to the servants' hall. Gathered around the table were Corporals West and Budge and the only two VAD girls who were not on leave this week: Mary Fuller and Sarah Ellis. All conjecture, speculation, and chatter came to an abrupt end as she walked into the room. Heads turned in her direction and curious eyes took in her clipboard with the hospital schedule attached to it. Corporal Budge had evidently told them that she had stayed behind to talk to Colonel Valentine.

"Good evening, everyone. Where is Sister Carter?" she asked, and Corporal Budge answered that she was still in the medical wing. Mrs. Jackson sat down at the table and looked around at their expectant faces.

"I am sure Sister Carter will talk to you when she has time. But I want to let you know what is going on, so far, with the police investigation into the death of Captain Bray."

"You mean murder, don't you, Mrs. Jackson." It was a statement, not a question; Corporal Budge was the straightforward type.

The youngest and prettiest of the Voluntary Aid Detachment girls, Sarah Ellis, bent her head and sobbed into her hankie, and Mrs. Jackson reminded herself to be patient. *How old is*

Ellis—twenty? My goodness, she is young for her age, she thought, not for the first time, as she watched a pink nose emerge from a damp handkerchief, the lower lip of the soft little rosebud mouth quivering in protest at distressing news.

It had taken Ellis weeks to learn the simplest of domestic tasks when she had arrived at the hospital fresh from VAD training. She had not known how to make so much as a cup of tea and was incapable of completing any task in a timely fashion, leaving most of them half-finished as she flitted on to something else. But she was sweet-tempered and Mrs. Jackson had trained less-willing girls in her time. "Ellis, I can see you are distressed by all of this, it is a most upsetting thing to have happened. Go and wash your face and hands and then come along to my office please." She looked around the table to Mary Fuller, the other VAD girl, who was still on duty in the hospital this week. "And, Fuller, I would like to see you after I have finished talking to Ellis." She waved the schedule to reassure the young women that this was about hospital business.

"Now then, about the police investigation into the death of Captain Bray: there has been no inquest yet, Corporal Budge, and until there is it would be unwise to talk of murder." She looked away so as not to see his derisive expression. "I expect that Inspector Savor will want to talk to each of you. He will get to you when he can, so be prepared for a late night. There is no need to worry or panic about what he is going to ask you. But it is important you are completely honest with him. Keep your answers clear and accurate and we will probably not need to see him again beyond tomorrow." This was probably not going to be the case at all, but from experience she knew how important it was not to set them all on the edge of their seats. The police would do that very well without her help. "That's all."

She picked up the tea tray Cook had prepared for her and left, hearing exclamations of impatience and frustration from the overworked male orderlies, and wails from Ellis and Fuller. She walked up the back stairs to the main floor of the house, crossed the vast marble hall, and pushed open the door to her office with her shoulder. The room was in half-darkness; she set down her tray, switched on the light, and sat down at her desk to pour herself a cup of the reviving brew. She had just finished her first cup when there came a knock on her door and she called out to come in.

"You wanted to see me, Mrs. Jackson?" Ellis had made an attempt to be presentable. Her cap was on straight over brushed red-gold curls and she had respectfully put on a clean apron. She came into the room and stood before Mrs. Jackson's desk and waited.

"There, that's better," Mrs. Jackson said with a brief smile of approval at her tidy appearance. "Now let's talk about where you were today, shall we? You were on duty in the kitchen before luncheon?" she asked, and Ellis nodded.

"Is that a yes?" she pursued.

"Yes, Mrs. Jackson. I was helping the cook, we cleaned and prepared vegetables. Mr. Thrower had forgotten to bring us green beans for lunch, so Mary . . . Fuller was sent to get some from the kitchen garden."

"What time would that have been?" She kept her voice low and calm. She wanted Ellis to have a chance to tell her account before she met with Inspector Savor; it would help the girl if she had already run through her movements ahead of time.

"I expect it was at twelve, maybe a few minutes after. Cook sent her off and told her to hurry back so that we could prepare them in time for lunch in the officers' mess."

"And what about you? What were your duties in the kitchen before you helped Cook with the vegetables?"

"I cleaned up after Cook while she finished the stew. We had already made the apple pies."

"And earlier, before you worked in the kitchen?"

The girl look puzzled for a moment. "Earlier? Mary and I put away the clean linen—we recorded everything in the linen inventory like you showed us." *That means there will be thirty pillow cases on hand even if the inventory ledger shows only three.* Mrs. Jackson did not sigh.

"Well, there is not much to do really when there are so few patients at the hospital this week, and we cleaned and tidied the officers' mess yesterday. So today we just dusted the porcelain collection, threw away dead flowers and arranged fresh ones." She thought for a moment and then added, "Oh yes, and Cook sent for me at eleven and told me to make up a basket lunch for Captain Bray and take it to him in the kitchen garden."

"Wasn't that a bit early?"

"Yes, but she was running behindhand and needed me back to help with the veg. It was just a pork pie, a piece of cake, and an apple. We often take it over early, we just put it down under the tree on the bench, so it's handy—not that he ever eats it."

This early delivery of Captain Bray's luncheon basket is an interesting change in hospital routine that I was not aware of. Mrs. Jackson sipped her second cup of tea as she considered the possibilities this alteration might have caused. "So you took him his luncheon in the kitchen garden, and then?"

The girl had started to cry. "I can't believe that someone . . ." Ellis wept, wiping her eyes with the back of her hand.

"Yes, it is very shocking, but in time the memory will fade. In the meantime we must try to carry on. Now use your hankie, that's the way, and answer my question. So you took Captain Bray his luncheon . . ."

"Yes, I took his basket over to him."

"And then?"

"Then I came back to the house."

"At what time?"

The girl's eyes slid to the left and then to the right and then fixed themselves firmly on her face. *Here we go,* thought Mrs. Jackson, *here's the first lie.*

"I forgot to wind my watch, Mrs. Jackson, so I can't be sure of the time."

She let that one go for the moment. It would be easy enough to check with the cook. Both Fuller and Ellis had developed a ridiculous infatuation for Captain Bray in the last few weeks, but it was nothing she thought she need worry about, it was mostly all in their heads. It gave them something to giggle about and whisper over to one another; all part of having to rely on immature young women for the war effort.

"And after luncheon, what did you do then?"

"Fuller and I cleared the table in the officers' mess and when everything was washed up we put away all the china, then it was time for us to take a ten-minute break. After that we were both scheduled for nurses' training with Sister Carter." Mrs. Jackson felt a momentary flash of pity for Sister if she had to rely on these two girls in a nursing emergency.

"Did you come back to the house directly from the kitchen garden after you gave Captain Bray his luncheon?" As she circled back to Ellis's delivering the captain's luncheon basket she watched the girl's eyes fill with tears. "There is no need to cry," she said quietly. "Come now, did you speak with Captain Bray when you took him his luncheon?"

"I called out a good-morning." Her voice faltered. "But he didn't say anything or turn around, he just carried on with his digging." Mrs. Jackson tried for more patience. The captain was indifferent to everyone, men and women alike, even if the women were young and pretty.

"Did he turn round, or wave, or anything?"

"No." Her eyes skittered off to a far corner. *Silly little thing,* thought Mrs. Jackson and smiled at the ineffectual fibbing.

"How did you know it was Captain Bray then?"

"What?"

"He was in uniform and his back was to you. So how did you know it was him?"

The young woman was so disconcerted by this question that she simply stared at Mrs. Jackson with her mouth open.

"Because of the color of his hair," she recovered herself, and her voice was defiant. "He wasn't wearing his cap; he never does in the garden when it's sunny. His hair is ever so, was ever so beautiful." She choked up and groped for her hankie. "Dark gold, like ripened barley." *Ripened barley? Oh good Lord above,* Mrs. Jackson thought, *was I ever this gormless at twenty?*

"For someone as young and energetic as yourself, Ellis, it probably takes all of ten minutes to walk from the scullery door of the hospital to the kitchen garden." The girl bowed her head, a complacent smile acknowledging her youthful energy. "And since you did not stop to talk with the captain it would only take a few minutes to put the basket down on the bench, under the walnut tree, wouldn't it?" From her dismayed expression, Ellis evidently didn't like this accurate summation of her minutes. "And another ten minutes to walk back to the house. So if you left at eleven o'clock you must have been walking back into the kitchen to help Cook at exactly twenty-three minutes past eleven."

Ellis dropped her eyes to the carpet, lips pressed tightly together.

"Is that a yes, or a no?"

"Yes."

"Are you sure about this, Ellis, that you were back in the kitchen by twenty past eleven?" The girl started to nod, thought better of it, and said, "Yes, Mrs. Jackson, I am quite sure."

"Very well then, Ellis, that will be all. Off you go, and start setting the table for dinner in the officers' mess, please. I will be along when I have finished talking to Fuller."

Ellis opened the door and there sitting on a chair in the corridor was her best friend, Mary Fuller. Mrs. Jackson saw Ellis give her friend a meaningful nudge with her shoulder as Fuller came into the office.

"Good evening, Fuller; just give me a moment please."

Mrs. Jackson got up from her desk and stood in the window looking out at the darkening evening as she thought through Ellis's version of her trip to the kitchen garden. When she turned back to the young girl sitting with her hands in her lap, she thought Fuller had the rather complacent look of a cat. Her small round face was turned up toward her, large clear eyes serene, mouth relaxed in a faint smile.

"What time did the cook send you over to the kitchen garden this morning to pick beans for luncheon?" The girl's expression became even more catlike in its inscrutability; she blinked once or twice and answered without hesitation, "It was midday, perhaps a few minutes after."

"So you went over to the kitchen garden and arrived there at what time?"

"It only takes me about ten minutes. So it must have been about twelve-fifteen. I had a lot of beans to pick and Cook had told me I had to be back by a quarter to one."

"So what time did you get back to the kitchen?"

"I was back when Cook told me to be back, at a little before a quarter to one. We topped and tailed the beans, and Cook had them ready by the time the soup was eaten." Mrs. Jackson remembered that the beans had been perfectly prepared when they were served and there had been plenty of them. She paused before she asked her next question so that her voice was without a trace of doubt as to the veracity of Fuller's bean-picking expedition.

"Did you happen to see Captain Bray in the kitchen garden while you were there?"

A pale smile and the girl put her head on one side. There was considerable competition between Fuller and her friend Ellis for the captain's attention it seemed. "Of course I did." There was no "of course" about it, the bean rows were at the top end of the garden and between them and the bottom of the garden where the captain would have been digging were rows and rows of raspberry canes, and if she was in that corner of the garden, the grape pergola would have completely obscured the line of sight from the bean terrace down to the root-vegetable section at the far end of such a large area. It was as if she had voiced her doubts aloud, and Fuller smiled again. "I met Captain Bray in the kitchen courtyard when I arrived. He was sharpening his spade in the potting shed. He followed me into the kitchen garden. I told him I was in a rush and he helped me to pick beans. He was ever so nice, he's always nice to me," She smiled and then her face crumpled and she put her hands over her eyes. "How could anyone have done something so terrible to him?" There was no drama here, just shock and grief. Fuller struggled, and Mrs. Jackson stood up and patted the young woman on the shoulder. "He was such a sa-sad man. I know he was missing some of his marbles, but he was always so nice to me." She looked up as Mrs. Jackson made soothing there-there sounds. *If what she is saying is true and she left the kitchen courtyard to be back at the kitchen by a quarter to one, Captain Bray had been alive at about half past twelve.*

Before she turned in for the night Mrs. Jackson decided to have a word or two with Major Andrews. Right from the moment the head medical officer had walked through the door of the hospital nearly ten months ago, something had clicked between them. Nothing that made things difficult or embarrassing, there was none of that kind of silliness. Mrs. Jackson prized her independence and was proud of her status as a single working woman, despite the many delightful letters she exchanged with Ernie Stafford, who was presently in uniform with the War Graves Commission somewhere in France—somewhere with an almost unpronounceable name.

What's the name again? "Auchonvillers?" She tried the name out loud and wondered if that was how it was said. She had looked it up on the map in the library. Ernie had mentioned in his last letter that his move to Auchonvillers meant he was closer to the Boulogne docks and he hoped to be granted some home leave for Christmas.

"Auchonvillers," she said again, as she crossed the echoing cavern of the great hall, her footsteps loud on the marble floor.

"Ocean Villas, did you say, Mrs. Jackson?" Corporal West, the younger and livelier of their two male orderlies, came out of Major Andrews's office and, guessing in which direction she was headed, stood to mock attention and held the door open for her. West was a pleasant and easygoing man in his late twenties, an especially skilled male nurse. He came from the East End of London and had all the outgoing charisma of a self-assured cockney. He was openly adored by the professional nurses for his ability to remain good-natured and even-tempered in the worst situations, as well as for his smooth, well-barbered appearance: neatly trimmed hair and perfectly clipped mustache as worn by the American moving-picture heartthrob Douglas Fairbanks.

"Is that how it is pronounced? I was wondering. Some of these French towns have such odd-sounding names."

"Horrible place that Ocean Villas, that's what the soldiers call it by the way. They've seen more misery there than in all the rest of northern France—barring the other Somme battlefields and of course Wipers." She smiled at the soldiers' slang for the French town.

"Ypres?"

"Spot on. I hope no one in your family is in Ocean Villas, Mrs. Jackson."

"Just an old friend but he's not in the fighting."

"Doctor, then, I expect?" he said, pushing for more information. Before the war Mr. Stafford had been the Talbots' landscape gardener and had been of great help to her with one or two of her ladyship's inquiries. But it would be the last thing in the world she would ever tell the gregarious and extremely inquisitive Corporal West, whose other attractions for the female staff included his love of gossip.

"He is with the War Graves Commission, well behind the lines." Mrs. Jackson stuck her head around the door of the doctor's office. "Do you have a moment, Major Andrews?"

A gray-haired man with the stooped shoulders of a scholar looked up from his desk. He stood up, took his pipe out of his mouth, and waved her into the room. "Mrs. Jackson, please come in. What a pleasant surprise at the end of a perfectly dreadful day."

She thought the hospital's chief medical officer looked more tired than usual, his plain, long horsey face was pale, and his coarse hair lifted in a double cowlick at the crown, giving him a permanently harassed appearance when he was one of the calmest men she had ever come across. She took a seat in the chair opposite his desk and placed a stack of requisition forms in front of him for his signature.

"I was wondering how our officers were doing, sir, any ill effects after this afternoon?"

He picked up his pen and signed the first form without reading it. "Phipps has withdrawn; he's still in shock. It's too soon to say for Martin and Fielding. Men who have been in combat rarely show emotion when one of their number is killed. But they are at home now in England, in a hospital where they believe they are safe, and Captain Bray was not killed in action, he was murdered. I expect Sister Carter and our orderlies will have a long night with some of them—especially Lieutenant Phipps. We might consider recalling Nurse White from home leave."

"Do you think Captain Bray was liked by the other officers, sir?" She had become used to the fact that there was rarely a question that this considerate man would not try to answer, if the questions were honest ones. If he thought she was intruding on patient confidentiality he would say so.

"Not actively disliked. They steered clear because he was so withdrawn. They rather admired him, I think. His war record was remarkable. No one doubted his courage or his dedication to the men in his company, so he had everyone's respect. But I am not sure how much they liked him."

"I am a bit worried about Inspector Savor." If she had had an older brother, or a brother at all, she liked to imagine he would have been like this quiet, reserved man who had such a capacity for understanding and such enduring patience. She never felt at ease with most men, except perhaps for Mr. Hollyoak, whom she had known for half her life, and Ernie Stafford, for whom she might or might not have particular feelings.

"You mean his rather contemptuous attitude? Yes, I think that's just a cover-up for his sense of inadequacy; he has rather an inferiority complex. Most policemen have a bit of a chip on their shoulders, unless they are really good at their job. The chief constable is a nice old codger though." He laughed. "He appears to be instinctively intelligent, straightforward, and well meaning."

"Whereas Savor might be a bit of a bully, sir."

He signed the last form and put his fountain pen down on the surface of the desk. Pushing back his chair, he folded his hands behind his head and considered for a moment. "You are concerned about his interrogation of the hospital staff and our patients?"

"Yes, I suppose I am, sir."

"I wouldn't worry, I am sure our staff can handle him. You should sit in on a Medical Board when they are 'interviewing' our patients to see if they are ready to return to duty, or if they are avoiding being sent back. If they can withstand those verbal drubbings,

Inspector Savor and his snide belligerence will be a walk in the park."

She wondered if it would be a walk in the park and felt a flash of dislike for the inspector. She had heard him say to his sergeant as she had left the drawing room, "Won't take us more than a minute to flush out our killer, Sergeant, they are all doolally"—he had tapped his temple—"even the ruddy doctors."

"The inspector will finish talking to the staff tonight. He'll start on our officers tomorrow. What room do you think I should put him in?" The major believed that surroundings affected mood: harmony created a sense of serenity, and clutter and chaos had a disruptive effect on his patients. He had insisted that the rooms the officers slept in were simply furnished and painted in the soft, muted colors found in nature. Green was a favorite with the major.

He laughed. "What about the old garden room, such a nice view of Captain Martin's late summer perennial bed. If it is a pretty day it will be warm in there and if we sedate him with a nice luncheon he will be less aggressive—any chance of steak-and-kidney pud?"

She reached across the desk and gathered the scattered forms into a tidy pile. "A good solid luncheon and with the afternoon sun warming his back our inspector will be as nice as he can possibly be, sir." She got up from her chair and then something else occurred to her. "Were you and Captain Pike with the cider detachment officers *all* morning? I mean right up until luncheon?"

He shot her a thoughtful look. "Yes, and if they were waiting for either one of us, Sister Carter gave them their physical checkups. All three of them were in the medical wing with Captain Pike, Sister Carter, and myself right up until we all walked over to the officers' mess for luncheon, except Phipps." She turned her head, perhaps a little too quickly, and noticed his faint smile before he continued. "Phipps went off to the orchard at about half past twelve—he wanted to get a start on apples for the pressing. I am afraid he will be at the top of Savor's list."

She didn't like this idea at all. "But Lieutenant Phipps is such a slight lad and Captain Bray stood well over six feet; it would have been hard for Phipps to have hit him on the top of his head."

The major tapped his forefinger twice on the arm of his chair. "Aha," he said. "So that's your thinking is it? But if Bray was bent over, or crouching to pick up potatoes?" He seemed so at ease with this discussion that she immediately asked another question.

"Might Lieutenant Phipps have been hallucinating, sir, and not known what he was doing?"

"Anything is possible, but it is highly unlikely that Phipps was hallucinating. Our inspector had better watch out, Mrs. Jackson, I can see your interest is piqued."

She wished him good night and hurried away. Major Andrews was a sharp one, and if she was going to get to the bottom of this situation she would have to be more discreet and work quickly. The War Office inspection and Medical Board review were at the end of the week.

Chapter Six

It was a preoccupied Clementine who changed into her evening dress and walked down to the drawing room half an hour before dinner. But she was pulled out of her introspection when she met Mr. Edgar Bray. The man who got to his feet by placing a heavy walking stick between his knees and pushing himself up with it was one of the most beautiful beings she had ever seen. She turned to the butler to give herself a moment to cover her surprise that Edgar Bray was such a stunningly handsome man. "We will eat dinner as soon as his lordship joins us, Hollyoak," she said, and then, her composure recovered, she gave her full attention to their guest.

"Good evening, Mr. Bray, I am Clementine Talbot. I am so sorry that Ralph and I were not here to welcome you. Oh please do sit."

He bowed his head in greeting and then lowered himself back into his chair and set his stick against its arm. "Not at all, no apology necessary. Lady Althea and Lord Haversham gave me tea, and we had a pleasant time comparing the delights of my native Cotswolds to the rolling hills of the Chilterns. Thank you so much for inviting me to stay with you, Lady Montfort. Elizabethan houses not completely ruined by our grandparents to bring them up-to-date are a charming rarity, and Iyntwood is a perfect jewel of a house."

Not only is he the most handsome man I have ever seen, but he is quite charming. Clementine looked into a face that bore all the hallmarks of beauty in a man. From the high crown of Edgar Bray's well-shaped head and his smooth high forehead to his classic jawline, his face was almost flawless. Dark straight brows, expressive and intelligent hazel-brown eyes, a straight strong nose that prevented him from looking too pretty, and a firm mouth that was neither too thin nor too full in the lip. He was of a good height, and his impeccably cut suit fitted him well across his broad shoulders. The only thing that prevented absolute perfection was that his right leg was turned at an almost forty-five-degree angle toward his left, which ever so slightly skewed the overall balance of his bearing. *But it does not mar his beauty at all,* she thought, *and with all the young men in Britain these days with missing limbs, even with his crooked leg he has such presence.* She also noticed that when he was not smiling, as he had been since she had come into the room, his mouth in repose turned down a little at the corners, pulled there by two deep lines from the edges of his nostrils to the corners of his mouth. The two deeply scored lines gave his beauty a truly human cast—otherwise she felt she might be overawed by his resemblance to a Greek god.

It must be exhausting to walk with that twisted leg. And then she realized that Edgar Bray had not been told yet of the death of his brother. She looked across the room at the smiling Althea, enchanting in a simple silk evening dress in royal blue, and at her son, who had also risen to his feet and was looking across at her with concern. *Harry knows that Captain Bray is dead, but Althea does not. Oh God, what a minefield this is going to be. Where on earth is Ralph?*

"My husband, Lord Montfort, will be with us directly . . . we were detained at Haversham Hall Hospital this afternoon." He didn't seem to mind in the slightest that neither of them had been here to welcome him at teatime. "How long did it take you to drive over from Gloucestershire, Mr. Bray? You live near Cheltenham, don't you?"

"I think it would have taken me about two hours, normally. But unfortunately I had a breakdown in my motor, so I was late to tea too." He shook his head as Hollyoak came forward to refill his sherry glass.

"How unfortunate. And how long were you detained before your driver sorted out the problem?" Hollyoak offered her a glass of sherry, even though brandy would have been more gratefully accepted.

"I drove myself," he said to her surprise. "My motorcar has been adapted so that I only need my good foot for the clutch and the accelerator; the brake is the old-fashioned type and I can operate it by hand." He seemed to be quite unselfconscious about his leg and his acknowledging it made her feel less strained. *What a delightful and unaffected manner he has,* she thought as she beamed approval.

"I hope someone was able to come to your aid. How long were you stranded?" She sipped her sherry. *I am certainly not going to be the one to tell him about the murder of his brother; why hasn't Ralph already spoken to him?*

"I had driven through Haversham village when my car conked out on . . . on Brook End Lane I believe it was. Not much I could do, the lane was completely empty—not a soul in sight. Just as I was giving up and thinking about sleeping the night there, as if by magic your daughter"—he turned to acknowledge Althea standing there in her pretty dress with her blue eyes shining in her sunny face—"came along and rescued me—such a competent mechanic."

"There are two mechanics in the Talbot family; my brother, Lord Haversham, is a most accomplished engineer. I learned very simple mechanics when I joined the Women's Land Army," said Althea with commendable modesty.

"So you were over at Brook End Farm this afternoon, Althea?" Clementine asked her daughter, who blushed very prettily.

"For most of the afternoon, off and on." Clementine caught Mr. Bray's admiring glance at Althea. *Being outside all day really agrees with her,* she thought, *she looks positively glossy these days.*

"So you must have organized the farm detachment then."

"Yes, I picked the officers up at Haversham Hall this morning and dropped two of them off at their farms. Lieutenant Carmichael and I were on our way to Brook End Farm when we came across Mr. Bray, sitting in a car that would not start."

Mr. Bray laughed. "The lieutenant had simply no idea what to do," he said with evident appreciation for his rescuer. "But Lady Althea had the bonnet up in a jiffy and spotted the problem in no time at all. Dirt in the carburetor wasn't it?" Althea's smile broadened and she said it was.

"Thank goodness help was at hand then," was all Clementine could think of to say as she raised her glass to her lips. *So if Althea wasn't picking young men up and dropping them off all over the countryside, she was mending motorcars.* Clementine realized she was feeling out of sorts and caught herself; *I am being old-fashioned in my outlook—again.* But the thought of her pretty daughter driving around the county unchaperoned, with young men she hardly knew, was something she should not ignore now that she had discovered that this was how Althea spent part of her day.

"How are our officers adapting to harvesting?" she asked, which was the only topic of interest that consumed the county at this time of year.

Althea glanced at her mother out of the corner of her eye as she replied, "Most of them come from families who own land and some of them even helped out with the harvest when they were boys—like we did." She waved her hand to include her brother. "I just dot them around the local farms for the day and then pick them up and cart them off home. The Land Army girls are more than capable of directing them—some of them have even learned to use a scythe without actually injuring themselves."

"So how are they doing over at Brook End—do they have all the wheat in?" Harry asked as Mr. Bray had fallen silent.

"Pretty nearly, should be done by tomorrow. Molly Anderson gave everyone a wonderful luncheon of rabbit pie, but we missed it as I was teaching Lieutenant Carmichael to plow—the old way, with a horse. Dolly can pull a single-furrow plow because the upper fields have such light soil." She turned to Mr. Bray. "In heavier soils two horses are needed, one walking on the land and one in the furrow. Most of the Land girls learned how last winter, they are getting awfully good at it. We are thinking of doing a plowing competition in November, you know, between farmers and the Land Army girls. First prize goes to the team that can plow the straightest and tightest furrows!"

"No luncheon, you must be famished!" Clementine thought her words sounded a bit forced or, even worse, jolly.

"Not at all, Molly sent us out a picnic lunch of bread and cheese. It was delicious; she sent cider too."

Us? Clementine felt the evening was slipping away from her. *What on earth is going on?* She couldn't quite remember this Lieutenant Carmichael who had spent most of the day with her daughter. Mr. Bray was drinking in all this bucolic countryside fun with appreciative interest, and Harry, who had been smoking cigarettes one after the other, looked across at his mother and shook his head slightly in commiseration with her that someone was going to have to tell this most pleasant Mr. Bray that he would not, after all, be reunited with his brother.

And then as if he had sensed her unease and recognized the need to come to her aid, the door to the drawing room opened and her husband walked into the room as if murdered bodies in his kitchen gardens occurred at Iyntwood every day of the week. *And why not indeed? At least we are not related to this particular victim*, thought Clementine.

"I am so sorry to have kept you all; I was with Colonel Valentine in my study." And to his wife: "The colonel will not be joining us for dinner, simply doesn't have the time." *So that's where you have been, chatting away with Valentine—without me!* She introduced their guest.

"Ralph, this is Mr. Edgar Bray. Mr. Bray, my husband Lord Montfort."

Introductions and small talk over, Lord Montfort invited his guest to join him in his study, where he might be given the news of his brother's tragic death in privacy. *What a terrible thing to hear in some stranger's house where he knows no one at all*, Clementine thought as she watched Mr. Bray make his way across the drawing room to the door.

"Hollyoak, perhaps you would wait outside his lordship's study and then arrange for Mr. Bray to take dinner in his room if he would prefer that to joining us. I am sure he will want to retire after he has spoken with his lordship." There was no need for her to inform her butler of Captain Bray's violent end as Hollyoak managed to acquaint himself with everything that happened in their lives. She was proved right by his response.

"I have asked Cook to stand by with a tray, m'lady, and I will be on hand to valet Mr. Bray. I have instructed our first housemaid Agnes to wait on you at dinner, if that will be all right." Clementine was utterly grateful for the old butler's foresight. Even with a depleted servants' hall Hollyoak managed to keep things running smoothly. She half smiled as she remembered his embarrassment when he had had to train Agnes and Mary to wait on them in the dining room.

Women servants in waiting in the dining room, unmarried girls out driving young men their families barely knew around the countryside, and on top of it all the brutal murder in their kitchen garden. Clementine trudged back across the room toward her very independent and, she reminded herself, adult children. *I don't seem to be as adaptable to change as I used to be,* she thought as she sat her daughter down on the sofa and brought her up-to-date about the death of Captain Bray.

"Oh no, Mama, no!" Althea was so shocked by the news that she was halfway to her feet. "How absolutely awful. Poor Mr. Bray; he was so overjoyed that he was going to see his brother again. He talked of nothing else when we got back to the house." Althea turned first to her mother and then to her brother. "Did you meet Captain Bray, Harry? He was such a nice, quiet man."

"Well, yes, I suppose he was. I knew him briefly—before the war." His mother noticed that he did not repeat his opinion of Captain Bray's rather Casanova attitude to life before he'd gone off to France.

"What a shock it must have been for you, Mama. I expect it was suicide. Mr. Bray told me that he believed his brother would probably never regain his full memory, he was simply hoping that Captain Bray would recognize him when he saw him. How terrible it would be not to know who you were, or who your family was, to not remember anything about your life at all," said Althea as Harry poured them all another glass of sherry.

"Althea, darling, we think—well, we know—that Captain Bray was murdered."

More cries of disbelief from Althea. Despite a determination to be independent, Althea had a sunny disposition, skipping through life with the belief that everyone in her world was kindness itself and that no one bore a grudge, or harbored envy or malice. "But who would do such a thing? Oh, Mama, not one of the other officers surely?"

"I don't know, Althea. But until we find out what happened, I don't think it is a good idea to drive about alone—or with people we don't know too well. They have orderlies at the hospital to drive the patients for you." Had she finished the sherry in her glass already? *We can't all fall into drink because Captain Bray was murdered on the day he was to be reunited with his brother.*

"I'll drive with her," said Harry, and to his sister: "No, Thea, you can do the driving, I'm just there for the look of the thing. You shouldn't be unaccompanied anyway, especially with all this going on," he added with brotherly severity. "Mama, what about the chaps in your hospital—I mean do their *problems* make them dangerous?"

"Harry, you make them sound like they are the insane. They are suffering from neurasthenia, for heaven's sake, it is not a disease, it is a symptom of stress, of battle fatigue. And yes, I know some of them; I knew Captain Bray because his condition was a little more pronounced than the rest of our patients, and I know Captain Martin and the chief medical officers. But they come and go, you know, and in uniform it is sometimes hard to remember one from the other. I am quite sure I have never met Lieutenant Carmichael but I think I have seen him once or twice." Her son was watching her with a particularly sympathetic expression on his face, as he no doubt recognized how much concern the self-reliant Althea always caused her. Ever since they were young it had been Althea who broke the rules, made up new ones, and often got away with behavior that their very proper and older sister, Verity, would have been thoroughly scolded for.

"If I go with her, Mama, will you be less anxious?"

Perhaps with something to do Harry would not drink quite so much, would stop fretting about being grounded. An active country life would help him relax and find himself again. But she said none of this, she merely patted his arm. "Thank you, darling, that sounds like a sensible idea, doesn't it, Althea? It will give both of you a chance to spend time together, as you help the local farmers with the harvest."

"Well that's settled then," said Harry and laughed at the mutinous look on his sister's face.

Chapter Seven

At half past ten the following morning, Mrs. Jackson finished her interview with Inspector Savor and, putting on her uniform straw boater, went out into a cloudless morning. She pulled her old boneshaker out from under the scullery-porch roof and pedaled off down the drive to Iyntwood. As she bowled along the dusty lane that connected the two houses she unclenched her jaw, which had become set with indignation during her interview with Inspector Savor. She lifted her face to the sun, relieved to have escaped from her encounter with the inspector with a mere bruising.

What was the term Corporal Budge used in the servants' hall last night after his bullying session with the police inspector? She smiled as she remembered it: *That's it, it was "a parade ground bully," another army expression, and a good one.* The inspector used his position of authority to browbeat people, something he clearly enjoyed doing.

"How did your interview go with the inspector, Corporal?" She had been able to ask her question quite directly as the corporal was the sort of man who was so unaffectedly open with everyone that it was easy to be straightforward with him.

"Is that what he was doing, Mrs. Jackson, interviewing us? Could have fooled me!"

"Oh dear." Her worst suspicions were confirmed. How on earth would the shattered Lieutenant Phipps fare with this man's methods of interrogation?

"'Oh dear' is roight." His West Country accent became thicker with his disgust. "The accusations were flying through the air like shrapnel. He asked me where everyone was by name, like, and I answered best I could and then whammo he laced into me—thought I was up for a rogue's salute. In the end I just got down in me crump hole and waited it out. Anyway he says he don't have time for you tonight, Mrs. Jackson. You're up first thing tomorrow." Mrs. Jackson's face was grim as she pedaled down the drive. Her own experience might not have been so ferocious but it had been unpleasant and insinuating.

"Where were you between the hours of eleven o'clock in the morning and half past two in the afternoon yesterday?" Inspector Savor had asked her when she had stepped into the garden room for her interview, unfortunately before luncheon and the soothing effect of Major Andrews's cunningly planned steak-and-kidney pudding. It was a question the inspector had been right to ask, but there had been no preliminary greeting. He had fired these words at her when she had been halfway through the door. His back, she noticed, was toward the pretty flower beds just outside the window. The world's simple delights held no pleasure for the likes of Inspector Savor, Mrs. Jackson had realized as she offered up two densely filled foolscap pages pinned neatly to a board. "As the schedule says . . ."

"I am asking you, not the schedule, Miss Jackson." She decided not to correct him, as he clearly did not understand that the title of Mrs. was one given out of respect to single women who ran the grand houses, or the hospitals, of the aristocracy.

"At eleven o'clock I was in my office, working on the hospital accounts."

"Alone?"

"Why yes, I was alone. At noon I made my rounds of the hospital."

He put a cigarette in his mouth and slapped his pockets for matches. When she had come into the room he had given her an appraising once-over, and since then had not so much as glanced at her when he asked his questions. Every movement he made was abrupt and impatient, and so was his tone.

"After checking that VADs Fuller and Ellis had tidied the officers' mess on the ground floor, I went down to the kitchen to check that luncheon was on schedule for one o'clock, that would have been about twelve-thirty."

"Who was in the kitchen when you got there?" He gave up on his coat and trouser pockets and picked up his overcoat and started to go through its pockets in his quest for matches.

"VADs Fuller and Ellis, the cook, and the scullery maid; I spent a few minutes with them and then I walked back up to the officers' mess with VAD Ellis and we set the table together. At one o'clock all the officers who were not away from the hospital that day helping out at our local farms, which would be Captain Martin, Lieutenants Phipps, and Fielding, came into the mess and were joined there by our medical officers Captain Pike, Major Andrews, and Sister Carter. I made sure they had everything they needed and then I left to eat my luncheon."

Now he deigned to look at the schedule. "What does this mean? It says here Farm Detachment." He pointed with a nicotine-stained forefinger.

"Farm detachment refers to the patient-officers from the hospital who volunteer to help the local farmers. For the past week we have been very busy with the harvest. As you see," she pointed to the list, "Lieutenant Carmichael was working at Brook End Farm, Lieutenant Standish at Dodd Farm, and Lieutenant Forbes at the Home Farm. Officers on farm detachment leave the house after breakfast and return just before sunset."

"What about Captain Bray, you don't mention him coming in to lunch." He threw down his overcoat and irritably returned to his jacket pockets.

She patiently answered a question that he had asked yesterday in the drawing room. "When Captain Bray worked in the kitchen garden, someone took a sandwich out to him." *Really this ferreting about in pockets is most distracting,* she clenched her teeth together to stop herself from betraying irritation.

"Ah yes, that's right." He tapped his finger on the schedule. "Special treatment, aye? Is that because he is a baronet and not just an officer?" He sneered and she ignored the question. "And what about you, where did you eat your noonday meal?"

"I took my *luncheon* with the staff downstairs and then came back up to my office and continued to work on my accounts until I was interrupted with the news that Captain Bray's body had been found in the kitchen garden."

"Who told you?"

"Major Andrews. When Captain Bray's body was found by Lieutenant Phipps, Lady Montfort was in the kitchen-garden courtyard with the cider detachment. Lieutenant Fielding was told to run back to the hospital to fetch our chief medical officer, Major Andrews. Lord Montfort was in the stables at the time, which are right next . . ."

"I know where the stables are." He had finished slapping and patting his pockets.

". . . *Next to* the kitchen-garden courtyard." She fixed him with her eye and continued. "His lordship had specifically asked that Major Andrews bring me with him as he was sure her ladyship would need me."

"And why would she need *you*?" He found and shook his box of matches, but when he opened it there were only three dead ones inside. Mrs. Jackson's eyes strayed to the chimneypiece. There were two unused boxes of matches sitting there begging to be used. "I have worked for the Talbot family for many years; I was her ladyship's housekeeper at Iyntwood before the war. It was natural that I go to her, she was suffering from shock." She tried not to bristle.

"Did you at any time between the hours of eleven and half past two leave this house for any reason whatsoever?"

"No."

"But you were alone in your office—do you have an alibi for that time?" Now he was looking at her, in fact he was staring at her: his brows down, his chin thrust forward. She noticed that he had missed a bit on his chin when he had shaved that morning. *He's a drinker*, she thought, *those bloodshot eyes, the lack of concentration, and his desperate need for tobacco. He has the same bleary-eyed pugnacious look that the Dodd Farm pigman has when he has had a few too many at the Goat and Fiddle.* It also occurred to her that he should be in uniform, and by uniform she meant as part of the British Expeditionary Force and not the South Bucks police, who had an easy time of it chasing around the countryside bullying villagers in their quest for stolen petrol.

She found his boorish questions provoking and wished she could have replied, *Did I say that I left the house when I accounted for all my movements for the time asked?* But she knew better than to antagonize, so she politely affirmed that she had been inside all day except for when she left with Major Andrews at getting on for three o'clock to go to the kitchen garden. "I can't be sure what time it was when Major Andrews told me I was needed in the kitchen garden." Let him work out how long it would take her to walk there, murder a man, and then walk back when she had been sitting in her office with her accounts.

"I hope you have been accurate with your information, Miss Jackson." She started to say she always strove to be accurate but he threw up his hand toward her, palm outward, as if she were a wandering pedestrian about to blunder into the traffic in Piccadilly

Circus. "If something has slipped your mind, or you wish to revise what you have told me, just make sure you come to me or the sergeant. Now I want to see Lieutenant Carmichael next, and have Lieutenant Fielding in waiting. I have far more important things to do with my time than find out why someone in this so-called hospital did away with a fellow lunatic." He had given up his search and now stood with his back to her, his hands in his pockets, glaring out the window at an abundant display of creamy-yellow dahlias, rich gold Rudbeckia, and the pale lavender of Michaelmas daisies, as if their rich colors displeased him in some way.

She felt the heat rise to her cheeks and, to her horror, for she was the most prudent of women, almost found herself asking when missing petrol was more important than the death of a twice-decorated officer whose service to his country had been so self-less that he had ended up in Craiglockhart with absolutely no idea of who he was. And at the same time her heart sank. *Why on earth is this talentless imbecile investigating a murder that if not solved quickly with the arrest of the right man, might result in our hospital being closed down by the War Office?* But all she said was, "There are matches on the chimneypiece behind you, Inspector." He spun around and seized them with such eager desperation that she thought she would take her time finding Lieutenant Carmichael. *Better give him a moment to enjoy his cigarette before he launches into his interrogation of a man who served his country in the war, instead of hiding out in Market Wingley harassing the local farmers. And while you are alienating everyone with your unintelligent questions and you're fumbling for matches, Lady Montfort and I will have this investigation wrapped up so fast it will make your eyes spin.*

She was still fuming as she came level with the kitchen garden and was even more irritated when she heard a telltale bumpity-bump as her bicycle slid to the right. "Oh for heaven's sake," she said aloud in her frustration. "Didn't I pump both tires the day before yesterday?"

She bent down and examined the rear wheel. Yes, it was a puncture. She spun the wheel searching for the cause, a nail perhaps? She could find nothing that might have made it deflate. Well, she didn't have far to walk, but the lack of a bicycle would make her late for the rest of the morning. She propped the bike up against an apple tree on the edge of the orchard and crossed the drive toward the north gate of the kitchen garden. If she was going to be late for everything she had to do today, she might as well have a good look around.

The kitchen garden was empty. She saw the disturbed earth where the body had lain and the thoroughly trampled area around it. But an investigation of the potato rows was not why she was here. Eyes down, she walked over to the bench under the walnut tree. The luncheon basket brought to Captain Bray by Ellis yesterday at eleven o'clock was nowhere to be seen. *Someone else might have taken it back to the house, but in all the fuss of finding the body, who would have thought to do that?* Perhaps Colonel Valentine and his retinue of coppers had noticed it and had decided that its being there held some significance, but she doubted it. She stood in the garden and considered the implication of the missing basket and then took from her pocket the list she had made that morning. She sat down on the bench and read it through before she walked on down the drive to Iyntwood.

Chapter Eight

Clementine's favorite place to spend the early part of her morning was in her sitting room, which adjoined her bedroom and had a southeastern prospect. This morning the sun poured in through the windows, lighting up the silver-gray damask walls and the deep china-blue chairs. A shaft of sunlight fell on her writing bureau and cast its warmth on her industriously bent shoulders. She lifted her head from the menus she was writing to gaze out across the smooth expanse of the lawn and considered whether or not Mr. Bray would wish to join them for luncheon.

Perhaps he would prefer the privacy of the Blue Salon, she thought as she wrote "veal cutlets with cream sauce" for today's luncheon. *What is the best thing to do in these sorts of situations?* After some consideration she decided it best to assume that he would join them if he felt up to it and that at the same time she would ask Hollyoak to inquire as to their guest's wishes for luncheon and dinner. *We don't want to intrude, but at the same time it is important to show that we are pleased to have him here as a guest no matter how tragic the circumstances are.* She was still fretting if this was the best approach to take when Mrs. Jackson knocked on her door.

"I was wondering if I was going to see you today, Jackson." She hadn't wondered at all. She had openly and honestly prayed that her old housekeeper would put in an appearance. They met regularly throughout the week on hospital business, so that Clementine might volunteer some activity or event to spur their patients on to returning to life as it might be lived. All summer, croquet had been played with an almost aggressive air of competition on the south lawn by officers who rarely displayed much zest for anything, while the more withdrawn of them had spent contemplative hours reading or, if they were moved to do so, weeding the rose garden, which at the height of its glory had offered an exquisite haven of scent and color. But on this glorious September morning it somehow felt like old times again. *Good old times,* she thought, and then a little ashamed at her enthusiasm at the prospect of another inquiry she corrected herself: *Good old times, under most unfortunate circumstances.*

"Do come in, Jackson." She waved to a chair by the window. "Now, first of all, how are our officers faring? Was it an awful night?"

Mrs. Jackson obediently perched on the utmost edge of the chair indicated. "Sister Carter said it wasn't too bad, m'lady. They were restless, partly because Lieutenant Phipps had a terrible time of it with nightmares. I expect Captain Bray's brother had a bad night too."

"It was a most distressing evening and such a dreadful shock for Mr. Bray. I have not seen him yet this morning . . ." She related the events of Mr. Bray's arrival after a long journey, the breakdown of his motorcar, Lady Althea's rescue, and the unhappy end to his day. "Lord Montfort told me Mr. Bray is now the only member of his close family left. Tragically, Captain and Mr. Bray's parents were killed many years before the war, leaving their two young sons in the care of an elderly bachelor uncle who had very little time for them. Apparently the brothers were deeply attached as only two young boys can be when they are orphans—the poor man is devastated."

She set her menus for the day aside and reached for her leather notebook. "I do hope that this most unfortunate occurrence in the kitchen garden will be resolved quickly, with the War Office and the Medical Board descending on us at the end of the week." She picked up and put on her new half-moon spectacles, glancing, with some trepidation, over the top of them to see how her fears for the hospital had been received. "If only for the sake of our hospital."

There were two faint vertical lines between her former housekeeper's brows. To Clementine's observant gaze they were the result of years of responsibility, but in the past few moments they had, she observed, deepened. She hesitated before she picked up her pencil. *I hope I am not being presumptuous in assuming that she is here to discuss Captain Bray's murder.* Clementine had learned in the past that it was not a good idea to assume Mrs. Jackson's willingness to be part of one of her inquiries.

But her housekeeper was simply searching in the pocket of her uniform, difficult to do when one is sitting down, so she stood up and tugged her notebook free of her dress pocket. Clementine was so pleased to see the familiar battered book in her hand, so rapturous that it no doubt contained notes of interest on the unfortunate occurrence, that she had difficulty in containing her enthusiasm when she said, "What are your thoughts, Jackson?"

The frown had gone completely now that Mrs. Jackson had her notes in hand, in fact she looked positively vital, and Clementine leaned forward feeling both excitement for the days ahead and great affection for this capable and most considering woman.

"I have consulted the hospital schedule, m'lady, and followed up where I could, and I do have some ideas."

Hooray, she has been thinking! And Clementine felt a giddy little thrill of delight.

"I wouldn't ordinarily make too much of this, m'lady, young girls being what they are and particularly with the hospital on a sort of standby with so few patients and staff this week. But I have a feeling something might be going on with a couple of our VAD girls. Do you by any chance remember Ellis and Fuller?"

"Yes, Jackson, I think I do. Ellis has very pretty hair, and Fuller is not quite so arresting but she has a particularly sweet expression—nice girls, I thought, both of them. But I can't believe that they are mixed up in this ugly business. Good heavens, Jackson, I have just remembered Lord Haversham told me that before the war Captain Bray had a terrible reputation where women were concerned. Please tell me that we are not talking about a crime of passion."

"Passion?" Mrs. Jackson sounded almost offended. "I am quite sure we are not, m'lady." Her frown had reappeared at the thought of such unattractive emotions where innocent young girls were concerned. "Both Sister Carter and I are very aware of the responsibilities we have to our VADs; most of them come from very good families and they are entrusted to our care. I don't for one moment suppose that either of the two girls are suspects, but something is not sitting quite right about their account of where they were yesterday just before luncheon." Mrs. Jackson paused—Clementine was used to these pauses. Mrs. Jackson was a scrupulous woman, always careful about how she ordered her thoughts and as a consequence how she uttered them.

"Sometimes it is just better to say a thing, Jackson."

"Very well then, m'lady. I'll just tell you what these young women told me, and you can decide if I am getting ahead of myself.

"At eleven o'clock yesterday morning the cook told Ellis, the one with the pretty hair, to take Captain Bray his luncheon—this was quite usual when the captain was working in the kitchen garden all day. Ordinarily it would take Ellis only about half an hour at the very most to walk there and back, especially since, as she told me, she did not stop to talk to the captain; he was digging with his back toward her apparently and did not turn around when she arrived. But when I checked with Cook she said that the girl had come back just after the midday hour and had been very defiant with her when she told her off about being late."

"So, she was gone for over an hour then. Perhaps she was just dawdling—you know how dreamy girls can be. It was a lovely morning, it wouldn't be surprising if she took her time." Clearly, Mrs. Jackson did not think so; there was no change in the expression on her face but her silence was heavy with meaning. Clementine was quick to ask, "What do you make of her story, Jackson?"

"Sunny weather and all of that aside, m'lady, I think Ellis was not being straightforward. At the very least it might be something quite innocent such as frittering her time away, as you say. But it is the luncheon basket I am thinking about, m'lady. The one she was supposed to have delivered to Captain Bray. Yesterday afternoon when we were all in the kitchen garden, did you happen to notice it when you were sitting on the garden bench? Ellis said she left it in the shade of the walnut tree. I checked this morning and it is not there now."

Clementine cast her mind back; it was hard to recall mundane details like picnic baskets when there was a dead man lying not twenty feet distant from where she was sitting. She closed her eyes and tried to remember the scene before her as she had sat on the bench.

She opened her eyes and looked at her housekeeper. "I'm afraid I was rather preoccupied with the garden's doors at the time. You see, Jackson, I was wondering why Lieutenant Phipps had come from the orchard with his barrow of apples into the kitchen garden to get to the courtyard. It would have been much easier for him to have wheeled his cumbersome barrow from the orchard up the smooth surface of the drive than to negotiate all those turns in the gravel garden paths, unless he had a particular reason for doing so."

Mrs. Jackson said nothing, so Clementine obediently closed her eyes again, the better to envision the scene. "Was it large, like a picnic hamper?"

"No, m'lady, just an ordinary little basket—with a folded white napkin covering the top."

Clementine shook her head. "I am sorry, really I am—does that mean there wasn't one perhaps?"

"I am not sure if there is any significance at all quite yet. I will check with Cook; she might be able to cast some light on it."

"What are your thoughts about this young Ellis, Jackson?"

Mrs. Jackson cleared her throat. "I am thinking that Ellis might not have been in the kitchen garden at all, m'lady. In other words, she might not have delivered the basket as she had been instructed to. She was particularly evasive when I questioned her about what time she had arrived and left. And it turned out that she was being untruthful about how long she had taken." Mrs. Jackson tapped her notebook lightly with her pencil and Clementine decided that a little perspective might be needed.

"She is not likely to have hit Captain Bray on the head though, is she? She is just a little thing, and Captain Bray was a tall man, well over six feet." She wondered why Mrs. Jackson was so concerned about the girl in the first place. "Was she distressed about the murder?"

"Yes, she was most distressed. And I imagine it was because she and her friend Fuller were quite infatuated with Captain Bray." At Clementine's I-told-you-so glance she rushed to say, "Nothing alarming, m'lady, just silly schoolgirl behavior. Ellis is a nice enough girl: willing and kindhearted, perhaps a bit too flighty for hospital work. But she might have seen something or someone and is scared to talk about it; there is something about her account that bears some checking out." She glanced down at her notebook. "Major Andrews pointed out to me that Captain Bray might have been crouched down to gather potatoes or just bent over when someone hit him on the head."

Clementine got up from her chair and, extending her arms, she clasped her hands together and swung them as if she were playing golf. "So he was not hit like that," she said as she energetically demonstrated a swift upward sideways swipe, which would certainly have landed her ball in the rough. "But more like . . . this." She raised her arms straight up above her head and, hands clasped together, swung them down in a chopping motion toward the carpet.

"Exactly, m'lady. The blows would have been downward to connect with the crown of his head, rather than sideways to connect with its side. Or at least that is what Major Andrews observed."

"When you talked to Inspector Savor did he mention whether they think the spade might have been used? It does have a long handle."

Her housekeeper looked disdainful when she mentioned the inspector's name. *Jackson does not approve of that particular individual either,* she thought.

"No, m'lady, Inspector Savor asks the questions and we do the answering. I can't imagine that anyone would ask him for information about the particulars of the murder—he is a most . . . impatient man."

"Yes, I imagine his preferred interview method would be intimidation. But what is alarming is that he seems to have formed a deep antipathy for our officers and the hospital. I am hoping he will not spend a lot of time on who murdered a man he has already dismissed as a coward, Jackson. In fact I think what worries me most is that the Market Wingley constabulary might simply turn this investigation over to the Royal Army Medical Corps for court-martial, which would put our hospital in complete jeopardy. Since Colonel Valentine's police force is suffering from a lack of experienced men, he might have already decided to hand this matter over for a military investigation." As she said this she felt a flutter of anxiety and noticed that Mrs. Jackson looked troubled, too. *This is what is propelling her into this inquiry with such zeal,* she thought. *Our hospital and its good works are at risk.*

"I do hope he has not, m'lady, I really do." Mrs. Jackson had not quite finished with her notes. Clementine craned her neck and saw that there were quite a few pages covered in her tidy, upright handwriting. "I have spoken to most of the staff at the hospital about where they all were yesterday up and until about half past two, and it is quite possible that Captain Bray might very well have been alive at half past twelve. Shall I read what I have, m'lady?" Clementine sat forward, pencil poised over her notebook, and nodded for Mrs. Jackson to begin.

"Of the people in the hospital, the last person to have seen Captain Bray alive, apart from the murderer, of course, appears to be Mary Fuller when she went to pick beans for Cook. She saw the captain when she came into the kitchen garden at twelve-fifteen; this would have been after Sarah Ellis had delivered the captain's luncheon basket. He was standing outside the potting shed in the kitchen garden, sharpening his spade. She told me that he helped her pick beans until she left him a little after half past twelve to be back at the kitchen by a quarter to one. So Captain Bray must have been murdered between about twenty-five minutes to one—I added a couple of minutes there for safety—and when his body was found at half past two."

"How can we be sure that Mary Fuller's story is accurate?"

"I checked with Cook: Fuller was told to go and pick beans a few minutes after twelve o'clock. She got back to the kitchen at a quarter to one with enough beans for everyone for luncheon. She would have had to have some help gathering enough beans for both upstairs and downstairs luncheon." Another pause as she considered. "For the time being, m'lady, until we have a clear idea of the time of the captain's death, Fuller might have been the last person to have seen him alive at twenty-five minutes to one."

"Twenty-five to one," Clementine wrote in her book. "And then Lieutenant Phipps discovered the body at half past two. Two hours." She looked up. "Well, that narrows down the field a bit, doesn't it? Something bothering you about Fuller, Jackson?"

An almost imperceptible shrug of her shoulders—*How she dislikes conjecture,* Clementine thought. "Impressions can be most enlightening sometimes, Jackson." This seemed to throw her assistant sleuth into a rash of indecision.

"It's just feelings really."

"Go ahead with them. Feelings, as Major Andrews says, are often the key to revelations."

"I am not sure I would agree with him, m'lady. I sometimes think that feelings can be very messy and unreliable."

"Well then let's just talk about your impression of Fuller's account of her time in the kitchen garden with Captain Bray."

"She was upset, quite naturally. She knew I was going to ask her about her trip to the garden: Ellis gave her a little nudge as she left my office, a sort of warning. But I felt that a lot of her account was like something from a stage play. Perhaps I am reading too much into things."

Clementine laughed. "I am quite sure you are not. This young Fuller sounds like a complicated sort.

"Do you have any information about our officer-patients who were still in the hospital that day?" Mrs. Jackson evidently did, Clementine thought, and did not look particularly happy about that either.

"After breakfast Captain Martin and Lieutenants Fielding and Phipps spent the morning hours in the medical wing in consultation with Captain Pike and Major Andrews, and if they weren't with them Sister Carter gave all three their monthly physical check-up. She occupies the old anteroom to the salon and the tapestry room, which are now the doctors' offices, and whichever officer was not with a doctor was with her, or waiting to be seen by her. Major Andrews and Sister Carter both say they were all in this area right up until luncheon. I am telling you this because Lieutenant Phipps was the only one of the three officers who left the hospital building before luncheon."

Clementine looked up, her eyes wide. "Phipps left the house *before* luncheon—what time did she say he left?"

"Sister Carter thinks at half past twelve and Major Andrews also mentioned it. Lieutenant Phipps said he was going to the orchard to bring apples up to the kitchen courtyard for the cider pressing. The rest of them—Sister Carter, Major Andrews, Captains Pike and Martin, and Lieutenant Fielding—walked together from the medical wing to the officers' mess, arriving in time for luncheon at one o'clock."

Clementine was writing as fast as she could. "Lieutenant Phipps . . . went to orchard . . . gone from hospital . . . half an hour or maybe longer . . . before luncheon," she said as she wrote, and then she looked up. "So at the moment our suspects must include both Fuller and Phipps, and even perhaps Ellis. What about the other members of staff?"

"I saw Corporal Budge off and on throughout the morning as we went about our duties. He spent some time with me in my office going over his requisitions for the week, and then I saw him again in the kitchen before he joined us for luncheon with the other staff belowstairs. After that he went off to the kitchen courtyard with the officers on cider detachment. I am not sure he would have had the time to go to the kitchen garden at all during the morning."

Clementine's right hand was beginning to ache. "To get to the kitchen garden from the hospital—what sort of time would that take, didn't you say earlier ten minutes?"

"On foot between ten to fifteen minutes at the very most, m'lady, but on a bicycle . . ." She paused. "It takes me about five minutes, but if you were riding at speed, two, maybe three minutes, it would depend on age and strength I suppose.

"I need to do more checking on Corporal Budge's morning," Mrs. Jackson said, and wrote a note before she went on. "To continue, m'lady. After luncheon when the cider detachment left the hospital, Major Andrews, Captain Pike, and Sister Carter had a meeting to discuss the next Medical Board review. I think they are all in the clear, as they were together right up until the time Captain Bray's body was found."

"Corporal West is the only one you have not yet mentioned; where was he?"

"He was . . ." Mrs. Jackson turned to the next page, and after a quick glance at what she had written there: "He had been on duty the night before and so he had the day off yesterday. After breakfast I saw him sitting outside the scullery door on the top step, polishing his boots. Then, according to the cook, he sat in the servants' hall with his newspaper and then left just before eleven o'clock, saying that he was going to walk down to the village to buy some tobacco. He was back just in time for luncheon at one o'clock. From two o'clock on he was asleep in his quarters."

Clementine clapped her hands together and her mouth widened in a smile. "You see, Jackson? You see? He *says* he went down to the village for tobacco at eleven o'clock and was back in time for luncheon at one o'clock. But even walking slowly he had all the time in the world to get there and back, perhaps dropping off at the kitchen garden to murder Captain Bray between the time Fuller last saw the captain at twenty-five minutes to one and luncheon." She got to her feet and paced up and down with her left forearm folded under her bosom and her right forefinger tapping her chin in thought. "If he cut through Crow's Wood and the cart track to the south-gate entrance into the kitchen garden, no one would have seen him. If Captain Bray was bent over to pick up a few potatoes he could have taken the spade and hit him on the head. If Fuller saw the captain alive at twenty-five to one, West could have been hiding down at the other end of the kitchen garden, waiting for her to leave."

Mrs. Jackson listened with her head ever so slightly tilted to one side.

"Does Corporal West have a bicycle?" As Clementine asked this seemingly ordinary question, Mrs. Jackson dropped her pencil on the floor, and then when she had straightened up after retrieving it she shook her head. "No, m'lady. The cook and her kitchen maid bike up from the village every morning for work and they keep their bicycles locked up in the coal shed next to the scullery, but I keep mine right outside the scullery door under the porch." And she disappeared off into a world of her own for a few minutes before she said, "I thought I would go down to the village before I return to the hospital. I could go to the tobacconist and check with Mrs. Diggory when Corporal West came into her shop. And as it was his day off, so he might have stopped for a pint at the Goat and Fiddle, or even gone to the post office."

"We seem to have four possible suspects then, Jackson: the unfortunate Lieutenant Phipps; VAD Fuller, who might have been the last person to see Captain Bray alive, other than his murderer; and Corporal West, who, so far, has no alibi at all for the time of the captain's death. Then there is VAD Ellis and her rather cagey account of her morning."

Clementine made some notes in her notebook before she looked up, her face bright with intention. "We have things to do, Jackson! See if you can dig up some more information on Lieutenant Phipps and his trip to the orchard before and after luncheon— Mr. Thrower might have seen him there." She threw her pencil onto the desk with all the heedless delight of a schoolgirl when she has finished her lessons. "And while you are doing that, I will talk to Lady Althea about the farm-detachment officers. Perhaps she can vouch for them being at their farms all day, though we might have to do some checking ourselves, just to make sure, because it seems that not all of her attention was engaged on the harvest yesterday. And I will simply ask Colonel Valentine when the coroner thinks Captain Bray was killed, and whether the spade was used as a murder weapon." *After all,* she thought, *the old boy is quite used to my interfering by now. He might even welcome some help.*

Mrs. Jackson closed her notebook as Agnes arrived to beg her ladyship's pardon for the interruption but Colonel Valentine was waiting in the morning room hoping to talk to her as soon as she had the time, and that Lord Montfort was also asking for her as Sir Winchell Meacham had come to call. "His lordship says would you spare him a moment or two with Sir Winchell, m'lady?"

"Sir Winchell? Oh dear me, is *he* here now?" On being assured that he was, Clementine's heart sank. She felt tremendous sympathy for their neighbor, Sir Winchell Meacham, whose life had been emptied quite tragically by the death of both of his sons. His eldest had been shot by a sniper at the Battle of Loos and the youngest, a pilot in the Royal Naval Air Force, had gone down in flames and his body never recovered during the Battle of the Somme. Unfortunately, their nearest neighbor was naturally of the sort of disposition Clementine described as agitated, and the death of his sons had made him even more high-strung than he had been before the war.

I simply don't have time for Sir Winchell today, she thought with exasperation. *And certainly not* this *morning; Ralph must fend for himself.* She lifted her hand in acknowledgment of Mrs. Jackson's sympathetic look that she had to deal with Sir Winchell, whose prickly reputation was well known.

"Off I must go, Jackson. Perhaps we might finish our conversation tomorrow, unless something interesting occurs in the meantime." And with that they parted company.

Chapter Nine

Clementine took a few moments in front of the looking glass to tidy her hair before going downstairs to join Colonel Valentine in the morning room. *How very nice it is,* she thought as she went down, *that one's chief constable for the county does not think twice about coming to consult on matters of murder.* And with this agreeable thought she crossed the threshold of the library and said, with the right degree of gravitas, her good-morning to the elderly colonel, who courteously rose from his chair and bent his head in his customary bow to her.

"I am really here to see Mr. Bray, Lady Montfort; I know I must not take up too much of your time. Last night he was in such a state of shock and grief that I was quite alarmed for his health."

"Yes, Lord Montfort told me that Mr. Bray was most distressed."

The chief constable made tutting noises and shook his head as he stared down at his feet. "But I also wanted to see how you were faring this morning after the shock of finding Captain Bray's body, and also," he paused and looked apologetic, "whether anything had occurred to you about that time after the fact, so to speak. If now would be a good time and it would not upset you too much to think about it."

Thoughts? She had had a hundred of them and all before breakfast, and she was enchanted by the colonel's invitation to share them. "Please tell me what I can do to be of help," she said, looking as modest as she could as she waited to be consulted.

"Oh, there is nothing you can really *do,* I am afraid, Lady Montfort. I was just wondering if there was anything you might have remembered about . . ." He left the words hanging as he looked everywhere in the room but at her, and then, brightening: "I spent quite some time with Major Andrews at the hospital this morning. What he is accomplishing there is most impressive."

It was important for her to be patient. *Why is it that some men have such difficulty in accepting that not all women faint at the sight of blood, especially these days?*

"We have so much respect for Major Andrews and Captain Pike. They work incredibly hard, and have been most successful with their patients. Captain Bray was doing so well under their care," she said, and the colonel nodded in agreement: an apparent convert to the cause of treating neurasthenia.

"Do you have any idea yet at what time of the day the captain was murdered, Colonel?" She slid this question in as a sign that she was his willing ally in this investigation.

There was a long silence as Colonel Valentine struggled with what he evidently felt was her unseemly interest. *Rank sometimes has its advantages,* she thought as she smiled at him until he gave in. "Certainly we do, Lady Montfort. Since Captain Bray was found so soon after his death we can say with reasonable certainty between the hours of half past eleven in the morning and about half past two in the afternoon. Give or take a few minutes, as he was in a shady part of the garden." She suppressed a smile of triumph. *So we were quite right: he was killed between twenty-five to one—that is, if Fuller was telling the truth—and when Phipps came through the kitchen garden at half past two.*

"Poor Lieutenant Phipps, he was most shaken-up. I am quite sure he still is." This was the closest she dared come in asking if the lieutenant was a suspect.

Valentine cleared his throat and, hands clasped behind his back, stared down at the carpet as if he might find some message written there in its pattern, and Clementine realized with a painful shaft of understanding that his asking for her thoughts was, just as his conversation had been with Major Andrews, the colonel's way of appeasing all involved. Her earlier buoyant mood began to dissolve. *Does this mean that he has already arrested Lieutenant Phipps and put him in Market Wingley jail?*

"I saw Mrs. Jackson leave the house as I was waiting for you." There was the slightest note of censure here: Colonel Valentine was quite familiar with Clementine and Mrs. Jackson's several successful inquiries into wrongdoings and it seemed to Clementine that the old man was nowhere near closer to accepting their help, and was as disapproving of their involvement as he always was— unless of course they were successful.

He knows we are already discussing things so it's best to be absolutely straight with him. "Yes, she was here to let me know, with her customary efficiency and eye for detail, that she is aware where all our officers were from just after breakfast until well after the time the body was discovered. There are some stray odds and ends out there that make one wonder . . . such as who might have visited the kitchen garden—off schedule, so to speak. This rather makes me think that perhaps Lieutenant Phipps simply had the misfortunate to find Captain Bray and that it might very well have been someone else who murdered him."

Colonel Valentine cleared his throat again and they both gazed thoughtfully out the window, she to a lawn that needed cutting and he no doubt to ponder the many gallons of missing petrol.

"I am sure you are aware, Lady Montfort, we are operating with at least half of our original number of police officers, but we are quite sure that all intelligence presently points to Lieutenant Phipps."

"Not actually arrested then?"

"Well, not exactly . . . but the Defense of the Realm Act does not require us to obtain a warrant for arrest these days."

She decided to delay if she could the young lieutenant's arrest. "Mrs. Jackson possesses a most disciplined and observant mind, Colonel. I think her opinion would be of immeasurable help in this investigation—if you would talk to her . . ." She did not add "leaving Inspector Savor free to return to his petrol investigation" but she prayed that this would be the outcome.

"That is very generous of you, Lady Montfort." He got to his feet. "I am hoping that we will be able to sew this one up quickly, and for the time being we must pursue an avenue that as I say points . . . very . . . significantly . . . And shorthanded as we are . . ." As Clementine's quizzical expression turned to naked distress, he coughed and tried not to meet her gaze. "Well now, I think I had better meet with Mr. Bray. I am sure he has questions for me, last night he was most troubled."

And Clementine realized with a mixture of both alarm and annoyance that however willing Colonel Valentine was to outwardly approve of the work Major Andrews was doing at Haversham Hall, the murder of a man with shell-shock by another man "while of unsound mind" was of lesser importance than recovering stolen government property. There was just one more question she needed an answer to and she asked it before the colonel managed to make his exit.

"Does the coroner believe that the garden spade dug into the earth next to where Captain Bray was lying might have been used as a weapon?"

His wiry brows shot up at her mentioning a weapon—she thought he looked rather like a startled elderly hare. "The coroner said the spade was not the murder weapon."

"Oh, I see, and why is that?"

"What? Um, because the head of the spade is a flat instrument and the weapon used to kill Captain Bray was narrow; most likely a length of lead piping, or something of a similar gauge." Having indulged her vicarious interest in the murder weapon, he nodded to the window as he said, "Your rose garden still looks quite splendid, Lady Montfort. It must be the fine weather we are having," as if hoping to distract her from the ugly topic of murder weapons.

"Thank you, Colonel, the rose garden is such hard work but I believe that it is worth the effort to be thorough when weeding." *Unlike your wretched investigation.* "I don't suppose your policemen found any lead pipe lying around the kitchen garden, did they?" She laughed to dispel some of the tension.

"No, I am afraid not, Lady Montfort, my men searched the garden and the surrounding area very thoroughly. Nothing was found that might have been used."

"But what about the potting shed?" She managed somehow to conceal her irritation. "The one in the kitchen-garden courtyard, could someone have used a different type of gardening tool and then returned it to the potting shed?" She heard the sharpness in her voice and modified her tone. But she was feeling quite dashed.

Colonel Valentine looked at her with kindness, the sort of patronizing kindness when one must disappoint. "We searched there this morning, Lady Montfort, as we came over to Iyntwood. Nothing was found."

Well, she thought, *at least I have the time of death to work with, and it would seem that a weapon might have been brought along for the job, so that rules out our earlier theory that whoever killed Captain Bray did it on the spur of the moment.*

"Did you or your sergeants happen to see a luncheon basket in the kitchen courtyard yesterday, or this morning?" He turned his head, looking first surprised and then annoyed, perhaps that his curiosity had got the better of him.

"A luncheon basket you say—whose luncheon basket?"

Clementine smiled. "It would have been Captain Bray's, and I am not altogether sure if it was there at all. And if it is significant,

I promise you I will let you know." And she turned away, hoping against hope that they were given at least this day to work things through before Lieutenant Phipps was carted off to Market Wingley jail.

Clementine's lighthearted mood that the colonel had come to consult with her now dashed to pieces, she decided to make for her favorite haven, her rose garden. Its tranquil beauty would give her the peace she needed in which to mull over the dangerously precarious situation the hospital now found itself in. She was almost to the terrace door when Hollyoak materialized from the small dining room. "His lordship asked if you would step into his study for a moment, m'lady, Sir Winchell Meacham is with him."

She suppressed a harrumph of irritation at having been caught before she could make her getaway but dutifully changed course toward her husband's study.

As soon as she entered the room she understood exactly why she had been summoned. Lord Montfort was sitting behind his desk, well back in his chair with his arms crossed rather defensively in front of him as he watched a rotund and gray-haired man in his middle years pace to and fro on the Turkey rug, talking at him in a high-pitched and fretful tone. Every so often Sir Winchell would pause in his pacing to lift his hands in the air and shake them in emphatic irritation.

". . . Every one of them are damned cowards I tell you; every one of them hiding out while brave men are falling left and right for their country. All this rot being spouted by the War Office about shell-shock is complete hogwash. Oh, good morning, Lady Montfort." Sir Winchell stopped mid-tirade and Lord Montfort turned weary eyes toward her. Clementine had already guessed that she had been summoned to pour oil on stormy waters. Sir Winchell might rave at her husband about the hospital, but he would behave himself with her, as he was particularly sentimental about the fairer sex since the death of his wife ten years ago.

"Hollyoak told me that you had dropped in to see Ralph, and I thought I would just pop in to say hullo." She waved her gardening gloves at her husband so that he knew she would not stay long.

"My dear Lady Montfort, you are looking remarkably well."

I wish I could say the same for you, Clementine thought. Sir Winchell had aged in the weeks since she had last seen him. His eyes were sunk deep and ringed with dark shadows, his face was deeply lined, and there was an overall sense that he was physically less robust than he had been two months ago. She felt even greater remorse for their neglect when she noticed that there was a tic working away at the corner of his left eye. *We should not be so preoccupied with our own troubles that we overlook Sir Winchell's misfortunes. We simply must invite him to dine with us more often.*

She guessed from the little she had heard when she walked into the room that Sir Winchell knew of the murder and was back on his latest hobbyhorse, that of closing down the hospital and returning every one of what he loved to refer to as "lily-livered cowards" to active duty.

"My dear Lady Montfort, I am so glad I had the opportunity of seeing you before I left," Sir Winchell said in a far calmer tone. And Clementine glanced over to her husband sitting silently in his chair, his face like ice. "I understand there was a murder at Haversham Hall and I am here to ask Lord Montfort, once and for all, to close the place down. Your patients will regain their self-respect a good deal faster if they are given the opportunity to be real men, and not hide out at your hospital playing croquet and painting pictures—assured as they are of your hospitality." His tic became more noticeable as he struggled to keep his manner polite. "As I was telling Lord Montfort, I feel it is my duty to write to the War Office and state as much in the most stringent terms."

"Of course we understand, Sir Winchell. We understand completely. In fact I was just talking to Colonel Valentine about the hospital. He will send a full report of this unfortunate incident to the War Office as soon as he has completed his investigation. You see, this matter is being handled by the chief constable himself—he left just a moment ago. But there is no need for you to worry yourself on our account." She smiled and put her hand lightly on his forearm. "I was hoping that perhaps you would join us for dinner? We are not entertaining much at the moment. What about tomorrow night—are you by any chance free?"

Clementine was careful not to look at her husband, whose face no doubt expressed nothing but polite invitation, but who would be most unwilling to listen to an evening of fuss and bother from a man he had always found acutely tiresome.

"My dear Lady Montfort, how kind; of course, I would enjoy that." And Clementine felt a prickle of remorse that in spite of his many acrimonious faults, Sir Winchell was after all grieving for the loss of his only children.

"We will look forward to seeing you tomorrow then, now I must go. I have taken on the care of the rose garden, and it takes up all of my time." And she left the room, completely aware that this was just a temporary truce and that if they did not discover the identity of the murderer soon, Sir Winchell would more than likely eat up every last piece of her husband's patience.

Chapter Ten

Mr. Thrower looked over Mrs. Jackson's bicycle with a critical eye as he spun the rear wheel back and forth a few times and exclaimed at its ruined state. "Yes, Mrs. Jackson, see here, the tire has been ripped, going over something sharp lying in the lane, but it is rather an old tire after all. I might be able to patch it for you, but you're probably looking at a new pair. Meantime, why don't you try this lovely machine out?" He wheeled forward Iyntwood's housemaid Agnes's gleaming bicycle and they stood admiring it in the bright sun. He tinkled the bell and then, taking the bicycle by its handlebars, ran it forward and applied the brake to make it stand on its front end in a most satisfactory way. "Drum brakes," Mr. Thrower said. "Lovely machine, that." He stooped and applied oil at several points along the machine's working parts.

Mrs. Jackson stepped through the bicycle's frame and raised the right pedal with her toe. "Thank you, Mr. Thrower, I will return it later today. Goodness me, is that the time?"

But farewells were never speedy with Mr. Thrower. He placed a restraining hand on the handlebars and fixed her with his mild gaze. Even though the old man's shoulders were bent from years of gardening, his calloused hand held the bicycle in place with surprising strength. Mrs. Jackson must listen to a few words of caution before she was allowed to go.

"Whatever you do, Mrs. Jackson, watch out for those Land girls, they cut across the end of the east drive, right there by the Home Farm, in a very reckless way, and the speed at which they drive their tractors is disgraceful: nearly sent Mrs. Thrower to her maker last Thursday." She assured him she would be watchful, and then, as if it had just occurred to her: "Were you perhaps in the orchard when Lieutenant Phipps came over yesterday morning before luncheon to collect apples?" He stood looking at her for a moment, whistling softly through his teeth.

"He must have, because the apple pile was a good deal lower when I came back through the orchard at half past one; but no, I didn't see him."

"And then later on he came back for another load after luncheon at about two o'clock, did you see him then?"

"Dunno that I did, I went over to the orchid house after I drove the geese up from the lake into the orchard. I had planned to work in the rose garden, but her ladyship told me she would take care of that. Oh and by the by, Mrs. Jackson, if any of the VAD girls," he pronounced VAD as a word and not as an acronym, "*must* pick beans in the kitchen garden, then ask them please to find me first so I can show them how to do it properly." His usually kind eyes blinked almost ferociously. There was not much that upset Mr. Thrower, he was the gentlest of men, but careless young women picking beans in his kitchen garden was clearly something he found hard to tolerate.

Mrs. Jackson arrived in the village on Agnes's wonderful new bicycle in double-quick time. *Is it the fat tires that make the going so true and straight? And whatever have they done to the springs that support the saddle?* She had not needed to raise herself up over every bump in the lane; her ride had been downright luxurious in a bouncy feather-bed kind of way. She idly wondered how much this gleaming machine would cost, with its safety brakes, its cushioned saddle, and its shining bell on the handle-bars instead of a rubber-bulb horn. She had bowled along at such high speed that she had to spend a good few minutes outside the village tucking her hair back up under her hat before she ped-aled sedately down the village high street and alighted outside the post office.

"Good morning, Mrs. Peabody," she said to the postmistress. "Just four penny stamps if you would be so kind." She opened her purse for the correct change. "Corporal West wondered if perhaps he left his pipe behind when he popped in here yesterday around noon?"

The postmistress shook her head. "It was a very busy day, Mrs. Jackson, lots of parcels being sent off to France, but it quieted down about midday; I would have remembered the corporal coming in and certainly no one left their pipe in here." Mrs. Pea-body was an angular and authoritative woman who ran the post office with the help of her husband, a small, inoffensive man who was deeply fond of stamping the daily post with a smudgy Royal Mail rubber stamp and lots of violet ink. Together they kept the tiny area of the shop dedicated to post office business in immaculate order.

Mrs. Jackson tucked her envelope of stamps into her handbag and stowed it away in the basket of the bicycle before wheeling it down the village street to the tobacconist. A tinkley bell and a strong waft of peppermint, tobacco, and newsprint welcomed her as she opened the door into the cramped shop.

The proprietor, Mrs. Diggory, was getting on in years but still moved with the energy of a younger woman. Her solace for the long hours she spent standing behind a counter at her age was the chance to gossip—all day. In Mrs. Jackson's long experience, Mrs. Diggory's chinwag always opened with routine observations about the weather, and at this time of the year the harvest, before picking a popular topic and expounding on it at length. This morning she exclaimed at the Land girls, not about their driving but about their morals, or what the village perceived as the lack of them.

She folded her arms up high under her bosom, her mouth turned down in a thin, compressed line. "Townies, that's what they all are—and certainly no better'n they should be." Mrs. Jackson nodded and smiled, hoping she might be allowed to leave within the next twenty minutes. "And what do you make of Miss Bottomley-Jones being frightened half to death in the lych-gate of the church?" Mrs. Jackson kept her expression bland, dreading what she would hear next. "Oh, you haven't heard, Mrs. Jackson? Well it was quite a carry-on; the Rev. Bottomley-Jones's gardener, Mr. Preston, told me all about it." Mrs. Diggory leaned on the counter, her hands clasped across her forearms. "Miss Bottomley-Jones had been doing the flowers in the church for Sunday service and was leaving just as it was getting dark. As she was walking down the path through the churchyard she thought she heard people talking, but on she went and when she got to the lych-gate she got the shock of her life. Screamed the place down she did."

"Good heavens, what can have happened?" In spite of herself Mrs. Jackson was drawn.

Mrs. Diggory leaned farther forward and whispered, even though there was no one but Mrs. Jackson in her shop. "A courting couple, that is what she saw. Some little hussy with a man in uniform—such a terrible thing for the vicar's sister to come across, the poor dear innocent. What do they call it when young girls behave badly, khaki fever? Who would have thought we would see that sort of behavior in the village? Poor Miss Bottomley-Jones didn't quite understand what she was seeing or what they were up to. And the next morning . . ." She paused to find suitable words for what was evidently the crowning piece of her gossip.

"The very next morning, guess what the verger found under the bench seat in that gateway?"

Mrs. Jackson was quite sure she did not want to know what the verger had found, it all sounded like the worst sort of music-hall vulgarity. She interrupted the older lady before she could speak her next words. "But there are no uniformed men in the village."

"Excuse me, Mrs. Jackson, excuse me. There are plenty of uniformed men staying up at the Hall. When Miss Bottomley-Jones screamed, she heard the man say as clear as clear, 'We'd better scarper, Maisie, see you next Friday.' Now what does that tell you?"

Mrs. Jackson said she didn't really know.

"Well . . ." Mrs. Diggory evidently did. "That the soldier was a Londoner, because Mr. Bottomley-Jones's gardener says that's the sort of language they use up there. And I'm quite sure that the girl he was with was one of them Land girls. There is no one in the village of that name."

Mrs. Jackson said nothing; her mind was busily sifting through the different possibilities presented by this information, and Mrs. Diggory, evidently bored with her as a possible confederate in her gossip, resumed her role of shopkeeper.

"So what can I do for you, Mrs. Jackson, a quarter of your usual mint imperials?" She reached for one of the many glass jars on the shelf behind her and carefully weighed out the sweets, and the rich peppery smell of mint intensified in the air.

Mrs. Jackson looked around the shop. "Did Corporal West perhaps leave his pipe, Mrs. Diggory, when he was in here yesterday?"

Mrs. Diggory didn't even glance around her cluttered counter space as she deftly swung the white paper bag twice to twist its corners closed. "Couldn't have done, Mrs. Jackson." Her face assumed deeply furrowed lines of disapproval—no doubt Corporal West was a Townie in her eyes, with his strong East London accent, and was more than likely the lecherous fellow in the lych-gate. "Mr. West didn't come in *here* yesterday, I most certainly would have known."

Mrs. Jackson held out tuppence for her sweets, wished the shopkeeper a good afternoon, and made a quick exit before she had to hear any opinions about Haversham Hall Hospital and its patients. Outside, she stowed the bag of sweets in the bicycle's basket before she rode off down the village street, calling out a good-morning to the verger on his way across the green to the church.

The very least I can do is check at the Goat and Fiddle, she thought as she passed the butcher sulking over his lonely side of beef and the greengrocer standing in the entrance to his shop in his brown apron with one bunch of overripe bananas artfully arranged between a generous display of local apples and a pile of King Edward potatoes.

She rode on toward the village green, and dismounting in the alley that ran alongside the Goat and Fiddle to its cobbled backyard, she tapped on the kitchen door of the public house.

"Good morning, Mrs. Jackson." The publican's wife opened the door and ushered her into her kitchen, where she was busy making mutton pies for the evening's customers. "How are things going for you up at the Hall?" Mrs. Jackson assured her that they were going very nicely—if the villagers had heard of the murder of Captain Bray they were all being uncharacteristically silent on the subject.

"I am running a few errands and I told Corporal West that I would inquire for him. Did he by any chance leave his pipe in the snug when he came into the village yesterday at midday? He didn't say he stopped here, but . . ." She smiled and shrugged her shoulders at the absentmindedness of men and their enjoyment of a pint in the middle of a day off.

"I wouldn't know, Mrs. Jackson, but I will just ask Fred," and without moving she called out, "Fred? Fred?," until her husband's shining red face appeared around the door, and he peevishly asked her not to shriek, he wasn't deaf.

"Was Corporal West in yesterday 'bout midday?"

Mr. Golightly saw Mrs. Jackson and raised his right hand to his temple in salute.

"Good morning, Mrs. Jackson. No, can't say as I remember serving Corporal West his usual half pint. And how are things for you up at the hospital these days?" His bright eyes appeared curious. *Aha,* she thought, *Fred Golightly knows about Captain Bray. So it'll be all round the county by this evening.*

"Fine, thank you, Mr. Golightly. Well, I must be on my way." She smiled and wished them both good day and left them to argue together alone in hushed tones about the inevitability of violent doings at the hospital.

She pedaled on out of the village and up Haversham Hill toward the Hall. On the downhill she felt as if she were flying as she swooped smoothly past the tall iron gates that now stood permanently open with the Ministry of War sign proclaiming "Haversham Hall Hospital" in black letters on a white board.

But she did not steer up the left fork of the drive to the back of the Hall and the scullery door but continued along the lane that led to Iyntwood. When the kitchen-garden wall loomed up on her left and the apple trees of the orchard were on her right, she hopped off the bicycle and wheeled it along the flint path that ran through the orchard to the boathouse. She wouldn't risk Agnes's lovely fat tires on this uncompromising path of Buckinghamshire flints. She propped the bicycle against the boathouse wall and walked up the steps and opened its nail-studded, neo-Tudor front door.

Many decades ago the boathouse had been a simple building in which to moor punts, rowing boats, and a little sailing skiff below it on the edge of the lake. When Lady Montfort had come to Iyntwood she had had the old structure torn down and this pretty little rustic cottage built in its stead. The ground floor consisted of a large and airy sitting and dining room to give shelter for picnickers and boaters should it come on to rain and had gone from there to become a comfortably romantic spot to linger on a summer's afternoon. It had been a favorite of the Talbot children—Lady Althea and Lady Verity had done their lessons there in the summer with their governess when they were little girls.

There was no electricity in the boathouse, but the windows overlooking the lake were big enough to admit plenty of daylight into its dainty interior. Mrs. Jackson did not pause to admire the view of swans, ducks, and geese in their allotted territories gliding on the mirror of the lake's surface, swept at its edges by the silver-green of weeping willows. Instead she went to the comfortable sofa in the middle of the room.

"Pork pie, a piece of cake, and an apple," she said aloud as she looked down at the sofa. Crumbs, of course there would be crumbs; she smiled as she gathered them up in her hand. Even carried halfway to her nose she could detect the rich scent of dried fruit—cake! She peered into the wastepaper basket in the corner, nothing at all. Opening the French doors, she walked out onto the veranda. The curve of the bank disappeared on either side of her under the boathouse. The right bank ran almost parallel with the edge of the veranda, and there, lying on its side, on the smooth green turf, she saw a brown apple core, the circle of skin around its stem already wrinkling. She closed the French doors—someone had forgotten to bolt them—and returned to the front door of the cottage.

Standing in the open doorway, she looked out into the orchard. It was a bucolic prospect: late roses swayed overhead on the porch arbor; the orchard was cool and shady with its gnarled apple trees and soft tussocky green grass. She could just about see the east drive and the kitchen-garden wall through the trees. Lips pursed, foot tapping, she stood in thought for a moment or two. And then she looked down and there on the bottom step of the porch was the dottle from a pipe. The ash, disturbed by the hem of her skirt, eddied around a little plug of unburned tobacco.

Mrs. Jackson wheeled the bicycle through the orchard to the drive and pedaled back to the hospital. She went into the kitchen where the cook was lifting a large, heavy pot from the stove.

"Shepherd's pie today for dinner, Mrs. Jackson. I know it is one of your favorites."

She made appreciative noises and watched the cook strain the potatoes and put them into a bowl for mashing. "Has the luncheon basket been returned from the kitchen garden by any chance, Cook? The one that Ellis took out to Captain Bray yesterday?"

The cook straightened up, her mind clearly on her minced mutton with onions and carrots; she tossed a large knob of butter into the steaming potatoes and picked up her corrugated masher. "Can't honestly remember, Mrs. Jackson. It would be in the scullery cupboard if it was brought back—top shelf by the window."

"And is there any fruitcake left, from the one you made the day before yesterday?"

The cook shook her head. "Last of it went into Captain Bray's lunch basket, poor man. It was a nice big portion, so was the piece of pork pie Ellis cut for him, and a couple of apples. At least he had a decent meal inside him when he went."

Mrs. Jackson retraced her steps and put her head around the door into the scullery pantry. There sitting on the top shelf was the luncheon basket. She stood on tiptoe and hooked it down. It was quite empty.

Chapter Eleven

Mrs. Jackson barely had time to take off her hat and wash her hands and face in the handbasin when there came a very insistent knock on her bedroom door. Patting wisps of hair into place, she crossed the room and opened it. Standing on the threshold, deeply flushed no doubt with the exertion of taking the stairs two at a time, was Corporal Budge. Her face must have registered the disapproval she felt that a young man should dare to pound on her bedroom door in such a forceful fashion, because the color of Corporal Budge's complexion deepened and he took a step backward. He said something in a tangle of thick, round vowels intelligible only to those from the Mendip Hills that sounded to her very much like "mongrel-wurzel." She shook her head.

He took a breath to steady his voice. "That there policeman has arrested Lieutenant Phipps for the murder of Captain Bray," he said, taking care not to put Rs into words that need not have them.

She said nothing for a moment and Corporal Budge said, "Oh, so you did know."

No, she had not known, but she had expected it; only someone completely bereft of intuition or intelligence would have arrested Lieutenant Phipps so soon in the investigation.

"Where are they now?" she asked, and when he hesitated she

said more firmly, "Where are Inspector Savor and Lieutenant Phipps now, still in the hospital I hope, Corporal?"

"Downstairs with Major Andrews in his office. All hell broke loose when the inspector arrested the lieutenant. Captain Martin went completely over the top and West had to restrain him from hitting the inspector, which sent him round the twist, striking out and screaming about Fritz, and leaving the trench mortars unmanned." From where she was standing Mrs. Jackson heard Captain Martin's distant cries echoing up to them from the hall.

"What about Lieutenant Phipps? I hope he didn't say anything . . . that would . . ."

"Not a word more than he didn't do it. Major Andrews insists that Lieutenant Phipps is in no condition to go to Market Wingley jail and . . ."

Mrs. Jackson brushed past him and walked down the corridor to the back stairs. Down she went, as quickly as the steep, dark staircase would allow.

"Where is Ellis?" she said to Mary Fuller as she put her head around the door of the servants' hall. From the kitchen she heard an excitable giggle.

"Ellis, upstairs to my office at once, please." On the way up the back stairs she came upon Corporal West coming down them. "If you wouldn't mind, Corporal, I would like you to come with me. At any moment Lieutenant Phipps will be taken from the hospital by Inspector Savor. Come on, the pair of you, we haven't a moment to lose." She went ahead of them up the stairs to the ground floor of the house. On her way across the hall she called out to Corporal Budge as he came down the main staircase.

"Would you please go as fast as you can to Major Andrews's office and tell Inspector Savor that I have some information for him? Whatever you do, do not let him take Lieutenant Phipps from the house." He was already walking down the corridor to the medical wing. "Thank you, Corporal," she called after him.

In her office she stood in the windows so that she could see out across the drive. Corporal West and Sarah Ellis filed in through her office door, both looking, she thought, guiltier than anyone could possibly imagine.

"All right, you two," she said. "No need to look so mortified your secret is out. And by the way, having a picnic together is not a crime, even if it was Captain Bray's luncheon. But we cannot let Lieutenant Phipps be arrested for something he didn't do, can we? So let's be straight here. I know you were together in the boathouse from just after eleven until noon yesterday." She had hazarded a well-educated guess from minimal clues, but her intuition about young people was rarely wrong. "Right?" And when Ellis rushed to protest, she held up her hand. "No, Ellis, I know you were both in the boathouse eating Captain Bray's luncheon together, just accept that I know. In fact, you didn't even walk to the kitchen garden to give him his basket, did you? Instead you borrowed my bicycle and rode it down the drive and along the path to the boathouse for a picnic with Corporal West." Ellis's bottom lip jutted in dissent. "What you need to tell me is whether you saw Lieutenant Phipps in the orchard loading apples into his wheelbarrow while you were there?" The girl started to cry but Corporal West shushed her.

"Don't cry, Sarah, we weren't doing nothing wrong, and this is important. Yes, Mrs. Jackson, we was in the boathouse and when Sarah went back to the hospital I stayed on for a smoke with my newspaper—not in the house itself," he added in quick apology— he had probably lit his pipe inside and then remembered to smoke it on the porch. "And yes, I did see Lieutenant Phipps. He came into the orchard while I was on the porch. He loaded apples into his barrow and then he wheeled it off up the drive."

"Up the drive, not into the kitchen garden by the north door?"

The corporal looked puzzled for a moment. "No, he went up the drive, it's quicker that way. I followed him up there a moment later, and he came out of the kitchen courtyard and walked on ahead of me along the lane to the hospital."

"What time was that, Corporal?"

"He came into the orchard about half past twelve and took a load of apples, then went up to the courtyard. He came out as I was passing the archway and we both walked back to the hospital just in time for lunch."

Then he could not have had time to kill Captain Bray before luncheon. But why did he go into the kitchen garden with his second load after luncheon? This wasn't making sense and she was running out of time. If Inspector Savor took the lieutenant off to Market Wingley jail it would be very difficult to obtain his release. Policemen, especially ones with little talent for their job, did not like their mistakes to be made public. Mrs. Jackson glanced at her watch and then out of the window. The inspector's motorcar was still parked in the drive, so it was not too late. She stood in silent thought, ignoring the sad little snuffles coming from Ellis.

Why would a man take the easy route the first time and the more time-consuming and difficult-to-negotiate path through the kitchen garden the second time—was it to murder Captain Bray? She was stumped. Looking up, she saw Major Andrews and Inspector Savor walking down the steps onto the drive from the front door, and following, at a slower pace, was Lieutenant Phipps between two police constables. Major Andrews was talking to the inspector with evident vehemence. At the same time, there was a knock on the door and Corporal Budge put his head around it.

"No keeping them, Mrs. Jackson. That inspector has nobbled our lieutenant for the murder."

She was so concerned that she uttered aloud the question she had no answer to: "Why did Lieutenant Phipps take one barrow load of apples up the drive from the orchard to the kitchen-garden courtyard before luncheon and the second barrow through the kitchen garden afterwards?"

And Corporal Budge, a countryman through and through, laughed and said, "Because Mr. Thrower drives the geese into the orchard after lunch to pasture there, that's why. Those geese are aggressive blighters and that gander doesn't like anyone near his apples or his females. Lieutenant Phipps is scared stiff of him. Most probably he saw the gander on the edge of the orchard as he came onto the drive and turned back to take the safer route through the kitchen garden."

Mrs. Jackson took one look out her window and started off at an impressive pace. "Come on, Corporal, we might still have time," she ordered as she dodged around Corporal Budge still standing in the doorway of her office. "Go and get Mr. Thrower, you will find him in the orchid house. Tell him that I need him to come up to the Hall and tell him it is important—even if he says he is busy, tell him he must come immediately." Budge set off ahead of her with surprising speed.

"Ellis, dry your eyes, and, Corporal West, I need you too. Don't just stand there, we haven't much time." And with Ellis still dabbing away with her hankie they ran across the hall and out through the front door.

"Just a moment please, Inspector Savor!" Waving her arm, she went down the steps and out onto the drive to arrive only a little out of breath and just in time to stop the inspector before he ordered the constable to drive off for Market Wingley.

"I am so sorry to detain you, Inspector, but you did particularly ask that I report anything out of the ordinary that happened here yesterday," Mrs. Jackson said to Savor, who had reluctantly returned to the house to stand in front of the fireplace in the officers' mess with his hands in his pockets. He waited sullenly for her to enlighten him as he stared at Lieutenant Phipps, who was still wedged between his two constables in the middle of the room. Gathered around them were Major Andrews, Corporals West and Budge, VAD Ellis, and Mr. Thrower.

Does the man get drunk every night? Mrs. Jackson wondered as Inspector Savor lit a cigarette with an unsteady hand and gestured impatiently at her with the spent match to explain her reason for impeding his arrest. She pitched her voice low so that it did not jar a severe headache. "Before luncheon Lieutenant Phipps went to the orchard for a load of apples to take to the kitchen-garden courtyard. He was seen by Corporal West shoveling them into his wheelbarrow at just after half past twelve." She turned to Corporal West. "Am I right, Corporal?" She waited only for an acquiescent duck of his head and then continued. "When the corporal came out of the orchard onto the east drive, he saw Lieutenant Phipps ahead of him pushing his wheelbarrow up the drive in the direction of the kitchen courtyard." She turned to the corporal and this time waited for his reply.

"Yes, sir, that's how it was."

She did not wait for a response from the inspector before she continued. "By the time the corporal had almost reached the entrance to the kitchen courtyard, Lieutenant Phipps came back through the archway and they walked on to the hospital. The lieutenant then went to wash up before going into the officers' mess for luncheon, is that so, Lieutenant Phipps?" The young man stuttered a yes. "And was just a few minutes late to join the other officers for luncheon."

Inspector Savor mashed his cigarette out in the ashtray. "And what about later, what about after luncheon? He went to the orchard for more apples, but on his return he went into the kitchen garden by the north gate when it would have been a lot quicker just to have continued up it, the way he did the first time. That's when he did it—that's when he murdered Captain Bray. He had it planned out right from the start—he brought along a weapon for the job and then hid it after he killed Captain Bray." He glared around him, daring anyone to contradict him.

For a moment Mrs. Jackson was almost stunned. *The potato spade was not the weapon!* Then it had not been, as she had thought, a murder of opportunity but one that had been planned. "Did you find the murder weapon, Inspector Savor?"

He scowled. "No, but we will." He jerked his head toward Lieutenant Phipps. "This one will sing a different tune when we get him down to Market Wingley. C'mon, matey, let's be having you." He turned toward the door

If the murderer had brought along a weapon then he had obviously taken some time to conceal it, if the police had not yet found it, or taken it away with him. *This is even better than I hoped it would be!* Mrs. Jackson took a step forward, her voice lifted in conviction. "The captain was already dead, Inspector, when Lieutenant Phipps went into the kitchen garden after luncheon. Captain Bray was lying at the bottom of the potato bed; one glance and the lieutenant saw the wounds on his head. It brought the death of his friend in the trenches back to him." Inspector Savor gave a derisive snort and rolled his eyes. But Mrs. Jackson continued on. "In his panic he let go of his barrow, spilling apples all over the path, and ran for help to the kitchen courtyard to Corporal Budge and his fellow officers. He arrived through the east gate into the courtyard at half past two, completely out of breath and very distraught."

"So why did he go into the kitchen garden then? Anyone in their right mind can see that it's slower going through the garden; much easier to wheel a heavy barrow up the drive like he did before. No, Miss Jackson, it won't wash." He waved his constables toward the door and they took hold of the lieutenant.

"But Lieutenant Phipps couldn't go up the drive, could he, Mr. Thrower?" Mrs. Jackson turned to the elderly gardener who was standing in a far corner of the room with his hat in his hands, summoned there by the fleet-footed Corporal Budge. The old gardener touched his forehead in respect to her and stepped forward.

"No, Mrs. Jackson, he could not. Not with old Bill doing sentry go."

The inspector stopped halfway across the room. "Old Bill—who the hell is old Bill?" He turned on the older man, his face scowling in suspicion as if someone was trying to pull a fast one on him.

"He is a gander with a powerful temper and Lieutenant Phipps avoids him as he would the devil. You see, sir, Bill is big even for an Embden goose, a most impressive size to go with a ferocious nature. That old boy will hiss and flap his wings at anyone on the edge of his orchard." The gardener laughed, and extending his arms straight out on either side he craned his neck forward in a droll imitation of the gander on the attack.

Inspector Savor had lost his scornful look. "Get on with it, man."

"Certainly, sir. You see, he's a bully is old Bill, but he sometimes takes a bit of a dislike to certain types. We had a gardener's boy once; Tommy was nice little chap but he was scared stiff of Bill. I swear that old bird would sneak about and hide to wait for Tommy if he so much as tried to creep up that part of the drive. Over six feet Bill's wingspan is, tried to measure it once and he damn near took me leg off!" His voice was rich with pride—he certainly had the inspector's attention. "Oh yes, he's an impressive sight all right when he's angry is Bill, and he has a hiss like a viper. No matter how hard Tommy ran, old Bill was on him. You should have seen the lad's calves—covered in great black bruises they were. And he had it in for the lieutenant." He nodded his head at Lieutenant Phipps, who was drooping in silent dejection. "He's a right old bugger, in't he, sir? Old Bill took a dislike to you the first time he saw you. Whenever Bill was on that side of the orchard the lieutenant would take the long way round."

Mrs. Jackson could tell that Inspector Savor didn't like any of this. He looked around the room and then over at his prisoner. "Sounds like a lot of mumbo jumbo to me," was all he could think of to say.

"That'll be because you are from the town, sir." Mr. Thrower was having none of this superior talk from a jumped-up Market Wingley lad. "Hard to understand country ways if you are born and bred in a town. If you want to walk down to the orchard along the east drive toward Iyntwood, let's see for ourselves if that old gander will let you pass. If he don't take a liking to you I hope you have a good pair of legs on you and know how to use 'em." Thrower's shoulders shook with a silent inner laugh, as he looked around the room to include them all.

Phipps came out of his reverie. "That goose," he said without regard for the gender of geese or those around him, "is a right royal bastard, sir." He addressed the only man with any real authority in the room.

Major Andrews had been listening to the gardener's story closely. "So do you think the gander can tell if people are intimidated by him?" It was clear that Major Andrews was interested by this information, for he muttered in an aside to Corporal Budge, "That could be quite a useful therapy, Budge, herding Bill."

"Yes, sir, old Bill knows who to pick on." Thrower turned back to Savor: "You have to have felt that powerful beak penetrating the tender flesh of your nether quarters to really understand how fearsome Bill is, Inspector." Mrs. Jackson wondered if gardener and gander shared the same likes and dislikes. "And what is more, I drive the geese off the lake every afternoon just after two in the afternoon. And yesterday," he pulled an old turnip-shaped watch out of his pocket, looked at its face, and then turned it toward them so they might verify its accuracy. "I was held up a bit by Mrs. Thrower and it was right on a twenty past two when I drove the geese into the orchard. I saw the lieutenant shoveling his apples and he still had a way to go. I expect old Bill spotted Lieutenant Phipps right off as he was leaving with his wheelbarrow and cut him off at the drive."

"So you see, Inspector," Mrs. Jackson so loved to have the last word, "Lieutenant Phipps left the hospital at two o'clock with everyone else, walked down to the orchard and arrived there at ten past two, spent fifteen minutes loading up the apples into his barrow and started up the drive, and there was Bill, so he turned around and went back to the north gate to take a detour through the kitchen garden. He must have spent barely two minutes in the kitchen garden . . . enough to take in what had happened to the captain, before he . . ."

Mr. Thrower liked to have the last word, too: ". . . Legged it for help. There'd be no time at all for him to conk the captain one on the head and then hide his weapon, that's for sure."

Chapter Twelve

Just after breakfast the following morning, Clementine managed to waylay her daughter as she walked across the drive to her motorcar. She noticed that Althea was wearing her Women's Land Army uniform in the khaki so loved by everyone in Britain these days, and decided not to comment on her whipcord breeches; try as she might, she found the sight of them jarring. *At least they are modestly covered by her tunic,* she thought as she took in a pair of driving goggles worn, as Harry wore his, over her cap, where they could do no possible good at all. For some reason that Clementine could not fathom, her daughter was carrying a riding crop in her hand. She wondered if this was to discipline her motorcar if it showed signs of lagging, or whether it was required uniform.

"A moment, Althea, please," she called, and her daughter half turned at the top step.

Everyone who met them remarked at how closely Althea resembled her; they had the same oval face and delicate chin. But the eyes that turned toward Clementine were the intense blue of her father's and brother's and her gaze was just as direct. "Good morning, Mama, I am awfully late." Althea greeted her in a brisk tone of voice—a warning for her to say what she wanted to without too much ado. To back up her need for haste she waved her crop at her motorcar, its coachwork shining in the morning sun and a Women's Land Army pennant—a sheaf of golden wheat on a green ground—fluttering in the morning breeze.

"I won't keep you long, darling. Do you know if the officers on farm detachment stayed at their designated farms all day yesterday?"

Althea's gaze became thoughtful. "Captain Standish was working at Dodd Farm—I dropped him off myself at about a quarter past eight. Lieutenant Forbes walked down to the Home Farm from the hospital—he was leaving as I arrived; I can't imagine that they left their farms. I dropped Ian at Brook End last, and he didn't go anywhere at all after that. Mama, I must be on my way . . ."

Ian? She must be referring to Lieutenant Carmichael. Clementine was so taken aback by the informality of her daughter referring to one of their officer-patients by his Christian name that whatever she was going to say next went completely out of her head. *Ian? Why on earth did Althea think it was acceptable to call this complete stranger Ian?* She recovered from her astonishment and decided that she simply must know more before her twenty-one-year-old daughter drove off for the day, no doubt to spend more time with this Ian. She walked down the steps and around the front of the motor, opened the door of the passenger seat, and got in. "Such a lovely morning, I'll come along for the ride." *That's the way, take a nice bright but firm tone with her,* she thought, *and don't allow yourself to be persuaded that her spending time quite alone with young men is acceptable because it is her job.*

"Mama, I simply don't have time to take you for a ride this morning." Althea was still standing on the drive looking particularly put out. *Is she alarmed at the idea of my accompanying her to Brook End Farm?* Clementine watched the expression on her daughter's face set and patted the driver's seat next to her in invitation. "One day when you are not too busy I would love it if you were to teach me how to operate a motorcar."

"I would be happy to. It does rather take more than a morning though. Perhaps when you and Mrs. Jackson have solved your crime, and you have some time to yourself, then we could dedicate a week or two to the business of teaching you to drive." Althea opened the door on the driver's side.

How on earth does she know about our inquiry? "Solving our crime?" she said, feeling almost guilty of breaking the law.

Althea was clearly enjoying the fact that she had surprised her. "Did you imagine for one moment that Harry wouldn't tell me? Darling Mama, I had absolutely no idea that it was *you* who worked out who killed Teddy until Harry told me how clever you were. And that business up in London at Hermione Kingsley's dinner party? I was simply amazed that it was you and Mrs. Jackson who got to the bottom of all of that." Clementine couldn't help but notice that Althea's eyes were shining with pure pleasure as she informed her that she knew about her rather eccentric interests. "I think inquiring must be a jolly sight more interesting than gardening. Exercises the brain and keeps you on your toes. It is not good for us to settle too thoroughly into a life of habit." She ended on this rather patronizing note as she slammed the door of her motorcar shut.

"A life of habit?" Clementine pretended to be taken aback. "Let's not talk about your addiction to world travel, then—a habit that only a war could break." She caught her daughter's eye and they both laughed, lightening the tension considerably. "Gardening and making inquiries are very similar interests: they both require patience, observation, and a strong appreciation of both harmony and things that don't fit together, as well as the willingness to painstakingly weed through either information or a herbaceous border." This made her daughter laugh even more, as if she had said something enormously funny.

"I am driving straight to Brook End Farm this morning. The Land girls have already picked up the farm-detachment officers and I will be spending all morning there. There is so much to do . . ." Blue eyes turned toward Clementine and a slight frown made a brief appearance. Clementine understood that she was not welcome on Althea's farming jaunt.

"That's quite all right, you can drop me on Brook End Lane. I will walk back to the house across the fields. A perfect morning and I could do with the exercise." She adjusted the brim of her hat and smiled, happy at the prospect of a drive with her daughter. "Where is Harry, by the way?" *So much for promises from reliable family chaperones.*

"He went over to Brook End Farm earlier; one of the tractors won't start. He bet me five bob that it wouldn't be long before I was interviewed, either by you or Mrs. Jackson." The motorcar was fitted with an electric starter and she put her foot down on the accelerator and started down the drive at a sedate pace. "This slow enough for you?" She gave her mother a cheeky smile. "Now what can I tell you?"

"It's about the officers on farm detachment. How, for instance, would you know if they had spent all day at their farms?"

"Well for a start, Forbes at the Home Farm was out in the fields and he would have not been working alone but with the Land girls and farmers. He doesn't know how to use a scythe so he was probably stooking wheat. Standish at Dodd Farm might have been actually at the farm because their crop is already in. But if either of them went off for an hour or two it would have been very noticeable. I will check if you would like me to."

"And the other officer, the one at Brook End, what about him?" Her voice must have sounded critical, because her daughter hesitated for the slightest fraction of a second.

"No need to check. I gave Ian . . . Lieutenant Carmichael a plowing lesson with Dolly in the morning. And then just before luncheon he took her down to the pasture and came back to the spinney, you know by the ten-acre, and we had a picnic there."

Clementine had been wondering about this picnic off and on ever since last night. She was quite aware where the spinney by the ten-acre was. It was a particularly picturesque spot, perched up on top of Marston Downs. A romantic place to spend time with a young man, she concluded, with a sizable flicker of apprehension. After lying awake at three o'clock in the morning for over an hour she remembered that she had met Lieutenant Carmichael outside the hospital as she and Ralph were returning home on the afternoon Captain Bray's body had been found. He was the one with the at-tractive, open, boyish face. *But there are so many boys,* she thought as she drifted back to sleep. *The world is full of them: polite, dutiful, patriotic boys all getting blown to bits in the war.*

But this morning was a beautiful one, and the little car zipped along the narrow lane with its tall hedgerows. The airy boughs of beech trees cast dappled, dancing shadows and the air had the sweet, rich smell of dew-soaked grass as it dried in the sun. Cle-mentine's reverie of the peaceful countryside was interrupted by her daughter's voice. "You have gone very quiet," she said. Althea's pretty bay-brown curls fluttered around her jaunty little cap as she glanced over at her. And Clementine decided that her con-cern for the unchaperoned picnic was not one that should be dis-cussed now. Timing was everything when you needed to make your point with firm emphasis.

"Really? I was just thinking that I didn't know you could plow."

"My plow lines are as straight as a die. Old Mr. Lawrence taught Harry and me when we were younger. Plowing, once well taught, becomes second nature; it's like riding a bicycle—once learned, never forgotten. There is a real art to it, Mama, you should learn, then you can help us with winter plowing."

Clementine's smile became a little fixed. Althea was teasing her. *She knows I disapprove of her spending time alone with this Carmichael—with any young man—and now she is being pert.* But she wanted information. "So, Lieutenant Carmichael and you spent the morning plowing and then he put the horse out to pasture, the one at the bottom by Brook End Lane?"

"Yes, that's right. And I went on up to the spinney and unpacked the luncheon basket." *Picnic baskets seemed to be popping up all over the place yesterday,* Clementine thought with a grim expression on her face. "And Lieutenant Carmichael joined me about twenty minutes later. So that would make me his alibi"—another glance to see how her mother was taking this rather startling information—"wouldn't it?"

At least she has stopped calling him Ian, Clementine thought, but all she said to her daughter was, "Any idea of the exact time?"

Althea blew her horn as they came up to a blind corner in the road. "Oh, Mama, you surely don't think that Lieutenant Carmichael could have murdered Captain Bray? What about the men back at the Hall? It must have been one of the other officers, one of the ones that failed their Medical Board review last week."

"Nevertheless, Althea, can you remember the time you stopped plowing for luncheon, the time that the lieutenant left you?"

"Well as a matter of fact I can: I said, 'No wonder I'm famished, it's nearly time for luncheon,' and he said, 'Back in a jiffy, poor old Dolly has earned her luncheon too,' or something like that. And off he went down to the pasture to let her loose, and I looked at my watch and it was just a little before one o'clock." She ended on what sounded to Clementine very much like a note of defiance.

It would only take him just few minutes to walk Dolly down to the pasture but it would take longer to walk back up the hill, it gets steep below the spinney. Say twenty to twenty-five minutes? Probably closer to twenty, maybe even less; he must have been awfully keen to join her for a picnic à deux. She pictured Lieutenant Carmichael throwing open the gate to the pasture and speeding the young mare through with a hearty slap on her rump before setting out up the hill at a vigorous pace. She gazed out of the window at the hedgerow flashing past them at an alarming rate, and thought that Ian Carmichael had the perfect alibi—her daughter.

"And do you happen to know how long it was before he joined you at the spinney?" She did her best not to sound too critical and she must have succeeded because her daughter answered quite unselfconsciously, "Yes, I do. He came puffing up the hill and said he was sorry to have taken so long, Dolly was playing up a bit, and I looked at my watch and it was just after twenty minutes past one."

"And after luncheon?" she asked, but with little interest for the answer except the hope that they had both finally rejoined the Land Army girls—who no doubt were all nudging each other in the ribs and rolling their eyes at Lady Althea Talbot strolling along in the company of Ian Carmichael. She gritted her teeth together. *Say nothing, wait until this evening.*

"Oh, afterwards we went down to the pasture to catch Dolly so we could take her back up to the fields to pull the big wagon. She made a huge fuss about it and was being very naughty; Lieutenant Carmichael was running all over place. We caught her finally and were just about to walk her back to the farm along the lane and that's when we saw Mr. Bray sitting forlornly in his motorcar." She slowed down as they crossed the narrow bridge at the top of Brook End Lane.

Clementine hardly dared ask what time that was and was not surprised when her daughter became vague about little things like the time of day. "I can't be quite sure of the actual time, but it was probably about half past three or so. It took ages and ages to catch Dolly." *I am sure it did,* Clementine thought, simmering at her daughter's reckless attitude to convention, and what was worse, she didn't, even now, seem to be aware of her tremendous breach of propriety, for on she went as if everything about her afternoon was quite acceptable.

"Crops are all in at Brook End, so we can concentrate on helping

Mr. Howard to get his wheat in. I simply can't believe how stubborn he is. I think he just doesn't like the idea of women working on his land, and he seems to have a deep prejudice against any help that isn't local." Althea skillfully negotiated a tight series of bends in the lane without slowing down, her right hand hovering over the electric horn, and pulled up at the bottom of the lane that led up to Brook End Farm.

"Which way are you walking, Mama? Footpath across Holly Farm's fields, or shall I drop you in the village?"

"Here will do very well, darling." Clementine got out of the motor and stood by the gate into the footpath through the wheat field. "Is this where Mr. Bray's motorcar broke down?"

"Right where you are standing, Mama. Have a lovely walk then. Got to dash now, cheerio!"

Clementine stood by the side of the road and watched Althea drive on toward Brook End Farm in a cloud of dust. Moments later a motor truck full of Land girls came speeding along the lane. She waved to the driver to slow down and a gloved hand lifted in greeting.

It is not a good idea for all these young women to be racing around the countryside, driving farm machinery, and picnicking alone with young men, she thought crossly as she opened the gate and set off along the footpath through the Holly Farm wheat field to home. *In fact it is a very bad idea indeed; no wonder Mr. Howard doesn't want the Land girls on his farm.*

Chapter Thirteen

After luncheon Clementine put on her hat, found her secateurs and heavy leather gardening gloves, and went out to work in her rose garden—an occupation that she usually enjoyed. But today there were so many unanswered questions teeming through her head that she didn't know which of her considerable problems to tackle first: the murder of Captain Bray; the War Office and the Medical Board review; the insistence by their neighbor Sir Winchell Meacham that the hospital be closed; her daughter's blithely unconventional behavior; their elder daughter Verity's determination to continue to stay on in Paris just miles from the fighting; or Harry's habitual brandy at breakfast. As the afternoon wore on, hard work stilled most of the arguments going on in her head, or at least distilled them into some sort of order.

If we are methodical we will sort out who killed Captain Bray, which will take care of the Medical Board next week. We have at least cleared most of our officers—not a single one of them could possibly have had the time to find his way to the kitchen garden at the critical time.

She bent down and pulled up a particularly stubborn weed before she returned to clipping off dead roseheads with her shears. *Althea is not a wayward girl, she is just carried away with all this independence, so it is important for me to be firm with her. And as for Verity, if the Germans break through the line there will be plenty of time for Etienne to bundle her and the children off to Chinon.*

She raked up garden debris and fallen leaves and realized that her greatest concern at the moment was for her son. His evident low spirits at being temporarily out of action did rather indicate that he had completely lost the capacity to enjoy simple, everyday life. *For the last two years combat has been his everyday life— the thrill of it, the risk, the camaraderie with the men he leads; sitting around at home waiting for his arm to heal must be absolute misery for him: it gives him far too much time to think.*

She tackled the painful business of tying back rose shoots and stems over the domed hazel withies that supported them. It was a job that took all her concentration if she was to avoid being badly scratched. *And as for Sir Winchell, poor old thing, I can surely persuade him to understand the hospital's value so he doesn't turn up at the Medical Board review and rave at them to close us down.* She looked up from tying back a particularly powerful and thorny stem and caught sight of her son, sprawled in a lawn chair apparently asleep under the chestnut tree. An hour later, in spite of her leather gloves, she came off worse in an altercation with a particularly vicious old damask rose and decided that it was time to call it a day.

The best thing about gardening, she thought as she surveyed the immaculate beds around her, *is that you can see results immediately.* She threw the last of the dead heads into the barrow. Her son was still recumbent in his wicker chair at the bottom of the lawn. Glancing at her watch and seeing that it wanted only half an hour until tea, she walked down to join him.

Harry was not asleep. He was lying inert in his chair, an empty brandy glass in his left hand, his splinted right arm in its sling resting on his chest. He was staring across the lawn toward the west, watching the late summer sun as it started to sink in the sky.

The shadows were lengthening on the lawn and the light had turned to the glowing green-gold of late summer as the sun's rays slanted through the canopy of the chestnut tree. Now that she was no longer active, Clementine shivered. She noticed Harry's leather flying jacket lying on the grass, picked it up, and slipped it around her shoulders. Its lambskin lining was immediately comforting. She sat down in the chair next to his and he turned his head toward her and smiled a welcome.

It had taken Clementine years to accept her son's love of flight. When she had visited the flying field at Eastchurch at the start of the war, she had been quite disappointed when she had seen her first aeroplane: an ungainly machine squatting like a giant toad in a field. She had half turned to her husband in surprise. "Yes, they are rather unimpressive on the ground," he had said, smiling at her disappointment. "But wait until they take off!" She had watched the machines clumsily bump across the roughly mown grass of the airfield, and thought how ridiculous they looked as they lurched upward in a roar of overworked machinery, leaving a trail of petrol fumes in their wake. She had lifted her hand to her nose at the thick, oily smell as Lord Montfort had lifted his to shade his eyes, the better to enjoy the spectacle. "Now look at them, darling, a little more interesting when they are up, don't you think?"

He had been enthralled with the skill of the young flying officers that afternoon as they watched the squadron of planes fly in formation, tumble and turn in the sky, and then surge upward to peel away left and right when she thought they might crash into a church steeple. "Superb!" Lord Montfort—the man who had for two years frowned at the idea that men should take to the air, especially his son—was captivated. "Oh marvelous, would you look at that? Absolutely splendid, what incredible skill! Can't believe how fast the things can go. And now look, they are flying like a flock of geese, wingtips barely feet distant from each other!"

Sitting in her peaceful garden, she felt a shiver of apprehension for Captain Harry Talbot, as he preferred to be called these days, who had chalked up seventeen aerial victories this year; he was one of the youngest flying aces of the war in France and the highest-scoring ace of his squadron. She shook her head to rid it of the image of her son in his fragile aircraft. Would he be able to reconcile himself to being a landowner when this war was over? How would any of these young men be able to return home and carry on as before?

"Beautiful afternoon," she said by way of a greeting.

He glanced at his empty glass and then down at the bottle of brandy sitting demurely underneath her lawn chair. "Quite lovely," he said politely, evidently wrestling with the idea of another drink with his mother sitting guard over the bottle.

"I went over to Brook End Farm this morning after breakfast with Althea. All her Land girls were gathering there to finish bringing in the harvest—such enthusiastic workers."

"Doing a capital job . . . every one of them. Jolly good show," he said.

"Did you have a moment to go there today, to Brook End I mean?"

"Helped 'em out for most of the a.m. Two of their tractors were kaput." This was how her son expressed himself these days. These brief utterances laced with the slang used by his fellow pilots were used as a polite wall to keep conversation on a superficial level.

"She said she was teaching Lieutenant Carmichael to plow, yesterday. I had no idea you both knew how to do that."

His response was glib: "Best thing about a country childhood. Plowing kept me on the straight and narrow all my life." He smiled at her and she heard the soft slur in his speech from an afternoon in company with the brandy bottle. "Althea does a crack job with her Land Army. Far better 'n I could." She guessed he was alluding not just to plowing, he was referring to his sister's love for the estate and its thousands of fertile acres. If Harry was completely honest, he found the land and all its attendant burdens terribly dull. She tactfully kept the conversation away from her son's interest in the estate.

"I do hope Mr. Howard comes off his high horse about the Land girls helping him with his crop."

"He will; they really know their stuff. It's 'stonishing how fast they can whip through a wheat field." He turned his head back to the western horizon.

"Have you met Lieutenant Carmichael? He is on farm detachment at Brook End."

Harry considered her question, his eyes half closed in the strong late afternoon side light. "Yes, I met him the other day. Seemed a decent enough chap—nice manners." He came out of his lethargy and sat up in his chair. "What's up, Mama, something wrong?"

"Something wrong?" Where has he been in the last two days? A man was brutally murdered in our kitchen garden, and he asks if something is wrong? She sighed—it was more of a huff of irritation.

"Of course you must be worried. It doesn't do for Althea, or any of her Land girls, to be anywhere alone when there is a murderer on the loose. I'll talk to her about it—please don't worry." He was concerned now, she realized; he had actually used a sentence with more than four words in it. *No matter how unhappy he is, he is still the same kindhearted soul he always was.* It was an inexplicable relief to see her son emerge at last from the preoccupied and withdrawn state he had been in for the last few days.

Her feet were cold. She got up from her chair and he joined her to walk farther down the lawn, where they stood looking out across the valley. A river mist started to drift into the water meadow, collecting in long thin golden strands at the bases of the trees. Cows slowly moved through the mist toward the gate at the far end, where they stood in a patient herd, waiting for evening milking. "The golden hour," said her son as they gazed down on the simple beauty of pastoral England. His voice was low, but not so low that she didn't catch his wistful tone. And then his mood changed. "It could be any one of them I suppose, your patients up at the hospital." She turned her head so quickly that he laughed. "I know, I know they are all perfectly harmless, but someone in our little world is a murderer, and it isn't one of our local farmers, is it?" He stamped his cigarette into the ground and put his hand on her shoulder. It was the first gesture of affection he had shown in the days since he had come home. She reached up and patted his hand.

"I worry most about Althea—I know she and her Land girls are together, for most of the time, but she doesn't stop to think things through very carefully."

"Yes, I know, Ma." He hadn't called her Ma since he was fourteen. "I am going to be with her wherever she goes from now on. I just had to be up at Brook End earlier than her this morning. We are going to Holly Farm together tomorrow morning, bright and early, to volunteer our help to Mr. Howard to bring in his harvest. All of us—the Brook End people, the farm-detachment officers, and our local Land Army volunteers—will spend every moment of the day with Althea, and if Carmichael or any of his brother officers try to lure her off for plowing lessons I'll give him a swift kick in his posterior." He took her hand, gave it a squeeze, and let it go. And Clementine felt such reassurance and gratitude that she stood on tiptoe and kissed him quickly on the cheek. A cloud of brandy fumes so strong that they made her eyes water engulfed her for a moment. But all she said was, "Harry, thank you. It is quite awful when murder happens in a small community. Everyone is suspicious of each other—and especially of our officers."

"I am sure you and Mrs. Jackson will work out what happened in the kitchen garden long before old Valentine and his policemen have even come up with their first suspect. You'll probably have pieced it all together by this time tomorrow."

They started to walk back up the lawn to the house; its windows reflected the glowing sun as it sank lower in the sky. Harry breathed a long sigh. Was it contentment or loss? She linked her arm through his and said, "When I came down to you just now, you were quite lost in your thoughts."

"It's the time of day I enjoy the most," he said; and aware that it was bad form for mothers to reveal too much concern, she said nothing. "I love the sky, 'specially in the early morning and evening. I think it is why I enjoy flying so much. But it is as clear as a bell here, not a plane in sight." He obviously decided that that was enough war talk for one day because he fell silent.

She was quite happy to change the subject. "Supposing you were at Dodd Farm and you wanted to get to the kitchen garden quickly without being seen?"

"So not up our drive, or on foot?" He shot her a bright, inquisitive look as she shook her head. He was evidently pleased to help her with this part of the puzzle, because he launched into considering it with enthusiasm. "A few of our farmers have motorcars and there are a good many tractors about. The Land girls have a lorry but it's a huge beastly thing. Anything with a motor would be noisy and could be easily spotted or heard coming along our north or east drives. But a bicycle would be quick, silent, and easy to ride on all of the footpaths and bridle trails around here that lead to the kitchen garden's south gate, and there are plenty of bikes about. One of the saddest things about the country these days is that there are no horses any longer, except Papa's Bruno and Dolly."

"Please come in, m'lady, and get warm. Once the sun goes down it gets quite chilly in the evenings, especially in this house."

Mrs. Jackson gave the logs a stir in the grate. Lady Montfort had arrived without announcement at the door of her office and it had seemed quite natural to ask her to join her in her evening glass of sherry. She hoped her ladyship did not think that she was being presumptuous, but if she felt at ease drinking a glass with her then surely that was all that mattered.

"Your health, Jackson," Lady Montfort said as she held up her sherry to the firelight in salute to her hospitality. "I have always thought amontillado is such a perfect drink for autumn." The pale gold of the wine caught the orange firelight and became a glowing amber, and she lowered the rim and took an appreciative sip. "I love these September days when they start to draw in earlier and it's hot in the day and the evenings are chilly enough for a fire."

"Autumn's not far off now, m'lady." They sipped in companionable silence for a while.

"So I hear you had rather a dramatic end to your afternoon, Jackson, with that dreadful inspector!"

With the first log fire of the season, a glass of sherry, and an attentive audience, Mrs. Jackson enjoyed recounting Lieutenant Phipps's near arrest. When she came to the part about Mr. Thrower providing an alibi for the unfortunate Phipps in the shape of an aggressive gander, they were both laughing. "Mr. Thrower really enjoyed himself, m'lady. You know how once he gets going he loves to tell a good yarn. I think this one will be repeated all over the county."

A merry laugh from her ladyship as she sipped away; she appeared to be quite delighted at the inspector's set-down. "And Inspector Savor will be portrayed as a witless city boy, Mr. Thrower as a wise old gaffer, and Bill will get bigger and meaner with each telling. I remember the Allenbys' eldest boy used to creep into the orchard to steal apples until he ran into old Bill." Lady Montfort was still smiling at the memory as she put her glass down on the little table at her elbow.

"I asked Colonel Valentine about the potato spade, Jackson, this morning. He very reluctantly informed me, as you already know, that it was not used to kill Captain Bray. Wrong shape—something more like a length of lead pipe, he said. Interesting, don't you think, that Inspector Savor was quite ready to arrest Phipps even without a murder weapon? Rather putting the cart before the horse I think."

"Yes, m'lady, the inspector is rather impatient, not a useful trait in a murder investigation, I would have thought."

Lady Montfort glanced at her wristwatch. "We should put our heads together, Jackson, before I have to run back to Iyntwood. Mr. Bray has decided he will join us for dinner this evening and I only have twenty minutes or so before the changing bell. Do you think Lieutenant Phipps is safe from arrest now?"

Mrs. Jackson gave the fire a stir with the poker and the flames leaped higher, sending sparks up the chimney. "The inspector still believes that Lieutenant Phipps killed Captain Bray, m'lady. He said that under the Defense of the Realm Act he could arrest and imprison Lieutenant Phipps merely on suspicion. But Major Andrews wouldn't back down. He said time and again that Phipps could not have had the time to kill Captain Bray and hide the weapon. In the end, the major threatened to take the whole business before a military tribunal, and since we are all in the army here, then military law takes precedence over civil law. The inspector left in a right sour mood. But until we can prove otherwise, Lieutenant Phipps is still a suspect and not allowed to leave the hospital building, even to go into the garden.

"Not one of our officers on cider detachment, nor any of the staff in the house, could have done the murder, m'lady. I have checked very carefully, none of them were alone or missing at the time Captain Bray was killed." She took a sip of her sherry.

"Before I forget, Colonel Valentine did confirm the time of death. The captain was killed between the hours of half past eleven in the morning and about half past two in the afternoon. Which brings us to the men on farm detachment: Lady Althea says that they could not have left their work in the fields without their absence being noticed—even when they stopped work for luncheon. I am not too sure we should be complacent about any of them, until we have checked on their alibis between those hours." And Lady Montfort gave the example of Lieutenant Carmichael's day with her daughter, embarrassing though it clearly was to her to have to admit that Lady Althea had not behaved in a way suitable for a lady.

What on earth are these girls thinking with their silly picnics with men unknown to their families? Mrs. Jackson wondered. Not that she could possibly imagine Lady Althea behaving badly.

"So you see, Jackson, Lieutenant Carmichael could not have made it from Brook End Farm, across the footpath that cuts through the Holly Farm wheat field, to the kitchen garden's south gate, murdered the captain, and then returned all in twenty minutes— even if he had a bicycle handy, which I suppose he might have. Well one thing has clearly emerged from today, whoever murdered Captain Bray brought a weapon along for the job and either took it away with him or hid it carefully perhaps to retrieve later." She got to her feet and warmed her hands in front of the fire.

"And if Ellis's account of her morning is reliable, m'lady, Captain Bray was last seen alive by her at twenty-five minutes to one and found dead at about half past two, which gives our murderer two full hours, more than enough time to get from Dodd or the Home Farm." Mrs. Jackson put her sherry down on the side table with such intention that the foot of the glass made contact with its wooden surface with sharp click. "Forbes at the Home Farm could have walked along the cart track straight to the south gate of the kitchen garden; it would take maybe just twenty minutes. He could have killed Captain Bray and then walked back within an hour, perhaps less."

Her ladyship didn't like this information any more than Mrs. Jackson did. She bit her lip and stared into the fire. "Then we must check distances, Jackson. In those two hours Lieutenant Standish at Dodd Farm could have walked or ridden a bicycle up to the south gate of the kitchen garden, too. And since this appears to be a premeditated crime, Carmichael could have stowed a bicycle under the hedge of the horse pasture and ridden up to the kitchen garden and back again." She paused, her brow wrinkled as she thought. "How long would it take on a bicycle, Jackson, to ride that distance—what is it, about three miles, perhaps a little more?"

"I can't be sure, m'lady. It takes me six or seven minutes to bicycle from Haversham Hall over to Iyntwood and the drive is well maintained and quite flat; how far is that, I wonder?"

"Lord Haversham told me once it was a little over a mile and a half, so it would have taken Lieutenant Carmichael all of his twenty minutes just to get there and back, and then he would have had to get up to the spinney afterwards."

Mrs. Jackson noticed that her ladyship's glass was long empty. "May I pour you another glass, m'lady?" She held up the decanter.

"Thank you, Jackson, but I must be going. I think I am crossing Carmichael off our list—time is against him. So, back to Lieutenant Standish: he could have easily walked to the kitchen garden using the footpaths from Dodd Farm, couldn't he? The quickest way to go would be the one to the footbridge across the river. But it is quite a distance even then."

"Yes, he would have to go down Cryer's Breach Lane to the top of Sir Winchell Meacham's drive, m'lady, and then through the withy gate onto the bridle path and across the little wooden footbridge, then up along the other side of the river. It would take over an hour on foot one-way. Even with a bicycle it would be slow going, the paths are very overgrown by the river and it is often a bit boggy there. He would be gone from Dodd farm nearly two hours." She put another log on the fire and they both watched the flames curl eagerly around it.

"We must check up on both Forbes and Standish and see if they left their work in the middle part of the day and if they did for how long. Oh my goodness, will you look at the time, I simply must go. You and I can easily check up on Lieutenant Forbes at the Home Farm, it is Dodd Farm that will be more of a problem; I can't remember the last time I went over there."

Mrs. Jackson couldn't imagine how they would phrase such a question to Mr. Dodd, either; like most farmers, he was a silent individual and probably only enjoyed a gossip with old friends, farmers like himself, after an evening at the Goat and Fiddle. She walked over to the bell pull. "I am going to ask Corporal Budge to drive you back to the house in Major Andrews's motorcar, m'lady. I don't think you should be walking alone when it's completely dark out."

Chapter Fourteen

Really Mr. Bray is a most pleasantly mannered man, thought Clementine as she ate her fish and listened to him chatting away to Althea on his right, *and Althea certainly finds his company enjoyable.* She glanced at her son, seated farther down the table; he had barely forced a bite throughout what was after all quite a reasonable dinner. The chicken that followed their local trout was roasted to a delicious succulence and had been stuffed with wild mushrooms, as a substitute for truffles, giving the bird a pleasantly woodsy flavor. *It is well worth the time walking on eggshells around Mrs. Thwaite in case she decides to desert us for the Banbury munitions factory.*

Turning her attention back to the conversation at the dinner table, or rather to the monologue from Sir Winchell that had started with the fish and was still going strong, she realized that he was already steamed up about what he described as the impertinent behavior of "the lower orders," an expression that made Clementine wince. She tilted her head to one side in a listening pose, a smile on her lips, and every so often she exclaimed, "Oh my goodness, how terribly upsetting," or, "Good heavens above, who would have thought it?"

"... So that put the fool of a man straight; I think Londoners become more disrespectful every time I go up to town." Sir

Winchell lifted his fork to his mouth and Clementine said, "It certainly is—I mean, they certainly are." She thought that no matter how many misfortunes Sir Winchell might have suffered and how sympathetic she felt toward him, he was still and always would be rather a swaggering and trivial man. She decided to make the conversation more productive.

"I spent such a pleasant morning away from household duties; I went over to Brook End Farm with Althea in her motorcar this morning and walked back along the Holly Farm footpath; they have not cut the wheat there yet and it was a particularly lovely morning."

"My dear Lady Montfort," he gave her a courteous little bow of the head, "you should have come by way of Meacham House; the footpath along the river is a far prettier walk to Iyntwood and I could have given you luncheon." And Clementine realized how welcome any visitor would have been to interrupt his lonely hours.

"How kind of you, but I wouldn't want to disturb your day," she said.

"Not at all, not at all, you would have been most welcome," he said. "I spent the better part of my day fishing on the river—didn't get a bite but it was a pleasant way to waste the middle hours of a lovely day. I could see trout hiding under the bridge, but they were too clever for me."

Clementine sat up and took notice. *So he was fishing from the bridge at about the time Lieutenant Standish might have left Dodd Farm, but which bridge?* There were four across the river in that area: the largest of them was Brook bridge, which connected the end of Brook End Lane with the beginning of Dodd Lane; the Iyntwood bridge, which spanned the river at the entrance to their north drive; and then the lake bridge outside their house, so she could eliminate that one, but there was the little wooden footbridge that she had been discussing with Mrs. Jackson earlier that evening. The bridge that Lieutenant Standish would have had to use!

"Harry and Ralph are always lucky when they fish from our lake bridge, Sir Winchell, something to do with the flag iris providing good cover for the trout as well as food for the hatch; you must have been fishing from the footbridge."

He nodded in acknowledgment. "That's right—I fished from there all morning and some of the afternoon." Her heart beat a little faster—he had been in a perfect place to spot any comings and goings from Dodd Farm either along the lane or the footpath to the bridge.

"Do you fish, Lady Montfort?" he asked, and she remembered hours of aching boredom as first her husband and then her son had attempted to teach her to cast on the lawn. "No, but I do have to listen to a lot of talk about it." She smiled, thinking of the earnest dinner conversations between father and son as to what the fish were biting and endless discussion on the tying of different flies. "Perhaps you were fishing in the middle part of the day? Ralph always says he avoids that bend in the river because the sun is too bright and it is quite busy along the footpath—on pretty days." She was on a fishing expedition herself, eager to discover if Lieutenant Standish had left Dodd Farm between the hours of eleven and half past two because Sir Winchell would most certainly have spotted him.

"I was out quite early and the footbridge was in heavy shade then, but I packed it in at about three o'clock, didn't see a soul all day." *Poor old boy,* she thought, *he must be awfully lonely.* "But it is a pretty spot. I had an apple or two in my creel and a substantial game pie, so I spent some pleasant hours just wasting time. I am not much of a fisherman, as you know I prefer the hunt."

Pleased with the information she had so effortlessly gathered, she ticked Standish off their list of suspects, and obliged their neighbor in a discussion popular in their area: foxhunting. "I think that one of the worst things about the beginning of the war was when our horses all went off to France; it nearly broke my heart when the Army Remount service came that day to take them. We only managed to hang on to Bruno because Althea told the War Office such a convincing story." She had felt nothing but misery at the thought of their horses pressed into service in muddy Flanders, and then careful not to be too low-spirited she said, "We had such wonderful meets at Cryer's Breach, didn't we?"

Their talk of horses brought Harry out of his inner reverie to join their conversation. "I took Bruno out the other morning, it was misty in the hollows and there was a chill in the air. As I came back through the village toward the green the old boy's ears came up and he started to look around. He thought for a wonderful moment that we were coming up to the green for a meet. And then Fred Golightly's old hound spotted him and set up a fearsome yell and Bruno perked up and moved forward like a five-year-old." He laughed down the table toward his father, whose stallion Bruno was as passionate about hunting as his rider.

"Good foxhunting country round here then?" Mr. Bray asked, turning away from an evidently fascinating conversation with Althea, who, Clementine noticed, was looking particularly alluring in ivory silk that dramatically emphasized her dark blue eyes and glossy bay-brown hair. "My estate sits right in the middle of some excellent hunting country. They used to hunt all through the season, never missed a day before the war." But his face was somber as if the memory was not a pleasant one, and Clementine realized that he was being polite and that her preoccupation with Lieutenant Standish's possible movements from Dodd Farm to the kitchen garden had distracted her from suitable dinner-table conversation. *Why on earth are we talking about foxhunting of all things?* Ralph had told her that Mr. Bray's horse had gone down on its side, trapping his right leg underneath its heavy body, and that he had been lucky that the leg had been saved. She glanced down the table at her husband, who was staring at her aghast as Harry launched into a detailed monologue about the agility of the

Irish sport horse as opposed to the more solidly built and temperamentally dependable English hunter. *Oh, Harry, please stop,* she sent a telepathic message to her son. *Talk about aeroplanes, motorcars— anything but hunting.* She glanced at Mr. Bray out of the corner of her eye: he was listening politely, his face impassive, and every so often he would nod his head, interjecting an opinion or two of his own on the best bloodlines for hunting. Evidently at one time Mr. Bray had been an active member of the North Cotswold Hunt because the points he made were well informed, but his courteous expression was becoming rather set and Clementine's mind was darting hither and yon for another topic.

She cut across Harry's rhapsodies about Bruno's offspring and said to Sir Winchell, "Harry's preferred method of transportation is mechanical, Sir Winchell. He fell in love with motorcars when he was about fourteen, and then when he was nineteen nothing fascinated him more than flying. He used to spend his summers with Tom Sopwith at his aeroplane manufactory in Kingston-on-Thames—my goodness, how we worried for his safety. And then the war came and it was inevitable that he join the Royal Navy Air Service—making us even more anxious . . ." She ground to a halt as she saw the frozen expression on the old man's face.

Dear God, she thought, *there is so much we must* not *talk about, I can't help but put my foot in it.* It was her fate to remember too late that Sir Winchell's second son had been shot down over France as he was flying a reconnaissance mission. *How long did that terrible news take to come through, was it just this summer?* Clementine flushed with embarrassment. *I wonder how many more gaffes I am going to make before this cumbersome evening is at an end.* She looked across the table to her daughter, who evidently understood her dilemma.

Althea laid down her knife and fork. "Harry is quite wonderful with engines, Mr. Bray, it was he who taught me how to clean a clogged carburetor, otherwise you might have been stuck at

Brook End Lane for hours. It is quite the emptiest road in the area." Clementine's sigh of relief was almost audible. *Thank you, thank you, darling girl.* She smiled grateful appreciation at her daughter.

Mr. Bray turned from his conversation with Harry. "But what about the farmhouse I could see from the lane? Is it deserted? It seemed very quiet. I tried waving and sounding the horn, hoping someone would walk down the hill and find me stranded there," he smiled at his rescuer, "but I am quite delighted that it was you who saved me from spending the night in my motorcar, Lady Althea." Althea took his compliment in her stride.

"The house you saw from your motor is Holly Farm, and the Howard family like to keep to themselves. But we are going there tomorrow to talk to Mr. Howard about helping him bring in his crop. Would you like to come along, Mr. Bray?" He earnestly said that he would love to.

And then to Clementine's horror Althea said, "We are going to offer the Haversham Hall officers' help at the farm tomorrow, they have all volunteered. You see, Mr. Howard has put his foot down about the Land girls—he says he won't have city girls ruining his crops. So our officers at Haversham Hall Hospital are pitching in!"

Clementine felt her forehead go hot and then cold and clammy. She glanced at Sir Winchell out of the corner of her eye. The color was rising in his face, and his eyes flicked nervously around the table as if to seek confirmation that lunatics were to be set free in the wheat fields of Buckinghamshire armed with scythes. *Someone, please say something! Talk about fishing, talk about gardening, talk about the wretched harvest festival.*

She was about to interrupt her daughter when there was a respectful cough on her left as Hollyoak presented her with a chocolate soufflé. Murmuring something about serving spoons, the butler bent forward, and Clementine watched with paralyzed horror as the serving dish started to slide on his silver tray. "Hollyoak!"

Clementine finally managed to get out as the dish gathered momentum. "The soufflé!" she cried as it hit the edge of the tray.

"M'lady!" The butler's horror echoed hers as the soufflé miraculously kept its shape as it flew undished through the air. "What have I done?" The butler's anguished question was answered for him as his lordship's favorite pudding filled his wife's lap.

Contrary to its light and airy appearance, it settled into the sagging cradle of Clementine's skirt in a most unpleasantly wet and weighty way. She heard her own shocked gasp followed by another from her butler. "M'lady, I will never forgive myself." Hollyoak closed his eyes, perhaps praying that when he opened them again the soufflé would be back in its dish on his tray.

Well, I was praying for a distraction and here it is—I never particularly liked this dress anyway. And she set about soothing her butler's distress at his clumsiness and beckoned to her daughter for help.

Althea with the aid of two serving spoons deftly served the soufflé back into its dish so that Hollyoak, his face set and his ear tips flame red, might make his escape to lick his wounds in the privacy of his pantry and then go and nag the cook about the instability of her serving dish.

Led by her husband and her son, there was a ripple of laughter around the table that gradually grew in strength as Hollyoak closed the door after him. *Well, I suppose a lap full of pudding is a small price to pay for such a thoroughly effective interruption.*

"Darling," her husband wiped his eyes with his napkin, "your face expressed the three stages of panic quite perfectly: mild surprise, changing to slight alarm, and from there to pure horror. I wish you could have seen it." And then: "It wasn't hot, was it?"

No, she assured him, it had not been hot, just rather an unpleasant sensation.

Mr. Bray had lifted his napkin to his mouth to cover his laughter, but Sir Winchell was frowning either because there would be no soufflé or perhaps because the lower orders were unreliable, but Clementine simply didn't care. This disastrous evening was nearly over.

"I like the way Althea put it back in its place," said Harry finishing the wine in his glass. "Do you think Hollyoak will survive the embarrassment? He would have had his footmen's guts for garters if they had done anything as clumsy."

"Poor old Hollyoak! Perhaps it is a good thing our footmen are not here, they would be giggling away for weeks. He insists on waiting without any help when we have company; the thought of either of our housemaids in waiting in the dining room is sacrilege to him when we have guests for dinner." And smiling serenely around the table: "Althea and I will join you in the drawing room when you have finished your port." She modestly draped her daughter's napkin across the stain in the front of her dress and left the dining room with her.

"I thought for one moment you had done it on purpose," Althea said, buttoning the back of her mother's dress. "What a terrible evening. First of all we talked about hunting, and I have to say that Mr. Bray was pretty decent about that considering how much he loved to hunt before his accident, and then we dropped that in favor of the dangers of flying. Harry wasn't offended but poor old Sir Winch was."

Clementine leaned forward to her looking glass and patted her hair into place. "Sir Winch, as you call him—and be warned, one day you will say it to his face—is offended by *everything*. An evening spent with that man is a minefield of hurt feelings and opportunities to fuss. But I feel quite terrible that we have neglected him these past months. It was wrong of us when he has no one." She sat down next to her daughter on the sofa. "Let's just wait here for a moment for them to finish their port and then we can go down and join them in the red room for our coffee. It will give Hollyoak a moment to recover. Besides, we need to have a little talk." And she began the business of explaining to her daughter how important it was that she did not go out in public alone in the company of young men.

"But, Mama, the world has changed since 1914, quite a lot in fact. No one in London even thinks about chaperones anymore."

"You are not a 'no one' though, are you? You are your father's daughter. And apart from that, someone was murdered in our kitchen garden, which means, Althea, that it is not safe to be alone outside of the house."

Althea looked crestfallen. "Yes, Harry has spoken to me about *that,* and I quite understand the safety side. But about the chaperone thing, I am sorry, Mama, really I am—I forget that the country is so much more behind the times than London." Leaving Clementine to wonder exactly how her daughter spent her time in Town when she was staying at the houses of Clementine's closest friends.

Pandemonium was perhaps too strong a word for what was waiting for Clementine and her daughter when they went down to join the men in the red room, but it came close.

Standing center stage and waving his arms and shouting almost incoherently at her husband was Sir Winchell. *If he carries on like this he will have a heart attack,* was all Clementine could think as she and Althea paused in the threshold of the drawing room, waiting to be noticed so that Sir Winchell could rein it in. And then as she heard the words "malingerers and cowards," she thought, *Oh no, it's the hospital again, but what can possibly have precipitated this display?*

"It is an outrage, a . . . disaster. Our boys are fighting fearlessly to protect our country and you harbor malingerers and cowards in your mother's house? I would never have thought in a million bloody years to see deserters given a holiday at a country house . . ." *And as for this this frightful language* . . . She coughed to alert Sir Winchell that the company was no longer exclusively male, but he was too enraged to care.

"All of them should be damn well shot for cowardice and desertion. I can't tell you how outraged everyone in the village is. They might not tell you, Lord Montfort, but I hear . . ." He started waving his arms again, his complexion deep red, his breathing harsh and labored. Her husband's face was expressionless. At one point he reached out a mollifying hand, hoping perhaps to calm the man, but Sir Winchell was beyond reason.

Edgar Bray, who was sitting by the fireplace, leaned forward on the stick he had planted between his legs. "I say, old chap, steady on. My brother was far from being a coward, he was decorated for bravery. One of the highest medals of honor our country can bestow!"

Sir Winchell rounded on him like an angry dog. "Then he needed to be back in the war, leading his men to victory, not cowering here digging up damned potatoes and whining about his fears to a doctor who would be more usefully occupied in a field hospital taking care of men who are . . . who are . . . dying in pain." His voice broke at this point, and it was clear to Clementine that he would either have an apoplectic fit or burst into tears.

"My brother was *wounded in action,* Sir Winchell," Edgar Bray said, his voice controlled but his eyes hard and bright with anger. "He brought back a man from behind enemy lines, after three harrowing days of battle. Saved the man's life, attempted to save the lives of others. He was mentioned in dispatches and awarded the Distinguished Service Order." Bray took a deep breath before he continued. "He was so exhausted he could hardly walk, and yet he returned to find his stranded men and bring the survivors back to safety. The next day he woke up in hospital and had no idea who he was." Mr. Bray's self-control threatened to unravel as he recounted his brother's bravery, and he ran his hand through his hair, his eyes miserable at the thought of his suffering. "He was a casualty of war just like any man who has lost a limb, or his sight." He looked across at Sir Winchell. "I am sorry for your loss, sir. I know how hard it is to lose the only member of your—"

"My sons died with honor . . . not hiding out . . . in a hospital for cowards."

Ralph interrupted, "That's enough, Meacham, more than enough."

Clementine realized that this could only get worse. "Sir Winchell . . ." she said as she went across the room toward him, but he was already walking to the door.

"They should be lined up against a wall and shot . . . every one of them." And he stamped through the open doorway and out into the hall, ignoring the butler as he proffered his hat and overcoat. The door slammed and silence rang through the room.

"How on earth did that happen?" Clementine asked her husband, who was still standing in the middle of the room look- ing at the door. "Someone should go after him, he is most terribly upset."

"He will do better on his own. He can walk his anger off on the way back to his house. I will go over and see him tomorrow. What- ever anyone says to him tonight will not be heard." He turned to his remaining guest, who was sitting quietly in his chair with his hands clasped around the silver handle of his stick, his head bent forward. "My apologies for our neighbor, he recently lost both his sons. Grief has made him unreasonable."

The younger man got slowly to his feet. "I completely under- stand, Lord Montfort, of course I do. I am afraid I might have made things worse, but it is hard to not say something. My brother had his faults, as we all do, but he was far from being a coward." He bowed his head to Clementine and then to Althea. "I think it would be best if I said good night. It has been a long day and I promised Lady Althea that I would accompany her and Captain Talbot to Holly Farm tomorrow. What time do we leave?" He turned to Harry.

"At about half past nine," said Harry. "We'll see you at breakfast."

The man took a step forward with practiced ease, his lame leg slightly behind his good one. He steadied himself, brought his weaker leg forward, and then walked across the room with immense dignity for one a little lopsided in his gait. At the door he stopped and turned to Clementine. "Lady Montfort, thank you so much for your hospitality. I had no idea until this evening how much your family has invested in your hospital for these stricken men. I am forever in your debt . . . for your compassionate understanding and care of my brother. Thank you." And with that he left them all standing in a room that still felt electrically charged with Sir Winchell's outrage.

"Time for a brandy," said Lord Montfort, and Clementine wondered if she had said the words herself.

Chapter Fifteen

The following morning Clementine awoke early to birdsong and a dewy lawn sparkling in the early light. She watched the last of a thin mist lift up through the trees and evaporate in the sunlight. *It's going to be a perfectly splendid day!* "And a hot one," she said to her wardrobe as she took out a white lawn blouse and a sensible walking skirt. *I might wander over to Holly Farm in the afternoon and see how the harvest is coming along.* She tossed a wide-brimmed rolled-straw hat onto the chair next to her clothes and looked for a pair of sturdy walking shoes.

The only thought in her head as she left the house through the terrace door and started up the drive toward Haversham Hall was that they could most certainly cross Lieutenant Standish of Dodd Farm and the happy-go-lucky picnicker Lieutenant Carmichael off their list of suspects, which left Forbes at the Home Farm still on it. Her step was light and brisk and she swung her arms purposefully, anticipating a day bristling with clues hitherto hidden and each now shouting to be acknowledged.

As she rounded the corner of the drive and the entrance to the north gate of the kitchen garden she was not surprised to see Mrs. Jackson striding toward her with a particularly intent look on her face. They met up at precisely the place where Bill the gander would take up his territorial stance in the afternoon.

"Good morning, m'lady." Mrs. Jackson was wearing her VAD shoulder cape in navy bordered with crimson, colors flattering to her pale complexion and rich auburn hair.

"Hullo there, Jackson, it's a beautiful day, let's go for a stroll along the lane and visit the Home Farm, we can say hullo to everyone and do some discreet inquiring. Have the officers all left yet for Holly Farm?"

"Not yet, m'lady. Lady Althea told me that once Lord Montfort had talked Mr. Howard into accepting their help, then the Land girls would drive our officers over and drop them at the foot of Holly Lane. We don't want Mr. Howard to see any Land Army girls today. It might be too provoking."

"And how is Lieutenant Phipps?"

"Sister Carter said he had a bad night of it."

"And our other officers?"

"Captain Martin has calmed down somewhat, but he is still on edge. Corporal Budge said there were no signs of his neurosis about whether his breakfast tea was made with muddy water, or that dropping crumbs on the cloth is a sign of a slack regiment. But the rest of them are in reasonable shape. Lieutenants Forbes and Standish are proud that they learned to use a scythe yesterday. They were all beginning to gather in the officers' mess as I left the hospital to go off to Holly Farm."

As they walked down the drive Clementine related her very useful conversation with Sir Winchell Meacham about his day of fishing. "Sir Winchell said that he spent those hours of the day on the footbridge, Jackson. So if Standish had wanted to get to the kitchen garden without bumping into him, he would have had to walk down Dodd Lane and cross the river at Brook End bridge and then come up the footpath through the wheat field that I walked the other morning. How long would that have taken him d'you suppose? Hours I would think."

"Certainly a long time, m'lady, and he could still have been spotted by Sir Winchell both coming and going along Dodd Lane from the footbridge."

Together they turned right into the lane to the Home Farm and arrived at the back of the farmhouse just as the farmer's wife, Mrs. Allenby, came out of her kitchen. She was a tall woman with dark hair drawn off her face and the tired and rather preoccupied expression that all farmers' wives wore these days. "Good morning, m'lady," a little bob, "and Mrs. Jackson," a polite nod of the head. "What can I do for you—Mr. Allenby is around somewhere, probably slopping the pigs. Ah, there's young Davey, he'll know." She waved her tea towel and a tall boy of about eight or nine came across the barnyard. He hastily raised his knuckles to his forehead when he saw Clementine and then looked down at his boots in embarrassment.

"Good morning, Davey, how are you today?" Clementine said, and Mrs. Jackson felt in her pocket for her bag of mint imperials. Davey had reached that awkward age when boys find it difficult to say hello to people they didn't know well.

"Is Lieutenant Forbes coming over to the farm today, Davey?" Clementine asked, and the boy finally mastered his reserve and lifted his head, but couldn't bring himself to look at them directly; he gazed shyly to the emptiest part of the barnyard. "Not today, ladyship."

"Ah yes, your harvest is in, isn't it? I expect you and your father will go over to help Holly Farm bring in their wheat this morning." He nodded vigorously that they were. "Then we shall have a nice old-fashioned harvest supper on the village green when it's all in. Won't that be lovely?" She turned to Mrs. Allenby to give her reason for their visit: "We are hoping you will make some of your wonderful blackberry-and-apple crumble for the harvest supper, Mrs. Allenby. We will be celebrating a bumper crop this year."

The farmer's wife said she would be happy to, and now used to the idea that he was expected to converse, Davey drew himself up.

"The lieutenant and me were soldiers on parade." He saluted smartly, and his mother laughed.

"He really enjoyed working with Lieutenant Forbes. Followed him everywhere, didn't you, Davey?" The boy nodded again, eyeing Mrs. Jackson's bag of sweets with interest.

"I don't think he has ever worked so hard before, and Davey is a hardworking boy." His mother reached out and ruffled her son's thick brown hair. "Says he wants to go away to war and become a soldier, don't you, lad?"

"I marched behind the officer all day. He said, 'Lift them stooks up onto the cart, Davey,' and I did. He said I was strong for my age—I'm ten next month." He pushed his chest out and his mother's tired eyes softened.

"Did he leave you in charge then, Davey?" asked Mrs. Jackson, opening her bag of sweets.

"Oh no, I was part of his work detachment. He called me Private Allenby and I had to stick close. I told him the names of all the birds and flowers in the hedgerows and he told me all about the different types of guns they use in the war. We was a fighting unit all day."

Mrs. Jackson offered her bag of sweets and the boy took one, hesitated, looked at his mother, and took another. "For later," he said as he stowed it in his trouser pocket, and because he knew it was bad manners to eat sweets in front of her ladyship, he held the second sweet in his hand.

"Don't let your sweet get all sticky. I don't mind if you eat it now," Clementine said. "So Lieutenant Forbes did not go off and leave you to work alone then?"

Was it her imagination or did the boy look embarrassed and unsure. It was hard to tell with boys as reserved as Davey. He looked down at his feet and then his eyes slid up to his mother's face. She nodded her head, no doubt to remind him that he must answer all questions politely, especially since this was her ladyship.

"No, m'lady, we was together all day." His indistinct reply came from around his sweet. "We marched out to the fields after breakfast with my dad and old Mr. Walsh and my friend Johnny and then Lieutenant Forbes and me loaded the stooks onto the cart. He even let me drive the tractor. It were a fine day. Me mam brung bread and cheese and some cider for our dinner and after that we had a smoke." He was scolded by his mother for the last part and looked off across the barnyard, seeking an escape.

"Well that sounds like a first-rate day to me!" Clementine laughed. "So it was just you and the lieutenant building stooks was it?" She saw that slight hesitation again before he nodded and she couldn't tell whether it was his natural reserve or he was being evasive. "He din't know how to build one but I did. I showed him how: twelve sheaves to a stook, I told him, got to make 'em stand tall so they can dry out."

His mother laughed. "You'll turn the lieutenant into a farmer yet."

"Mam, I must go to me dad and help him with the pigs." They said goodbye and Mrs. Jackson gave him another sweet for later on.

"He has certainly shot up this year," Clementine said as they watched him turn the corner of the piggery.

"Yes, he has, m'lady. I'm praying that this war will be over and done with soon. It's the only thing he talks about, being a soldier." She turned briskly back toward her farmhouse, tucking her tea towel into the waist of her apron. "It's getting warm, going to be a hot day. I have just made some lemon barley water; can I offer you a glass?"

And as they sat on a bench in the shade of the front porch, Clementine said, "Such a nice straightforward boy, young Davey; he will miss working with the lieutenant as he will most likely pass his Medical Board review in a few days."

Mrs. Allenby sipped her lemon barley water. "Yes, Davey misses his brother and the lieutenant is about the age our Tom was when he went off to fight a year ago. Lieutenant Forbes is a very decent gentleman—all your officers are. Pity they have to go back to that war, you would have thought they had done enough, wouldn't you?" And with a polite good-morning the farmer's wife went back into her kitchen, leaving Clementine and Mrs. Jackson to walk back to Haversham Hall.

"Let's go along the cart track to the kitchen garden," Clementine said, and they turned left up the lane and set out along the dusty track toward the south gate of the kitchen garden. "Well, it would seem that all the young men at the hospital are in the clear, Jackson. Although it is rather a chancy business to rely on the memory of a nine-year-old boy."

"And especially one who was not being strictly truthful, m'lady."

"Do you think Davey was lying to us, Jackson?"

Her housekeeper shook her head. "Not lying exactly, but something was troubling him."

Clementine waited; Jackson was after all the one who understood young people—especially those who might be intimidated by her own lofty position.

"What makes you say that?" she asked as they walked up the track, careful to keep to the shady side. She thought she knew, but she wanted to hear what Jackson was thinking.

"He was evasive when you asked him if Forbes had left him alone, m'lady. Something about his demeanor was uncertain, embarrassed. Perhaps he had been asked not to mention the lieutenant's absence. I am not sure."

She had seen Davey's hesitation, too. "He wanted us to stop questioning him. Oh dear, Jackson, this doesn't look good for Forbes, does it?"

Mrs. Jackson didn't answer immediately. She smiled and said, "I like young Davey, he's a straightforward sort of lad. Perhaps it would be worth my while to drop in on him again." And Clementine understood that she would go alone.

"Good idea, Jackson. And don't forget to take your bag of sweets with you. Do you remember Lord Haversham's addiction to those colossal bull's eyes they sold in the village when he was Davey's age?"

Mrs. Jackson started to laugh. "He would wrap it in his handkerchief and hide it in his pocket when he had to come into the house, m'lady. It used to drive Nanny mad. I don't think Mrs. Allenby would thank me if I arrived with one of those jawbreakers for Davey."

They had come to the south gate and Clementine looked at her watch. "Just fifteen minutes to walk along the track to here. But they were out in the fields to the east. So add another twenty minutes or so . . ." Someone had closed the heavy gates and together she and Jackson pushed one side of them open. "So where are we with our suspects, Jackson? I think we have cleared all of our officers except for Forbes."

"I can account for all our staff at the hospital. Not one of them was without an alibi, often two or three since we all work so closely together. Except of course for VAD Fuller, who was the last person to see Captain Bray alive, and whose only alibi is that she came back to the house with enough beans for luncheon upstairs and down. But I can't imagine her capable of that sort of violence, m'lady. It would be completely out of character." She stopped for a moment, fanning her face as the morning was becoming hotter by the moment.

"Out of character? Jackson, haven't we always said something like this before and then there was a horrible 'aha' moment at the end?" Her ladyship produced a handkerchief and dabbed her upper lip.

"Have we, m'lady?" Mrs. Jackson almost wrinkled up her nose in disbelief.

"Well yes, I think we have. I remember once being completely taken off guard, dangerously so. VAD Fuller could have killed Captain Bray before she left the kitchen garden, they were completely alone together here." They had stopped to catch their breath under the shade of walnut tree and Clementine threw out her arm to indicate the great open space before them completely enclosed by ten-foot walls. Mrs. Jackson lowered her eyes.

"Well first of all she would have to have killed him after he helped her pick beans, m'lady. But now I come to think of it, Mr. Thrower was rather irritated by the mess they left his vines in."

Clementine tried not to laugh at her housekeeper's earnest face. "I think it would be a good idea to dig around a bit there, Jackson. For instance, why did Captain Bray offer to help her pick beans, wasn't that rather out of character? The captain was closed down almost to the point of being antisocial, so why would he go out of his way to help a young girl who had an embarrassing crush on him?"

"You are quite right, m'lady. I will see what more I can find out about Fuller and Captain Bray."

"Thank you, Jackson." They walked on together toward the north gate of the drive. "And another thing, I am wondering if Carmichael could have ridden Dolly up through the wheat field by Brook End Lane to the kitchen garden and back again in twenty minutes. It wouldn't do to be caught off guard by that possibility either." And with that they said goodbye for the time being and went about their morning, Mrs. Jackson to return to do more of what she privately called snooping, and Clementine to continue on down the drive, hoping to find out how Lord Montfort had fared with Mr. Howard at Holly Farm.

"Oh dear, now why are they back from Holly Farm already?" she said out loud as she rounded the corner of her house in the direction of its main entrance to find her daughter's little Morris and the Iyntwood Daimler drawn up in the drive. "Surely that wretched Howard has not turned down our help again!" Her frustration evident, she marched around to the front of the house, where annoyance turned to alarm. For there, in the great sweep of the north entrance to the house, was an ambulance and the chief constable's Lanchester.

Mrs. Jackson was feeling just a little grumpy after Lady Montfort left her at the north gate of the kitchen garden. She walked along the gravel paths under the grape pergola toward its east end. *Well, they evidently picked from there,* she thought as she contemplated the rather chaotic tilt at the far side of the long bean arbor. *What a wicked waste,* she thought, tutting as she surveyed shriveled beans hanging from broken stems.

"You see, Mrs. Jackson, this is exactly why I told the cook not to let the VADs come in here and gather vegetables. Look at this." Mr. Thrower appeared on the other side of the vines and waved a disgusted hand at its lopsided end. "There was weeks of eating left in these two plants."

"I am so sorry, Mr. Thrower, I will most certainly talk to the cook about instructing our volunteers. I am surprised they made such a mess of it."

"'They'?" Mr. Thrower propped his rake against the arbor. "They—who else has been meddling in my garden?"

She felt that little prickle of excitement when something is in the air, the beginning of something momentous. "Why, Captain Bray of course, it was he who helped Fuller pick them." Mr. Thrower was shaking his head. He pushed back his battered felt hat and scratched his forehead.

"He never did this sort of damage, you can be sure of that. The captain was a careful man, methodical in his work. He would never have made such muck of it. It was not the captain, God rest his soul, who tore away at these vines, I can tell you that for nothing."

Mrs. Jackson was momentarily at a loss. *Then who?* she wondered and went hot and cold at her next thought.

"Well, I won't detain you in your workday, Mr. Thrower," she said as she walked back to the central garden path and stood staring down it in the direction of the shady walnut tree and its bench where the captain had taken his ease to eat his luncheon. *But he had no luncheon at all on the day he died,* she reminded herself.

She shaded her eyes against the sun and thought about VAD Fuller and her bean-picking expedition. If she had gathered the beans alone, that would explain the havoc she had left behind. And if Mr. Thrower believed that the captain was too careful and respectful to have torn at the vine, then why had the girl told her that Captain Bray had helped her? She walked back down to the potato bed and, lifting the hem of her skirt out of the little hillocks of soil, walked to where the captain's body had been found. She crouched down briefly and looked up the garden back to the east wall. All she could see from here were beds stretching to the left and right. She stood up; even standing she could just see the far wall, but not the beans vines, as that quadrant of the garden was completely obscured by the pergola and the raspberry canes.

"I met Captain Bray in the kitchen courtyard when I arrived. He was sharpening his spade in the potting shed. He followed me into the kitchen garden. I told him I was in a rush and he helped me to pick beans. He was ever so nice!" She saw Fuller's complacent, cat-like smile as she remembered her words. And then she stood up and walked back up; the garden again, through the gate, crossed the kitchen-garden courtyard, and continued on to the hospital.

When Mrs. Jackson sat down at her office desk she discovered that she had little interest in the hospital inventory and what Cook had done with twenty-eight pots of strawberry jam in just under two months. She did her best to apply herself to the endless forms and requisitions the War Office demanded of its clerical staff, but she was too restless to concentrate. She had promised Major Andrews that she would sort out the paintings done by Haversham Hall's patients in the art room. She stopped off in the old servants' hall to enlist Fuller's help, and together they went up the stairs and along the corridor to the little-used east wing of the house and the large sunny room that had become the hospital's art studio.

"It's quite simple, Fuller, I will go through this stack of paintings and you can make a group of the ones I select in that corner." She walked to the far end of the empty room and, rolling up her sleeves, started to go through a stack of canvases propped against the wall. "It's interesting how it's always the new patients who spend most of their time in here when they arrive," she said as she went through paintings of muddy landscapes with harsh colors emanating from the centers of the canvases and black curly spirals and tangles of what she took for barbed wire.

"This one is quite colorful, Mrs. Jackson." Fuller turned with a painting in her hands—it was black with a massive ball of orange and red in its center.

"Yes, put that with the others over there. Look, this one is rather pretty in its own way," Mrs. Jackson selected a pastoral scene with rolling green hills covered in neat white squares, blue sky, and puffy white clouds, "except for the headstones. Yes, it's a recent one by Captain Martin. He was obsessed by graveyards when he first came, he still is really. Put that one over there with the others."

Major Andrews had put together a group of the officers' paintings he wanted to keep against the far wall by the door, and out of curiosity Mrs. Jackson started to flip through the canvases. Each was labeled with the name of the artist, the date on which it had been painted, and sometimes, if they had given their work a name, its title. She turned a painting toward her and tilted the canvas and the midday sun shone full on a rather crude resemblance to man with yellow hair and blue eyes. She turned the painting more fully toward the light of the window. "No bombs going off in this one," she said more to herself than to Fuller. "Why, it's by Captain Bray. What a terrible thing to have happened. I hope it has not made you and Ellis anxious about going into the kitchen garden." She turned toward the young woman, the better to concentrate on Fuller's response.

There was no answer but Fuller blinked her eyes furiously, her breathing became uneven, and she ducked her head. Mrs. Jackson put down the painting and steered the girl over to the window seat and sat her down. And then she waited. But Fuller did not speak; she bit her lip and kept her head down. Mrs. Jackson reached over and patted the girl's shoulder. Often the simplest acts of sympathy can precipitate a strong response when someone is struggling to maintain control. But she was shocked at the great gasping sob that finally wrenched free of the tensely held body sitting next to her.

"My poor, dear girl," she said with genuine compassion. Her kind words and gentle tone completely undid Fuller, whose shoulders shook as she struggled to calm herself. "Would it help to talk about it?" After a while Fuller lifted her head. Her eyes were dry, but there were dark circles around them, as if she had not slept for weeks. The pale face that lifted to hers was so drawn that Mrs. Jackson felt real alarm. *These young girls are in my charge,* she thought. *It is my job to look to their welfare here. I have been so bound up with this inquiry that I have neglected to notice that this young woman is suffering.*

All thought of finding out more about Fuller's alibi in the kitchen garden evaporated. She must sit here patiently and wait for her to speak. After a few minutes Fuller said something that caused Mrs. Jackson even greater alarm than the agonized tearless sobs.

"I don't think he knew how much I c-c-cared," the young girl managed to get out as she balled up the handkerchief in her hands. "I tried to talk to him when Cook sent me to the garden to fetch vegetables. You see," she struggled to steady her breath, coughed, and after much throat clearing managed to continue, "I told him how much I admired him. How much I . . . loved him . . . and he just walked away." She worked at the handkerchief in her hands, balling it up and then smoothing it across her knee, her movements jerky. Mrs. Jackson's eyes had nearly popped out of her head. *Oh dear God, and what did you do after you told that deeply troubled man that you were in love with him and he ignored you?* It was quite clear from her wide, staring eyes and restless hands that Fuller was far from calm or even rational. *Did you hit him over the head?* was the first question on her lips, but all she said was, "Did this happen on the morning he was killed?"

"Oh no, it was about a week or so ago. He has avoided me ever since then." Her voice broke and she shook her head as if to rid it of a painful memory.

"Have you told anyone about this?" She wondered if Fuller had confided in Ellis. Of course she had.

"Yes, I told Ellis that I loved him, and she laughed at me." There was some satisfaction in her voice. "But she would, wouldn't she? She is *such* a flirt." Said the sweet little flibbertigibbet who had told a man suffering from the acute stress of war that she loved him, when all he had wanted to do was dig in a garden and listen to the birds sing.

Why on earth does the VAD send us such babies? Mrs. Jackson wondered, remembering that Fuller's father was a bank manager in Liverpool. *These immature, overprotected middle-class girls have no idea of the havoc they cause with all their emotions . . . and feelings. A sensible, mature woman from the village would be far more useful to us.* But she knew she must not underplay the genuine hurt that Fuller felt.

"I understand why you are so upset, Fuller. But you see, the captain had been seriously ill for quite some time. He was recovering slowly from months of stress and anxiety in the most terrible of conditions. Why, just three weeks ago he was hard put to remember his name; can you imagine what that must be like? I am quite sure he was confused when you told him of your feelings for him. I think we need to arrange some home leave for you." She kept her tone professional.

"No, thank you." The girl smiled. It was a smile full of courage. "He did his duty and I will continue to do mine, even more so now that he has . . . gone." Her words sounded like lines from a play, the whole thing sounded like the worst sort of romance novel. *Oh my giddy aunt* were the words that bubbled to the surface and Mrs. Jackson shut her lips firmly against them. Then inspiration came.

"Yes, sometimes it is best to be occupied when we feel sad. But you have a responsibility to the men in this hospital, don't you?" Fuller evidently approved of this idea, as she nodded, her face serious. "And as you say, duty comes first! Our patients have been through a most harrowing time and they are still suffering from severe shock. So we must be quite sure that all of us who look after them are able to cope with what are often the most distressing situations. Now you are grieving for a man you admired . . . and cared about." The girl nodded and licked her dry lips. "And if you would like to continue here it is important that you tell me *exactly* what happened while you were in the kitchen garden on the morning Captain Bray was killed. Do you understand the importance of being accurate with your account? Major Andrews"—at the mention of his name the girl straightened her back—"will need to be convinced that you are capable of continuing to work here. No detail is unimportant, Fuller, do you understand?"

There was a long silence. "Thank you," said VAD Fuller, putting her grubby handkerchief away. "I would like that."

Chapter Sixteen

"Harry, what on earth is going on?" Clementine made short work of crossing the gravel sweep of the drive as her son walked out from behind the Red Cross ambulance. "Why aren't you all up at Holly Farm?"

"Lieutenant Carmichael has been found—dead, I am afraid. They are bringing up his body now." Clementine turned and looked down the north drive. And there across the bridge that spanned the lake, at its narrowest part, was a procession coming through the trees toward them.

"An accident? An accident at the farm?" Her heart sank.

"No accident I am afraid, Carmichael was shot. We found him by the drive just after the lake bridge. He must have died sometime last night; his body was soaked with dew when we found it."

"What was he doing up here by the lake, and does anyone know who shot him?" And then she answered her own question with another: "Oh, Harry, he didn't shoot himself, did he?"

Her son shook his head. "No, he was shot in the back. No sign of a weapon anywhere, but I am sure it was an army-issue revolver, you can't move in England for them these days. Don't say anything for a moment—Althea is awfully upset. You see it was she who spotted his body." They watched the procession cross the bridge onto the drive, feet crunching on the gravel as it made its way toward them.

"Spotted his body—do you mean as you were driving off to Holly Farm?"

"No, as we were driving back from a rather unpleasant meeting with Mr. Howard, which I will tell you about later. Althea slowed down before she got to the bridge and as she negotiated the turn she said she saw something flash in the sun under the trees."

"Gunfire?" She couldn't help but interrupt him.

"No, Mother, please listen. It was most probably the sunlight catching his cap badge. When we left this morning we didn't see him, probably because the mist gathers quite deeply in that little hollow. On our return, the area where Carmichael's body was lying was in sunlight. Althea saw what she thought was someone lying on the ground, so we stopped and I went to investigate and there he was."

Two constables carrying a stretcher covered by a canvas sheet came up onto the circle of the drive. Behind the stretcher, as if they were mourners at a funeral, came Lord Montfort walking protectively at his daughter's side and then a little behind them Colonel Valentine. There was no sign of Inspector Savor, Clementine noticed with relief. *Perhaps we have seen the last of him since this murder cannot possibly have been committed by Lieutenant Phipps, safely locked away in our hospital.* She started to walk toward her daughter, who broke free of her father's arm and ran to her.

"Ian . . . shot," she said, and Clementine turned her daughter toward her, to shield her from curious eyes. Althea put her head on her mother's shoulder and soaked the light material of her blouse with her tears.

"There, there, my poor darling. Come along now. Let's go inside, away from all of this." She walked a weeping Althea through the front door of Iyntwood, where her butler stood waiting for them.

"Will you bring some tea to the morning room as quickly as possible please, Hollyoak?" And she steered Althea across the hallway and into the sunlit warmth of the room. "Here we are, darling." She handed her daughter her handkerchief and sat with her arm around her as she waited for the shock to ebb a little. But not all her attention was directed to Althea, as her brain could not help but click through the possibilities that popped into her consciousness, demanding to be examined.

"There, there," she soothed. "There, there, darling. Nice, slow, deep breaths. I know, I know, my poor dear girl, such a terrible thing to find."

Of all people, she wondered as she soothed her child, *why was Carmichael shot?* Her first thought was that the two murders were tied to each other. Perhaps Carmichael knew, saw, or heard something that had resulted in his death last night. *How long was he lying by the side of the drive? Was he killed yesterday evening or later that night?* She would check this with Valentine. *But what was Carmichael doing at Iyntwood?* Surely the staff at Haversham Hall would have noticed his absence last night or earlier this morning. *Why has no one said anything?* Mrs. Jackson would surely have the answer to this one.

Had Carmichael come up to the house to meet someone? Clementine felt a flutter of anxiety. *Surely Althea did not leave the house to meet with this man after her promises to be sensible about her behavior?* Her daughter made a loud trumpeting noise into her handkerchief. *No, it can't be possible, Althea is a flirt, most girls are, but she would never arrange a clandestine meeting with Carmichael.*

Althea had found the body this morning, quite by accident. If she had known of the murder last night she would not have swanned down to breakfast in her breeches and trench coat full of bobbance and bounce, ready to bring in the harvest at Holly Farm. As her hand gently stroked her daughter's rather clammy one Clementine continued to sift through the possibilities.

Surely we would have heard the shot so close to the house. And then she knew what time it had been. *Just after Sir Winchell had left the house and Mr. Bray had retired to bed. Harry, Althea, Ralph, and I were still in the drawing room.* Harry had laughed as he had said, "Old Meacham is still stamping down the drive to his house. I can guarantee you that a strongly worded letter will be written to catch tomorrow morning's first post—to the War Office."

"But what on earth made him so frightfully angry? He seemed quite reasonable at dinner; you just have to skirt around certain subjects," Clementine had answered, privately thinking that neither her husband nor her son could be trusted with their touchy neighbor.

"My fault," Harry had said. "I forgot how peppery he was. I was talking to Edgar Bray about his brother. You see, I knew Captain Sir Evelyn Bray before the war. He was seen everywhere in London—belonged to all the clubs. He was what we called a boulevardier; there was always a pretty girl on his arm, never the same one twice. He was perfectly pleasant, a complete gentleman, but aimless and irresponsible. A life dedicated to pleasure. I told Mr. Bray that the war had turned up some oddities. Men who you thought would be great officers and leaders folded up, and the ones you believed would be hopeless surprised you by their courage and bravery. Evelyn Bray was the last sort: the war brought out the best in him. He had the common touch: his men trusted him completely; he was a born leader—and, as it turned out, most awfully brave."

Lord Montfort had interrupted. "Sir Winchell had had far too much port and he started up with the usual guff. 'Then what the hell was your hero brother doing in a place for crackpots and cowards?' he said, and you heard the rest. Of course Bray didn't know that Sir Winchell is devastated by the death of his sons. It was an awful moment, we did our best to divert an argument, but once Meacham's dander is up . . ."

It was a little after half past ten when Althea and I returned to the drawing room to witness this embarrassing scene. Clementine calculated that it must have been about a quarter to eleven when Sir Winchell had stamped off home. Mr. Bray, looking quite exhausted, had immediately apologized. And then, after thanking them most courteously and sincerely for the work they did for the hospital, he had left the room. *What happened next? Ah yes, Harry heaped logs onto the fire and for the first time in weeks we all sat together, it was almost pleasant.*

Lord Montfort had chided Harry about creating an inferno so powerful that he was dying of heat, Althea had said she was looking forward to roasting chestnuts in the evenings. And Harry had said that some of the logs were perhaps a bit unseasoned when one practically exploded and the deliciously pungent scent of hot pine sap filled the air. *If there was a shot then, would we have heard it over the hiss and crackle of our fireside evening?* Clementine wondered. It was perhaps an hour after that they had all retired for the night. Althea's room was in the front of the house, in the corner looking out toward the lake and the bridge.

"Althea, did you hear anything after you went to bed last night?"

Her daughter visibly pulled herself together. "Are you talking about a shot, Mama?"

"Yes, I am."

"My windows were open, so I would have heard something like that. Colonel Valentine said Ian had probably been shot early last night. We were probably all still in the drawing room when he was killed." Her face was woeful but she was had stopped crying.

It was hard to reconcile the lively Althea of last night and the stunned and frightened girl sitting next to her now with her white face and tear-stained cheeks. She was such an outgoing and confident young woman that one tended to forget she was still so very young. "The image will fade in time, Althea, it really will, darling."

She lifted her face from her hankie. "I know it will, Mama. Just such a shock to see him lying there." She shuddered. "All he wanted was to go back to France to his unit. You see he was not from our background at all, no Eton or Harrow for him, and then a commission in some fashionable regiment; just a nice, ordinary young man, willing to do his bit." She started to weep again and Clementine lifted her hand and stroked her hair until she fell quiet.

"There, there, darling," she murmured.

The door opened and Harry, Lord Montfort, and Colonel Valentine came into the room, closely followed by Edgar Bray, whose alert eyes went straight to her daughter sitting on the sofa, recovering from her tears. There was concern on Mr. Bray's face and for a moment it looked to Clementine as if he might cross the room to join them on the sofa. But he had too much tact for that and she was grateful that he remained where he was, and said instead, "I am so very sorry you were the one to find him."

Althea straightened her back and stopped sniffing. "Thank you, Mr. Bray," she said under her breath.

Lord Montfort looked across at his wife, his eyebrows slightly raised, perhaps with hope that she and Mrs. Jackson would sort out this awful mess before the War Office and Medical Board arrived next week. Summoning all her energy, Clementine got up and walked over to Colonel Valentine, who had already stepped forward to claim her attention.

"If I may intrude at this time, Lady Montfort, just for a brief moment before I drive over to Haversham Hall. I have spoken with those of your family who found Lieutenant Carmichael. When did you last see him alive?"

"I only met him a couple of times. It was probably days ago. He has been at the hospital for such a very short time. I think it would be a good idea if you and I were to drive over to Haversham Hall and on the way I will tell you what I can. If you will give me a moment, I must see that everyone has what they need and then I will meet you in the hall." She desperately wanted to talk to Mrs. Jackson as soon as she could, but before that she needed more information from her family before she left. She turned to her husband. "What happened at Holly Farm?"

"Absolutely nothing at all. Howard was at his most adamant. He believes he will have brought in all his crops from the edge of Brook End Lane all the way across to Oddman's Folly by the end of the week. How he imagines he can accomplish that with two young boys, his brother, and their wives, I don't know. And the barometer is dropping, so it will be a wet end to the week—but there you are, nothing I said could shift him. But if he lets us down I will take away his tenancy of the farm." *Now is not the time to ask him further about what has clearly been not only a fruitless but unpleasant morning.* "I am going over to the hospital with Valentine. Will you please keep an eye on Althea?"

"It was an awful experience but she is much more resilient than we imagine. Will you be back in time for tea?" She said she would.

Deciding that it would be better to give Althea something to do, she returned to the sofa. "I am going over to the hospital for an hour or so with Colonel Valentine. Please tell Hollyoak that you will be four at luncheon, and will you take my place, darling? I really shouldn't go and leave you all like this but . . ."

Althea put away her handkerchief. "Of course, Mama, I will just run upstairs and wash my face and change. In the meanwhile I will ask Hollyoak to offer sherry."

Relieved that her daughter seemed to be rallying—a hot meal and the kind solicitude of Mr. Bray would improve things greatly—Clementine made for the door.

To her surprise it was Harry who opened it and walked out into the hall with her. "There is something odd going on at Holly Farm," he said to her.

"There is something odd going on all over the county," she replied. "For one thing, the way the police have been dealing with this inquiry is quite laughable. I would not be surprised if Sir Winchell is arrested for shooting the lieutenant; they seem to jump to the first most-likely suspect. But what do you mean about Holly Farm?" They trudged up the stairs together.

"Mr. Howard is hiding something or at the very least covering something up. I knew it the moment I saw him last week. He and his family have always been reclusive but never devious—he looked downright shifty the other afternoon last week when I dropped in on them, and when I first arrived this morning he was defensive, almost truculent." Clementine didn't like this description of a man who farmed so many of the Talbot acres, but she was pleased to see that her son appeared to be far less withdrawn this morning. *Inquiries keep us on our toes and in the moment,* she thought before she returned to the topic of Farmer Howard.

"What do you mean by 'shifty'?" she asked as they reached the top of the stairs. Harry pantomimed: hands in pockets, shoulders drooping forward, he lowered his head and glanced up out of the corners of his eyes, and Clementine laughed. "You look like Fagin in *Oliver Twist,*" she said.

"Bang on the nose, Mama. He looked furtive, deceitful, you know—shifty! Althea and I took the dogs across country one evening last week. As we neared Holly Farm from the Iyntwood side, the land lifts sharply and on the highest part of the rise is the Holly Farm barn. Well, I have keen eyesight, and flying makes you acutely aware of any movement above you." *If you are not half cut with brandy,* thought Clementine, but wisely said nothing. "I saw someone running across the barnyard. For one split second I was quite sure that it was a young man, but the bushes on the side of the barn cut my line of vision."

"A boy or a man? Don't forget Howard's younger sons are twelve and fourteen or something like that, you know how fast they grow at that age."

Harry smiled at her and said he knew the difference. "This was a grown man."

"In uniform? Was it one of our officers?"

"One of your patients, you mean?"

"Yes, a man in uniform, officer's uniform."

He shook his head. "No, he was wearing what looked like an old brown corduroy coat and a flat cap."

"Who did you think it might have been?"

He sighed and pursed his lips. "I don't know. I thought it might have been a tramp. But later on when Althea and I dropped in at the farmhouse, Mrs. Howard was not particularly happy to see us; I know she is a reserved woman but her hands were shaking. I think our dropping-in not only surprised but scared her. I accept that the Howards keep to themselves, but usually she has enough composure to say good afternoon without falling completely apart. And then Howard came out of the barn with that shifty look and when he saw it was us he looked almost angry. Althea said it was because he doesn't hold with the Land girls but I think we had taken him, both of them, unawares." They had reached the top of the stairs and she stopped and looked back down the graceful curve of the flight to Colonel Valentine waiting patiently for her in the hall. "I simply can't see a tramp having the cheek to wander about the Howards' barnyard in broad daylight with them both at home."

Clementine's frustration with the Howards was running high this morning, as they kept getting in the way of her train of thought. "Just a moment, Harry, if you saw a strange man there, running for cover in the barn, then he might very well be the man who killed first Captain Bray and now Lieutenant Carmichael!"

But her son shook his head at her. "Yes, that would be convenient wouldn't it, Mama? But however much the locals don't quite approve of your hospital for the shell-shocked, they are hardly likely to be quietly bumping them off one by one. I think your villain is one of the officers. One of them who has gone completely dotty and thinks it's his job to protect Haversham Hall from a German attack; don't people suffering from shell-shock keep reliving the worst bits of their war?" She decided not to take issue with this ridiculous thinking.

"But what I came to suggest was this." Harry was smiling now, a broad, pleased smile, his eyes shining with pleasure at the prospect of an entertaining diversion. Standing in front of her was the Harry of old; he put his hand on her shoulder and held her gaze, his face a picture of boyish enthusiasm.

She started to laugh. "Suggest what?"

"That after luncheon Althea and I take a nice country walk together. It will take her mind off of Carmichael, and perhaps we might see something at the Holly Farm barn."

He looked so pleased with himself that she had to stop herself from saying, *Oh no you don't!* Instead she said, "You mean you are going to spy on Mr. Howard." Her eyes narrowed. *Ralph most certainly would not approve of this idea at all.*

"Spy? What an unattractive suggestion. We are going to reconnoiter. Althea and I, together, it will be fun! Althea needs a distraction, otherwise she will mope about the place feeling sorry about Carmichael. What harm is there, Mama, if we are careful?"

There might be useful information to be gained, but with Harry's rather flippant attitude and Althea's earnest determination to be of practical use on behalf of the Land girls, they might cause irritation and foster even more obstinacy from the farm, and Ralph would be livid if any of the precious harvest was lost. She wasted no time in offering some cautionary advice.

"Whatever you do, Harry, please do not intrude on the wretched Howards—it will only make a muddle. Just go for a walk and observe from a distance and perhaps keep a lookout for this man in the brown corduroy coat—though doesn't every farmer in the county wear a brown corduroy coat in summer? And lastly . . ." because there is always a last thing when one is giving instructions to one's son, "on no account, if you discover that all is not as it should be, ought you to do something about it. This is a reconnaissance mission and not a surprise attack," she said as she held her son's gaze, willing him to be cautious.

"I understand you completely, Mother," he said, gazing back and matching her tone exactly. "And hopefully one of these days you will understand me, and stop worrying every time I have a brandy. It's what we have for breakfast in the RNAS."

She lifted her hand and patted his cheek briefly but with great affection. "I know, my darling, but your feet are firmly on Talbot land right now."

Chapter Seventeen

"I didn't tell you earlier this morning, Jackson, but we had quite a dreadful dinner with Sir Winchell last night. You know the usual rubbish. Angry displays about the hospital—that sort of thing. The upshot was he just stormed off into the night, with all the drama of a Wilkie Collins novel. And the next thing we know is that this morning Lieutenant Carmichael is found shot dead practically outside our front door. But that is not quite all, I am afraid: on the way over here Colonel Valentine told me that Inspector Savor drove over to Meacham Hall and took Sir Winchell into custody on suspicion of the murders of both Captain Bray and Lieutenant Carmichael." Lady Montfort lifted both hands to heaven as if asking for divine intervention before she added, "Of all the stupid men I have come across in my life, this Inspector Savor really takes the cake. He periodically arrives out of nowhere and without asking any of us a single question makes one daft arrest after another."

Mrs. Jackson could only nod as she struggled to take in all this information. Her ladyship had arrived minutes earlier with flashing eye and heaving bosom and had barely planted herself in the privacy of her office before she had delivered this disturbing news at top speed. *You only left me a couple of hours ago and now this?* Her ladyship's quivering hat feather was the only indication that she was waiting impatiently for her response. When she did not immediately comply, her stunned silence was evidently taken for something else.

"Did it ever cross your mind that it might have been Sir Winchell, Jackson? I mean have I missed something?" Her ladyship sounded so plaintive that it was easy to see that not only had her dignity been deeply offended by Colonel Valentine appearing to ask for her advice only to ignore it, but that her confidence was beginning to fray a little around the edges. "Did you for one moment suspect Sir Winchell?"

"Certainly not, m'lady, I think it is one of Inspector Savor's rushed jobs." This was all she could really think of to say to this astonishing account of what had happened in the last few hours. Apart from a perennial tetchiness to his nature, and a reputation as a fusspot, Sir Winchell was referred to in the village by everyone as a harmless old duffer. *But there again, even a harmless old duffer can turn nasty, given the right circumstances.*

"I can certainly understand that the inspector might suspect him, Jackson. But arrest him just because he left Iyntwood last night in a very distressed frame of mind? It would be ludicrous if it wasn't so disturbing. Even Colonel Valentine seems to believe that Sir Winchell bumped into Lieutenant Carmichael as he walked down the drive, and in his rage at finding one of our cowards wandering about the grounds quarreled with him and shot him."

Mrs. Jackson ventured a question: "Shot him, m'lady, with a gun?"

Lady Montfort's eyes widened and her brows rose a fraction. "That is usually how someone accomplishes such a thing, I believe."

"I apologize, m'lady, for not being clear. I was thinking that if it was an army-issue revolver it might suggest the murderer was one of our officers, but that would be difficult because small arms are banned from hospital premises. But if it was a shotgun, that might point to one of our farmers, or anyone locally. Do Colonel Valentine and Inspector Savor believe that Sir Winchell came to your house for dinner and brought a service revolver with him or his shotgun? That does seem rather strange."

"Well, exactly, it is hardly the sort of thing that a gentleman would do. After all, this is not the Wild West, one's guests do not come to dinner armed to the teeth. But the belief is that Sir Winchell has lost his marbles: the strain of bereavement, Valentine called it. He had the gall to tell me that he thinks that when we opened our hospital it in some way tipped the fragile balance of Sir Winchell's sanity, and that he decided to eliminate some of our malingerers. A sort of one-man court-martial, I suppose." Her indignation was so great that her already straight back grew another two inches in her chair.

"And he is also being charged for the murder of Captain Bray too, m'lady?"

"Yes, Jackson, for that too. You see, Sir Winchell was fishing from the little footbridge on the day Captain Bray was murdered. He was there from ten in the morning until three in the afternoon. All he had to do was walk along the footpath to the south gate of the kitchen garden, kill Captain Bray, and return to continue fishing. He has no alibi for those long hours. No one saw him there, no one was with him. All the farmers and their families were busy harvesting."

Mrs. Jackson thought about this one for a moment and then she asked the inevitable: "Does Colonel Valentine have any idea why Lieutenant Carmichael was on the grounds at Iyntwood last night?"

"I don't know what the colonel is really thinking. I don't know whether it is his age or the long hours he is working, but he is most distracted, and Inspector Savor is hardly the man to think through any situation with calm logic. It makes sense to *them* evidently that Sir Winchell murdered both men. And quite frankly, Jackson, you only have to hear Sir Winchell raving away about shooting lily-livered cowards to see that he is far from stable. Was no one at the hospital aware that Carmichael was not in his quarters?" Her ladyship got up and wandered over to the window, pushing the looped swags of the heavy plaid curtain back against its frame. She held it there so she could more clearly stare out at nothing at all. Only the light tapping of her forefinger on the window frame was an indication of her irritation.

Mrs. Jackson, reluctant to interrupt her ladyship's annoyance, waited a moment or two before she said, "Lieutenant Carmichael was in the officers' mess for dinner. I am not sure at all about after that, though. I will ask Corporal West, he was on duty last night. If you will excuse me a moment, m'lady." She was through the door and before ten minutes were over was back again. "Corporal West says that Lieutenant Carmichael retired to bed directly after dinner. When the corporal checked in on him, at a quarter past ten o'clock, he was sitting up in bed reading a newspaper. We have a curfew here at the hospital, as you know, m'lady: after ten no one may leave the grounds." Lady Montfort turned from the window.

"How would he leave the house without being seen?"

"None of our officers are particularly interested in leaving the hospital or its grounds, so unless their condition is chronic no one really checks up on them. So he probably just walked down the stairs and out of the door. But if Lieutenant Carmichael was shot at eleven o'clock or thereabouts, he had only just left the hospital. He might have just wanted to get some air, or maybe he had an appointment with someone, though goodness only knows who it could have been."

Lady Montfort's gaze wandered back to the window, where she continued to stare at nothing.

What on earth is going on with her? thought Mrs. Jackson. *There's something she is not telling me. Well, if it's to do with these murders she will get to it in her own good time.*

She respectfully waited a few moments and then related her conversation with Fuller in the art room.

"She did what?" Lady Montfort's incredulous response to Fuller's love confession was almost gratifying. "I told you, Jackson, that this might be a murder of passion!"

"Not at all, m'lady, far from it in fact. This unfortunate girl was living in a daydream that she had made up about Captain Bray. First of all, she took his silence as some sort of shy acquiescence that he was in love with her too—or cared for her. But when she actually told him that she loved him, he snubbed her."

Lady Montfort started to shake her head. "Poor Captain Bray, how awkward and embarrassing; what is wrong with these modern young women?"

Mrs. Jackson didn't say that the upbringing of sheltered girls did not prepare them for hospital life, but continued on with her account of Fuller's infatuation. "She said that on the morning that the captain was killed, she went to the kitchen garden to pick beans and he walked straight past her from the potting shed back down the garden to his potato rows as if she wasn't there. So she went and stood under the pergola and watched him, hoping he would notice her there and come and talk to her."

"Oh good Lord above!" Lady Montfort put her hand over her eyes. "It actually makes you cringe; what can she have been thinking? But she told you originally that he helped her pick beans. What happened to that story?"

"It was just a story she made up to impress her best friend Ellis and ended up believing, I suppose. She says what really happened that morning was that she watched Captain Bray digging at the end of the garden, wondering whether to go and talk to him again, then she realized the time and had to pick beans as fast as she could to be back to the hospital on time, which explains why the vines were in such a . . ."

"Did you believe her? I am sorry to interrupt you, Jackson."

Mrs. Jackson smiled. "I believed her, m'lady. I told Major Andrews her story and he had a talk with her. He said that she is suffering from a form of hysteria: a compulsion to form a romantic attachment with a man in uniform, and in Fuller's case she was impulsively drawn to heroes. Major Andrews told me that at the beginning of the war they had to enlist special women police constables in some towns near army training camps to enforce a curfew because very young women were behaving so outrageously toward the soldiers that they would run if they saw them. 'Khaki fever' they called it. Major Andrews says her condition is aggravated by the shock of Captain Bray's murder and the fantasy, as he referred to it, of her imagining herself in love. He said it is not unusual for girls of her age to make up stories to sound more interesting, especially as her friend, the much prettier Ellis, is so popular. Fuller is such a young and impressionable girl and is far too suggestible to be working in a hospital like ours. We are giving her some home leave and after that we will decide if she is cut out for this sort of work."

"She could not have killed Captain Bray then in that 'hell hath no fury like a woman scorned' sort of way then?"

"I asked the same of Major Andrews, m'lady," her expression sheepish as she remembered the major's rather derisive laughter, "and he said it was most unlikely."

Clementine walked back to Iyntwood in time for her meeting with Mr. Hollyoak to plan the harvest supper for the local farmers and villagers on the village green.

"If I may say so, m'lady, it would seem that the barometer is not predicting auspicious weather for an outside supper at the end of the week," was her butler's first contribution and it went on from there. Clementine resolved to be firm but patient.

"I am quite sure we will have brought in the harvest by Tuesday, Hollyoak. So we should plan for the village green, and then if it looks rainy that afternoon we can always move the celebration to the great barn at Brook End Farm." She could tell by the expression on his face that he didn't approve of the barn any more than he appeared to like the idea of the village green. *Oh where on earth do you want us to have the celebration for heaven's sake?* She wanted to ask him. But this was not the way to deal with elderly butlers whose professional lives had changed so drastically since the war. Hollyoak was pining for the formal celebrations at Iyntwood of two years ago; he brooded alone in his pantry on the grand balls and house parties for forty guests before the war had come and spoiled everything. Any opportunity to flog himself and his seriously depleted staff into the ground to make a grand occasion would be a welcome distraction and an opportunity to polish every piece of the Talbot silver.

"I particularly do not want to hold the supper here, Hollyoak," she said cautiously, watching his back stiffen. "It has always been a village occasion. We will provide the food and drink—cover all the costs, in fact, but I don't want to turn it into a big house event, especially not now."

"If I may presume, m'lady, the local people enjoy a big house event. We are the focus of a large community here at Iyntwood."

No, it is you *who likes a big house celebration,* she thought. *You seize on any opportunity to overdo the simplest dinner party as its solo performer.* Without Mrs. Jackson's steadying influence on the old man, Clementine was already dreading preparations for Christmas.

"I want this to be a celebration for our farming community, and an opportunity to include our officers. The farmers' wives love to show off their best cakes and pies. We will supply cold chickens, hams, and a side of beef to roast, as well as the beer and the cider, and we mustn't forget lemonade, the fizzy kind, for the children."

He looked away, clearly offended that she might think he was incapable of organizing the celebration, and said in a sniffy sort of voice, "Yes, it is unfortunate that Mrs. Jackson is unavailable these days to organize things properly, m'lady, employed as she is by the War Office." He was clearly determined to suffer from hurt feelings, she realized, and decided that commiseration was not the best course. "Yes, it is a pity, Hollyoak. But there is a war on and we have all had to cut back and expect less. But I need you to liaise with Mr. Golightly at the Goat and Fiddle and make sure that he has everything he needs to lay on a decent supper for all our people. The farmers' wives will take care of the rest. And if you can scrape up enough players from the villagers to make up a small band, that would be quite wonderful."

She got up from her chair and walked toward the door, to signal that their meeting was at an end, and wondered how long it would be before Althea and Harry came back to report on doings at Holly Farm.

Chapter Eighteen

"There *is* someone hiding up at Holly Farm, Mama, we saw him!" Althea cried out as she and her brother came across the lawn toward Clementine. She had taken refuge in the rose garden after tea and as a result was feeling rather overwhelmed at how quickly the weeds had grown back under the rose shrubs. Mr. Thrower was doing his best, but she had noticed that he had more or less retired to the orchid house, where he spent hours fiddling about with rare specimens that he believed could not be abandoned, even with the labor shortage caused by the war. She straightened her back and, taking off a glove, looped back a strand of hair that had fallen from under hat so that she could see them clearly.

She could not help but smile at the sight of her two adult children marching across the lawn, their faces beaming with enthusiasm. *Harry hasn't even had the time to pour himself a brandy today and Althea is almost over the horror of Lieutenant Carmichael's murder.*

Her son threw himself down on the freshly cut lawn. "Making polite inquiries with Althea is like running rabbits to earth with a terrier." He laughed at his sister, who was cutting roses and threading them around the brim of her uniform cap.

"And what did you find out, my darlings?" Clementine purred as she stirred her son with her foot to organize a wicker chair for her comfort so that she might listen to their report.

"Althea should go first," Harry said as he seated his mother and returned to his supine position on the lawn, a grass stalk in one corner of his mouth, his splinted arm across his eyes to shield them from the sun. *I hope they weren't seen;* Clementine mentally crossed her fingers.

"We walked up from Brook End Lane through the wheat field and took the left fork of the footpath; you know the upper part where you can look down on the Holly Farm barn, before you drop down through the woods above the farm?" Clementine had taken the right fork the other morning when she had walked home. She nodded that she knew the route they had taken and, reaching down a hand, adjusted the dark red rose in the front of Althea's cap so that it sat squarely in the middle of the band. "And by the way, they have made absolutely little to no progress on their harvest." Clementine waved an impatient hand at infuriating behavior. *Drat all Howards,* she thought with a flash of her earlier irritation.

"We must have sat up there for ages just watching the farmyard. Don't look anxious, Mama, we were hiding out among the trees, they couldn't see us. How long were we sitting there for, Harry, it must have been easily an hour?"

"'Bout ten minutes and it is not called watching, Althea, it is called spying." He rolled away from his sister to avoid a playful cuff.

"Well, it *felt* like all afternoon. Anyway, Mrs. Howard came out of her kitchen door and pegged up some washing on the line. Then she came out again and threw a bucket of water down on the cobbles of the yard. It was getting hot and we were thirsty and thinking of abandoning the whole idea. There was no sign of Mr. Howard, his brother, or the two boys."

"They were off working the fields on the other side of the river," her brother said, throwing his grass stalk away. "Tell her about Mrs. Howard. Mrs. Howard—" he started to explain.

"No, I'm telling this." Althea sat up. "Mrs. Howard came out of her kitchen with a blue-and-white-checked bundle. She looked around her in a most furtive way."

"No, she didn't, she was behaving quite normally."

"She went across the barnyard and into the barn. She was in there an awfully long time—"

"About three minutes."

"And then she came out again and walked back to the farmhouse—but, Mama, she did not have the bundle with her!" All the roses on Althea's cap were quivering with her excitement.

"What happened next?" Clementine asked, impatient for a sighting of some man who was no doubt the individual who had conveniently killed Bray and Carmichael.

"Mama!" Althea exclaimed, taking off her cap and tossing it carelessly to one side. "Think what I have *just* said. She took a bundle wrapped in a tea towel into the barn and came back empty-handed. I won't go on until you acknowledge that this was a discovery." She did not allow Clementine to say a word, though. "She was quite obviously taking *food* to someone in the barn."

"It certainly was a discovery, darling. Well done." Clementine knew when to be obedient.

"We decided to walk on down through the wood to the edge of the barn. We hoped that perhaps we would be able to pick our way through the gorse on the north side and peek in through a knothole or something." Althea turned to her brother and magnanimously commanded him, "Go on, Harry."

"Oh, my turn? Righto then. We came up on the barn from the north side completely unobserved. This was about sixteen hundred hours, exactly twenty-five minutes after Mrs. Howard had returned to her kitchen."

"Sixteen hundred hours?" Clementine asked.

"Twenty-four hours in a day, Mama. Sixteen hundred hours is four o'clock; you take noon as twelve and then count forward throughout the last half of the day and toward midnight as twenty-four-hundred hours, saves a lot of confusion." Clementine didn't think so but she acknowledged that she understood yet another aspect of how war had changed everything—even how one referred to the time of day.

Althea had no tolerance for this dull sort of reporting, so she took over again. "Harry and I found largish knotholes and peered into the barn. We had to move up and down that side until we could find a clear view of the lower half of the building. And as we were standing there getting bits of dust in our eyes and being bitten by midges, who do you think came down the ladder from the upper part of the barn? Who, Mama? Go on, guess!"

Harry sat up; he was laughing as he picked daisies and threw them at his sister. Clementine had not seen him in quite so light-hearted a mood for months. He pelted his sister with daisy heads and bits of grass and taunted, "Althea can't stand not to be the one to tell!"

"It was Walter. Walter Howard," Althea said quickly so that she was not preempted in their great discovery.

Clementine's heart sank. "Home on leave?" *Oh why does it have to be Walter Howard? Such a mild-mannered, quiet young man, the last person in the world to bash people's heads in or shoot them in the back. But wait a moment!* "What on earth was *he* doing having his tea in the barn? If he is on leave, why wasn't he helping his father and his brothers out in the fields? Oh my goodness, he wasn't home on leave, was he?"

"If he ever joined up at all. He was conscripted earlier this year. Do you remember how devastated the Howards were when he went off to war?"

"A deserter—dear God!" Clementine felt such profound shock at the idea that the Howards' son had run away that she put her hand up to her mouth to stifle her exclamation.

"Yes," said Althea happily. "Explains everything, doesn't it? Explains why the Land girls are not welcome at the farm, or our officers—or anyone at all who is not family. *And* poor Mrs. Howard's shaking and trembling when we dropped in at her farm bright and early and took her by surprise, frying up eggs and bacon for Walter's breakfast."

Clementine looked over at her son, who was gazing out across the lawn to the horizon; his preoccupied expression had returned as he squinted at the clouds coming up in the west. *What does he see, Junkers fighter planes in our peaceful skies?*

"Harry," she said, and he turned to look at her. "What are we to do about this?"

"Well, we can't ignore it, and there will be all hell to pay if Walter has deserted. He will be shot. If he didn't enlist as he should have done, they will come for him and off to war he will go, and Mr. Howard might be sent to prison for hiding him. When the War Office started conscription they meant it. Every one of us must to do our part if we are to win this war."

"Poor boy . . ." Clementine allowed herself to feel some sort of pity for not only Walter but his family. "What on earth made them think they would get away with it?"

"They didn't think they could get away with it, they only hoped they could," said her son. But Clementine was not listening to his answer.

"Mrs. Howard," Clementine called as she knocked on the door of the farmhouse kitchen. "Good afternoon, so sorry to drop in on you like this late in the day, I didn't mean to startle you." She stepped into the kitchen and was immediately stricken by the fearful expression on the face of the woman who turned from her stove.

"M'lady." Mrs. Howard bobbed and her eyes shifted to look over Clementine's shoulder through the open kitchen door toward the farmyard and the barn. "I am afraid he won't change his mind," she said, obviously referring to her obstinate husband and not her eldest son's decision to avoid conscription. "He is quite sure he will be able to get the crops in by Tuesday."

"No, he won't, Mrs. Howard. He doesn't have enough help. And if you will trust me then I think we can achieve both things, bring in your harvest with the help of the Land girls and the officers at the hospital, and avoid a most unpleasant scene with the Market Wingley recruiting officer." Clementine felt pity for the poor woman as she watched Mrs. Howard's cheeks flush and then drain of color.

She had not seen the farmer's wife in months, but this once-sturdy woman was now quite gaunt. She had never been a pretty woman but she had always had the gloss of health about her. Clementine noticed that her formerly abundant shiny hair was dry and dull and her eyes were shadowed and sunken in her thin face. Here undoubtedly was a woman who lay in her bed every night sleepless from worry, and who daily looked over her shoulder expecting to see the army-green motorcar of the local recruiting officer from Market Wingley puttering up the hill to her house. *Of course she is sick with worry, it is what we mothers dread most, that our sons will be taken to be badly wounded or killed.*

Mrs. Howard continued to stand with her back to the kitchen stove, a soup ladle in her right hand, transfixed as Clementine asked, "Did Walter actually join up?" *Please say he did not. Please say he has not deserted.*

Mrs. Howard shook her head and Clementine's shoulders came down a notch or two.

"He got his papers in April—he was to report in May. He said he couldn't go to war to kill other men just because they were German or Turk. His nightmares were something awful and we would find him sitting here at night," she waved the soup ladle at the kitchen table, "reading the papers and all the terrible things that were going on around the world. He said he was a conscientious objector. He said he would go to prison rather than kill someone just because he had been told he was the enemy."

She put down the soup ladle in the stone sink carefully as if it were made of fragile glass. "I am sorry, m'lady, quite forgetting my manners. Please will you come into the front parlor for a cup of tea?" The invitation to drink tea was a welcome one. It would give this unhappy woman something to do.

"Yes, thank you, Mrs. Howard, that would be most welcome, but I don't want to take you away from preparing your dinner, I am quite happy to sit in your kitchen." She pulled a wooden chair away from the table. "I have heard that conscientious objectors are treated very badly in prison, Mrs. Howard. I am not sure what the penalty is for evading enlistment but I am sure it is quite severe. You cannot continue to hide Walter here. Conscription is the law once a boy reaches the age of eighteen, and the War Office keep very good records. My son told me that he was surprised that the recruiting sergeant hadn't come for Walter already."

It was hot in the kitchen even with the door open.

"They did come, about four weeks ago, and my husband told them Walter had already left to join up." Mrs. Howard filled the kettle and put it on the hob to boil. "So we thought they would not return to look for him here." She reached up to a crock on her Welsh dresser and placed three oatmeal biscuits on a lace doily on a plate. "Mr. Howard told them Walter had left in May on the train for Birmingham, just like his call-up papers had said he should. But they will come back, won't they?"

"Yes, I'm afraid they will. And anyway you can't hide your son away from the war, it isn't right. Thousands of families say goodbye to their sons, their brothers, fathers, and husbands every day. We do not have a choice in this, Mrs. Howard, not when our country is at war." Even though the woman's head was bowed Clementine could see her mouth tighten.

"I'm afraid you are in a very bad position indeed. Both your husband and your son could be put in jail for the rest of the war. Then what would happen to the boys and this farm?"

Mrs. Howard's head came up. "You are going to tell them, aren't you?" It was not an angry accusation, just a sad statement of fact.

"No, I am not going to tell them. I am going to ask your son to do his duty. And . . ." She held up her hand against a flow of objections. "There are many ways he can do his part without killing the enemy. For instance, he can register as a conscientious objector and volunteer as an ambulance driver, or a Red Cross stretcher-bearer or even a hospital orderly."

"Those are jobs that women do now."

"Men do those jobs too, and there are many men who go out at night after a battle to find men who are injured or killed and bring them back behind the lines to field hospitals or to bury them. It is a much-needed and vital job. It is a dangerous one, but it will give Walter an opportunity to contribute. And it will help give him back some of his self-respect." Her voice grew more stern: "Because hiding out in a barn is not the way. It is not good for a man to hide from his responsibilities; it will do more harm than anything. I think you know that, Mrs. Howard."

Now all she could do was sit there quietly and wait. Always a tremendous challenge when one is on the edge of one's seat, but she made herself be still even if her mind was ticking along at a great rate. She wanted to talk to Walter, she wanted to make sure he understood what sort of position he was in and the very real danger he was to his family by breaking the law. And she wanted to find out what he could see from his aerie in the barn, where all he had to do all day was watch the countryside below him. Walter had a perfect place to observe all the footpaths, bridle trails, and lanes that stretched across some several miles of Talbot land and she was trembling with anticipation for what he had to tell her.

"Mr. Howard will never ever agree to let our Walter go off to this war, Lady Montfort. And once Mr. Howard makes up his mind, then that's that." She plucked nervously at the edge of her tea towel.

Then he's a stupid obstinate fool, because you and your entire family could be languishing in Market Wingley jail within the next few days for aiding your son to break a very strict and unbending law.

A long evening shadow fell across the scrubbed pine kitchen table with its teapot comfortably puffing steam, the blue-and-white cups and saucers, and the beaded mesh doily decorously covering the milk jug. It was a particularly homey scene, except for the shadow. For there in the doorway stood Walter Howard.

Good Lord, he is huge, thought Clementine. *I never realized before how big he is.* She could think of nothing to say, she felt only apprehension at his immense size, blocking all hope of a quick exit. Dropping his head as he came into the low-ceilinged farmhouse kitchen, all anxiety evaporated. The eyes that looked down at her were gentle; the face frowned not in anger but in perplexity at his tangled situation. He pulled out a chair and sat down. "I agree though, Lady Montfort. I been listening to what you said about the Red Cross. I don't want to hide out in that barn another day. All I ever think about is when they will come for me. It's giving me the gyp and I want it over and done with."

His mother started in with a rush. "Whatever you do, Walter, don't do anything hasty right now. We must talk to your dad about this."

"No, Mum, I'm eighteen and a half. I have made up my mind. I made it up days ago, just couldn't quite work out the best way out of it," he waved his arm to encompass their home and the farm, "without getting you and Dad into trouble too."

He turned to Lady Montfort. "Can you help me?"

She knew she couldn't but she prayed that her husband might.

"I will talk to Lord Montfort, Walter. I am quite sure he will do everything he possibly can—if you are willing to do the right thing. If you come forward and volunteer for the Red Cross, and not sit up in that barn waiting for them to come to you. With your strong shoulders and sturdy frame you would make an excellent stretcher-bearer. There is no shame in helping the wounded. But if you run away it will ruin your life."

Walter reached out and took his mother's hand in his. "It will be all right, Mum," he said. "I really want to do it this way. I'll tell Dad when he comes home tonight that it is all settled. There, there, don't take on so. I will be safe, I promise you." And Clementine turned her head away because no one could offer any guarantee that Walter Howard would remain safe in the chaos of war.

Chapter Nineteen

"So that's why Howard wouldn't let anyone near his farm, the damned fool. But what on earth makes you think I would intervene on their behalf? They broke the law. On top of that, Howard has put his entire crop in jeopardy by protecting a man who is little better than a deserter." Clementine noticed that her husband's mouth was turned down at the corners and his eyebrows were up. *I should have known he would say this,* she realized, feeling anxiety on Walter Howard's behalf. *Men always see these things so differently.*

"Yes, they have behaved selfishly and stupidly, but Walter does not believe it is right to kill men because his country has told him they are the enemy. It has been a most burdensome four and half months for him and he is ready to do the right thing. I talked to him about the Red Cross."

A deep sigh—silence—another deep sigh, as Lord Montfort drummed his fingers lightly on the arm of his chair. Clementine waited for him to finish fuming.

"All this time Howard has been saying no to help from the Land Army because he didn't want anyone anywhere near the farm. What a pigheaded ass he has been when we are all stretched way beyond our usual capacity. I won't help him." He slapped his hand palm down on the arm of the chair. "I won't bail the man out."

"But would you at least talk to Walter? Not everyone believes it is right to go to war against another country, and Walter is awfully young. He has been badly advised by his father and is asking for a second chance; will you at least think about giving it to him?"

He laughed, and she relaxed. He had said many times that she would have made a marvelous criminal defense lawyer if women were ever allowed to do such things.

"Very well then, send for Walter Howard. Not his father, I don't want that turnip head in my study. If I think Walter is not swinging the lead, I will do what I can for him to be conscripted into the Red Cross and sent off to France so that he may see for himself why there should no more wars—ever."

Mrs. Jackson had settled herself once again at her desk to catch up on her neglected administrative duties when she was interrupted by Corporal West's knock on her door.

"Beg pardon for interrupting, Mrs. Jackson, but there is a lady here to see you," he said. "One of the locals," he added. And before she could ask who, Mrs. Allenby was ushered into her office.

"Oh, good afternoon, Mrs. Allenby." She rose from her desk and offered her visitor a chair. "I was just about to have a cup of tea."

The farmer's wife sat down and took off her gloves, which she kept on her lap as she declined tea. "I only have a moment, Mrs. Jackson, but I felt that you and her ladyship were owed an explanation of some sort for the other morning, when you came to talk to Davey."

Mrs. Jackson tried not to show her surprise. She had intended to pop over to the Home Farm and have a little chat with Davey Allenby, and now here was his mother quite evidently on a mission of her own. "I'll come straight to the point, Mrs. Jackson, it will save time." She looked up from the business she was making of folding her gloves. "I think I know why you were asking Davey about his day with Lieutenant Forbes. Perhaps you were wondering if the lieutenant had left the farm on the morning that the officer was killed in the kitchen garden." Mrs. Jackson's eyebrows came up. "The village," Mrs. Allenby's laugh was a little forced, "has been buzzing with gossip ever since."

"Ah yes, the village."

Mrs. Allenby fixed her eyes on her strong brown hands lying in her lap, her face without expression, and continued as if Mrs. Jackson had not spoken. "I noticed Davey's hesitation when you asked if the lieutenant had been with him all day. First of all I thought it might just be his shyness. And then I thought that it wasn't so much a hesitation because he felt awkward, but more likely that he was embarrassed and not just for himself."

Mrs. Jackson decided to play along. She didn't like being put on the spot about being a busybody but it was clear that Mrs. Allenby's quick mind had grasped exactly why she and her ladyship had been chatting away to a nine-year-old boy. "All young lads are shy at that age. But you obviously think differently, Mrs. Allenby." The woman smiled to herself as if she had proved her point. *Now everyone will know that her ladyship and I were asking questions.*

"My boy is particularly fond of Lieutenant Forbes. We all are; he is a very nice young man and I don't want the lieutenant to be implicated in this terrible business up at the hospital. Lieutenant Forbes *did* spend his entire day with Davey and Mr. Allenby. He did not go off by himself at any time so he could not have murdered Captain Bray."

Well that's very direct! "I am glad you came to me, Mrs. Allenby. But before you say anything I should let you know that I will share this information with . . . the police."

It was only good manners that prevented Mrs. Allenby from laughing, but she smiled her reassurance. "But that wouldn't do much good, would it? Everyone in the village expects her ladyship to get to the bottom of this ugly business like she always does, with your help too of course, Mrs. Jackson." Now she laughed outright as Mrs. Jackson clenched her jaw tight to stop it from dropping. To save her any further embarrassment, Mrs. Allenby continued to come straight to the point.

"On the day that the captain was murdered, Lieutenant Forbes was showing young Davey how to drive that tractor just before I took them their midday dinner. Nasty faulty things, they are, and they smell terrible; there is nothing like a dependable Shire horse. But anyway, the tractor had stopped and wouldn't start. So I left them their dinner and went back to the farmhouse. But when I talked to Davey this morning about his day with Lieutenant Forbes, he told me that after they had eaten their dinner they went back to the tractor to see if they could get it going so they could use the combine harvester. Well, it started all right, there was a loud bang, and it sort of lurched to a stop and started again with another terrific bang."

"It backfired." Mrs. Jackson supplied a term beloved of Lord Haversham in his motorcar days.

"Yes, that's it. It backfired. A very loud and explosive sound, and Davey said that Lieutenant Forbes started to shake. His hands shook so hard he couldn't steer the thing properly and it rolled across the meadow, completely out of control, and hit a tree stump. No harm done to the tractor or anything. But Lieutenant Forbes was a right mess, he couldn't stop shaking. It frightened Davey. He was so dismayed he ran through the gate to the field, leaving the poor man sitting there shaking, to get his dad." Mrs. Jackson straightened in her chair. "No, he was not gone for long, Mrs. Jackson; my husband was on the other side of the hedge in the wheat field, just seconds away. Mr. Allenby knew right off what the trouble was. He has a cousin who is suffering from what we call war-nerves. Can't walk straight most of the time and he wakes the house every night with his screaming."

Mrs. Jackson reached for a pencil. "What time do you think that was, Mrs. Allenby, any idea?"

She scribbled down the woman's answer: "About one o'clock it would be, or so my husband said it was. I had taken them their dinner at midday, and this was after. Anyway, Lieutenant Forbes had a cigarette and calmed down after a bit. But I wanted to let you know that he did not leave the farm for the whole day. And that was why Davey hesitated about being with the lieutenant all day, he didn't want to talk about something that had upset him and he probably didn't know how best to explain." This was said with a great deal of finality. Mrs. Allenby began to put on her gloves and Mrs. Jackson realized that her visit was over.

"Thank you for coming to see me, Mrs. Allenby. Davey must have been most upset by the lieutenant's fit of the shakes." She had seen what happened to their patients if they were having a bad day; any loud or sudden noise could reduce some of them to trembling wrecks. She also breathed a long sigh of relief as she was also particularly fond of Lieutenant Forbes. He was such a wholly decent young man. "Thank you so much for taking the time to tell me this, Mrs. Allenby. I really appreciate it."

"You are most welcome, Mrs. Jackson, anything I can do to help. I am sure you and her ladyship, with your quick, clever minds, will get to the bottom of this soon."

Chapter Twenty

At five o'clock, as the staff gathered belowstairs for tea, Mrs. Jackson took advantage of the rapidly cooling evening and went outside for a breath of fresh air. As she cut late-blooming dahlias and early-blooming Michaelmas daisies for the officers' mess she mentally reviewed the list of suspects she had so confidently put together with Lady Montfort just a few short days ago. It took her less than a second, because there was no one left on it. *We are nowhere near closer to understanding who killed the captain and the lieutenant than we were at the beginning of all this, and we are running out of time.* She stood in the shadow of the laurel hedge as the sun began to dip behind the trees and until she felt too cold to be outside any longer. *There is something waving away at me, something I have overlooked,* she thought and turned to walk briskly up the path to the welcoming light of the house.

As she came back through the front door there was her ladyship, waiting for her in the hall. "There you are, Jackson!" she said and walked ahead of her down the corridor to her office, where she sat herself down in a chair. She was evidently here for more than a minute, because she took off her hat. "I have so much to tell you. I simply don't know where to begin."

You would probably like to begin with a glass of amontillado, because I know I would. Mrs. Jackson bent to light the twist of paper under the kindling in the fireplace. "There now, m'lady, that should make us feel a bit cozier; the chill strikes even colder after such a hot day. A glass of sherry might warm us up a bit too." She took out her sherry glasses, gave them a quick polish, and poured a generous thimbleful for each of them.

"This afternoon, Jackson," her ladyship announced after they had raised their glasses in silent salute and had taken a sip, "I think we were handed a gift, a considerable step forward in our inquiry. And it just goes to show that there is a right way of handling a tricky situation and an altogether wrong way." She paused for effect, so that her final revelation would be appreciated. *Well, it is quite clear that she handled it the right way,* thought Mrs. Jackson. She consciously fixed a concentrated look of incredulity on her face and took a cautious sip of sherry, but her stomach fluttered with anticipation. Discoveries were always so thrilling and she had been quite convinced that they had reached a stalemate.

"We have achieved two things today: the exposure of a dark and shameful secret," Lady Montfort extended an upright forefinger, to be rapidly joined by her middle finger, "and a very credible witness." And she waved them both as she began to relate Lady Althea and Lord Haversham's discovery at Holly Farm.

"Walter Howard is a conchie, m'lady?" Mrs. Jackson was so shaken at this news she could not help but blurt out the unattractive expression. It was the worst curse imaginable in this day and age to have a conscientious objector in the family. *How, for heaven's sake, did a farmer's son raised with the slaughter of spring pigs, the castration of calves, and the general butchery that goes on in the countryside find killing his country's enemies repugnant? Why, this is even worse than harboring cowards in the name of neurasthenia,* she thought and wondered what the village would make of this revelation.

"A conchie?" Lady Montfort had clearly not heard the expression before. "Oh! Ah yes, I see. Yes, I am afraid that poor Walter

Howard is a conchie." With a merry little laugh she sipped her sherry. "But," her face became solemn, "I am hoping that we can save the poor wretch before he is clapped in irons and sent to the brig." Mrs. Jackson made a mental note to provide some cheese biscuits next time she served sherry. She squinted at her ladyship's glass, she had filled it a moment ago, and her own was still two-thirds full, but her ladyship's was quite empty. She got up and poured her another splash.

"You were saying about Walter Howard, m'lady?"

"Discovering Walter Howard in his father's barn is not the best part of this tale. You see, from his perch Walter could see out across the valley almost all the way to the village."

Walter Howard saw something! Mrs. Jackson found that she was holding on to her glass quite tightly. She set it down on the table next to her.

"Walter Howard observed two most useful things on the day Captain Bray was killed. After his noonday dinner, which he ate in the open gable door of the hayloft, he dropped off for a moment or two, but he awoke with a bit of a start to hear the unfamiliar sound of a galloping horse."

She paused and Mrs. Jackson quickly acknowledged the moment: "A horse? Was it his lordship's Bruno perhaps?"

Lady Montfort shook her head. "No, it was not Bruno, Jackson. When Walter opened his eyes he saw a large gray horse, with a rider on its back, being galloped for all it was worth along the footpath that leads from Brook End Lane through the wheat field in the direction of Crow's Wood. The very same path I walked the other day."

"Could he see who the rider was, m'lady?"

"No, Jackson, he could not identify the rider. But I promise you I asked all the right questions. Was the man in uniform? I asked. He wasn't sure, he said, it was difficult to tell from that distance. Was it a woman or a man? And he said that it was most probably a man—as the person was riding astride. I didn't remind him that many women have abandoned riding sidesaddle."

Mrs. Jackson made no comment for a moment and then she asked, "Did he know what time it was, m'lady?"

"Most certainly he did! Walter's long days in the hayloft weigh heavily. Breakfast, dinner, and supper times are the highlight of the day—I suspect it must be the same for all prisoners. He ate his dinner promptly at noon, and when he awoke from his nap he looked at his watch and it was just after one o'clock."

The time Lady Althea was laying out her picnic in the spinney, while Lieutenant Carmichael was setting Dolly loose in the pasture by Brook End Lane, Mrs. Jackson thought, smiling. "Then it must have been Dolly," she said.

"Yes, it was certainly Dolly, but I am not sure," her ladyship said rather wistfully, "that it was Lieutenant Carmichael upon her back because he had only been gone for twenty minutes or so when he joined Lady Althea at the spinney. I don't think a horse as heavy as Dolly could gallop that distance and back in the time. But then her stride is particularly long, so it might just be possible."

"At that time of day, riding in that direction, m'lady, it might very well have been the murderer."

"Yes, I think it must have been. We are close." Lady Montfort held up her forefinger and her thumb in a pinching gesture. "This close." She looked down into her empty sherry glass and Mrs. Jackson refilled it.

"I am not quite finished with what Walter saw, Jackson," said her ladyship when she had resumed her seat. "While he was sitting up in the hay loft that day, he saw someone else."

Mrs. Jackson felt the tremor of excitement she was meant to feel and took a sizable sip of sherry.

"The hayloft has a gable at each end, and earlier that morning Walter had watched from its west side as Sir Winchell came to the river and settled himself on the footbridge for a day of fishing. The distance between the barn and the river is quite close and he could see Sir Winchell clearly. Oh, how Walter, imprisoned up in his dusty loft, envied him sitting on a cool riverbank with his creel and his rod! Sir Winchell fished up and down that short stretch of the river for hours, frustrating poor Walter with his inept casting, hanging over the bridge so the fish could easily see him, and standing with his back to the sun to cast long shadows onto the river. But he said at no time did Sir Winchell leave the riverbank until well after three that afternoon."

Mrs. Jackson raised a polite hand from her lap. "Except for the time, m'lady, when Walter took his dinner over on the other side of the barn, during the crucial hours." She put her sherry to one side, the better to keep east separate from west.

"Aha, Jackson, I said exactly the same thing! But before Walter sat down with his dinner on the east side of the barn, he said Sir Walter had been trying to disentangle a long length of line that he had caught up in a bush—it was in a terrible muddle. After Walter had watched the horse galloping along the footpath, he wandered back over to the west gable to see how Sir Winchell was faring. And there he was, no longer surrounded by lengths of tangled fishing line but with his rod and line tidily propped against a tree as he ate his luncheon. I think we can safely say that Sir Winchell did not have time to walk to the kitchen garden, murder Captain Bray after twenty-five minutes past twelve when VAD Fuller left the kitchen garden with her beans, walk back, and untangle his fishing line all by one o'clock. A younger man might have done it if he ran all the way there and back, but Sir Winchell is very stout."

Mrs. Jackson smiled. "Then Walter can give Sir Winchell an alibi for the day when Captain Bray was murdered. And once again Inspector Savor has arrested the wrong man," she said and felt a wave of pure happiness that the inspector had once again proven his worthlessness.

"Of course he has, Jackson. That incompetent individual has no more idea how to conduct a murder investigation than he has of tracking down all those gallons of stolen petrol. Sir Winchell is undoubtedly innocent of both murders, we knew that all along. But I do believe if we find out who was riding that horse then we will be close to understanding who killed Captain Bray."

"And Lieutenant Carmichael?"

"Perhaps."

"What happens next, m'lady?" Mrs. Jackson reached for her notebook.

"I am hoping that Lord Montfort will intervene on Walter's behalf with the Market Wingley recruiting officer, and when all that has been taken care of I will arrange for Walter to talk to Colonel Valentine. I don't want Walter anywhere near that dreadful Savor. And I somehow think it would be better if Walter did not talk to Colonel Valentine too soon, as I want our murderer to think he is off the hook and that Sir Winchell will be tried for murder in his place."

Mrs. Jackson was not terribly sure that this was the right thing to do. It made her feel uneasy. "Isn't that called withholding evidence, m'lady? If we know something for a fact and deliberately do not inform the police?"

"On no, Jackson, I shouldn't think so. It is not withholding information, it is merely delaying it." Lady Montfort waved a dismissive hand at the idea. "And anyway it will not do Sir Winchell any harm to think about losing his temper quite so thoroughly in future. Gentlemen, however frustrated and unhappy they are, should not shout and carry on in that way." *So it is one of her oblique little lessons on self-control*, Mrs. Jackson thought as she watched her finish her sherry with evident enjoyment. "And perhaps," her ladyship said softly under her breath, "the next time Colonel Valentine appears to want my advice and I give it to him, he should listen to it." She put down her empty glass and Mrs. Jackson decided it was time to bring her up to date from her end.

"I think we can cross Lieutenant Forbes off our list, m'lady." She briefly related her conversation with Mrs. Allenby.

"Very glad to hear it, Jackson. I like young Forbes, he is such a decent sort—all of our officers are.

"Now with this information about Dolly's gallop I really think we should give some more thought to Lieutenant Carmichael. I only met him a couple of times; what did you make of him? Was he a decent sort, too? He was certainly an attractive young man with all that curly golden hair." It was a lighthearted observation but it stopped Mrs. Jackson in her tracks. Into her mind flashed an illustration of a fairy tale prince, with yellow hair and large blue eyes. Where had she seen that image—in a children's picture book? She frowned and closed her eyes in concentration, and saw once again the caricature of a man with golden hair.

"Do you have time to come up to the art room before you leave, m'lady? There is something I want to show you up there that I think might be helpful. It's something I noticed yesterday just before Fuller made her startling statement about Captain Bray. And then it went completely out of my mind until just now."

You had to hand it to her ladyship, she never hemmed or hawed about the time of day, and, having to be somewhere else, she was already on her feet and off they went together to the art room.

Chapter Twenty-One

It was nearly dark and Mrs. Jackson lit a lamp for each of them as they walked into the dark of the art room. "I was sorting through these paintings with Fuller, m'lady, and there was one here done by Captain Bray that was quite interesting. Let me see now, where did I put it." She turned to the stack that they had started to make by the window.

"Every painting our officers did when they first came here was labeled with their name and the date it was painted. Some of them even gave their work a title." She flipped through the stack. "Ah yes, here it is." She lifted up a canvas and glanced at the label on its back. "Yes. Captain Bray, April 1916. Do you recognize the man portrayed here, or am I imagining things, m'lady?"

She held the painting toward the light. "Let me turn up the lamp. Yes, that's better." The light shone on a simple rendition of the head and shoulders of a man with yellow hair and large, round blue eyes.

"Oh good heavens, Jackson, for a moment I thought it might be Lieutenant Carmichael. But it can't be. Do you see the man in the painting is not wearing the collar and tie of an officer's uniform, but the woolen battledress of an enlisted man. Hm, I have to say it is a little like him, though." She didn't look particularly enthusiastic about the similarity.

"A very similar likeness, though, m'lady. Do you see his ears sort of jut out a little at the top, just like Lieutenant Carmichael's did, and his right eyebrow lifts a little higher than the left? I always thought that Lieutenant Carmichael often looked as if he were about to ask a question," Mrs. Jackson said as they gazed down at the painting.

"I only saw him a couple of times, I'm afraid I don't remember. This man's chin is very weak for a man, almost girlishly so," said Lady Montfort, her eyes narrowed in what appeared to be dislike. "Was Carmichael's chin really that negligible? Oh look, there is a name or something down here, I can't quite make it out."

Mrs. Jackson peered down at the far right corner, for there printed quite neatly in black paint was a name: D. Or was it a P? Hector. "Hector?" she said the name aloud, and almost startled when Lady Montfort jumped in.

"Well, that explains it, it is a portrait of someone the captain knew in France, a soldier who served under him and who happens to look rather like our Lieutenant Carmichael." She turned the painting this way and that at arm's length, and then turned it to read the back. "And the date is all wrong for Carmichael, Jackson. You see it was done earlier this year in April. Carmichael had only been here a couple of weeks. Yes, it's definitely someone who served under Captain Bray—probably in his regiment."

They were interrupted from their contemplation of the portrait by a cheery "Hullo!" as a head popped around the door before Major Andrews entered the room. "You are working late, Mrs. Jackson. Oh, and good evening, Lady Montfort, so sorry to surprise you. Going through the paintings are you? Some of them are most interesting." He joined them in their study of Captain Bray's portrait. Lady Montfort glanced at Mrs. Jackson and she understood that they should hear the major's reaction to the portrait unprompted. He took his time as he squinted over Mrs. Jackson's shoulder at the canvas

"That's rather interesting—who did that?"

"Captain Bray, sir."

"So he did! Never out of the art room when he first came to us. It looks as if he painted a portrait of one of his fellow officers here, poor chap." He frowned. "And it is not a particularly flattering portrait of him, either." He took the painting from her. "It is quite a crude, almost childlike portrayal, but like many childlike observations it is honest. It certainly bears a strong resemblance to Carmichael. Hah, Bray saw him as weak—interesting, I would have said the same. Yes, I have seen that expression of his sometimes in our sessions; a watchful, rather cynical look. But see here, this is odd: Bray has painted him in the uniform of an enlisted man. Perhaps that's how he saw him."

He sighed and pinched his lower lip between finger and thumb in deep thought. He must have noticed that their interest had sharpened because his face assumed the bland expression of the professional who kept his patients' secrets safe. "Yes, I think we should perhaps hang on to this one. Look at this." He tilted the picture. "There something written here on the front. I don't have my spectacles."

"It says 'Hector,' some man he knew in France probably . . ." said Lady Montfort, and Mrs. Jackson thought her expression was rather forbidding. *She is almost determined that it is not Carmichael,* she thought.

"So is it Hector or Carmichael? Most intriguing—I expect that is what Captain Bray was trying to find out. There's the dinner gong, have to dash; perhaps you would join us in the officers' mess for a glass of sherry, Lady Montfort—unless you have to return to Iyntwood?" He had put the painting back against the wall, but he was still looking at it.

"Thank you, Major Andrews, how kind of you, but I am already late as it is!" Lady Montfort's smile was polite, but it was clear that her mind was a thousand miles away. And when the major left she was uncharacteristically silent.

"Perhaps Lieutenant Carmichael had a brother or a cousin, an enlisted man, in the same regiment as Captain Bray. But it is a strong . . ."

Her ladyship's hand flew up to her mouth and then to her forehead. She looked so stunned for a moment that if Mrs. Jackson had not been aware of her distress, her expression would have been laughable. "Oh dear God, Jackson," was all she said, looking for all the world like a landed codfish. "This might very well be a portrait of a man *called* Hector, but Major Andrews also recognized the likeness as being our Lieutenant Carmichael, which might very well mean . . ." She stopped and glared at the portrait. "I can't believe that *this* man came here as some sort of imposter . . . the . . . the impudence of it!"

Mrs. Jackson understood what was upsetting her. "Can we really believe that the man we know as Lieutenant Carmichael came here pretending to be someone he wasn't? It just isn't possible, is it? It's a very serious crime to impersonate an officer."

Her ladyship's laugh was scornful. "More serious than murder, Jackson? And not a completely *impossible* thing to accomplish in the confusion of war. I think," her face in the darkened room looked severe, "it would be quite possible if a man was both unscrupulous and clever." She had clearly convinced herself that Lieutenant Carmichael was definitely not who he said he was.

"In that case, m'lady, I think it is important to find out if this man had the time to ride up to the kitchen garden from the horse pasture and back again on Dolly." It was all she could come up with and was relieved to see her ladyship put her best foot forward.

"Quite right, Jackson, quite right." She turned and started for the door. "We must get to the bottom of all of this. It's time to concentrate our efforts; we have to find out who this young man in Captain Bray's painting really was." It was reassuring to see Lady Montfort had recovered from the stunning possibility that Carmichael might not be who he had appeared to be; her ladyship's look of confusion had gone, and now there was only implacable disgust. If Lieutenant Carmichael was not already dead he would have been in serious trouble.

Mrs. Jackson had waited patiently for this moment ever since Major Andrews had also recognized the portrait as that of an enlisted man. "I believe we might accomplish it quite simply, it is just a question of going to the right source. We have the War Office files for both Lieutenant Carmichael and Captain Bray and I am hoping that by using their information we will find out if Captain Bray and Lieutenant Carmichael were in the same regiment, even the same battalion, and if there is indeed such a man as P. or D. Hector. I can write to Mr. Stafford, he might be able to help us solve this puzzle. I just hope we can get the information from him in time."

Lady Montfort perked up. *However upset she is, she doesn't waste time moping about.*

"I knew it, Jackson, I simply knew you would not be presenting this puzzling painting without a solution! Where is Mr. Stafford these days—somewhere useful?"

"Most useful, m'lady. He was drafted into the Graves Registration Commission and is presently stationed in Auchonvillers in northern France. The Auchonvillers commission keeps records of all casualties and deaths in northern France. It would be quite easy for Mr. Stafford to look up the identification information for Lieutenant Carmichael and find out if he is alive or dead, and perhaps he can find out if there is such a man as P. Hector, too." It was a relief to see Lady Montfort's tension lift. "Should I write to Mr. Stafford, m'lady?" She dropped her voice as they reached the bottom step of the marble staircase and her words echoed in the cavern of the hall.

"Yes please, Jackson, first post tomorrow. How long does it takes for a letter to get to France?"

"The postmaster general told the newspapers only the other day that the post office guarantees that all letters reach France in two days now, m'lady—it is important for our troops' morale apparently. If Mr. Stafford can find the information we need quickly, perhaps we will hear in four or five days."

Evidently this was not a welcome answer, as Lady Montfort's chin came up and she frowned. "We don't have the luxury of five days! We have the wretched War Office and Medical Board inspection in four, and we must get Sir Winchell cleared before he is tried for murder."

"It would be so much better if the murderer turned out to be a civilian than one of our officers," Mrs. Jackson heard herself say, and then, horrified at the audacity of the idea, she instantly wished she hadn't said such a thing, for her ladyship turned to her, eyes wide with shock. *There now, this is what happens when you take succor in the bottle,* she thought. *What can I be thinking?*

"Perfectly brilliant of you, Jackson. If we have not solved our crime before then, we can just keep silent about Walter Howard as Sir Winchell's alibi for his uninterrupted day of fishing until after the Medical Board have completed their inspection and gone away."

And it was Mrs. Jackson's turn to be shocked.

Chapter Twenty-Two

Mrs. Jackson was up, washed, and dressed and by half past seven the next morning was reading through her letter to Ernie Stafford.

Well, I hope that will do, she thought, as she skimmed through her opening paragraphs. She seemed not to have the flair for written conversations and the confidences that some letter-readers enjoy and often require. *What a dismal job he has been allotted in France.* Burying the dead; burying Britain's hope, as Ernie Stafford called it: young men barely out of boyhood and men with wives and children praying for them at home. He had told her that part of his job was finding the right sort of terrain to create new graveyards. He did his best to find land on the rise of a hill where the earth was dry and clean and the air sweet. She thought of all the beautiful gardens that her friend had created over the years, and how saddened he had been on the day Britain had declared war on Germany. She read again what she had written.

I am pleased to hear that they have moved your headquarters further back behind the lines. Your description of the countryside reminds me of the Yorkshire dales with its sheep pastures and gray stone villages.

I walked over to Iyntwood last week and received a very

heartwarming welcome from Lord Haversham, who came home to recover from a broken arm.

And then she described as clearly and concisely as she could the events that had taken place at the hospital, playing down the murder because she did not want to alarm him.

It would be useful if you could help the hospital confirm the identity of two of our patients. We are sure Captain Bray is who he says he is, but it is Lieutenant Carmichael that we are puzzled about.

She copied down the identification number, name, and regiment, the Gloucestershires, for both Captain Bray and Lieutenant Carmichael from her patient ledger.

And if you could also look for a man with the last name of Hector, initial P or D, who might also have been in the same battalion of the Gloucestershires, it would be most useful. And need I say that speed is of the essence?

And then, because her letter should contain some personal details:

Did I say how much I am enjoying my new job? The treatment of our patients is most interesting and I am beginning to believe that perhaps this business of talking about the things that trouble and worry us, usually never mentioned so as to not burden family and friends, does seem to be helpful, if not taken too far.

And as it would amuse him, she told him about his old friend Mr. Thrower and his triumph over Inspector Savor.

I think we were all hoping that the inspector would want to check up on Bill's aggressive nature himself. But unfortunately he decided against such a course, which was a sore disappointment to Mr. Thrower. You know how he proud he is of Bill's efficiency as a watchdog.

She signed her letter, folded the three sheets of closely written pages, and slid them into the green envelope, a signal to the censor that the letter was from an auxiliary hospital and not to a man in a fighting unit and need not be opened and read. Leaving her envelope in the hall postbag, she let herself out of the front door of Haversham Hall and walked in the direction of the kitchen gardens.

Mr. Thrower was planting winter-cabbage seed, and he lifted an arm in salute as he saw her, but he did not stop to come over. With her eyes down she walked along the grassy area under the walnut tree toward the half-open double gates that led out of the kitchen garden on its south side. The grass felt brittle and dry underfoot. There was no sign of footprints anywhere in the hard earth: not from a human shoe or boot, a bicycle's wheels or the imprint of a horseshoe. On she went out through the open gate to the cart track that ran along the outer side of the kitchen-garden wall. The early morning sun struck hot on her forehead and she pulled down the brim of her hat to shade her eyes.

On the other side of the track was a tall hedge separating it from the wheat field. *If the man on the horse had ridden up the track, he would have been completely concealed from the field—even from the vantage point of the Howards' barn.*

She followed the track along the wall of the kitchen garden until it dodged out from behind the hedge to become a public footpath. Here it linked up with all the footpaths and bridle trails in the area as they rambled and meandered across the county to connect hamlet, farmhouse, croft, and village to others and thence onward across the entire country, providing the ancient network of rights-of-way that the people of Britain had walked for centuries. Someone had told her that it was possible to walk the length and breadth of the country on its footpaths and bridle trails, as the law forbade any landowner, city council, or industrialist to either obstruct a right-of-way or deny access.

Talbot land stretched in each direction for mile after fertile mile, and its public footpaths were well maintained by the Land girls even in these days of war. Hedgerows were trim and ditches clear of weeds. She glanced at her watch, turned left, and with her eyes on the tracks' hard and rutted surface she set a brisk pace in the direction of Crow's Wood.

Tall wheat, yet to be harvested, stretched away from her in a long sweep burnished to a rich, deep gold. The sky, a blue of such exquisite clarity that it was impossible to mimic its likeness in fabric or paint, provided a perfect backdrop to the rounded expanse of swaying gold. She stopped, lifting her hand to shield her eyes from the sun, and looked around her, partly to assess the distance, up on its rise, of Holly Farm and its barn standing in a ruffle of dark green woodland, and also to enjoy the simple delight of the pastoral beauty of England. The bent ears of wheat, heavy with grain, rippled and surged like the waves on an inland sea as a breeze blew up the valley. She might walk off the path and stand almost chest deep in the crop it was so tall. She stretched out an arm and palm-down brushed the edge of the field's tawny back, but she didn't slow her pace. The cart track in front of her widened and continued across the bottom end of Iyntwood's empty horse pasture to the Home Farm and was intercepted by a footpath that curved south to skirt the deeply shadowed fringe of Crow's Wood. A wooden fingerpost informed her MARKET WING-LEY 22 MI.

She stopped briefly in the shade of oak trees. The surface of the path was rich with damp leaf mold, the grass on either side a lush, soft green. Her eyes searched the ground as she walked slowly forward. *There!* She stopped and crouched down. Pressed deep into the soft earth was the great round print of the only Shire horse in the area.

Dolly's iron shoes were heavy: the six square-headed nails that secured shoe to foot were set three each side of the deep V of the frog of her hoof, clearly visible in the print. The mare was a strong-boned and stalwart creature standing almost eighteen hands at her withers. If she had cantered along this path on the edge of the woodland her stride would easily measure thirteen or fourteen feet depending on her speed. Eyes down, Mrs. Jackson walked forward.

Well for heaven's sake! Mrs. Jackson's exclamation was triumphant. *Here are Dolly's hoofprints going both ways: two here and a third one there going north, nearly obliterating a fourth southbound print.* She hurried forward, eyes down. *Now that is very interesting,* she thought, *there is no sign of any other type of tracks. No wheel prints from the tire of a bicycle, or cart, and the path is certainly not wide enough for a motorcar at this point.*

She was clear of the protection of the wood and now the wheat field stretched out on either side of her and the full force of the sun fell on the path as it ran ahead, hard-packed and as straight as a die right down the middle of the field. Not a hoofprint to be seen anywhere. She was halfway across the field now and on her right, to the west, she saw the rise on which Holly Farm house sat with its tall barn. She could easily make out the open gable door on the second story where Walter had whiled away his lonely days, a fugitive from the war. He was not there today. *He is probably just finishing his breakfast with his family, poor lad,* she thought as she remembered that this morning Walter would go down to Market Wingley with his father and Lord Montfort to turn himself in. She resumed her brisk walk across the field.

Ten minutes later she could see the hedge at the field's edge, another ten and she came up to the big five-bar gate. She leaned against its top rail to catch her breath and gazed out onto Brook End Lane and checked the time. It had taken her almost an hour to walk from the kitchen garden to this gate and she breathlessly realized that she had been going at quite a clip. *That's a distance of at least three miles, maybe even a little more,* she thought as she opened the gate to the meadow where Dolly had been let loose to enjoy a break in her workday.

Poor Dolly, she thought, *instead of an hour or two of cropping meadow grass and staring contemplatively into the brook that flows into the river at its border, she was made to gallop across country.* She walked down to the little stream and checked along its edge, and under the shade of a willow tree in the soft mud she found what she was looking for: the large, almost circular prints of Dolly's hooves.

Lieutenant Carmichael had certainly brought Dolly down to the pasture, but instead of letting her loose, had he jumped up on her back and ridden her as fast as she could go across the wheat fields and up to the kitchen garden? She imagined him sliding off the blown horse at the south gate of the kitchen garden and loosely tying her halter to it. "Hullo there, Evelyn, digging potatoes again?" he might have called out as he sauntered across the lawn under the walnut tree, mopping his brow from his gallop. She saw Captain Bray start to straighten his back, head turned toward Carmichael, and in one swift bound the lieutenant sprang forward and, lifting his right arm, hit the captain a stunning blow on the top of his head. *He brought a murder weapon with him,* she thought as in her imagination the captain fell like a stone facedown in the earth of the last potato row.

If it was Lieutenant Carmichael who had ridden Dolly, he would have known where to find the solitary captain; he would have carefully set up his alibi and arranged transportation. He had galloped with one hand on the halter because in his other he was holding his weapon. She felt most uneasy as she stood on the edge of the pasture, her head bent deep in thought.

It all fits together quite well, but did Lieutenant Carmichael have enough time to accomplish all this in twenty minutes? She had walked as fast she could for the most part, slowing down only slightly as she checked the path at the edge of Crow's Wood. How long would it take to gallop three miles? Dolly's stride was long, but, as her ladyship had pointed out, she was a heavy animal built for hauling, not racing.

Mrs. Jackson had not worked for the Talbot family for as long as she had without picking up some information about horses. Thoroughbreds on the racetrack were capable of the highest speed, and Bruno, Lord Montfort's stallion, a tall strongly built hunter bred not just for speed but for the endurance of the chase, would probably be able to run three miles quite easily and in a matter of minutes. But Dolly was not built for the raking speed of a Thoroughbred or the pace and endurance of a hunter. Would she even be able to sustain a full-out gallop for three miles? Lady Althea had said that Lieutenant Carmichael had taken twenty minutes to turn Dolly out in the pasture and then join her for a picnic; could he possibly have climbed on Dolly's back, galloped to the kitchen garden, killed Captain Bray, and then galloped back?

We'll have to ask Lord Haversham, he'll know. When he was fourteen, before he had discovered motorcars, the Talbots' son had been given a very severe dressing-down by his father for joining in a steeplechase on one of his lordship's hunters. The Talbot family revered their horses; there was never any question of their being whipped across country, taking all fences and hedges regardless of the dangers in a reckless steeplechase.

But if Lieutenant Carmichael murdered Captain Bray, then who shot the lieutenant? she wondered, before reminding herself not to go too fast and overwhelm her thinking.

She felt at this moment that the answer lay in the painting in the art room, depicting a likeness of Carmichael but with the name Hector painted in the lower right-hand corner. And with this thought in mind she set off as fast as she could in the direction of Iyntwood to find Lady Montfort and Lord Haversham.

"Ah yes, I see what you mean, Jackson, and your calculations are probably quite right so far as a Thoroughbred or a hunter is concerned. In the old days, before the war, a lot of farmers hunted on their plow horses, you know. They were such wonderfully steady beasts and quite talented jumpers. They did not have the speed of a horse bred for the track, or the hunt. I can't imagine Dolly, even though she is a young horse, managing six miles in twenty minutes, she would have been exhausted at the end of it, blown and lathered." She shook her head. "But as you say, we should ask Lord Haversham."

"Harry," Lady Montfort said when he had been sent for and had said good morning to her and Mrs. Jackson. "How long do you think it would take Dolly to go at her top speed from Brook End Lane along the footpath through the Holly Farm wheat field toward Crow's Wood and then along the track to the south gate of the kitchen garden? We think that distance is about three miles."

He laughed and said he thought Dolly would take the best part of a morning. "Would she be pulling a plow?"

His mother smiled. "She was probably being ridden, Harry, from the pasture by Brook End Lane. So, how long would it take her with a strong rider on her back to make the distance?"

"Are you serious, Mama? Ride Dolly, who is a particularly lazy horse by the way, three miles at her top speed?" And catching sight of his mother's expression: "Ah, it's a serious question then."

She beamed at her son in reply. "Dolly is a willing plow horse, but I don't suppose she has ever been under saddle."

"The Brook End Farm children get on her back. I have seen all four sitting up there like birds on a branch."

"And Dolly, what was she doing?"

She shrugged her shoulders. "She was cropping the grass, as placid as can be."

"So Dolly, who as far as we know has never been under saddle, would be an unwilling partner in a ten-minute gallop across a wheat field." He described the arc of her run with his splinted right arm across the room.

"But it was Dolly, wasn't it, Jackson? First of all Walter saw her, and Mrs. Jackson has just walked that way and she saw Dolly's hoofprints, didn't you, Jackson?"

"Yes, m'lady, I believe it was Dolly. I compared the prints by the stream in the meadow with the ones by Crow's Wood and they match. Big as soup plates they were and almost completely round." Mrs. Jackson did not ride but she did know the difference between the prints of a plow horse and those of a hunter.

"Well, Harry, are you going to commit to how long it would take Dolly to gallop three miles?"

Her son gazed at the far wall in concentration, as if he was doing mental arithmetic. "If you could get her to canter it would be a miracle, and you would have to have spurs and a whip even for that." He shook his head as he contemplated Dolly's merits as a racehorse.

Her ladyship sighed. "Yes, I think he is right, Jackson. I would not envy anyone trying to get consistent speed out of her."

Lord Haversham gave it some more thought. "Ten minutes one way if she was not tired, if it was not a hot day and she was willing, and even then only if you were a good rider with a strong leg." He was curious now and taking their idea a little more seriously.

His mother said, "Walter saw a gray horse being *galloped* across the wheat field. It could only have been Dolly and she was *galloping*."

"If she was being ridden from Brook End Lane, then that was the beginning of her journey and she might have been galloping at the beginning but she simply could not keep it up. You know what, though? I'll ride Dolly from Brook End Lane to the kitchen garden and back again. I will make her go as fast as I can, and we can time her. I think it is the only way to find out." He had evidently not forgotten his steeplechasing days.

"No, Harry, please don't get up on Dolly, she is as wide as a barge, and if you come off your arm might be seriously injured this time."

"I am hardly at risk riding a plow horse. Where is your sense of adventure, Mama?"

And so it was agreed that Lord Haversham would drive over to Brook End Farm and borrow Dolly for an experiment in time and speed.

"I will be riding her with a bridle and a whip, and a saddle if I can find one wide enough. And no betting," he said as he left the room, "this is a scientific study, not an opportunity to make a bit of money on the gee-gees."

But Lady Montfort had already said that half a crown would see Dolly there and back within thirty minutes. "Don't forget to spend at least four or five minutes giving the poor thing a rest outside the kitchen garden before you turn and take her back to the pasture," she called after her son.

"What happens during those minutes?" he called back as he went through the door of her sitting room.

"That is how long it will take you to come into the kitchen garden and bonk Mrs. Jackson and me on our heads," his mother said, as if he was being particularly dense.

"How long have we been sitting here now?" Lady Montfort asked for the third time, and Mrs. Jackson looked at her watch.

"About forty minutes, m'lady."

"Oh, Jackson, I do hope that Dolly has not bucked him off." She didn't look too concerned, though, in fact quite the opposite. *As cool as a glass of water despite this sweltering afternoon,* Mrs. Jackson thought as she looked up at the sky, which had clouded over in the past hour, to hold in the noonday heat like a tin lid on a saucepan. It was the sort of stultifying, humid weather that heralded a storm. *That's what we need,* she thought, *a storm to clear the air—but not until our harvest is in.*

A sigh from her ladyship. "What on earth can be keeping him?"

"His lordship has probably only just managed to catch Dolly, m'lady," she said and settled herself to wait for another twenty minutes or so. She was wondering how Lord Haversham could catch and saddle up a horse with the use of only one arm. "It will be quite authentic if his lordship rides her with just one hand," she added as she remembered the weapon.

"I do hope he notices the time before he sets off from Brook End Lane. And anyway, Jackson, what is it going to prove if he gets here in fifteen minutes, riding poor Dolly into the ground in this terrible heat?"

Jackson didn't answer, because she could not imagine that Lord Haversham would do anything of the kind, he was far too considerate.

They sat on in the silence of the afternoon and after a while they heard in the distance the sounds of hoofbeats drawing closer. Lady Montfort sprang to her feet. "Here they come!" she cried as if she were waiting for news on the eve of the Battle of Waterloo. "Can you hear them, Jackson? That's Harry on Dolly!" And they both made their way across the grass toward to kitchen garden's south gate.

It was Lord Haversham indeed and Dolly was evidently having the time of her life, cantering gaily up the track toward them in a cloud of dust. And on her back, with legs that spanned the mare's broad back, was Captain Harry Talbot, the Viscount Haversham: his face was scarlet and covered in dust, his hair was standing on end in the front, and there was an interesting smear of bright green on his cheek and his white shirt as he brought the mare to a halt.

"Harry," cried his mother, with no thought to the fact that her son could barely speak he was so winded. "How long did it take you?"

He slid off Dolly's back. The mare was lathered and steaming, and all the veins stood out on her gray body now black with sweat. Harry leaned his head against her broad chest, and she gave him a playful shove with her great Roman nose. He shook his head as he tried to regain his balance.

"She was hell," he said, still breathless from his ride. "What an opinionated, stubborn, and thoroughly miserable plug she is." Dolly shoved him again, leaving a bright chlorophyll-green smear on his coat shoulder.

"How long did it take you, Harry?"

"Catching and tacking her up was almost too easy; I had to find the longest girth strap and make an additional couple of holes, that's what took the time. Then I climbed up on the stile at Brook End Lane and got on her back and she was lovely, as docile and mannerly as you like. The moment we got into the wheat field I gave her a nudge in the ribs and she just stood there. I kicked her and she just stood there. I cut a switch from the hedgerow and gave her a good whack, and off we went hell-for-leather. And then just as we were coming up to the wood she shied. Stopped dead in her tracks and just stood there snorting. She refused to go forward. I gave her another whack and managed to get her going again. But she was clearly blown, and so we ambled along until she realized that the wood wasn't going to attack her. And then off we went at a sloppy canter—I think she even enjoyed it, the great lumbering fool."

"Did you by any chance look at your watch before you came up through the wheat field?"

"Oh yes, Mama, and again as we came up to you. Oh, Dolly," he turned to the mare and patted her on the neck, "you silly, useless girl. It's back to the plow for you, you will never win the Derby."

"Harry, please."

"Nearly seventeen minutes. And whoever rode her up here would have had to know how to ride. I mean *really* know how to ride, because Dolly hasn't a clue. If you are wondering if it was Carmichael who rode this horse, you have another think coming. The man didn't have an ounce of muscle to his leg. He was the sort that indulges in drawing-room chatter, not country sports. He could never have made her go fast enough, if he could have stayed on her at all." He wiped his sweating forehead with his handkerchief.

"If it took you seventeen minutes, Harry, then I am quite sure Carmichael could not have done better," Lady Montfort said with maternal loyalty.

"Thank you. Does that mean that I don't have to ride her back again?" her son asked, looking so hopeful that Mrs. Jackson had to look away so that he did not see her smile. "Does that mean I can walk her back? Because she is a completely different horse when you are leading her, a perfect sweetheart in fact."

"No, there is no need to ride her back to her pasture, darling, and thank you so much for helping us out." Lady Montfort turned away, looking quite crushed. "I think we can eliminate Lieutenant Carmichael as our culprit. We are nowhere nearer to an answer, it would seem."

"But Dolly was ridden here on the morning that Captain Bray was killed, m'lady," Mrs. Jackson pointed out, "if not by Lieutenant Carmichael then certainly by someone else." She could tell that her ladyship was scraping herself back together after a severe disappointment.

"Walter saw rider and horse just after one o'clock in the wheat field. Whoever rode her up to the kitchen garden had all the time in the world to murder Captain Bray by half past two o'clock."

Chapter Twenty-Three

Two days later, Mrs. Jackson was pleasantly surprised to find a yellow telegram envelope sitting on her desk. Her heart gave a little leap when she saw that it was from Lieutenant E. Stafford of the Graves Registration Commission in Auchonvillers, France. She groped for the back of her chair and pulling it aside was already halfway through its cryptic message before she sat down.

```
PTE. P. HECTOR KIA B. OF BEAUVILLE WOOD 16 MAR. 1916.
LIEUT. I. L. CARMICHAEL INJ. B. OF BEAUVILLE WOOD 16 MAR. 1916
CAPT. SIR EVELYN BRAY INJ. B. OF BEAUVILLE WOOD 16 MAR. 1916
THERE WAS ONLY ONE OTHER SURVIVOR AFTER THE BATTLE IN CAPT.
BRAY'S COMPANY 16 MAR:
PTE. S. GLENN INJ. B. OF BEAUVILLE WOOD 16 MAR. 1916
WHAT IS GOING ON?-E.S.
```

She read the telegram through several times. *So there is a connection between Bray, Carmichael, and Hector: they weren't just in the same battalion of the Gloucestershire Regiment, they were all in the same company, too,* she thought as she made sense of the abbreviated forms. *KIA means killed in action and I expect Inj. is an abbreviation of injured.* And someone else had been there too on that particular day, a Private S. Glenn, who had survived the battle along with Lieutenant Carmichael and Captain Bray.

It is not unthinkable that this P. Hector is the enlisted man in Captain Bray's portrait. Following on this revelation came the immediate question: *If all four men were in Captain Bray's company, then why didn't he acknowledge one of his own men, whether he was Carmichael or Hector, when he arrived at Haversham Hall two weeks ago? Perhaps he did and that is the reason why he was murdered, or perhaps his memory was not sufficiently formed to remember him!* And finally: *There is a connection between Hector and Carmichael, we just don't know yet what it is!*

She sat, brows down, and tried to find the sense behind this new information. Hector, Carmichael, Bray, and Glenn. Three of these men might have survived the Battle of Beauville Wood, but now two of them were dead. *And who is this Private Glenn?* Was he still in France after his injury or was it a "Blighty one"—an injury bad enough to return him home to Blighty as the soldiers nostalgically referred to England. And if this was the case he must have survived the war so far, otherwise he would have been listed in the telegram as killed in action.

Mrs. Jackson sat on in the quiet of her office. She heard distant footsteps along the corridor outside her room. A door opened somewhere and then slammed shut. Her frown grew deeper. Surely Major Andrews might shed more light on what had happened to Lieutenant Carmichael after the Battle of Beauville Wood. *But will he give me information about his patients?* She pushed back her chair and got to her feet. *He has all the reason in the world to help me solve this mess before the men from the Medical Board arrive with their attaché cases, dossiers, and forms in triplicate.* Picking up a stack of requisition forms that needed the major's signature, she left her office and walked down the corridor, hoping that she would find him in his office.

"Come!" the major's voice called out as she tapped on his door.

"Ah, good afternoon, Mrs. Jackson, yes, come on in. Now what can I do for you?" He was sitting in the bay window with a file in his lap and a cup of tea on the table next to him. He got to his feet and turned the chair next to his away from the direct sunlight. "Would you like a cuppa?" Without waiting for her answer, he opened the door to the orderlies' office and returned with a cup and saucer. "Don't suppose Lady Montfort has heard anything from Colonel Valentine or Inspector Savor? Do they really believe that Sir Winchell is our murderer?" He made an attempt to be lighthearted, but she could tell by the lines of fatigue around his eyes that he rather hoped that Sir Winchell's arrest meant the end of this ugly business. It would sit better with the War Office bureaucrats that murder had been committed by an angry old man in the neighborhood, rather than one of their patients in the hospital.

She took a sip of tepid tea and decided it would be best if she avoided an answer to this question. "Do you remember we found that portrait painted by Captain Bray, the one that had a strong likeness to Lieutenant Carmichael?"

He leaned forward, and his intelligent eyes met hers and held their gaze. "Yes, but he had painted the name Hector at the bottom of the painting, not Carmichael, most intriguing. I have it over here, brought it down from the art room this morning." He jumped up from his chair, walked over to the wall and picked up a canvas leaning against it. Then, standing close to the window, he held it at arm's length. Mrs. Jackson joined him. "Such a good portrayal of Carmichael," the captain said. "Almost a caricature: the oiled-down yellow hair. It is unmistakably Carmichael—his ears sort of winged out a bit at the tip and he had that habit of quirking his right eyebrow. I think Bray captured his characteristics really rather well." He looked up from the painting; his face had the encouraging sort of look that expects an observation to be acknowledged.

She could not help but agree. "Yes, I have to admit it is very like him." She hesitated. "Except for the name." Major Andrews tilted the painting and they looked down at the bottom of the canvas.

She decided to take the plunge, what was there to lose? "Private Hector actually, sir, a Private P. Hector was killed on the sixteenth of March at the Battle of Beauville Wood. You see, sir, it would appear that Bray, Carmichael, and Hector all took part in the battle that day. Hector was killed and Captain Bray and Lieutenant Carmichael were injured. I think there might be a connection between the three of them. And I am hoping that with a little more information we can give this information to Colonel Valentine so he can solve the rest of this mystery." He had listened to all she had said in silence, but she could almost hear him processing the facts and then carefully storing them away.

"Yes, I suppose they might have been in the same regiment, but there are or were probably over a thousand men in the Glorious Glosters, they couldn't all have known each other. Now if they were in the same battalion or better still the same company, that would be another thing entirely." Major Andrews put down the painting, straightened up, and stood there looking at her. "And what I would like to know, Mrs. Jackson, is how did you manage to come by this information? How did you know both Carmichael and Bray were in the same regiment at Beauville Wood?" His eyes were no longer thoughtful but alert and curious. *Oh my Lord, what have I done? In my impatience I might have completely ruined all our work.* Gone was the easygoing Major Andrews; he was looking at her in a way that made her feel distinctly uncomfortable, as if he was in the middle of making a difficult decision.

She drew herself up. *Whatever you do now, Edith, you have to be straight with this man, he is far too perceptive and much too intelligent to brush off with some incidental excuse.* "I have a close friend who is with the Graves Registration Commission in France. After I found Captain Bray's painting I wrote to him about these men:

Carmichael and Bray. I included the name of Hector since that was the name on the painting. And he sent me a telegram with the information I just gave to you. I know it is none of my business, but if you are willing to help me find out a little more, we might be able to help the police clear up this mess before the Medical Board review. Her ladyship does not want the hospital closed, Major Andrews, any more than you do."

He stood tugging on the corner of his mustache for a moment or two. And then to her relief she caught the bright, humorous glance of his eyes as he said, "Yes, I see exactly what you mean. Something happened between the three of these men, didn't it? Something conveniently hidden, perhaps by Captain Bray's amnesia." They gazed down at the portrait of Lieutenant Carmichael or Private Hector. "Bray had still some way to go to regain his memory when he painted this in April," the major said almost to himself. Then he gestured with his right hand toward his desk and the chair on the other side of it. Teatime was over, and their meeting had become formal. Mrs. Jackson sat down in the upright chair on the other side of the desk from the major. His face was empty of expression. She was still unsure which way this conversation was going to go.

Major Andrews leaned forward, resting his folded arms on the top of his desk. "Like all war heroes, Captain Bray took risks—he took tremendous risks to save his men, and he was well liked and respected as a leader. He was mentioned in dispatches, recommended at one time for a Victoria Cross. But what a price these heroes pay." He rapped the top of his desk lightly with his knuckles as he recalled Bray's history. "According to the filed report, Captain Bray and a small group of his were cut off from the rest of his company at Beauville Wood. We have no idea what happened because when Bray struggled back to our lines two days later he was pretty much done for. He brought with him a private whom he had half carried, half led for miles. The man had been wounded in the head and had lost his sight. Bray was in a pretty bad way, he had sustained a minor injury, but he was completely exhausted, drained from months of combat. The only thing he could report was that out of the four of the men stranded near to the enemy lines, only he and the private had survived so far. He had left a dead man behind and he thought that a fourth man was missing; he was practically incoherent. That is all his commanding officer entered in his report for that day, but it was the eighteenth of March when Captain Bray made it back. When he regained consciousness two days later, his memory had gone completely—he was no longer lucid—and he was sent home to Craiglockhart with amnesia as a direct result of battle fatigue and what the newspapers like to call shell-shock." He sat back in his chair and folded his arms. It was up to her to ask her next question.

"Sir, would you be prepared to take a look at Lieutenant Carmichael's file, to see if there is anything in there that mentions Beauville Wood and the battle that day?"

He was already pulling open desk drawers and searching for a key to the cabinet in which he kept his patients' information. "Carmichael, Carmichael," he muttered as he flicked through the card dossiers in the top drawer. "Yes, here it is." He walked back to his desk, tossed the file down on its surface, and stood over it turning pages. Mrs. Jackson forced herself to stay in her chair.

"Yes, it says that Lieutenant Carmichael survived the Battle of Beauville Wood with a mild injury to his head, which may have caused him to suffer shock. He was rather a puzzling patient." He looked across the desk at her and she felt a little stir of excitement. *Now we are getting to it,* she thought as she watched him look back down at the closely written pages. She had noticed before that when the major was pondering a problem he often hummed in a soft, tuneless drone, but now he was completely silent.

"On the day he arrived here, Carmichael was suffering from mutism. But within twenty-four hours of his arrival he was struggling to form words and then within two days only occasionally suffered from blocked speech—stammering his consonants just slightly. It is easy for men at the front to pick up on the outward signs of neurasthenia, you see, because sufferers exhibit certain symptoms of what they call shell-shock for quite some time until they break down completely and have to be given local leave, or in more serious cases are sent home to us in England."

"Are you saying that Lieutenant Carmichael had learned one set of symptoms in France, and that after he arrived here he displayed another?" She noticed the slight dip of his head before he looked down to turn a page of notes.

"In other words, was Lieutenant Carmichael pretending to suffer from neurasthenia?" she pursued, and he smiled and raised his eyebrows. "He was, wasn't he, sir?"

He smiled at her in a particularly congratulatory way and then turned his attention back to his notes. "To form a diagnosis on a man's mental state is often a lengthy and time-consuming business, Mrs. Jackson. But if you are going to simplify things it would seem that his symptoms varied perhaps more than most patients' suffering from neurasthenia."

She wondered how best to get the answers she wanted and realized that sometimes all it took was a directly honest question. She tried again. "I think that perhaps the man we know as Lieutenant Carmichael was not only faking neurasthenia, his change of symptoms tells us something else too," she said and watched him closely.

"Sounds like you have formed an interesting theory, Mrs. Jackson." His smile was encouraging and so she continued.

"I understand that studies of battle fatigue and neurasthenia show that the men, the enlisted men, lock down in complete silence or mutism as you call it."

"Yes, that is so, they withdraw; they are physically unable to speak."

"But officers do not suffer in the same way. They try to communicate no matter how distressed they are. They stutter and stammer; what you call blocked speech, am I right?"

"Yes, that is so."

"When Lieutenant Carmichael came to Haversham Hall suffering from mutism, might he have taken a good look at the patients here, our officers, and parodied their symptoms? Did he realize that he was faking the wrong symptoms for an officer?" Major Andrews was gazing at her across his desk with a particularly intense expression. "And then perhaps if he was faking his symptoms," she tried not to sound too excited, too triumphant, "he was also faking his rank and possibly who he was."

Major Andrews brought his right hand down and placed it on top of his desk in a sort of "right on the money" motion, his eyes wide as if he too had just learned something quite useful. "Now, if you will forgive me, Mrs. Jackson, I must leave you, I have a consultation with Lieutenant Phipps, who is waiting for me in the medical wing." And with that he walked across the room and out of the door, leaving Mrs. Jackson still sitting on the other side of his desk, looking at the open dossier on its surface.

Chapter Twenty-Four

She sat quite still in Major Andrews's silent office for a moment or two after he left, her eyes on the dossier. *Oh for heaven's sake, woman, have a look.* Upper servants did not, and did not allow those who worked for them, to read other people's letters or diaries, and they did not creep around people's offices reading confidential documents. It simply was not done. *But you are not sneaking, Edith; he gave you a very clear go-ahead before he left. Just have a good look before you leave. This will be your only chance.*

She reached out and slid the dossier across the desk toward her. She would not read the notes Major Andrews had written about his patient, all she needed was the War Office information at the front of the file. She turned back the pages. And there it was, a form pinned to the inside of the dossier's front cover, neatly filled in blue ink. Name: Ian Livingstone Carmichael, Second Lieutenant, Company A, Eighth Battalion, Gloucestershire Regiment. Born: 5th August, 1890. Religion: C. of E. Next of kin: a dash indicated there were none, and then the town in which Carmichael had joined up as Cheltenham in Gloucestershire. At the bottom of the page was a note by his commanding officer of the Eighth Battalion, Colonel Varron; the writing was cramped and small and stated mild head injury on sixteenth of March at the Battle of Beauville Wood. Lieutenant Carmichael had been separated from his company and had somehow made his way back to friendly lines and reported to another regiment in the St. Cyprien area ten miles to the south of his company's position on 20th June, 1916—suffering from shell-shock. There was one more file out and it was sitting in a flat wicker basket. She turned the basket and read, "Captain Sir Evelyn Bray, DSO, MC." She slid the file across the desk and cracked it open at the first page. The form was completed with almost the same information as Carmichael's. Captain Bray had been the commanding officer of Company A, with the Eighth Battalion of the Gloucestershires, wounded on 16 March at the Battle of Beauville Wood. Date of birth was 3 January 1886, with the address of Brayley Hall, Brayley, Gloucestershire. His next of kin was Edgar Laurence Bray, brother. And she noted that he had also joined up in Cheltenham.

Yes, they knew one another all right, they had both joined in Cheltenham as well as being in the same company and the same battalion. She closed the file and put it back into the basket. And with her hastily scribbled notes she left Major Andrews's office and made her way back to her own.

She closed the door quietly behind her as if she was worried someone would hear her, and feeling quite shaky with the enormity of her discovery she walked over to her desk and sat down. Something Mr. Hollyoak had told her flashed into her mind about the men who had volunteered at the beginning of the war: "When Lord Northolt's son joined up in 1914 he took most of the young men from the surrounding area with him. His valet and two footmen from the house, the vicar's son, several boys from the estate and the tenant farms, and even the local squire's son had all joined on the same day. They made up an entire company when they went marching off to war. And then after the Battle of Ypres, which took such heavy casualties, the telegrams came pouring in. Pretty near half of the village, the men on the estate, and the cream of the county all went in one day. Wiped out just like that. It doesn't bear thinking about, does it?"

Is this what happened in the case of Captain Sir Evelyn Bray? Did he go off to war with boys from the estate and village, and sons of the local gentry? If this was true, then surely it would be easy to find out more about this Private Hector and Lieutenant Carmichael, and perhaps if they were lucky to speak to this other man who had been there on that day, who had presumably been invalided out of the war if he had lost his sight. What was his name again? She opened the telegram: Private S. Glenn. *If they were all in Captain Bray's company they might have known one another before the war.*

There was now only one man alive out of the original four who might be able to help them with what had happened in northern France on the sixteenth of March, and it was Private S. Glenn.

Mrs. Jackson pulled writing paper toward her and picked up her pen. When she had finished her letter she put it in an envelope, walked to Sister Carter's office, and hunted through regimental directories until she found the address of the Gloucestershire Regiment's headquarters. She addressed and stamped the envelope and tucked it into the postbag in the hall. And because she was now very behindhand with her duties she busied herself to finish the roster of work to ready the hospital for the Medical Board's inspection so that she could go over to Iyntwood and report in to her commanding officer.

"Yes, do come in, Jackson, I can tell you have made discoveries." Her ladyship was dressed for dinner but she waved her housekeeper to her customary chair, her eyes bright with curiosity.

"Here is a telegram from Mr. Stafford, m'lady. And I had a most interesting and useful conversation with Major Andrews." She wasted no time giving her a detailed account of the information he had made available to her from his files. When she had finished, her ladyship sat staring at her with a gratifying expression on her face that said: *How on earth do you do it?*

"When he was last on home leave, m'lady, Mr. Stafford told me about these identity disks all our men wear in combat carrying their name, regiment number, and religion. There are two of them: an octagonal green disk attached to a long cord that goes around the neck, with a second circular red disk attached by a six-inch cord. When a man is killed in action the red one is taken by whoever finds his body and they turn it in to their commanding officer so that men can be accounted for just after battle. The green disk remains on the body for future identification and is only removed when its wearer is buried." Her ladyship was nodding along, waiting. Jackson took a deep breath. "If, after a battle, a man wanted to change his identity, then all he had to do was switch his identity disks with a man who had been killed. And if he was an enlisted man and he wanted to assume the identity of an officer, he could exchange his battledress for the shirt, tie, and tunic of an officer. It would be that simple."

"What about their trousers: enlisted men wear puttees, don't they, and cavalry officers wear riding breeches and riding boots?" her ladyship asked.

Mrs. Jackson almost blushed. "I believe that officers rarely wear their cavalry boots at the front, m'lady, when they are in combat. Corporal Budge told me they wear puttees like the enlisted men, stops them being identified by enemy snipers."

Lady Montfort frowned. "But his comrades would recognize him, Jackson."

"Of which there were very few, m'lady. It appears that Company A, Captain Bray's company, only had three survivors after the Battle of Beauville: Captain Bray, who had lost his memory; Private Glen, who had lost his sight; and Lieutenant Carmichael, who went missing after the battle and turned up further down the line with a mild head injury and shell-shock. It seems everyone else was killed."

"How on earth did you manage all of this, Jackson? In such a short space of time, I mean? In just twenty-four hours you have moved us forward with this marvelous work—well done."

Mrs. Jackson felt the tips of her ears grow warm. However wonderful it was to be congratulated, she felt that all she had really accomplished was deepening their inquiry into a darker abyss of perennial what-ifs.

"The information was there for us, m'lady, it was just a question of knowing where to go for it. And in war the system is in place to document everything, but as we realized the other day, after battle it is probably easy for people to disappear, or even switch their identity. Now I just hope we can work out the rest of this riddle." But her ladyship appeared to be quite undaunted by the prospect of more unraveling. Her eyes glowed as she reviewed this new information.

"So really what we are looking at is that these four men—Bray, Carmichael, Hector, and Glenn—were together on a particular day in an event that happened after they survived the Battle of Beauville Wood. Of whom one died of his injuries, one was separated from the others, and one was injured, to be brought back by Captain Bray to safety. And it would appear that this incident was pretty much the last straw for Captain Bray because he lost his memory." Mrs. Jackson remained silent, and waited, as she watched her ladyship think this through. *If anyone will see a way, she will, her mind leaps over the little things like practicalities and rules and she will see what my methodical thinking often misses.*

Standing tall and slender, a silver column in her evening dress, her half-moon spectacles glinting in the lamplight, her ladyship continued. "So this Private Glenn might be able to help us understand the missing details of what happened on the sixteenth of March. But in the meantime, there are some things we have already deduced that point the way." She lifted her right hand, and Mrs. Jackson smiled. *Here we go,* she thought, *this is where she takes off,* and she waited to be enlightened. Her ladyship was a little erratic in her approach sometimes, relying as she did on instinct or intuition or whatever you chose to call it, but she always turned up interesting ideas and stimulated their thinking.

"First of all, Captain Bray, helped by the therapies of Major Andrews, is emerging from the clouds. The portrait of Private Hector is a direct message from the foggy mind of Captain Bray." Mrs. Jackson nodded in agreement. "When Private Hector turns up at my hospital masquerading as Lieutenant Carmichael with his fake neurosis, Captain Bray does not appear to recognize him, but he is killed less than ten days later, which means that Hector came here with a plan." She paused and smiled. "He came here to kill the captain before his memory returned completely, before he could have Hector arrested for desertion and for impersonating an officer.

"And if Captain Bray and Lieutenant Carmichael knew one another before the war, then surely Mr. Edgar Bray would have recognized Hector as an imposter on the afternoon of his arrival? Were they working together?"

Mrs. Jackson looked doubtful for a moment. But her ladyship was off again: "Hector alias Carmichael contrived a strong alibi for the day of Captain Bray's murder: he spent the morning with my daughter, took Dolly down to her pasture, and then joined her for a picnic luncheon just twenty minutes later." Her ladyship drew in a breath and fell silent for a moment. "Perhaps this is what happened. At the end of their plowing lesson, Hector alias Carmichael came down to the pasture at Brook End Lane and set Dolly free. Mr. Edgar Bray was waiting for him in his stalled motorcar right there on the lane. Off they go up to the kitchen garden together in Mr. Bray's motorcar." Mrs. Jackson's expression changed from doubtful to disappointed. "Everyone was having luncheon,

Jackson, there was no one to see them. Hector alias Carmichael kills the captain and they drive back to Brook End Lane, where Hector goes off to his picnic with my daughter, and returns afterwards with her, where they bump into the stranded Mr. Bray." She was now speaking through tight lips, practically spitting out her words. "Lady Althea mends the motorcar and on they all go."

Mrs. Jackson almost shook her head. "But, m'lady, who was that on Dolly, seen at exactly the right time of the afternoon riding in the direction of the kitchen garden? There are even hoofprints going in both directions. Mr. Thrower could have easily seen or heard a motorcar on the drive."

"Oh bother! And I suppose a motorcar could not possibly go up the footpath!"

Mrs. Jackson sighed in sympathy. "Yes, you are right, m'lady, it all falls apart right there." Lady Montfort got up and raised the lower sash of the window, letting in hot and humid air, and continued as if Mrs. Jackson had not voiced the big hole that was Dolly's inability to thunder across country like a Thoroughbred. "Well, never mind that bit for a moment. If Mr. Bray and Hector-Carmichael planned this murder together, why would Mr. Bray arrange to meet him just outside our house and shoot him?" She stopped, her hands palm upward, her face beseeching. "Oh bother it all!"

"Yes, it is rather unlikely, m'lady, when all Mr. Bray had to do was point out that the man posing as Carmichael was an imposter with an ulterior motive for killing his brother. Everyone would believe the brother rather than a cowardly imposter. And we are not able to prove that the man we know as Lieutenant Carmichael was really Private Hector. "

Lady Montfort stood in the window, her arms folded, and glared at a sparrow singing his evening song on a branch outside. "I am quite sure he was an imposter and one with an ironclad alibi, which prevents him from being Captain Bray's murderer—it is up to us to break his alibi, Jackson."

It is the How that we always ask ourselves at this point, Mrs. Jackson thought. *How did Carmichael get to the kitchen garden and back on Dolly in twenty minutes? We have struggled with this one for days now and where are we? Nowhere.* It was time, Mrs. Jackson thought, to help them look at it another way.

"Might Mr. Bray be connected more closely to the death of his brother, m'lady? Do we know what time his motorcar broke down?"

"It was well after one o'clock. I am not quite sure what time Carmichael and Lady Althea finished with their picnic." Her ladyship had lost her spark; her voice was quiet and her manner almost apathetic.

"But Mr. Bray does have a motive, doesn't he, and a good one I would have thought, m'lady. With the first son dead, who inherits?" For the first time since the beginning of this inquiry, Mrs. Jackson felt that this question should perhaps have been asked before. Lady Montfort evidently did not, for she sighed about the heat of the afternoon, before she rallied.

"Now there's an interesting topic—the business of inheritance, such a complex issue in this country, Jackson, especially where title and land are concerned. I see your train of thought with this one, because it makes sense to consider it. The Bray family is rich, their estate, Brayley, is quite considerable and has been in the family for centuries, and I believe if memory serves that the Brays own the mineral rights to coalfields in Derbyshire. They are a rich, landed, old family. So Mr. Bray, now that his brother is dead, will become Sir Edgar Bray—considerably better placed in society with a much larger bank account than he had when his brother was alive. He has every motive for murder."

Mrs. Jackson politely cleared her throat.

"So, m'lady, Mr. Bray comes down to visit his brother with the intent of killing him. He stops at the kitchen garden on his way to Iyntwood, kills the captain, and then organizes the breakdown of his motorcar to give himself an alibi."

"Yes, that would be absolutely acceptable, but Mr. Bray is severely incapacitated, he can only walk with the aid of a stick—he can't even climb the stairs in the house without help. He would have had to walk into the kitchen garden and I am not sure he is steady enough on his legs to have killed a very fit man." She looked across the room at her housekeeper. "Why the frown, Jackson?"

"It's Dolly, m'lady. We know that Walter Howard saw a horse and rider going along the footpath at the time the murder could have been committed."

"Maybe it was a farmer's son who decided to take the horse for a gallop? Dolly's run from the lane to the kitchen garden might have nothing to do with the murder at all."

Mrs. Jackson felt almost annoyed. "Mr. Bray was at Brook End Lane in his broken-down motorcar, right by the horse pasture. M'lady, I am wondering if Mr. Bray rode Dolly?"

But her ladyship was already shaking her head. "No, Jackson, it simply won't wash. If you saw Mr. Bray you would understand, his right leg was badly damaged in a hunting accident. He can no longer ride. It cannot have been him. And another thing, perhaps Mr. Bray did not recognize Private Hector being introduced to him as Lieutenant Carmichael because he had never met him." She closed her eyes and lifted both hands to hold her head as if to stop it from spinning. "I need to have a talk with my daughter," she said, "get her impressions of their meeting in Brook End Lane, and we should be ready to run off to Gloucestershire as soon as we can locate this Corporal Glenn. Because we certainly need more information about who is who, and this Glenn person might be able to supply it."

Chapter Twenty-Five

Clementine was up early and ready for whatever the morning would bring. *It can't be this hot so early in the day,* she thought as she walked along the corridor to her daughter's room before Althea left for Holly Farm.

"Are you coming too, Mama?" Althea asked as she took in her practical gardening clothes.

"No, darling. I thought I would show Mr. Bray the rose garden, since he cannot come with you to the farm, and he must be bored to tears sitting in the library all day. But before you go I wanted to ask you something." Althea's face assumed an expression of daughterly obedience. "How was Mr. Bray when you came upon him in his broken-down motorcar the other day?" Althea looked at her as if she hadn't understood. "I mean what was he doing, just sitting in his motor?"

Althea looked even more puzzled. "Yes, he was sitting in his motor." She hesitated and then added, "He was awfully pleased to see us."

"How did he know who you were?"

"I introduced both of us. He said something like, 'Rescued at long last, I've been stranded here for hours. I'm on my way to Iyntwood and my wretched motor stalled and I can't get it going.' I told him that Papa was the Earl of Montfort and who I was. And he said his name was Edgar Bray and I realized that he couldn't have gone very far for help because of, you know . . . his leg."

"And Lieutenant Carmichael, where was he when this conversation was going on?"

"Just standing there; I introduced him, and he said he knew nothing about mending engines, poor Ian." Her face fell at the thought of the murdered man.

"You didn't get the impression that they might have known one another. Perhaps met before?" Clementine asked before Althea could dwell too long on poor Ian.

Althea looked so startled that her voice was almost loud in the quiet corridor "No . . . of course not—why would you think that?" and Clementine hastily tried to cover her tracks by saying, "I am sorry darling; it must be the weather, such a headache this morning. I can't imagine how they could have met before."

Clementine worked methodically through the rose bed closest to where Mr. Bray was sitting, reading a pamphlet on cross-strains of sheep bred to produce both high-quality wool and the springtime lamb that graced every table in the country with a roast joint on Sunday. Occasionally she threw the odd remark or question at him, until with the utmost patience he put his pamphlet down and gave her the attention she required.

"I think we have become a much closer farming community here since the beginning of the war. Don't you find that we depend on our neighbors even more than we did a couple of years ago?" She kept to the only interest in common they might have, that of being a landowner or a woman married to one—he certainly couldn't care tuppence for roses since scarcely an exclamation of appreciation had he made on their arrival in the garden. He had patiently waited for Hollyoak to organize a lawn chair and set a jug of lemonade on a little table next to him in one of the most acclaimed rose gardens of the decade without even a glance at its exquisite symmetry of design and equally glorious specimens.

"Arable farming must be hard with so many men in the military. Sheep farming has always been about the shepherd and his dogs. And since most good shepherds are elderly men I have been most fortunate. It is lambing time and shearing that present the real problem. Lady Althea suggested I talk to my local Land Army office, she has been most helpful."

She bent down to tie up the heavy head of the Madame Plantier rose that tended to flop a little on its slender stem; its scent filled the morning air and she stopped work to enjoy it. "Yes, so much has changed, and not just in the country. Althea says that London is full of young men and women going to nightclubs, but I have not had the time to go to town since we opened Haversham Hall."

"Never go there myself, can't stand the place," he said as is eyes wandered back to his pamphlet. "Like your lovely daughter, I am quite contented in the country." *And unlike your man-about-town brother,* she thought as it occurred to her that even before the war this brother had stayed at home to run the estate, while the other had enjoyed a more cosmopolitan existence. They had undoubtedly moved in different social circles and perhaps did not share the same friends. But Lieutenant Carmichael was from Gloucestershire and he had joined up in Cheltenham, so there was a very strong chance Edgar Bray knew him. She decided to keep Althea the center of their conversation and lead it back to the day his motor had broken down on Brook End Lane.

"We offered our London house to the War Office as a private hospital," she explained. "But Althea has no interest in nursing, she is far more interested in the business of farming," she tested, also hoping to find out whether or not this man had any interest in her daughter, or whether he was still a guest in their house for other reasons. She had his immediate attention. "She is immensely knowledgeable for such a young woman."

He put down his pamphlet and poured two glasses of lemonade, and getting to his feet he picked one up and with the aid of his stick walked very carefully to her. He had not filled it quite to the top, so it didn't spill. "Hot work gardening in this weather, Lady Montfort." He offered her the glass. "Your garden is quite lovely." He looked around him at the house, its grounds, and out toward the sweep of land below them with approval. "No wonder Althea is so happy here."

"Thank you." She sipped lemonade and thought of her daughter's addiction to travel before the war. "Yes, she has always loved the country, far more so than our son. Harry is passionately interested in anything mechanical. Althea should have been a boy!" She handed him her empty glass and bent to tie a strong knot to anchor the wayward rose in its place.

"That would have been a terrible waste." His smile as he referred to Althea was tender, and was it the heat of the morning or did Clementine imagine that he colored? She beamed her approval and managed to bite back an exclamation of annoyance as Madame Plantier sprang away from her gloved hands and scratched the tender inside of her arm.

"Althea had just finished giving Lieutenant Carmichael a plowing lesson the morning you arrived, before she found you on Brook End Lane," she said as they walked back to the table together and sat down in the shade. "Actually, Lieutenant Carmichael told Althea that he came from your neck of the woods. I am surprised you did not know him." She put down her half-finished lemonade, as someone in the kitchen had put in too much sugar and it was far too sweet for her taste.

"Gloucestershire is a large county, Lady Montfort, and the estate keeps me continually busy so I am afraid I don't accept invitations as often as I used to. My brother is, I mean was, far more sociable than I am. We did not see much of one another in the last couple of years, but it is hard to believe he has gone," he said, and she turned her head away and gazed at her rose garden, feeling gauche and unmannerly.

"So awfully upsetting for you . . . for all of us . . ." she said to cover her embarrassment at her uncomfortably direct questions.

He quickly made it all right for her: "Yes, after everything Evelyn went through it was his fate to bump into that very unhappy old man. I think we sometimes forget that grief can unhinge even the steadiest of us. Any news of Sir Winchell's trial?"

"Quite soon I expect."

He nodded, and taking his stout walking stick he planted it firmly so that he could get to his feet, and Clementine glancing over her shoulder saw the distant figure of her husband approaching across the lawn. "This business is most distressing for you and your family, Lady Montfort, especially since Sir Winchell is an old friend." She looked up; his eyebrows were raised in regretful commiseration as he started to get to his feet, and she saw, too late, that his heavy stick was caught between the chair leg and its stretcher. A look of acute alarm crossed his face as he put his weight on his good leg and tried to bring his stick forward and could not. For a moment he panicked, abandoning his stick and reaching back for the chair's arm for support. Clementine whipped around the table and took him firmly by his upper arm and held him until he regained his balance. There was a moment of silence, and then Mr. Bray laughed. "So sorry about that, Lady Montfort." He shook his head, his face rueful. "Thank you, you saved me from a tumble there, well at least the lawn is soft." And then as if nothing had happened at all he disentangled his stick and walked forward to greet her husband.

It took this considerate and thoughtful man nearly fifteen minutes to walk to the rose garden, a distance I can easily cover in less than five. How could I even imagine for one moment that he walked up to his brother and hit him hard enough on the head to kill him without completely losing his balance? Clementine felt so unimaginably disgusted with herself that she returned to her rose beds and snipped off withered blooms left and right to avoid joining the two men standing in the sun discussing with considerable energy the many men who were languishing in Market Wingley prison as conscientious objectors.

Chapter Twenty-Six

"Good morning, Jackson. Anything from the Glorious Glosters?" Her ladyship loomed out of the bright light of day and into the gloom of the hall looking tired and dusty in her broad gardening hat.

"Good morning, m'lady." She tried not to notice that her ladyship had tracked in a considerable amount of planting compost. She was not used to seeing Lady Montfort in such a state of dishevelment. "Nothing in the first post, I'm afraid."

Mrs. Jackson had spent a busy and frustrating morning with VAD Ellis, Corporals Budge and West, and the scullery maid organizing for the Medical Board inspection. She concentrated her hope that even if two of their officers had been brutally murdered, the five bureaucrats who would decide the fate of the hospital would find the gleaming floors, shining windows, and the orderly medical wing complete compensation for a hospital that evidently had no control over its patients. *And not only close us down,* she worried as she had paced between the medical wing and the officers' mess, holding a duster and being unnecessarily critical to her scurrying workers, *but decide that Major Andrews is an incompetent commanding officer and his compassionate treatments complete nonsense.*

"So all of our officers are over at Holly Farm today. Did they let poor Lieutenant Phipps out of his room yet to join them? Though I hardly envy him in this terrible heat."

"Yes, m'lady, Lieutenant Phipps went off with the others. They certainly came home tired out yesterday but they ate a decent dinner and turned in at nine o'clock. And every one of them is looking forward to the harvest supper tonight. I think that our officers' helping with the harvest has done a lot for local acceptance of the hospital." *Not that their good opinion will influence the War Office when they decide to close this place down.*

They walked down the corridor together and into her office. The heat in the room was stifling. Mrs. Jackson opened the heavy sash windows as far as they would go, but it made no difference. A bead of sweat trickled down the nape of her neck into what had been a stiffly starched collar this morning and was now mercifully softening its tight grip around her throat.

"Mrs. Jackson?" Corporal West was standing in her open doorway. "Sorry to interrupt, Mrs. Jackson, but this dropped out of the postbag when you were looking just now." Corporal West had in his hand a buff envelope. "Didn't know you had a family member with the Glosters."

Lady Montfort practically pushed her out of the way to take the envelope. "Thank you very much, Corporal," she said, and then remembering herself she turned to her housekeeper and handed over the letter. "I am so sorry, Jackson. How awfully rude of me, it is the anxiety of waiting, my apologies." But Mrs. Jackson had already torn open the envelope.

Dear Madam, she read aloud.

In answer to your letter . . . she skipped down to the next paragraph. *Private Samuel Glenn was invalided out of the regiment on 30th March of this year, and after treatment has returned home. All correspondence to be*

*forwarded to 10 Balaclava Street, Cheltenham, W.
Gloucestershire.*

She held out the letter to her ladyship, who read it through and
then waved it in the air. "The wonderful, wonderful Private Glenn
is in Cheltenham! At last, there is someone who can throw some
light on this mystery," and then as was customary when Lady
Montfort rushed too quickly to enthusiasm: "But we don't have
two whole days to waste with polite letters asking to visit, and
hopefully a pleasant response saying, 'Yes, how delightful, come
for tea.'"

"I am quite sure the Glenn family would understand if we were
to arrive unannounced on official business, m'lady." Mrs. Jackson was already searching through her desk drawer for a Bradshaw's
Guide. She thumbed through the pages. "Unfortunately, our train
journey just to Cheltenham would take the better part of today,
that is if we caught the twelve-fifteen from Cryer's Breach and there
are two . . . no, three changes of train."

"Train, Jackson, why would we take a train? Lord Haversham
will drive us—there and back—in the Daimler. He can manage
to drive it quite well with one hand. It will take only a few hours
and I am quite sure this most useful and necessary Private Glenn
will be at home when we get there." Lady Montfort had returned
to her earlier mood of triumph, and she clapped her hands together, her face beaming out from under the shadow of the wide
brim of her hat. "Now, call in Corporal West and tell him to bicycle
over, fast as he can, to Iyntwood. No, on second thought, tell
Corporal West to drive me home in Major Andrew's motorcar,
and then he can go on to Lord Haversham while I change. Lord
Haversham and I will come over and pick you up in about an
hour." She stopped for a moment. "I will have to leave Lady Althea and Hollyoak in charge of the harvest supper, I am afraid.

Goodness only knows what they will come up with together. Would you ask your cook and scullery maid to offer their help, Jackson? If I am not there to restrain him Mr. Hollyoak can be somewhat grandiose, in which case he will need more than a few helping hands." And with that she was on her way, leaving Mrs. Jackson to hurry to the kitchen to give last-minute instructions to Cook.

"What do you have there, Jackson? Oh my goodness, sandwiches, how sensible of you, and what's in that?" Lady Montfort asked as Mrs. Jackson stowed away the cumbersome metal thermos flask somewhere near her feet.

"I thought we had better take some tea, m'lady," she said as if this were the rarest of commodities in England, not to be found anywhere outside of Iyntwood. They couldn't possibly make any journey without supplies.

Clementine leaned forward and slid open the glass window that separated the front of the Daimler from the back. "All right then, Harry, off we go," and her son, immaculate in his RNAS uniform, touched the brim of his hat with his right hand before he pulled out through the gates of the hospital.

"How long will it take to get there do you think?" Clementine asked for the second time as they swung down the east drive to the village at the sort of speed that Corporal West had probably employed as an ambulance driver in Boulogne. "If the roads are clear, probably a little under a couple of hours," her son answered just as patiently as he had the first time. But as they left the village of Cryer's Breach he had to slow the motor down to a walking pace not once but several times.

"Oh not another cart—how maddening. We will never find a place to get around it on this narrow stretch. The wretched thing is taking up the entire road!" Clementine exclaimed, and then stopped herself, as she knew she must not give way to despair quite so readily.

"Mama, half the countryside is bringing in the last of its harvest. I am afraid until we are on the other side of Market Wingley it will be slow going. But the road from there will be good to Oxford, and from Oxford we will take the Grand Trunk Road west to Cheltenham."

Clementine sat back and made herself relax. There was no point in badgering her son to drive more quickly, he was doing his best. She turned to Mrs. Jackson, who was looking marvelously official in her navy-blue VAD dress uniform. "If uniforms still stand for anything in Private Glenn's life, I am accompanied by a very smart and official-looking pair," she said and settled herself down to wait.

"I haven't been to Cheltenham in years, such a pretty spot—a Regency spa town, Jackson, and Gloucestershire is a lovely county. We used to come over here before the war to Lord Worley's house, the Worleys threw such lively house parties." She leaned forward to look out of the window at the quiet, tree-lined squares and terraces of houses. They drove down Montpelier Terrace and out of the town to a suburb on its western side.

Balaclava Street was on the outskirts of Cheltenham, part of a series of drab streets of meanly built Victorian domiciles built to house the working people of the town. "I am not terribly sure I can get the Daimler down Balaclava Street." Lord Haversham, nervous about little things like scratches on the coachwork, pulled the motorcar to a halt at the top of the narrow street. Their arrival immediately attracted the attention of several small boys who gathered around them as Harry peered anxiously down a street they evidently inhabited, or at least considered part of their territory. He leaned out the window. "Hullo there, I am looking for number ten Balaclava Street."

"Yus, sir." A little boy elbowed his way to the front of the silent crowd. "See that blue door?" His thin arm extended well beyond the edge of his frayed and buttonless cuff as he pointed a grubby forefinger. "That's number ten. Course yer gonna avta leave yer big posh motor 'ere, won't be able to fit down our street."

"Oh dear," Lady Montfort said, looking at the group of threadbare boys who were either crowded around the motor or, if they were older and taller, leaning back against the grimy brick walls of the street's terrace of houses, their arms folded. "Better stay here with the motor, Harry."

"I am not letting you out of this car on your own," her son said firmly. "I am quite sure they are perfectly decent boys . . . really."

"Are you the queen, then?" A skinny little boy with a runny nose and his hair sticking out from under his cap asked Clementine hopefully.

Clementine smiled. "No, I am afraid not," she said. She was used to the candor of the village children but no country child was ever this thin and worn-looking. "I am Clementine Talbot, and what is your name?"

"Cloive," the boy said in the round vowels of Gloucestershire.

"Well, Clive, do you know the name of the gentleman who lives at number ten?"

"Yus, 'is name's Mr. Glenn. 'E lives with 'is mum, Mrs. Glenn."

"You in the war then?" An older boy still propping up the wall levered himself forward with one elbow to address Harry. "How did you 'urt your arm?"

"Flying. I am a pilot in the Royal Naval Air Service." Lord Haversham got out of the motor and the group straightened up with new respect, and one of the smaller boys saluted and Harry returned it. "Now then, chaps, we are here to see a war hero on this street. We have come on special army business."

"Mr. Glenn was messed up good and proper in the war, are yer giving him a medal?"

And the one with the runny nose piped up, "Come on, sir, follow us, we'll take you to 'im."

"Good show," said Harry, and reaching out his hand he straightened the boy's cap. "Let's look smart about it then, and you . . ." He turned to the tallest boy, who had joined the small-fry on the curb, eyes alert for opportunities. "What's your name?"

"'Arry," the boy said.

"Same as me," said Harry. "I am Captain Harry Talbot. You?"

"'Arry Smith."

"Right then, Harry Smith, I want you to keep an eye on things here. Look after the motor and see no one touches it." Harry jingled loose change in his trouser pocket in an encouraging sort of way, and then opening the door for his mother and Mrs. Jackson he handed them out onto the street.

The gang of children marched up the street and stood in a group around them as Harry knocked on the door of number ten. Clementine was struck by the bleak poverty of the street she found herself in: not a tree gave shade in the relentless heat of the afternoon, paint had long peeled from casements and doors, and wherever there was space that offered bare earth there grew clumps of straggling weeds. As she stood in front of the shabby front door she realized that working-class people, especially those in the towns, were having a far worse time of it than anyone she knew in the country. She glanced at Jackson. "Well here we are, Jackson, let's hope that the Glenns are at home to see us." Mrs. Jackson evidently felt the same way as she did about the street and its inhabitants. She had opened up her handbag and was rapidly dispensing mint imperials to the youngest boys closest to her.

The woman who answered their knock was a tiny little thing. Seeing the smartly dressed trio on her doorstep, she lifted a soapstained hand to push wispy graying hair back away from her forehead. Her expression remained unchanged as her tired eyes took in their uniforms, coming to rest last of all on Clementine, who was standing behind the tall figure of her son. Her eyebrows lifted a little and Clementine stepped around Harry. "Good afternoon, I am Clementine Talbot and this is my son, Captain Harry Talbot, and Mrs. Jackson of Haversham Hall Hospital. I am hoping you are Mrs. Glenn?" She surely was Mrs. Glenn, as she looked old enough to be the mother of the twenty-two-year-old Private Glenn, and not his sister.

The woman wiped her hands on her apron. "Yes'm," she said, "I'm Mrs. Glenn. Have you come about Sam?" Clementine felt relief wash through her like a cool glass of water—so he was still living here and not tucked away in some out-of-the-way hospital. "Yes, we have come to see your son. Might we come in for a moment or two?" The door was opened wider to admit them, and they filed in. "I am afraid we are a bit cramped in here at the moment, Mrs. Talbot. I am staying with my daughter and her two young boys, all our men being at the war, except Sam." She stood to one side in invitation to walk down the narrow corridor that ran from the front door to the kitchen at the back of the narrow house, where several people were gathered eating what was evidently their cooked tea, as a strong smell of haddock wafted up to them.

"Mrs. Glenn, perhaps you should know that this is . . ." Mrs. Jackson started to say that Clementine was not Mrs. Talbot but the Countess of Montfort, but she shook her head. They were three invaders into the privacy of this woman's house, best not to overpower the situation with titles and rank.

Mrs. Glenn opened a door to the right and showed them into the stale, airless heat of her front parlor: a cramped room with a strip of drugget on bare boards, dark wallpaper, and three worn chairs arranged around a low deal table on which were the framed photographs of the men in Mrs. Glenn's family. All three of them were in uniform.

It was a moment before a young man came into the room accompanied by a thin woman in her late twenties whom Clementine judged to be Private Glenn's sister, for they bore a strong family resemblance to each other. Until the young man turned his head Clementine did not at first see the disfigured side of his face, puckered and seamed with recent scars, which pulled the eyelid and most of his cheek down on the right side of his face, almost to the edge of his nose. They were followed by two very young boys who stood looking at the three strangers towering over them. Mrs. Jackson groped in her handbag for the depleted bag of mint imperials.

"What do you say, Herbert?" the young woman said, pouncing on her eldest child as he thrust the offered sweet into his mouth, his eyes wide with delight. "What do you say to the nice lady?"

Herbert managed to say, "Thank you, miss." He looked up at his mother uncertainly; he was about five years old. "And God bless yer," he added as he took in Clementine's hat, perhaps wondering if she had anything interesting to offer.

Mrs. Glenn dusted off a horsehair chair with the tea towel she had been holding when she opened the front door. "Please to take a seat, ma'am," she said to Clementine and pulled a cretonne-covered side chair forward for Mrs. Jackson.

Clementine waited for everyone to settle themselves. Corporal Glenn, she noticed, had recovered some of his sight because when he turned the smooth, undamaged side of his face toward her, his left eye, which gazed thoughtfully at her, was quite clear. It was easy to see how this young man had looked before the war: a well-proportioned pleasant face, a firm jawline, and intelligent and alert brown eyes.

"I am awfully sorry to barge in on you like this without writing first, but we are here on a very important matter and must be as speedy as possible."

Clementine was hastily assured by the entire Glenn family that she was most welcome.

"Corporal Glenn, may I ask if you served under Captain Bray of the Gloucestershire Regiment when you were in France?" In the silence that followed her question, Clementine wondered if he had heard them, for the damaged half of his face remained completely devoid of expression. He turned his head to look at his sister as if asking her a silent question. When she nodded, he said, "Yes, I was. Old Hee-haw we used to call him." He almost smiled as he referred to his commanding officer, and Clementine remembered that Captain Bray's laugh, on the rare occasions she had heard it, had been rather like his name.

"And were you with Captain Bray and several other men on the sixteenth of March this year, when they were cut off from their company at Beauville Wood?" Another pause, and then Corporal Glenn said, "Yes, it was on the sixteenth at Beauville Wood, or what was left of it. I'll never forget it."

"I am sorry to bring back unpleasant memories, but do you remember the names of the other men with you?"

No pause this time. "Private Hector, Lieutenant Carmichael and me, and of course the captain." Lady Montfort glanced at Mrs. Jackson; her eyes were positively gleaming with triumph.

"Thank you. Would you please describe Lieutenant Carmichael for me? I mean height, build, coloring, that sort of thing."

If he found her question strange he did not look put out by it but said immediately, "He was a tall man, lanky like—brownish hair, dark eyes, ordinary-looking sort of bloke."

Clementine smiled her thank-you. "And what about private Hector? Can you describe him?"

Private Glenn almost smiled. "Hector was a good-looking chap and made the most of it at the town estaminet with the local girls. Goldish hair I suppose you would call it, and blue eyes. He was tall, well built."

Clementine caught Mrs. Jackson's eye; they were certainly on the right track so far.

"Thank you, Private Glenn. Now would you be prepared to tell me about that day, that is after you were cut off from the rest of your company?"

If he was puzzled why an upper-class, middle-aged woman was sitting here in his sister's parlor asking questions about battles in France, he had the manners not to look surprised. But he hesitated as if reluctant to put into the words the horrors of that day. Clementine leaned forward and said in her calm and unemphatic way, "We believe that something occurred on that day that later resolved itself in the murder of Captain Bray several days ago. Whatever you can tell us about what happened during or before the battle might be of great importance."

"The captain was killed here, at home, after all he went through?"

"Yes, I am afraid he was, and we need your help to see if we can discover who killed him." He turned the scarred side of his face away from them for a moment. "I am sorry to hear that he is dead, I can't imagine why anyone would want to do a thing like that. But war can have a strange effect on some people. I would be happy to tell you all I know if it would help; you see Captain Bray was one of the bravest men I knew," he said with quiet sincerity. "He was the best officer in our battalion. I am proud to have served under him, and lucky he was with us that day, otherwise I wouldn't be here. It was all about the men for the captain, you see. It will take a little time for me to tell you what happened, if you will bear with me." He cleared his throat.

"After the second day of the battle we went back for the men who were stranded after the attack earlier that day—the men in Captain Bray's company who got separated from us out there. The captain and me had to wait until it was dark and then we made our way forward very slowly—crawling we were because the ground was uneven after being blown to bits all day. It was as black as pitch and it seemed to take hours just to move about twenty feet. We knew that several of our company was lying low in a shell crater. When we got to them we found that four had died of their wounds and Private Hector and Lieutenant Carmichael were the only two alive, but the lieutenant had been wounded: he had been shot in the leg. Captain Bray asked the lieutenant about the rest of the men and he said they were either dead or maybe taken prisoner. As we came out of the crater a land mine went up on our right. We saw it going sky-high, a huge mass of soil. It alerted the Germans and they opened fire . . . there were bullets everywhere, like a swarm of bees round you, you could almost feel them plucking at your clothes." He paused. "I got caught by a bullet." He lifted his hand to his face. "It knocked me for six: went straight up the side of my face and through the side of my helmet and I couldn't see a thing for the blood. I don't know how the captain got us into the shelter of the wood, I really don't. I just held on to the edge of his coat, and stumbled on as best I could, because he was carrying Lieutenant Carmichael . . ." He glanced at both women. "In the dark and the confusion we didn't know which direction we were going in." He paused and dropped his gaze, as if recounting the horrors of that night had brought back memories he would have preferred to forget.

"Did you get the information you needed?" Lord Haversham had been called away halfway through their visit with the Glenns; Clive had come to the door and said that most of the street were sitting in their motorcar.

Lady Montfort leaped into the Daimler with such nimble speed that Mrs. Jackson had trouble keeping up with her, but she understood the urgency. Their conversation with Private Glenn had rightfully put the fear of God into her mistress. "Drive, Harry. No, we don't have time to stop for a quick bite at a public house, we have to get home tonight, I don't care how hungry we all are." Her ladyship was a little out of breath with the speed at which she had raced up Balaclava Street, that and the anxiety caused by Private Glenn's account of the Battle of Beauville Wood. "I simply can't believe that our hospital has been so unfortunately used by such an unscrupulous and cowardly individual," she said as her son obediently started the motor and drove back toward town.

"What a tale! What a frightful story of betrayal and cowardice." Mrs. Jackson could almost see Lord Haversham's smile at his mother's rather colorful beginning.

"You have evidently been given more than you had hoped for," he said, turning his head now that they were on the open road outside of the town.

"Yes, we have, and the sooner we get back to Iyntwood the better. How long do you think it will take us?" She looked out of the window at the peaceful pastures of grazing sheep they were passing in the last of the early evening light.

"It's nearly six o'clock and the light will last another hour or so. We might be lucky and be back in Haversham by eight o'clock at the very latest." He pressed his foot down on the accelerator and the powerful motorcar surged forward. "So are you going to tell me what you both learned in there?"

"I don't know quite where to start." Lady Montfort's earlier energy was beginning to dwindle and she sounded tired and anxious as she began to relate Private Glenn's story and their rescue of Lieutenant Carmichael and Private Hector. "Captain Bray wanted to get Carmichael, Hector, and Glenn into the shelter of the wood before going back for help. Private Glenn said that Hector was in a terrible state, babbling on about the wood being full of German soldiers waiting there with flame-throwers and refusing to leave the shelter of the crater, until the captain told him to pull himself together or he would be up on a charge for disobedience. But somehow Captain Bray managed to get them into the safety of the wood."

There was silence in the motorcar for a moment. The sun was sinking lower on the horizon, turning the woods and fields around them into a deep rose gold. "Well, there they were in the shelter of the wood. Captain Bray did what he could for Lieutenant Carmichael, who was weak from loss of blood and incapable of moving. Glenn, who could no longer see a thing, said that he sensed they were in a dip in the center of the trees and Captain Bray covered both him and Carmichael with dead leaves to keep them warm as it started to rain. After a while Private Hector pulled himself together and asked the captain how they were going to get back to their lines. Hector said that they should make their way southwest, away from enemy lines, and Bray said no, they should go southeast. Hector insisted he had kept his bearings straight in his head as he had lain in the shell crater, and in the end Bray left to reconnoiter the area to the southwest of the wood. Glenn lay there blinded, in pain and unsure how it would all end. At one point he said he started to pray, he was so sure they would not make it back. As he lay there in the dark he said he could here Carmichael's groans on his left. Even though he was confused and in pain, he says he felt quite sure that Carmichael's last cry had been stifled, as if someone had put a hand over his mouth. He guessed it was Hector, worried that if Carmichael made too much noise they might be found by German soldiers. He asked, 'Hector, is Lieutenant Carmichael still alive?' But there was no answer. Every so often he would ask, 'Hector, are you there?' But there was no answer at all from Hector and complete silence from Carmichael. And then he heard what he took to be, hoped to be, Hector uncovering the leaves around Carmichael to see if he could perhaps make him more comfortable. He asked Hector several times: 'Is the lieutenant alive? Any sign of the captain?' but there was no answer either from Carmichael or Hector, just what he took, at the time, to be Hector perhaps seeing to the field dressing that Captain Bray had put around Carmichael's shattered left leg. He thought at one time that the wound in his head had made him hear things, and he was parched with thirst. 'Do you have any water, Hector?' he asked, and there was no reply from Hector. He thinks he must have lost consciousness for a while because he came to and felt completely bewildered by the silence. He wondered if Captain Bray had returned and taken the other two back, and that he was now lying in the wood alone. He got to his hands and knees and started to crawl first this way and then that. Then he found a body, he assumed it was Lieutenant Carmichael, and if it was he was quite dead; he groped around, searching for a canteen of water. But there was none. He realized at this moment that Hector had gone. That he was indeed alone, and he lay back down and prepared for the worst."

"You mean this Hector character had just abandoned him?" Lord Haversham asked.

"Yes, he had deserted them. But the worst didn't happen to Private Glenn, as Captain Bray came back. Hector had sent him off in the wrong direction, but he had managed to get his bearings and had cut around behind the wood to get back to them. He told Glenn that even in the dark he would be able to get him back safely to their lines. It was then that Glenn told him that Carmichael had died and that he thought that perhaps Hector had run off. He remembered quite clearly the captain saying, 'Yes, you are right, the vengeful little swine sent me off into enemy fire, and now he's probably run off in the direction of Guillement. He's deserted us.'

"All Glenn can remember after that was Captain Bray half carrying him, half leading him. As they made their way along the uneven ground, at one time the pain in his head was so bad that he blacked out. Later on, when he came to, he was in a field hospital and the orderly told him that Captain Bray had brought him back to safety and that they were the only survivors of 'A' company. In the days that he lay in the field hospital waiting to be shipped back home, he remembered thinking over Captain Bray's words: 'Yes, you are right, the vengeful little swine sent me off into enemy fire.' And wondered what reason Hector had to do such a thing when the captain had risked his life to save him. He said that Hector had always been a sly one—he knew him, you see, because every one of them in their company had all come from the *same village* in Gloucestershire. Their captain was the owner of the Brayley estate, and Glenn and his father had worked on the estate all their lives. Private Glenn was a hedger and ditcher before the war, and his father a gardener at Brayley House. And this character Hector was the son of the estate steward. Lieutenant Carmichael was a solicitor's son from Cheltenham, but the other men who had died that day had all been from Brayley. They had all joined up on the same day."

"Are you saying that this Hector stole Lieutenant Carmichael's uniform and identity and then ran off?" Harry turned his head and looked over his shoulder at his mother.

"Yes, I am, but wait until you hear the rest of it. So, four days later Private Glenn was shipped back home with a Blighty one. He heard that Captain Bray had recovered from a slight wound sustained when he was reconnoitering the best way back to their lines, and that he had also returned to England. Glenn was so ill after he returned home that all he wanted to do was to forget everything that had happened. He wrote once to Brayley, to Mr. Bray, to inquire after Captain Bray, but had had no reply." Her ladyship's voice now that her story was told sounded tired and depressed. "So you see there is indeed a connection between all of these men. The Bray brothers, Sam Glenn, Ian Carmichael, and Private P. Hector."

"And this character who came to Haversham Hall calling himself Carmichael was really Hector?"

"Yes. When he explained that a Lieutenant Carmichael had come to our hospital, and described him, Glenn said that Hector must have taken the lieutenant's uniform and exchanged his identity disks for Carmichael's when they were waiting in the wood for Captain Bray to return." Lady Montfort turned to Mrs. Jackson to acknowledge Mr. Stafford's telegram that showed the death of Hector in his official records. "And then he abandoned Private Glenn, hoping that Bray would be killed as he tried to find a way clear to get them all to safety. Hector, the man who was shot outside our house, was a coward and a deserter. Captain Bray would more than likely have had him court-martialed when he recovered, but he had retreated into a world that had no past. He remembered nothing of those two days or even his life before the war. That is until he came home to England to be helped to begin the business of reclaiming his life by Major Andrews."

Now that she had finished, Lady Montfort sat quite still, looking out into the darkening evening. Lord Haversham had switched on the Daimler's powerful headlights and they lit up the country road ahead of them flanked on either side by high hedges. A great golden moon lifted up into the night sky just above the horizon.

"A harvest moon, look, Jackson, how beautiful it is. It is hard to believe on a night like this that a battle like the one at Beauville Wood could possibly be going on in France right now, isn't it?"

Lord Haversham glanced up automatically into the night sky and pressed his foot down on the accelerator. The only sound was the motorcar's powerful engine as it covered the miles toward home. Mrs. Jackson sighed, a long sigh. "But that is not all, m'lady," she reminded her ladyship. "That is not quite the end of it, is it?"

"No, Jackson, it is not," Lady Montfort said as she came out of her thoughts. "If you can make this thing go any faster, Harry, I would be very pleased if you would."

"The harvest home supper will be in full swing by now, Mama, we have definitely missed it."

"No, it's not that, Harry; I want to get home as quickly as I can, because what is troubling me most of all is that if Hector was well known to Captain Bray, then he was also known to his brother, the three boys grew up together. Mr. Bray met Private Hector when he and Althea found him on Brook Lane in his broken-down motorcar. In fact, Althea introduced Private Hector as Lieutenant Carmichael. But Edgar Bray never said a word, did he, Jackson? He never admitted to knowing Hector, and Hector did not admit to knowing Mr. Bray. So what do you make of that, Harry?"

Lord Haversham slowed to negotiate the narrow streets of Oxford. They drove up the deserted High Street to Magdalen Bridge, and as the moon shone down on the smooth surface of the water below them, the other side of the riverbank was lost in the blackness of the night sky, and Mrs. Jackson had the horrid feeling that the bridge would just go on and on into darkness and that they would never reach the other side. She shivered in the stifling heat of the night.

Lord Haversham said, "Captain Bray's murder was planned, planned so that Hector would not be exposed as the coward he was, and also so that . . ." They reached the other side of the river and the companionable comfort of the bank and he slowed the Daimler as it started the climb up Headington Hill.

"So that Mr. Edgar Bray would inherit the estate in his brother's place," said Mrs. Jackson, eager to make her point.

"Exactly, Jackson, you speculated as much earlier on and you were right," said Lady Montfort. "Harry, can't you go a little faster?" A roadside public house had come up on their right; its white walls gleamed in the Daimler's headlamps and Lord Haversham slowed to take the bend in the road. "We'll be home in an hour or so," he said, and then: "So Bray killed his brother so he could inherit?"

The turn negotiated, Harry again pressed the accelerator and the motorcar leaped forward once more.

"Yes. Bray, convinced that he is the new lord of Brayley Manor, is swanning around Iyntwood being handled with kid gloves as he mourns the death of his murdered brother, and waits for Sir Walter Meacham to be brought to trial for the murder of both men. I am quite sure you can go a little faster, Harry."

Mrs. Jackson held on to the roof strap as they swayed around another corner. *Yes, but we don't want to end up in a ditch, and we have to get home as quickly as we possibly can because Lady Althea, bless her innocent little heart, is spending an awful lot of time with a man who probably murdered his brother and then disposed of the man who had helped him to do it.*

Chapter Twenty-Seven

The night air was heavy. Clouds coming in from the east had gathered in a great banks along the horizon and were now moving in overhead, obscuring the moon, as Harry drew up outside the great barn at Brook End Farm. Clementine felt such anxiety that she barely noticed how hot and airless the night was. Her only thought was for her daughter. As she got down from the motor she saw to her relief that Althea's little motorcar was parked demurely next to the gleaming coachwork of Mr. Bray's splendid Lanchester. *She is safe then, she is in the barn with everyone else.* She crossed the cobbled courtyard toward the light streaming out through the doors of the barn, thrown open to the night air. From the sound of it, the harvest home supper had turned itself into a harvest home dance. She could hear the scrape of fiddles overriding the notes of a piano that was in bad need of tuning, and someone had dug up a cornet and was doing his best to keep three-three time. As she stood in the threshold of the barn, blinking in the light, she was joined by Mrs. Jackson and, behind them, Harry.

"I can't see her anywhere," she said, scanning the red and perspiring faces of farmers, their wives, and some of their children as they swirled past them to the quick tempo of a sprightly waltz. Festive red, white, and blue bunting was strung across the rafters, bales of hay were covered with old horse blankets to provide seating, and down one side of the barn were trestle tables offering great pink hams, cold chicken, and dozens of cakes and pies. Clementine's gaze swept on to the top table and there was her husband, standing with a tankard of ale in his hand, gravely listening to the Reverend Mr. Bottomley-Jones, who was more than likely making one of his gentle and persuasive pleas for funds to repair the bellows of the church organ, or a trip to the seaside for the local children. The noise from the music and the voices of those dancing rose up to them in a wave of celebratory cheer, its volume encouraged by a large keg of beer standing next to the trestle tables of food. "Can you see Althea anywhere, Harry?" Clementine shrieked into her son's ear, and turning to Mrs. Jackson she mouthed, "Lady Althea?" And together they scanned the dance floor.

"Can you see Edgar Bray?" Harry shouted back to his mother, and again all three of them searched the crowd.

"There is Colonel Valentine." Mrs. Jackson touched Clementine's arm and nodded toward the chief constable.

"Good," said Clementine, although neither of them heard her. "We are going to need him." She caught her husband's eye and immediately had his attention, for he excused himself and started to make his way down the side of the barn toward them.

As they stood waiting for him, a flicker of lightning lit up the dark cloud outside and almost immediately was answered by the rumble of thunder as it rolled toward them across the heavens. "You are over two hours late. Where on earth have you both been?" Lord Montfort looked quite angry, and Mrs. Jackson took several steps back, determined that she not invade the privacy of a family argument.

Clementine paid absolutely no attention to her husband's annoyed greeting. "Where are Althea and Edgar Bray?" she asked—almost accusing him of the sort of negligence one reserved only for negligent chaperones at a debutante's ball.

"Here, celebrating the harvest with Althea's Land girls and *our* farmers," her husband reminded her, as if she had forgotten her duty as the wife of the county's most prominent landowner. "I didn't see her in there," Clementine said. "Harry, did you see her?" but Harry had disappeared back into the barn's stifling interior.

"What is going on, Clemmy?" Her husband caught her anxiety. "Where on earth have you been? Would someone," he turned to Mrs. Jackson, "please tell me what is going on?"

Harry emerged from the barn. "I walked around, she's not in there, and neither is Edgar Bray."

"Well, I expect they have walked over to the stables. Bray wanted to meet Dolly."

"He met Dolly on the day he arrived," Clementine said. "He said more than just hello to her, he took her for a gallop across the wheat field from her pasture, all the way up to the south gate of our kitchen garden, where he beat his brother to death." Her words caused her husband to turn to her with such a look of incredulity that ordinarily it would have been remarkably droll if their daughter's safety had not been in such jeopardy. "Ralph, we must find Althea; if she is with Mr. Bray then she is in considerable danger. Once we have her safe I'll tell you everything."

"Are you sure they went to the stable?" Harry asked, and behind him the sky lit up with a brilliant flash as the storm moved in directly overhead. A resounding crack and crash of thunder and the air was filled with a particularly pungent smell as if someone has just struck a light from a tinderbox.

"The last thing I heard Bray say, about twenty minutes ago—of course you can't hear a damned thing in there—was that he wanted to meet Dolly, and Althea told him that the stable was next door." He was already walking ahead of them toward the stable. As the four of them rounded the corner another great flash lit up the barnyard, and to Clementine's utter relief she saw a faint light shining through a chink in the stable door.

As they approached the open gate into the stable courtyard her husband lifted his hand. "Clemmy, stay here with Mrs. Jackson. Come on, Harry, we'll just wander in and send Althea back out to you. And then we can have a little talk with Mr. Bray."

With her heart beating away in a breathless sort of way, Clementine watched them open the door and walk down the wide aisle between empty horse stalls toward the pool of light at the stable's far end.

"Spoiling Dolly with too many carrots will make her lazy," she heard her husband say, and to her immense relief she heard Althea's light voice reply, "But she has worked so hard, Papa, and she is such a good girl." And then the hairs on her arms lifted at the sound of Edgar Bray's smooth-toned voice: "I think what I admire about her the most is that she is so biddable, so sweet-natured." Just the sound of his voice caused Clementine's heart rate to pick up in a sickening thud that filled her throat. Even the reassuring sound of her husband's voice—calm, reasonable, and just a little chiding, the voice of a father who is surprised to find his daughter alone with a man in a barn—did little to quell her rising anxiety. "Althea, your Land girls are looking for you. I think they want to drink a round of toasts to their first harvest. Will you come along now? Your mother is here and she's waiting for you."

And then to her horror she heard her daughter say, "Is she back from Cheltenham? I would have thought she would spend the night there. Didn't you say it was a terrifically long journey, Mr. Bray?" *Silly, silly girl*, Clementine thought in exasperation, *why does she always have to say whatever comes into her head?* And then the smooth voice replied, "Must have been awfully important for her to rush off to Cheltenham and back in one day." And before anyone could stop her Althea piped up, "Well, she *was* in a rush; I think it had something to do with one of the soldiers in your brother's regiment. She thought he would have information that would help her solve these awful murders."

She must stop these rash revelations! As Clementine ran forward into the stables, Edgar Bray turned a look of such malignancy toward her that a surge of adrenaline prickled up the backs of her legs. Althea must have heard herself and sensed the change in the man who had been chatting away so pleasantly about horses and harvests. She stopped laughing as she lifted her head from kissing the nose of the gray mare and within the tick of a second was pulled toward Mr. Bray. In his hand was an army-issue service revolver. *And without any doubt,* Clementine thought as ice-cold fear froze her into immobility, *the service revolver he used to shoot Private Hector in the back.*

"Best to put the gun down, Bray, and let Althea come over to me." Lord Montfort extended his arm to Althea.

Harry started to move forward, and Bray's grip tightened around Althea's waist, holding her tightly against him.

"Stop, both of you," he said. His anger that all his plans for a perfect future were now in ruins was so powerful that his once pleasing features were almost unrecognizable. "All of you, into that empty stall." He gestured to the right with the muzzle of his revolver, but they all stood rooted to the spot, staring at him as if they could not understand a word he was staying. Bray's arm slid up Althea's body until his forearm was across her throat and she gasped, her eyes staring at them in fear. He jerked Althea closer to him and she gave a little cry of pain, which was hastily snapped off by his strong arm. Her eyes bulged, her white face started to suffuse with blood, and her mouth gaped in a silent scream that they do as they were told so that she could breathe again.

Clementine moved into the stall, followed by her husband and son. Harry stood as close to the door as he could. "Close the door," Bray said, and he removed his arm from Althea's throat. Clementine heard her gasping for breath as Harry reached out and swung the door to, but held it as if it were closed. "And put your hand through the bar and latch it. That's it. I don't want you to stir from that stall until you are quite sure that I have gone. Now, Althea, walk forward, and do exactly as I say, or I will shoot you."

They will never hear, they will never hear a thing in the barn. The waltz came to an end and within two beats the musicians launched into a polka. Clementine put her nose up against the bars of the stall and peered out to see her daughter take a step forward away from the horse and toward the center of the aisle, and Edgar Bray, holding the gun steady, leaned on his cane and took his first step to follow her.

It was at this moment that Dolly woke up from a deep dream of days standing up to her hocks in meadow grass with the warm sun on her back and found to her annoyance that no carrot was on offer. She didn't appreciate Althea's moving away from her, and as Edgar Bray came alongside her she gave him a vigorous nudge to remind him that a treat was needed. She caught Edgar Bray in mid-step and he was thrown sideways, his weight falling on his useless leg, and came crashing to the ground. Before Clementine's horrified gaze, Harry slipped the catch on the stall door, and was through it in a moment, catching his sister by her waist and whisking her to safety. Right behind him, Lord Montfort leaped out of the stall and brought his foot down on Mr. Bray's right wrist before he could reach for his revolver. Bending down, he swiftly relieved the man of his gun, and Harry joined him to lift Mr. Bray up off the ground.

Out of breath, Lord Montfort clapped his son on the shoulder in congratulation. "Put him in a stall, and make the latch secure with a stud chain or something. And then go and get Valentine. We need to sort this one out before everyone comes looking for us."

"I will go and find the colonel," Mrs. Jackson said; and looking at Harry with his cap off, his hair on end and his face hot and angry, Clementine had to agree that this tall, unruffled woman would cause less of a stir in the barn full of revelers than would her son.

The last thing they wanted was to have the entire party out there to find out what was going on.

"Do what you want, you fools, there's nothing you can prove." Edgar Bray, supporting himself with his stick, sneered at them as Harry marched him into the stall they had occupied just minutes ago. "It was the coward and deserter Hector who rode the horse to kill my brother, he had all the motive in the world. And it was Sir Winchell Meacham who shot Hector, not I. What a bunch of interfering idiots you all are."

"Would you please stop scoffing and sneering, Mr. Bray, it makes you look quite common. And I wouldn't be quite so quick if I were you, we know a good deal more of your story than you think we do," Clementine said. "But I only have the energy to tell it once, so I think we will wait for Colonel Valentine." She had to lean up against the wooden wall of the stall nearest to her for her legs felt boneless, and her hands were shaking.

Another sneer. "That old codger, and what do you think he will do?"

"Why, arrest you for the murder of your brother and Private Hector," said Clementine, and turned to put her arms around her daughter, who, white-faced and weeping with fear, needed her mother to tell her that everything would now be quite all right. "There, there." She took her clean handkerchief from her pocket and wiped the tears from Althea's pale face. "You are quite safe, thanks to your friend Dolly. I am so sorry I didn't warn you about Mr. Bray before I left, it was so silly of me. I worried about you all the way home, my darling." She kissed her daughter's wet cheeks over and over again.

And then turning to her son, she said in a murmur, "Harry would you please look inside the boot of Mr. Bray's motorcar? I think you will find something there that will be most useful to us and I am rather curious to hear what you think of it. Don't bring it in here; put it in the Daimler so we can take it up to the house."

She looked across the aisle of the stable to Mr. Bray, who was standing silently in his stall, watching her through the bars. *Yes, I see that you are looking a little less sure of yourself now, Mr. Bray,* and then her chest felt tight as she thought of this creature manhandling her daughter, making use of her all these days as he sat in their house and engineered his alibis for two murders, quite confident that he would go home as Sir Edgar Bray, to run his estates and lucrative coalfields. "It was not Private Hector alias Lieutenant Carmichael who rode Dolly up to the kitchen garden, Mr. Bray; it was you, wasn't it? How clever you must have thought you were."

I don't know how they do it, Mrs. Jackson thought, as she offered ham sandwiches hastily made for a ravenous Lord Haversham and as ballast for her ladyship, who was already sipping her second glass of brandy. The family was gathered in the drawing room at Iyntwood with Colonel Valentine. *You would never think from the pleasant way they have of chatting together that they have a dangerous murderer pinned down in a corner of this lovely room.*

"Clemmy, you have kept us in suspense for far too long," Lord Montfort said. He kept his back to their erstwhile guest, who had been handed over to Haversham village's stolid police constable who was standing guard of Mr. Bray. "I simply can't wait to hear what you have to say." He turned to his son. "Your mother is such a dab hand at wrapping things up, Harry."

"Actually," Lady Montfort finished her sandwich, took a sip of brandy, and smiled across the room toward Mrs. Jackson, "Mrs. Jackson is the dab hand; I am merely the one who sits by in amazement. You see it was Mrs. Jackson who very cleverly discovered that Lieutenant Carmichael was not Lieutenant Carmichael but someone else entirely. Isn't that so, Jackson?" The housekeeper smiled that this was so but she said nothing at all. "I wish you would tell this part, Jackson, I still get rather confused about who is who."

Mrs. Jackson was never one for the limelight, but she couldn't bear to think that this part of the story might be muffed as her ladyship was clearly exhausted and brandy on an empty stomach does sometimes have a somewhat paralyzing effect on continuity. So she readily pitched in with a clear account of what they had learned not only through discovery but from their conversation with Private Glenn. So clear, in fact, that she noticed with some satisfaction that even Colonel Valentine was nodding as she laid the complicated events of the Battle of Beauville Wood before him.

"So it was really Private Hector who came to our hospital, calling himself Lieutenant Carmichael and suffering from a confusing array of shell-shock symptoms, m'lord," she said as she described the events of the past few days, culminating in the murder of the man they had all known as Lieutenant Carmichael. She turned to address Mr. Bray directly: "Private Hector was the son of your estate steward at Brayley, you all three grew up together, didn't you, sir?" It was clear by Mr. Bray's face that he saw where this was going. "When Private Hector left the battlefield at Beauville Wood he had assumed the identity of a second lieutenant. Did he come home to you at Brayley, sir?"

"What if he did?" Bray asked. "It proves nothing, I had no idea he had run off. All he was to me was the son of my steward."

"Sir Winchell was right in one respect then, we were harboring at least one rascal after all." Lord Montfort did not look at Mr. Bray in his chair. "And right from the start this was a ruthless plan to eliminate Captain Bray by a couple of cowards."

Mr. Bray lifted his head from sneering at a very fine Persian carpet and said something indescribably vulgar.

"There is a good deal more to the story than that, my lord."

Mrs. Jackson stood quietly in the middle of the room, basking in their evident admiration—it was better by far she thought than a double brandy on an empty stomach. "Her ladyship should tell the next part."

"You know as well as I do what transpired, Jackson," Clementine encouraged.

"But I like the way you tell it, m'lady," she said.

"Very well then, I will continue, but first here is to a first-class brain that got us started down the right path in the first place: to Mrs. Jackson." And everyone lifted their glasses to the elegantly composed woman standing among them before turning expectant eyes toward Clementine.

"From the start Mr. Bray's plan was to get rid of his inconvenient brother, and for that he needed the help of Private Hector, or, as he had most usefully become, Lieutenant Carmichael. And just as equally Private Hector needed Mr. Bray's help, too, because the moment Captain Bray's memory returned Hector would be court-martialed and probably shot for cowardice and impersonating an officer, and Mr. Bray would have to surrender complete control of his brother's estate and everything that went with it. When Hector came back to Brayley it was then that they hatched their plan to be rid of Captain Bray. It does seem a tiny bit unfair," she smiled at Althea, "that Mr. Bray spent all his adult life running an estate he would never inherit, as his brother enjoyed himself in London. But that is the way with entails, isn't it?"

"I didn't collude to have my brother killed. I didn't need to. He was incompetent, incapable of running the estate." Edgar Bray spoke for the first time without sneering. "I brought Brayley back from nothing, single-handedly, while he gambled away the family money in London. And then he went off to war and obviously couldn't even cope with that. I knew that I would have to keep running things, even if he regained his memory. I had no reason to kill him. But it is evident that Hector did."

Clementine continued with her story as if he hadn't spoken. "The war came. Sir Evelyn Bray became Captain Bray and joined the regiment of the Gloucestershires and his younger brother, Edgar Bray, stayed at home and ran the estate just as he had always done. Two years later, Edgar Bray was informed that his brother was missing in action and believed dead after the Battle of Beauville Wood. Finally he would inherit! A triumph short-lived because not days later another telegram informs that Captain Bray was alive, but unlikely to recover from amnesia. This was not perfect but at least Edgar Bray could continue in control of the estate and with time have complete control if his brother remained so incapacitated.

"But Captain Bray was in the capable hands of Major Andrews and little by little was beginning to regain his memory. We wrote to you with such evident enthusiasm for your brother's future, Mr. Bray. How upsetting that must have been: the estate would revert back to Captain Sir Evelyn Bray, and after all your hard work you would be left out in the cold."

Mr. Bray scowled at her across the room. *I can't imagine why I ever thought he was a good-looking man.*

"On the day that Edgar Bray motored over to be reunited with his brother, the man known to us as Lieutenant Carmichael had organized everything quite beautifully. Edgar Bray would park his motorcar on Brook End Lane right by the gate into Dolly's pasture. Captain Bray was predictably ensconced in his favorite part of our grounds, contentedly digging over the potato bed. Staff and patients at the hospital were all gathered for their one o'clock luncheon. It was the perfect time for Edgar Bray to arrive in the kitchen garden, murder his brother, and then return to his broken-down motorcar.

"As arranged, Hector alias Carmichael brings Dolly down to the pasture, tacks her up with bridle and a saddle brought along by Edgar Bray, and off he goes on Dolly to the kitchen garden.

He murders his brother and returns to his car, where he releases Dolly and simply sits there to wait. Then an hour or so later along comes our impersonator Hector-Carmichael with Althea, to find Mr. Bray sitting helplessly in his broken-down motorcar. Althea unclogs the carburetor that Hector has very competently clogged, and Mr. Bray motors on to our house, where all he had to do was play the part of the bereaved brother and charming guest." *And flirt with my daughter.*

"Very clever," Mr. Bray said over his shoulder. "None of it plausible, none of it even remotely possible. You forget that I am incapable of moving at anything other than a snail's pace. How you imagine I could get up on the back of that clod of a cart horse and get her there and back to the kitchen garden I have no idea. But I am quite sure you will dream up something, Lady Montfort." Mr. Bray's expression was derisive, but lines of tension deepened across his forehead.

Clementine took the merest sip of brandy from her glass. "I already have," she murmured and nodded to her son.

"Never taunt a woman, Bray, it is not only ill mannered but foolish," Harry said as he left the room and returned a moment later with a curiously constructed saddle and a long girth. "Poor Dolly," Harry said as he set the saddle over the back of a wing chair. "It must have been very uncomfortable for her to wear this thing perched on her back. It is clearly made for a large horse; I imagine you usually ride an Irish Hunter, Mr. Bray, but not one with a barrel quite as wide as our Dolly's." He patted the pommel and smiled at a man who was no longer sneering. "No need to look away, old chap, I know you recognize the saddle because I found it in the boot of your motor. Fire away, Mama."

"I happened to mention to Private Glenn during our visit to him this afternoon that I had no idea how you could have made the distance from your motorcar on Brook End lane to the kitchen garden, since it is easily three miles just one way. And he told me that three miles was nothing to a man who regularly spent the day in the saddle as he went about estate business. Of course you didn't really need to gallop Dolly all the way there and back, but you were probably a bit worried about your motorcar being discovered even though your accomplice had assured you it was left on a very lonely stretch of road.

"Dolly was thundering along at such a rate that the sound of her hoofbeats on that hard ground through the wheat field was carried all the way across the field to the top of Holly Farm barn. And young Walter Howard woke up from his noonday nap and saw you. Dolly is remarkable only in that she is the only gray Shire horse for miles around, you see." Clementine walked over to the saddle and lifted two long, narrow leather straps that ran through the ring on the pommel, and Mrs. Jackson turned to Mr. Hollyoak, who was standing holding the brandy decanter, and gave him a look that said, *This is what happens when you trespass on the sensibilities of a protective mother.*

"We did a sort of run-through of Dolly's journey that day with Lord Haversham. Even riding with one hand, we knew that your friend Hector-Carmichael could not have been the one riding Dolly because he had made sure to establish an alibi with Lady Althea, and his twenty-minute trip to the pasture was not near time enough for him to ride up to the kitchen garden and back again. You must have a very good saddler, Mr. Bray. This one has been adapted most cleverly for a man who has lost the strength of his right leg."

She stood and admired the saddle in front of her. "So, your right leg is held firmly in place across the upper part of your leg by this sturdy strap and then once held in place this block here gives support to it." She picked up what looked like a long leather rein. "For stability, this strap runs from the back of the saddle under the upper leg and through a ring on the pommel. When you pull it you exert pressure on the horse's right side. Quite ingenious because

you can release the strap to come off the horse, which is important in an emergency, and the lower strap gives support if the
horse jumps sideways. All you needed then was the help of your
friend Hector to tack up Dolly with an extra-long girth to encompass her broad belly, and his help to mount. And then off
you went. You were quite able to dismount without help by the
boot of your motorcar when you returned, put the saddle into it,
and then send Dolly back into her pasture. I have to congratulate
you on insisting you do your own dirty work by murdering your
brother."

Colonel Valentine, Lord Montfort, and Lord Haversham clus-
tered around the saddle. They were all riding men and saw exactly how the straps worked.

"Yes, clever but not unusual; I knew quite a few fellas after the
Boer War who having lost a leg didn't give up hunting, thanks to
a good saddler. Don't know why we didn't think of it sooner!"

Lord Montfort's brows rose at their chief constable's understandable arrogance and asked his wife, "But how did you work all this
out?"

"Well I didn't really, Mrs. Jackson did. She discovered the connection between Captain Bray, his brother, and this Private
Hector, who came to the hospital masquerading as Lieutenant
Carmichael. From there we discovered that Mr. Bray here had ridden Dolly from Brook End Lane to the kitchen garden. And since
he was particularly coy with us about not being able to hunt or
ride, it took us longer than it should have done to work out how
he had accomplished that. And then it occurred to us when we
were with Private Glenn that since Mr. Bray had had his motorcar adapted, he might have devised some method of being able
to ride a horse. The only man who had the time to ride up to the
kitchen and back again on Dolly was Mr. Bray. Corporal Glenn
confirmed two things: one, that Private Hector had indeed stolen Lieutenant Carmichael's identity that night in Beauville Wood,

and the other was that Mr. Bray did all his business around his estate on horseback even after his hunting accident."

"And the murder weapon?" Harry asked.

"Harry, would you borrow Mr. Bray's walking stick for a moment please, I want to show it to Colonel Valentine."

Harry delivered Mr. Bray's stick into Valentine's hands. And the old man swished it through the air a couple of times. "Ah, yes. Hmm, yes I see! A particularly sturdy stick, rather heavy; I will ask the coroner to look it over. Feels like . . ." He swung it up and down, causing Mr. Hollyoak and Mrs. Jackson to wince as he narrowly missed a priceless piece of jade. He inspected the stick's end, slipped off the rubber cap that stopped it sliding, and took it to the table lamp. "Um, yes, see here, Lord Montfort, there appears to be a metal rod running down the length of the wood—a most formidable weapon. And what about this Hector fella, Lady Montfort, what happened there?"

"Well, Hector was just as unscrupulous and unpleasant as Mr. Bray here. And he had something on Mr. Bray as his direct accomplice to murder. I am guessing that he wanted money, or perhaps something Mr. Bray did not want to part with. Bray probably arranged to meet him after dinner on our lake bridge on the night Sir Winchell came to dine with us. Hector thought it was a meeting to discuss terms, and so it was because Mr. Bray shot him." She smiled around the room.

"During dinner we provided Mr. Bray with the perfect dupe for his plan to get rid of his friend Hector and make sure he was not relying once again on his leg as his alibi. After all, you can still shoot someone even if you cannot run, walk very far, or ride a horse. Sir Winchell Meacham is a particularly unhappy man, with two sons recently killed in the war, and our hospital at Haversham Hall shelters officers whom he considered to be cowards. After dinner Mr. Bray took the opportunity of encouraging Sir Winchell to drink more port than he should and also spent a few moments stirring him up into a state about the malingerers at the hospital. It doesn't take much to push Sir Winchell into a temper about our hospital, and when he does I am afraid he does sound awfully violent. Sir Winchell, always true to character, threw a paddy and stormed off into the night to walk home. And just after he left, Mr. Bray made his way to the bridge where he met Hector and shot him, leaving him right there by the side of the drive, where not minutes before Sir Winchell had stamped along it in a fury about the injustices of life. Well done, Mr. Bray, for quick thinking and making the very best out of a situation." The look she was given in return was a particularly unpleasant one. And Colonel Valentine decided it was time to remove their culprit.

"So Sir Winchell is completely in the clear, poor old chap," said Lord Montfort as Edgar Bray was taken from the room by the village constable, who had never spent such an entertaining evening in his life.

"He most certainly is, because Walter Howard not only saw Mr. Bray galloping Dolly up to the kitchen garden to murder his brother, he also saw, from the other side of his barn, Sir Winchell fishing on the river. Sir Winchell fished from the footbridge all day, and so he could not have gone up to the kitchen garden to kill Captain Bray. So I would say Sir Winchell was wholly in the clear, wouldn't you, Colonel?"

Colonel Valentine put down his empty glass on the tray to follow his constable and Mr. Bray from the drawing room.

"Indeed he is," Colonel Valentine agreed, looking, Mrs. Jackson thought, not the least embarrassed. He had, she noticed, not caught Lady Montfort's eye during the last part of her story. But he came forward toward her now and congratulated her most chivalrously on the cleverness of their deductions.

"It is Captain Bray who has all my sympathy and pity. It's the old Cain and Abel story," Lord Montfort added, as he extended an inviting arm for Colonel Valentine to leave them, as it was get-

ting late, and after the exhausting business of murders, conscientious objectors hiding on his land, and bringing in the harvest,
it had been quite a reducing several days.

Mrs. Jackson accompanied the colonel into the hall. "Can I drive
you back to Haversham Hall, Mrs. Jackson, since I am going that
way?" The elderly man bowed to her most respectfully as a Black
Maria came up the drive to take away Mr. Bray.

"Thank you, Colonel, it is a particularly unpleasant night." They
stood together in the doorway and stared at the wall of rainwater
falling heavily on the drive as two Market Wingley constables
opened up the double doors of the police van. "Thank goodness
the harvest is safely in," she said as the colonel put up his umbrella
to escort her to his motorcar. "But where is your inspector, sir? I
don't think I have seen him in a while." For Detective Inspector
Savor had been conspicuously absent ever since the arrest of Sir
Winchell.

"My dear Mrs. Jackson, how interesting you should bring that
up. Detective Inspector Savor has made himself most useful over
this business of the stolen petrol, but I am afraid he simply has
no talent for understanding people. You see, Mrs. Jackson, I understood right from the start that you and her ladyship were far
more suited to deductive reasoning than Inspector Savor ever will
be, so I just arranged for him to stay out of your way." And
Mrs. Jackson had to look away and bite the insides of her cheeks
so that he did not see her smile.

"There you are, Jackson." Her ladyship put her head around the
door of Mrs. Jackson's office. "I was hoping I would find you
here. My goodness, what a to-do at the Market Wingley inquest,
and thank goodness for the Defence of the Realm Act and his
lordship's determination that neither of us should get up in front
of a court full of curious people and testify."

"Well that is certainly good news, m'lady." Mrs. Jackson was heartily relieved that they had not been gawked at like a couple of exhibits at the fair.

"Yes, indeed. The whole inquiry was revealed by the wonderful Private Glenn, the intelligent Major Andrews, the records from the War Graves Commission, and of course Captain Bray's painting. Then there was Mr. Bray's saddle and Walter Howard's observations from his barn, and to pull things all together the ringmaster was once again Colonel Valentine. Between us we certainly manage to make our dear colonel look like Sherlock Holmes, don't we, Jackson?" And with her customary generosity: "And why on earth not, after all the fun is in the puzzle, not in standing up in court and showing off!"

Mrs. Jackson lifted her seriously depleted sherry decanter. "And it was just in the nick of time, m'lady, that the inquest was held so quickly and everything officially resolved before our Medical Board review." When she said "in the nick of time," she meant it. The day after the arrest of Mr. Edgar Bray for the murder of his brother had been a whirlwind of activity, culminating with the arrival of the War Office and the Medical Board's most supercilious bureaucrats who had cluttered up their time for three exhausting days.

"And particularly good news from the War Office just now, Jackson, by the way."

"Good news, m'lady?" Mrs. Jackson turned with a glass of amontillado in her hand, which she offered to her ladyship.

"Thirty-five officers will be arriving at the hospital after Christmas along with an additional medical officer! Hard as it is to find good workmen, we will have the guest wing cleaned up by the end of November and ready for our patients' families when they wish to visit. Major Andrews says family visits do wonders for men who are suffering from neurasthenia."

Now was the time for her to ask a favor of Lady Montfort, something she was most uncomfortable about. But it seemed that, as usual, her ladyship had done one of her intuitive leaps over small details such as actual information or the need to utter every single little thing.

"So, I thought perhaps when Mr. Stafford is next on leave, he might like to come and spend some time with us—we will be able to offer him a nice room here, if he wouldn't mind staying in a hospital. And then we could thank him for his help. After all, if he had not been in a position to give us access to the War Graves records, Mr. Bray would be a baronet and galloping about being lord of Brayley Manor." She laughed, and Mrs. Jackson lifted her glass of sherry.

"So when is Mr. Stafford next due for some home leave, do you happen to know, Jackson?" She gazed across the room at her, her face quite empty of expression, but did she detect a glint in her ladyship's eye?

"Christmas week, m'lady, and I am quite sure he would be happy to accept an invitation." *There is no point in being coy,* Mrs. Jackson thought, and wondered if Mr. Thrower might be talked into parting with another goose for Christmas dinner.

Author's Note

Craiglockhart Hospital and the Treatment of Shell-shock in 1916

I have to thank the Royal Journal of the Society of Medicine in London for most of my information about shell-shock as it was called then and now referred to as post-traumatic stress disorder. Craiglockhart Hospital in Scotland is perhaps the most famous shell-shock hospital of the Great War. It was set up to deal with the epidemic of psychological casualties created in the muddy trenches of the Western Front; and, in particular, with the huge increase of casualties following the Battle of the Somme in 1916, the year in which *Death of an Unsung Hero* takes place.

Craiglockhart's fame is unsurprising in that two of the finest poets of a war overflowing with poetic voices were treated there— Wilfred Owen and Siegfried Sassoon. It was Sassoon who nick-named the place "Dottyville." The hospital's literary importance has been established by Sassoon's memoirs, and Pat Barker's *Regeneration* trilogy and a film version of the first of Barker's novels, all of which contributed insight and historical context in the writing of this book.

Craiglockhart also has an important place in the development of British neuropsychiatry. The concept of a psychological stressor resulting in physical symptoms was still a relatively novel one in

1916; the necessities of coping with an epidemic of psychological casualties in the context of the war allowed some fundamental aspects of Freud's ideas regarding repression and the unconscious to gain greater acceptance in the medical profession.

Just like my fictitious Haversham Hall Hospital, Craiglockhart was inspected twice by the War Office: on each occasion the commanding officer was relieved of his position and another appointed. These administrative shake-ups illustrate the differing views held by the War Office and the civilians in uniform working at Craiglockhart. The traditional military (and often societal) view was that shell-shock sufferers were "lead-swingers" and malingerers who should be treated in an appropriately punitive fashion and not sent on holiday in the Scottish countryside.

I modeled Haversham Hall's chief medical officer, Major Andrews, on two notable doctors at Craiglockhart: Dr. John Rivers, who believed in the benefits of "talk therapy" to a generation and class of men who were brought up to repress emotions and feelings in times of stress, and Dr. Arthur John Brock, whose active and behavioral approach created what he termed "ergotherapy," or the cure by functioning. Brock believed that the shell-shocked needed to rediscover their links with an environment from which they had become detached. They could do this only through active and useful functioning: through working. He organized many activities in the hospital to provide his patients with a means of helping themselves back to health often based on writing poetry, painting, and participating in sporting events. He also organized temporary teaching posts for soldiers at local schools, jobs at local farms assisting undersupported farmers, and he even fostered links with an Edinburgh sociological group to open the eyes and the ears of the men to the social deprivation and inequalities in the home-front society.

Between October 1916 and March 1919, 1,736 patients with

shell-shock were treated at Craiglockhart. Of these, 735 were listed in the registers as "D. M. U."—discharged (or declared) medically unfit. Some 89 were recorded as having been given home service—usually in administrative or bureaucratic roles. There were 78 listed as having been discharged to light duties, commonly training new recruits or assisting with military bases in Britain. Some 141 were transferred to other units for further treatment or because there were more appropriate places for their treatment to be continued elsewhere; and 758 in total were listed as having been returned to duty.

It is easy to be misled by the stiff-upper-lip and the forced jollity of both officers and enlisted men at this time into underestimating their intense degree of suffering, and the often limited degree to which that suffering could be alleviated by the caring and the expertise of the medical profession, as this stanza from a poem clearly indicates:

> *Craiglockhart memories will be sad,*
> *Your name will never make us glad;*
> *The self-respect we ever had*
> *We've lost—all people think us mad.*

The Women's Land Army

Three million British men fought in World War I, but just as important to the war effort were the women they left behind. By 1915 Germany's best chance of victory lay in starving Britain into surrender through a naval blockade, so the country had to become more self-sufficient. The Board of Agriculture set up the Women's Land Army and over a quarter of a million volunteers flocked to help. Most of them were city girls and were not particularly welcomed by farmers, but by the end of 1916 nearly all work done on farms was accomplished by women.

Awards and Medals

There were many awards that an individual might receive for a conspicuous and gallant act of valor, usually in the presence of the enemy, while serving in the British, Dominion, and Colonial armed forces during the First World War. Listed below in order of precedence are those mentioned in *Death of an Unsung Hero*:

Victoria Cross (V.C.)
Distinguished Service Order (D.S.O.)
Military Cross (M.C.)

The Battle of Beauville Wood

The Battle of Beauville Wood is a fictitious battle, but it is based on the Battle of Delville Wood (Bois d'Elville) which was fought between 15 July and 3 September 1916, part of a series of engagements in the 1916 Battle of the Somme in the First World War.